Mercy's Shame . . .

Suddenly they were clutching at each other, his arms tight around her. She could feel his desire throbbing against her, a strange and quite terrifying experience filling her with the overpowering sensation of sensuality she did not know she possessed; she was trembling, shaking violently.

He held her tightly to him, crushing her lips against his, his hands searching, exploring. In a moment he picked her up bodily, and the touch of flesh was irresistible. He strode with her to the shore and laid her very gently on the dark green moss, then crouched beside her and looked into her eyes with great tenderness. She lay quite still as his hands moved over her—there was a heating of the blood, and she wanted to writhe but dared not.

She said at last, with terrible contained quietness, "Clifford, there is something I must tell you. I am . . . *despoiled*."

His lips were close to hers. "Sshh . . . be quiet. If you love me . . . as I love you . . . as I believe you do . . ."

"But you deserve so much more."

"More? What more is there in the whole wide world? I love you, Mercy. I love you so dearly."

She could fight against her will no longer, and reached up hungrily. . . .

Tropic of Desire

Antoinette Beaudry

PINNACLE BOOKS • LOS ANGELES

TROPIC OF DESIRE

Copyright © 1978 by Antoinette Beaudry

An original Pinnacle Books edition, published for the first time anywhere.

First printing, August 1978

ISBN: 0-523-40344-5

Cover illustration by Bill Maughan

Printed in the United States of America

PINNACLE BOOKS, INC.
2029 Century Park East
Los Angeles, California 90067

Tropic Of Desire

CHAPTER ONE

Mercy Carrol's little astrological handbook told her quite distinctly that this was going to be a difficult day, and it worried her.

She rested the book in her lap and looked out through the prettily curtained window of the drawing-room, rocking herself gently in the cane-backed chair and watching the rooks that were feeding off the rubbish that lay in the gutters.

The costermongers out there were closing up their stalls for the day, though it was only four o'clock in the afternoon, and there was a hurried, furtive look on some of their faces. They seemed apprehensive, almost frightened; and idly, she wondered why.

She watched the blind beggar who always sat on the corner of Carrier Street, where the Duke of Bedford had sold so many of the wretched houses

1

in this slum to make way for the new road. The beggar's name was Ephraim and he was a scrawny man in his forties who never seemed to stop scratching at the lice on his body. He was removing the patches from his eyes now and carefully counting the farthings he had collected on this long and rainy day. He put his patches back on again, and hobbled off, using his cane to walk, leaning on it heavily until he was out of sight of the Rookery.

Mercy smiled and said, "Blind Ephraim had a good day. He is gloating."

Her father's voice was gentle and sad. "Perhaps someone gave him a threepenny bit by mistake."

She nodded. "I hope so." She eased the embroidered cushion at her back, wondering why there were so many people on the street at this hour of the day.

Her father said, "Ephraim is a cheat, child. He asks for the pity of all who pass by, pity for a blind man who can see better than I can."

"Yes, I know that. I still feel sorry for him."

"You must never cheat, Mercy. Never cheat anyone. The world is a hard enough place to live in as it is."

"You know I never will, Father."

He said fiercely, the pain gnawing at him, "And never ask for pity. It's the . . . the ultimate humiliation."

"Yes. I know that too."

She got to her feet and went to the big dulled mirror over the mantleshelf and began braiding her hair. Close by, her father was watching her, a woollen blanket over his shoulders, looking somehow small and shrivelled in his wheelchair by the empty grate. He was smiling at her now, though

2

his gray eyes were still clouded. He said, "I must tell you, Mercy, how much . . . how much I admire you."

The practiced fingers stopped among the long braids, and she echoed him, surprised: "Admire me, Father? Why, whatever for?"

He sighed and gestured vaguely. "I will never be able to tell you that."

Impetuously, she crouched down beside him and kissed him on the cheek. She drew the blanket closer about him and held his hand, saying, "You're so cold . . . shall I light the fire? We still have some coal."

He shook his head. "We must keep the coal for when the winter comes and we need it."

"I'm sure Luke will be visiting us again, quite soon now."

"Ah . . . Luke!" He said gently, "We must never count on his charity, child, even though we know it is always there."

"Not charity, Father. Friendship."

"Yes. I suppose we can call it that. It's a softer word."

"It's the right word. *Friendship.*"

"And have you ever stopped to think what would happen to us, if we did not have Luke?"

She leaned her head against his side. "Yes, I've thought of it."

"I would be out there in the street, alongside Blind Ephraim."

"No. I would find more work."

"It's hard enough now. . . ."

"Don't think about it, Father. We live from day to day, and this year . . . the stars are very good for us this year, did you know that?"

3

"Of course . . ."

She went back to the mirror and finished braiding her hair. He watched her, realizing with a little shock just how beautiful she had become.

She was tall and slim, and just over twenty-one years old, with huge brown eyes—like her late mother's, he thought!—and long auburn hair that she let fall loosely down to her shoulders, except when she went out. Then she pulled her hair severely to the sides of her head and plaited it. After all, there were certain decencies to be observed, a tone to be kept up in spite of the poverty around them.

She wore a long skirt of dark gray wool, the two patches on its side so neatly stitched as to be almost invisible. Her white cotton blouse was buttoned up to her throat and hid the proud breasts that seemed to her a portent of a force she had already experienced, but did not fully understand.

She was very conscious of her body. She had even examined it carefully on those occasions when she had rebelled against her Aunt Melissa's admonitions so far as to take her almost-weekly bath without the discreet covering of her shift. . . . There was a bright and gleaming water heater in the kitchen, a relic of her father's more prosperous days. It was made of brass and copper and she polished it every morning, her first chore of the day. There was an ornate plaque rivetted to its flank, all covered over with little curlicues, that said: *The Geyser Company of Birmingham; Suppliers of Water Heaters to the Gentry.* Concerning the water heater, her Aunt Melissa had told her sternly, "I will not have you looking at your reflection in the geyser, child. When you use the hip bath, you

4

will always wear a shift. And when you wash between your legs, be sure to turn your face away. We will have no indecencies in this house."

But sometimes, out of curiosity (and feeling guilty about it) she disobeyed the injunction and stripped herself quite naked, even though the strange feelings—alarming and exciting at the same time—that coursed through her young, vibrant body, disturbed her because she could not fully understand what they meant. . . .

Her father was still smiling at her, thinking what a lovely child she was. He said, "What were you watching out there? It seemed to interest you greatly."

She laughed. "There were three rooks fighting over a rotten apple that lay in the gutter, and while they were pecking at each other furiously, a rat sneaked up and ran off with it. I could almost see the surprise on their faces. One of the rooks flew after him, squawking, trying to peck at the back of his neck. But he disappeared down a drain. It was so funny. . . ."

The room was small and tidy, with not a speck of dust anywhere, even along the tops of the doors. The furnishings were old but well kept up: a cretonne-covered sofa and two armchairs to match (their colors faded now, the worn patches hidden by embroidered antimascassars); a rockingchair by the window, a tall cabinet of dark-red mahogany holding an assortment of daguerreotypes, lithographs, and woodcuts, with a few pieces of fine china that were only brought out on special occasions; a small Chippendale table covered over with a lace cloth; and a standing bookshelf that held her father's history books and her own collection of astrological writings. There was a very large lithograph on the wall—depicting Wellington's meeting with Blucher at Waterloo—a formal portrait of the Queen to one side of it, and a pen-and-ink drawing of her mother as a young girl on the other.

Her father's wheelchair was in its habitual position by the fireplace and the fire ready laid with kindling and lumps of shining coal, but not yet lit. There was an ornate ormolu clock on the mantleshelf, with a reclining gilt cupid atop it, flanked by a flowered Japanese teapot on one side and, on the other, a beautiful Chinese vase that had once been broken and carefully rivetted together again.

Her father looked up at the clock and wondered about the hour. "You're shopping early today."

She was tying small green ribbons in the ends of her braids. "Yes," she said, nodding. "They are closing the barrows already."

"At four o'clock?"

"I can't think why . . . but from the way they're hurrying, this is the time to buy vegetables. The leeks were a ha'penny a pound this morning, can you believe that?"

"When I was your age, you could buy a whole week's supply of food for a ha'penny."

The hair was finished, and she took her bonnet and set it just so. Draping the black woollen shawl over her shoulders, she said, "I'll get leeks and turnips—we still have potatoes and onions—and I'll make you the best soup for tonight that you ever tasted."

"Your aunt is coming, don't forget."

"I know. And she said she'd bring a piece of beef."

"Good."

"I'd better hurry or they'll all be gone." She looked out of the window again and said, "Did you ever see so many people on the street? Is it a holiday?"

He shook his head. "I don't think so. Why should it be a holiday? But the Rookery is getting so crowded these days . . . Lord knows where they all come from. Or why."

She bent down and kissed him again. "Give me my tobacco jar before you go," he said, "I think I'll enjoy a pipe."

She placed it on the little table beside him, together with a wooden box of Lucifers and a piece of glass-paper to light them with. There was a warning printed on the box, in the ornate penmanship of Samuel Jones, the maker, that said: *If possible, avoid inhaling the gas that escapes from the combustion of the black composition. Persons whose lungs are delicate should by no means use Luficers.*

She waited till he had tamped down the Nosegay tobacco in his calabash and was holding one of the phosphor-sticks over the bowl. Watching the blue smoke rising around his head, she said, "I won't be long."

She took her shopping basket and left him there to his dreams.

Twenty-three years ago, when Elton Carrol had carried his beautiful young bride over the threshold of the house he had just purchased, St. Giles Rookery had been a fine and genteel place to live in. The trees—even then black with the rooks that gave the area its name—were green and healthy, and the water that flowed down the gutters to the Thames was still fairly clean. But then, the old sewers, put down by the Romans nearly two thousand years before, had become so corroded and clogged that the refuse in the lower-lying areas close by London Wall had begun to back up. And no one had seemed prepared to do very much about it.

For a few years, the Aldermen would sometimes send a laborer, equipped with long poles to ram down the sewers and clear them, to the Rookery, but it was a feeble attempt at best. The rats began moving into the pig sties and bullock stalls, nesting in the rafters and becoming a menace to people and livestock alike. Three times in as many years a terrible plague of yellow fever had broken out there, and soon, the clerks and merchants began moving out and finding more salubrious quarters. It was apparent that where one family moved out, a dozen or more moved in to take its place, crowding into the little houses in unbelievable congestion.

The filth that now began piling up in the streets gave off the most offensive and overpowering stench, and by the time Mercy was born, the city's Aldermen were already drawing up plans to clear this noisome slum by driving a new road through it, to be called New Oxford Street. There was talk in the family of moving out and finding a small house closer to the school on Milk Street where Elton Carrol taught history.

But then, when Mercy was seven years old, the timbers of the Covered Market had given way, and the ancient building had crashed to the ground in rubble. Eleven people had been killed, and one

8

hundred and fourteen injured, some of them very badly. Elton Carrol had been crippled for life, and his lovely wife had died a week later from multiple internal injuries. All thought of moving house had had to be thrust aside. Elton Carrol could no longer make his way to the school and his source of income had been abruptly cut off. There had been a few guineas paid in compensation, then he had been left to his own devices. His limited savings had quickly gone.

And now, the Rookery was worse than ever.

When half or more of the area had been demolished to make way for the new road, all of the inhabitants who chose to stay had been driven into the remaining ninety-five wretched houses. The whole area was barely an acre in size, and nearly three thousand people were crowded in there, sometimes sleeping, incredibly, as many as fifty to a single room. Often they were laid out on the bare boards and covered over with ragged blankets that were themselves as stinking as the filth on the streets outside.

The little Carrol house was a bastion against the encroaching squalor. Besides the neat little drawing room downstairs, there was a dining room (seldom used now) with a small scullery and a larger kitchen. The big iron range there was polished daily with stove-black, and the wood-plank table scrubbed to a pale buff luster. The house also had a small hall where the weather-coats were hung and the umbrellas stored; and outside, close by the kitchen door, a small leanto that was the coal-shed, and a smaller one that housed the latrine bucket. The latrine was emptied weekly into the trough that was supposed to carry the feces down to the river but never did anymore; the water had long since ceased to run there.

Upstairs, there were two small bedrooms and an even tinier one that was Mercy's, the bed covered over with a patchwork spread which she had made herself. An airing cupboard in the hallway held the family linen, most of which was now worn thread-bare and seldom replaced, but all of it immaculately washed and ironed.

It was all clean, neat, and orderly. Mercy would rise at five o'clock every morning, polish the geyser and the range, scrub the front and back doorsteps with a mixture of red-ochre and water, and sweep and dust all the rooms. She packed the tiny grate under the scullery cauldron, where the Monday wash was done, with faggots that would smoulder there and keep the water permanently warm. (Except on Mondays, when the little fire would be allowed to flare up and boil everything.) At eight o'clock she would lay out her father's clothes and help him dress—a long and painful process for him—and twice a week, on Tuesdays and Fridays, she would hurry off to the haberdashers where she would work till sundown selling lengths of muslin, calico, and wool for three shillings and fourpence ha'penny a week.

Every month or so, that good man Luke Doren would come by and visit his old school chum, now reduced to such a dire state of health and fortune; and every time he left, the tin box on the mantleshelf that held the family funds would mysteriously be replenished again.

And so, they managed.

It was time now, surely, for another visit from Luke. Mercy counted the coins in her reticule as she moved among the costermongers' barrows, filling her string bag with vegetables and wondering just how far the pennies and the farthings would go. She was at her favorite barrow, talking to the monger, a big, hearty man in his sixties whose name was Silas: "But I need two or three tomatoes, no more, a pound is too many . . ."

He grinned at her, chuckling over some secret thought. He said, "Go on with you, Mistress Mercy, you can have the bleedin' lot for a ha'penny. There'll be no more trade this day, once the boyos get here."

She was puzzled. "The boyos?"

He was dropping tomatoes into the string bag, eight, ten, a dozen of them, and saying cheerfully: "A ha'penny, and enough juicy tomatoes to last you a week, it's a good day coming for all of us . . ." He saw her look of bewilderment. "You didn't know?"

She shook her head, mystified, looking around and wondering where the crowd on the street was coming from. It was so dense now that she could hardly move; and she saw that most of them were strangers, rough working-men who seemed just to stand there as though waiting for something to happen.

Silas began slapping the boards onto the top of his barrow and tying them in place. When they were secure he leaned in to her and said confidentially, "It's O'Connor's boys, they're marching again."

But there were more important things to worry about. She saw the barrows being closed and said urgently, "No, wait, please. I need a few turnips, and some leeks, and perhaps a couple of carrots if they're not too expensive . . ."

He was standing there, with the last board poised like a shield, and he looked around and said, "Take what you need, Mistress Mercy, I won't even ask you for any more money, a day like this. . . ."

She took a few vegetables eagerly, amazed about her good fortune. When she turned to thank him she saw that he was staring up at the roof of the granary, on the corner of Carrier Street; his eyes were grave now, the good cheer gone from them and only worry in its place. "Well," he said, scratching an ear, "take a look at that, Mistress Mercy. They meant what they said, didn't they? Nobody believed them . . . but they meant it."

She did not know what he was talking about, and she could hardly move in the throng around her, it was so tightly packed; and that worried her. A barrow-man was pushing his handcart angrily through the crowd, shouting out, "Way there, way there . . . Way!" He rammed the little barrow into the crowd, forcing a passage.

There was a long line of uniformed men moving over the granary roof, carrying guns on their shoulders. Mercy felt a sudden shudder of alarm, not knowing what it could possibly mean.

She heard Silas say, a whisper now, "Soldiers, Wellington's men."

He was looking off toward the far end of Church Lane, and she could hear a muted, strangely ominous sound coming from beyond the ramshackle houses at the bend there, a sound that was not of marching feet or shouted voices, but

12

perhaps a combination of them both. She thought of it as the sound of anger.

Somewhere, a whistle blew, a shrill penetrating sound that was followed by another and another, and Silas, alarmed now, said to her urgently, "You'd best be getting back to your house, Mistress Mercy. I've a feeling there's trouble in store for the Rookery this day." He was kicking away the blocks from under the wheels of his cart and throwing the straps of the shafts over his shoulders. He began shoving it into the crowd, shouting, "Way, way, way there. . .!" But nobody made way for him now, and he could hardly move it. He turned back to Mercy and, gesticulating at her as she tried to shoulder a way through the crowd, said, "No, it's too late now . . . you'd best stay here. If you run now, there'll be naught but trouble in store for you, so put a smile on that pretty face and pretend you're with them."

She could not believe that so many people could be squeezed so tightly into such confinement. There was a sweating, pressing mass of humanity all around her and movement was out of the question. She heard Silas, who was grinning foolishly now, though his eyes were frightened, say, "Stay close to me, Mistress, I'll see no harm comes to you." There was fear in his voice and she thought wildly: *In two or three minutes I could be home, but I can't move an inch. . . .*

And now, close by them, a tall, lanky man wearing a threadbare topcoat tied around his skinny waist with a length of rope and a battered tophat on his head, was clambering up the wooden framework of the old water tower—long since dry and rotting—and hooking a leg around a timber. He untied the rope from around his waist and secured himself there with it, twenty feet above them. When his precarious perch was safe, he put his two hands to his mouth and hollered out at the top of his voice, "Good people of St. Giles! Listen to me! Come out from your hovels and listen to me!"

He fell into a savage fit of bronchial coughing and, when it had passed, he shouted again, "Come and hear me! Some of you good people . . . don't know me! You soon will! Ask your neighbors what my name is, and by God, they'll tell you! So listen to what I have to say!"

Scattered along the street now, the full length of it, there were a dozen or more young men— strangers, all of them—standing on the tops of the costers' barrows, holding up their arms and yelling almost in unison, "Quiet! Silence! Quiet!"

Mercy could feel the strong and friendly hand of Silas gripping her arm, and she heard him say quite calmly, "Don't let them see that you're frightened, Mistress Mercy. It's only their enemies are frightened of them."

The unexpectedness of it all frightened her. "Silas," she asked urgently, "who are they? What do they want? What are they doing here?"

The broad smile was still there, frozen on his face. He said quietly, "They are the Chartists, and they mean trouble for all of us."

Now, from the other end of Carrier Lane, a mob of two, three, perhaps four hundred people was pressing into the crowd. Some of them were carrying clubs, waving them over their heads and chanting something she could not clearly hear. It sounded like "*Master Jenkins, Master Jenkins, Master Jenkins . . .*" The young men atop the barrows

14

were shouting for quiet again. As the sound diminished, the man on the water tower was speaking again, his arms thrown out, a red kerchief in one hand, a black one in the other. He was waving the kerchiefs like a maniac and shouting now; his voice was a scream.

"The time has come, my friends!" he yelled. "The time has come to show the stinking, pot-bellied aristocrats who lord it over us . . . those vermin feeding off the honest labors of the working man . . . that we will tolerate their abominations no longer! And if it needs a revolution to put food on our empty plates, then by God that's what we will have—a revolution! And the time for it is *now*!"

A great roar of approval went up from the crowd and one of the men atop his barrow shouted gleefully, "We're with you, Master Jenkins, every man Jack of us!" A woman echoed shrilly from the crowd, "And every woman too!"

The press of bodies around her was so tight now that Mercy thought she was fainting. The tomatoes in the string bag were squashed to a pulp against her blouse, staining it almost like blood. She tried to force a way toward her house. There was a young man on the ground at her feet, crawling along the gutter to reach the front of the crowd, and she stumbled and lost her balance. A large, heavily built woman behind her moved away, and Mercy fell. There were feet all around her, some of them heavily booted, but most of them bare. Her bonnet was all awry and she struggled with it, while the woman bent down and dragged her to her feet, shouting at her, "It's a great day for all of us, duckie!" She could smell the strong odor of

15

fish; it emanated from Betsy, the fishmonger's wife from Church Lane, shouting now with the rest of them. Mercy said, struggling: "I have to get home . . ."

But even as she spoke, she knew that no one was paying any attention to her at all.

A thick-set young man, his sleeves rolled up to show off powerful biceps, was thrusting his way forward. He gripped Silas by the collar of his worn-out coat and thrust a finger under his nose, shouting, "Are you with us, old man?"

Silas nodded vigorously: "I'm with you, I'm with you, as all good people are."

"Then let me hear you cheering, old man." He had the harsh accent of the North, from Birmingham perhaps, where all this had started. And he moved on, aggressively, forcing his way through with broad and powerful shoulders.

The stench was terrible—the smell of rotting vegetables fortified by the sweat of the crowd. Master Jenkins was exhorting them again, but he had changed his tone. He was no longer a screaming maniac, but a calm and forceful orator. Cupping his mouth again, framing his words distinctly, he shouted down, "We march on Westminster! Now listen to me, friends! Call me by my name!"

Led by the young men on the barrows, a great chant went up from the crowd : "*Master Jenkins, Master Jenkins, Master Jenkins, Master Jenkins!*" It went on and on, and now the whole street was echoing the slogan. At last Jenkins threw out his arms for silence and shouted: "Enough! Enough, you oafish louts, you scum of London!"

There was a fire in his eyes, as he gauged carefully the results of his insults. And when the shouting had died away, he spoke more quietly now so that they would be forced to strain their ears to listen. "Yes, that's what I called you, oafish louts and the scum of London! And let me tell you *why*, my friends! Those are the very words . . . said today in our Parliament of parasites . . . by a man you all know well! Shall I name him for you? Robert Peel!"

There was a sardonic note to his voice now. "I meant to say, of course, *Sir* Robert Peel! His Lordship! The man who beat down our Irish friends into the state they suffer today! The man who wants to emancipate the Jews . . . and Catholics . . . who prey on us! The man who decided we need a policing force to hold us down where we are—in the gutters! Well, my friends, my good friends and fellow scum, that is what his Lordship called us today, before he went home in his fine carriage to his fine house and his fine food and his seven fine children all clothed in the finest silk! Is there a woman among you with silk on her back?"

A great guffaw went up from the crowd, and when it had subsided, he shouted, "Because if there is, then bring her to me so that I may tear the silk off her perfumed body!"

The crowd roared and Jenkins looked down on the massed faces, saying, "Notice, my friends, that I said *perfumed*. Because the likes of Robert Peel and his cohorts smell sweetly, while you and I . . . the scum of London . . . we *stink!*"

The crowd was delirious, taking up the slogan again, and Jenkins shouted, "Yes, Master Jenkins is my name, and I have the ear of the great Fergus O'Connor himself! And these are his instructions! We march on Westminster, and we march in two

17

columns. The first, by way of the new street they're building for the carriage of the rich, and which they call . . ."

He broke off, and when they had waited just long enough, he went on, "They call it New Oxford Street, after the *Earls* of Oxford, after the aristocracy, did you notice? They never thought to call it "New Jenkins Street," after the humble working man Master Jenkins, now did they?"

The crowd was cheering him, and the young men had climbed down from their perches and were passing free ale around. The men cupped their hands under the spigots of the little barrels, catching the ale as it spilled down onto the cobblestones.

Jenkins exhorted the crowd: "The boyos with the red bands on their sleeves will take this route, down New Jenkins Street, so some of you follow them. The boys with the black bands on their arms—black because the stinking aristocrats are trying to bury us—will go by Chancery and along the Strand. Follow, my friends, whichever of the boyos takes your fancy, but *follow* them! There'll be fights, and there'll be burnings, and by God, we'll make our presence *known!* Remember, my friends, we are Chartists!"

He was coughing again, and when he had recovered, he went on, shouting louder now, "The great Fergus O'Connor has told you, time and time again, that change will only come through force! The time for talk has gone! And the time for change is . . . *now!*"

From the roof of the granary, a single shot was fired.

For a moment or two, in their delirium, the

18

crowd on the street had no clear idea of what had happened. They saw Master Jenkins twist round on his perch and dangle there, secured by the rope around his narrow waist, his back bent over and a huge bullethole in his chest.

Then, another shot was fired, followed by another and another. And as they fought each other to escape, they knew, at last, that they had fallen into a trap set for them by the angered, and anxious, authorities.

Mercy was shoved roughly aside by a screaming costermonger whose shoulder had been shattered by one of the terrible ovaloid balls from a Greener gun. As he fell to the ground his clutching arm dragged her down with him and there were heavy boots stamping on her arms, her legs, her shoulders.

She could not know it, but the guards were charging into the crowd, using the butts of their guns and sometimes firing them too. There were dead eyes staring into hers and she screamed . . . then, she lost consciousness.

Sir Robert Peel—no enemy of the people, but their staunch friend—had described the city of London as "heaving with discontent, teaming with conspiracy, and on the verge of rebellion." And the government of Lord John Russell, a Prime Minister of markedly liberal persuasion and a bulwark of the Whig Party, had taken action. (The term "Whig," the Scottish Gaelic word for a horse-thief, had been introduced one hundred and sixty-nine years previously as a term of opprobrium for those of liberal leanings; in contrast, "Tory" was simply an Irish Gaelic word meaning plunderer.) To forestall the open rebellion preached by O'Connor and his

19

Chartists, London had been garrisoned so heavily that the troops seemed in some places more numerous than the citizenry.

The danger of that open rebellion was very real. The Chartists had come into the forefront of England's social conscience some ten years previously. The movement was destined to die a natural death, caused by its own excesses, two years later. They derived their name from "The People's Charter," a bill introduced into Parliament through the political efforts of the London Workingmen's Association, and their aim, simply stated, was social equality.

A previous effort towards this goal, the Reform Bill of 1832, had already enfranchised the middle classes, but it denied the vote to those whose contribution to the welfare of society at large could not be shown. And the Poor Law, now in effect for twelve years, offended them deeply because of the Machiavellain cunning with which it ensured that idleness should not be more rewarding than gainful employment. The Factory Act of the time, intended to lessen the burden of the unskilled worker, had merely succeeded in limiting the number of hours worked by children under eleven years old to no more than twelve a day.

For the Chartists, this was simply not enough. Spreading out from the industrial North to all the major towns of England, their speakers and organizers roamed the country, exhorting the poor and the oppressed to take by force what had not been given to them by arbitration. The Chartists were strong, they were angry, and they were very, very violent.

The London Democrat, a newspaper of somewhat innocent philosophies, had phrased their demands aptly: ". . . that all shall have a good house to live in, with a garden back or front just as the Occupier likes, good clothing to keep him warm and make him look respectable, and plenty of good food and drink to make him look, and feel, happy . . ."

Noble sentiments indeed! The idea of "a chicken in every pot" had been postulated many times in the past, all over the civilized world. But the means by which this Utopian state was to be achieved were not so clearly indicated, and the general trend toward at least some kind of equal opportunity (which the Chartists did not regard as quite what they were after) was not enough for them. They preferred the one, succinct word: *rebellion.*

Their leader was Fergus O'Connor, a fiery man whose Irish penchant for colorful invective made his name a rallying cry for the underprivileged. His reference to the aristocracy, in his highly successful newspaper *The Northern Star*, as "pig-bellied, little-brained, numbskulled, platter-faced, amphibious politicians" had already made the Parliament of even so ungrudging a man as Lord Russell the laughing stock of the country. And the only way to put them all out of business, O'Connor insisted, was by violence.

On that memorable day, August 2, 1848, the march on Westminster was stifled in its infancy. The government was ready and waiting. Twelve thousand troops of Wellington's Army—in a period of stagnation since the end of the Napoleonic Wars—had been prepared for the Chartist uprising, four thousand of them in London alone, and three hundred and fifty in St. Giles Rookery. This

21

highly trained and disciplined force was bolstered by one hundred and twenty-seven of Sir Robert Peel's new police force. One hour after Master Jenkins's call to action, the incipient march on Westminster, with its promised fury and turmoil, had been stopped at its very beginnings; the Rookery streets were empty, save for those who were dragging away the dead or stealing the boots of the wounded.

Eighteen people had been killed. Eleven of them were Chartists or innocent bystanders, and the remaining seven were members of the Armed Forces, including the Peelers. And there were many, very many, who had been injured. Most of them were able to drag themselves away to their homes or into hiding.

Not Mercy. Her unconscious body had been bruised and battered by the boots of the frightened, angry crowd that had surged about her. She lay there, half under Silas's overturned barrow, in complete oblivion of all that was going on, of the furious stampede, and of the silence that followed it.

CHAPTER TWO

The sun had long since set when she regained consciousness and there was no way for Mercy to know how long she had lain there.

She was wet through from the gentle rain that was falling, and as she gazed up at the stars in a moment of what seemed to be complete recovery but was not, she became aware of Jupiter up there. And she thought for a moment vaguely, that it was in quite the wrong place.

There were hands grasping her ankles and she felt herself being dragged along the wet cobblestones. Then, quite unaccountably, there was straw beneath her and an offensive smell was assaulting her nostrils—the sickening stench of the ordure of animals, perhaps pigs or cattle.

She looked for Jupiter again and could not find it, but there was a flame there now, very faint. She peered at it as though it might be the most important thing in her life and saw that it was coming from a piece of string floating in a tin of tallow wax . . . a candle. She closed her eyes again and sighed to herself, fancying that she was back in her bed and not knowing why the candle was in a tin instead of the prettily painted little Faenza holder her father had given her for—what was it?—her fourteenth birthday?

The straw under her was tickling her bare shoulder blade and she made a semiconscious movement to push it away.

She heard a voice, an uncouth, hoarse voice coming to her out of the void: "She's coming round . . ."

Another voice, strangely younger-sounding than the first: "Good, it's best she knows what's happening, I like it when they fight."

The first voice again: "She won't fight."

"She will. And I like it. A tit that don't fight . . . it ain't the same thing."

"I'll put a shilling on it."

"Where would you get a shilling, now? She'll fight. You'll see."

What were they talking about? And who were they? Were they in her room? And what time of the day was it? There was work to be done, the range to be shined up, and the tin of stove-black was almost empty; she had forgotten to buy a new one.

The voice again, and it was clearer now, much clearer: "I want her when you're done with her."

The voices came and went, and came again out of the darkness, just as the light of the candle was coming and going. Mercy rolled over onto her side and opened her eyes again.

24

There were four women sitting there in the hay, in shawls and bonnets, and she thought that perhaps she knew one of them. Who was it? The wife of the ship's chandler on Carrier Street?

A huge, very fat pig was close beside her, sniffing at her, and she tried to push it away. The straw was worrying her again, and she eased her body and groped for a blanket that wasn't there; all she wanted was sleep. The presence of the women worried her. What were they doing in her room? She thought to herself; no, it's not the chandler's wife, it's the mother of the boy who repairs . . . the cane-backed chairs . . . going from house to house with bundles of split cane wound around his waist . . . and what is all the straw doing here? It isn't even clean. . . .

She was delirious; there was a terrible pain in her head, and she thought: I will sleep now till morning, I will lie in bed late, and Father will wheel himself around the kitchen while he makes the porridge, and all will be well . . .

And then, with a sudden sense of shock: why are my shoulders naked?

Her hand went instinctively to her breasts. They were naked too and she thought of the brightly shining geyser in the kitchen and of the reflection of her body that so worried her good and dear Aunt Melissa.

The delirium flooded over her again; for how long? An hour? A minute? She had no way of knowing. She heard the voice again, the young one: "I think she's ready." A coarse laugh, then, "I know I am . . ."

There was guffawing all around her, the sound of the women's voices in it, echoing and reechoing, coming to her out of a great hollow pit of her own imaginings, fading away and then returning, and she was still not yet fully conscious.

There was a hand on her breast, moulding it, crushing it cruelly and hurting her. She woke up. She stared in horror. A young man who could not have been much older than her own tender years was poised over her, his eyes alight with a kind of crazed excitement. It was his eyes she became aware of first, very pale and seeming to bore into her own. And then she saw the growth of a scraggly beard on his chin, ragged and unkempt and very juvenile. He wore a heavy knitted jersey of dark wool and breeches tied at the waist with a length of string.

She was suddenly aware that her own legs were widely spread, and that the young man was kneeling between them, his hands fumbling at the front of his breeches. In a sudden moment of panic that was, at least in part, instinct, she twisted violently around and tried to close her thighs, but there were other hands on her ankles now, dragging her legs apart again.

She screamed, a long and piercing scream of terror, cut off as a hand covered her mouth and gripped her cheeks. It was one of the women—thin and worn out and middle-aged, with a gray bonnet all askew on piled-up hair in which some pieces of straw were sticking—and she was hissing at her, not even angrily, "We don't want no noise, duckey, the Runners might be prowling."

She fought against the hand, but it was very strong, hard and calloused, grinding her lips against her teeth. She tried again to turn her body sideways, but could not; the woman's other hand was at her throat now, forcing her head down into the straw till she could feel the hard stones beneath it. The voice went on, almost pleasantly, "Now you lie still for my boy, he's a right good boy . . ."

The young man was gripping both her wrists in one of his hands, holding them back over her head. Laughing at her struggles, he pawed at her breasts again and then the hand slid down and yanked her long skirt up around her waist, and pulled at the drawstring of her pantalettes till it broke. She could feel his fingernails on her bare stomach, and was aware, even, that one of them was broken, the sharp edge of it drawing blood. She fought with a strength she did not know she possessed.

There were two other faces leering at her now, older than the other, and she kicked her legs free savagely and heard the young man swear. He was wrestling with her, and he said angrily, "Her feet, get hold of her feet."

The pantalettes were pulled down around her knees, then to her calves, her ankles . . . and there were other hands holding her legs apart and her thighs were bare. There was the touch of hot flesh against them, and the panic was extreme. She tried to scream "No, no, no!" but scarcely any sound at all escaped from her bruised lips.

The voice was furious now, raised in frustrated anger, "Keep still, damn you." and the horror of what was happening to her was quite insupportable. Her eyes were wide and staring, and in a moment of terrified bewilderment she saw what looked like a cudgel, poised very briefly over her. She was certain it was going to come down onto her forehead, and she turned her face away from the blow.

The hands had left her throat and her face, and

they were gone from her ankles too. She saw the cudgel swing sideways and back again and she recognized it now for what it was—a belaying pin from a ship, the kind the sailors always carried around town. As the recognition came to her she saw it strike the bearded young man full in the face. She saw him reel over backwards and fall and she began screaming again, twisting her shameful body to the side and instinctively covering herself with her skirt. She rolled over onto her knees and tried to stand up, but collapsed against the timbers of a stall, staring in shock.

The brawny young man in a buff-colored hairshirt, the sleeves rolled up about the elbows, was swinging the belaying pin again at the other two men, who leapt to their feet and tried to scatter as the blows rained down on them. She saw that the four women had risen too and stood there in a hushed and frightened little group; one of them was rapidly blinking her eyes as though not really aware of what was going on. Then, quite suddenly, they turned and scuttled away, and she was left alone with the brawny young man.

He stood there, with a look of embarrassment on his handsome face, and she was conscious, first, of the strong bare arms, held akimbo now; and then, the long, widespread legs, with trousers of heavy wool bound at the ankles with strips of canvas. It was hard to raise her head, but when she saw his eyes, they were filled with a fierce anger tinged with—what was it?—compassion?

He stooped down and picked up her shawl and handed it to her, then turned his face away and said gravely, his voice surprisingly soft and gentle,

"I hope . . . I hope I was in time, Mistress, to put a stop to those ruffians' plans."

It was not phrased as a question, but she found herself nodding blankly. She drew the shawl over her shoulders and her breasts, trying to bring together the torn pieces of her bodice with hands that would not stop their shaking. There were tears of shame streaking her face, and her voice was a whisper: "Oh God . . ."

She pulled herself together with a conscious effort, and saw his eyes drop briefly—eyes that were soft and gentle now too!—and she bent hastily and pulled up the torn pantalettes. He averted his gaze again while she found the broken ends of the drawstring and tied them, her fingers still trembling terribly. She could hardly catch her breath. "I thank you, sir," she stammered. She knew that she was blushing, the humiliation almost more than she could bear. "Yes, they did not . . . did not . . . I thank you . . ." Tears filled her huge brown eyes.

He still kept his look turned away as she busied herself with her clothes. "The water here will not be very clean, Mistress, but if you would like some . . . if it would help?"

She nodded and he slid the long cudgel into his broad leather belt, went to the water trough, and scraped the scum on top of it out of the way. After tasting the water, he found an empty tin and brought her some. He was smiling now, perhaps a little hesitantly. "Not the finest water in London, Mistress, but perhaps, under the circumstances? . . ."

She began to drink, but he stopped her quickly, saying, "No, no, not like that! Permit me to show you. With your permission, Mistress?"

He took the tin from her and lifted the end of

29

her shawl, folding it into a few thicknesses and draping the material over the lip of the tin. Then he handed it back to her and said, "This way, the worst of the refuse can be strained out."

She drank gratefully. The water was good, tasting of wet straw and only very slightly of animal manure. She looked into his eyes and said steadily, "I have to thank you, sir, for coming to my rescue. I think . . . I think they would have killed me."

He shook his head slowly. "I fear that it was not your life they wanted. And I am happy that I came in time. My name is Clifford Hawkes, Mistress, and I am at your service."

"Clifford . . . Hawkes?"

"And I am a sailor from the *Northern Wind*, tied up for repairs at the West India dock." He was smiling broadly now and she was suddenly conscious that he was talking deliberately to take her mind off what had happened. It surprised her, but she was sure that it was so, and she was grateful for it. She said quickly: "They tell me the West India dock is full of whalers now."

He nodded. "And that is what the *Northern Wind* is—a whaler, the best in the fleet. Only, we ran into a hurricane on the way home, and . . . we were lucky to reach port before she split her hull wide open." He did not change the tone of his voice. "And if you are ready now, Mistress, I will take you to your home."

She remembered her manners suddenly and said, abashed, "My name is Mercy, Mercy Carrol, and I live with my father on Carrier Street. I am not quite sure where we are now, but I think Carrier Street is close by?"

"We will find it, Mistress Mercy. We are behind the granary. Perhaps you would take my arm?"

He was so very, very courteous. With manners far beyond the station of an ordinary seaman! She was about to lay a hand on his arm as though they were to go for a stroll together in the park, but she said quickly, conscious of the dreadful state she was in, "But . . . I cannot go home like this! . . ." There was a kind of desperation in her voice. "A few minutes, please, to do what I can?"

"Of course." He was very grave.

She lifted her heavy skirt delicately and tore off a piece of one of her petticoats. After she had gone over to the trough and washed her face carefully with it, she looked back at him as she fumbled with her shawl.

He turned away, smiling, and she slipped the shawl off and pulled her torn bodice together, pulled up her blouse and buttoned it again, and patted at her hair, wishing she could find a mirror. Remembering, she said in dismay, "My reticule, it's gone!"

He looked around the stable floor, but she shook her head. "No," she said, "I was out there on the street . . . I don't know for how long, lying unconscious under a costermonger's barrow."

"Then it will have gone," he said sadly. "Was there much of value in it, Mistress Mercy? If you would like me to go and search? . . ."

"No. As you say, it will have gone." She was almost wailing. "If only I had a comb!"

He came to her, solicitous and somehow amused. "If you will allow me?" he said.

His hands were at the sides of her head, easing the braids into their proper place, and he pulled out

31

a few pieces of straw and showed them to her as though it was all a huge joke. And then, it seemed as though he became aware, quite suddenly, of what had happened to her; he touched her very lightly on the shoulders, not quite holding her but just . . . touching her.

"I admire your . . . your fortitude, Mistress Mercy," he said earnestly. "What you have been through would have given most young ladies, I fear, a severe attack of the vapors. I wish I knew what . . . what words might comfort you."

The tears were in her eyes again, but now for a different reason. "You are so kind, sir," she said slowly. She moved back a step and spread her arms wide. "Am I almost respectable?" she asked. "My father is very sick, and I fear that if I present to him . . . an image of what might have happened . . ."

He looked her over very carefully and picked up the tin with the burning rope-end in it. He held it high and peered at her, saying at last, "A bruise, I fear, on your cheek. Two buttons missing from your dress, but your shawl will hide them, and your eyes . . . they are red with weeping, and I could wish that I had arrived a little earlier. I could, perhaps, have saved you those tears."

How kind he was! She laid a hand now on his arm, and when she stumbled, it was around her waist at once supporting her, a look of sudden alarm on his face. "If you would like me to carry you?" . . . he said.

"No, no, thank you. It is all right, a little faintness, perhaps. It will pass."

He steadied her and waited, then they moved off

32

together out into the faint gray drizzle that was falling over the Rookery.

Some of the costermongers' barrows were still there, abandoned now and stripped of all their greengrocery, their shafts forlornly on the ground as though waiting for their owners to come and lift them from their dejection. She looked around to get her bearings, and said: "Yes, the granary . . . Carrier Street is this way."

His strong arm was still around her waist, his other hand at her elbow, and she threw him a look and murmured, "You are very kind, Master Clifford."

He laughed suddenly, an open, boyish laugh of good humor. "*Master* Clifford? No, Mistress, not *Master*. I am just a common deckhand, I fear. The lowest form of life on board a whaler."

"But you saved mine, and I will address you as Master. And you talk . . . May I say it? Like a gentleman, of very good breeding."

"Ah . . . the gentry."

He fell silent for a moment, and then, "Once, I had a family who could, perhaps, be called gentry. But . . . there was some doubt about the circumstances of my birth, and there were brothers . . ." His eyes were troubled now, and he said gently, "I will not distress you with problems that I solved many years ago. Your own, I feel, are urgent enough."

His reticence disturbed her and she wanted so much for him to continue. But he had fallen into a brooding silence. When at last they reached the little house, she saw the silhouette of her aunt framed in the window, the yellow light of the lamp

33

behind her, the curtain drawn back by an impatient hand.

The door was flung open before she had even reached out for the bronze bellpull that hung there and her Aunt Melissa was throwing her arms around her, contriving to brush away tears at the same time and saying urgently, "You poor child. We were so worried, are you all right, are you hurt, are you? . . ." She seemed to become conscious suddenly of Clifford's presence and Mercy said quickly, "Yes, Aunt Melissa, I am all right, thanks to this gentleman here. Master Clifford Hawkes, my Aunt Melissa."

He bowed and said, "Your servant, Ma'am," and then Aunt Melissa was pulling them into the house and closing the door behind them. She said, as though conspiring, "Who knows if this evil day is over yet? The Chartists are gone, but are they? Will they still be skulking in dark corners, in the gutters where they belong?"

Her father was wheeling his chair swiftly into the little hall and Mercy saw with a sense of shock that his eyes were red too. He held out his arms for her, and she dropped beside him and embraced him. For a long, long time he said nothing, just held her tightly against his chest.

He said at last, "Are you all right, child? We saw the fighting out there, from the drawing-room window, and we were frightened for you, so frightened . . ." The tears were welling into his eyes now. "I felt so . . . so very *helpless!* Are you all right?" His eyes went to the bruise on her face and the rent in the sleeve of her blouse. "What happened, Mercy, my darling child?" There was a

34

great fear in his eyes now and she said quickly, "Nothing, Father. Nothing."

She pulled away from him and, indicating Cliffordord, said, "Master Clifford Hawkes, my father, Elton Carrol. I was dragged into the stable behind the granary, Father, by three . . . three evil young men. And they . . . they tore my clothes, and they tried . . . they tried . . ." The memory was flooding back to her, and she bit her lip and said, "Master Clifford came to my rescue. With his cudgel, his . . . what is it called? His belaying-pin, he put them to flight before . . . before any harm could be done. Without his help, I would have been . . . very badly hurt."

For a moment, Elton stared at her in shock, the realization dawning on him. He looked at Clifford and back to his daughter. "He saved you . . . from what, Mercy?"

She steeled herself and tried not to bite her lip. "He came in time, Father," she said gently. "If he had not . . . Yes, it would have been terrible. He came in time."

Her Aunt Melissa fainted away, falling carefully onto the sofa. Mercy went quickly to the kitchen and came back with the smelling-salts and held the little blue bottle under her nose, then looked at her father and said again, her voice very controlled, "He came in time, Father."

Elton, his eyes brimming, stretched out his arms to Clifford. Awkwardly, Clifford held out his hand, and Elton took it and held it firmly. "How can I . . . how can I thank you, sir?" he said, his voice quivering. "How can I *ever* thank you? There is little in this house except, perhaps, pride. Now it is

35

filled with gratitude, filled to overflowing. My only child . . ."

He broke off and dabbed at his eyes, covering his confusion by wheeling his chair around and leading them all back into the drawing room.

His eyes on Mercy, Clifford said, "I am grateful for your gratitude, sir. But it is not called for. I did no more than any other decent man would have done."

"More, sir. Much, much more."

"And it was the purest chance that I was passing by. I'm glad of it now."

"Chance? Perhaps not." Elton's eyes were alight now, the words tumbling out, seeking relief. "When were you born, young man?"

Clifford stared. "I beg your pardon, sir?"

"Your birthdate, Master Clifford?"

"My birthdate, sir?"

He said impatiently, "Yes, yes, the day of your birth."

"I was born, sir, on the twenty-ninth of November, in the year 1822."

"Ah! Sagittarius, I should have known it. One look at you, and I should have known it."

Clifford was quite bewildered. "I don't think I understand, sir. Who is . . . Sagittarius?"

"You have arthritis, young man?"

Clifford was positively staring now. "Arthritis, sir?"

Impatiently, "Yes, yes, a weakness in the bones? Perhaps a little trouble with the liver too? . . ."

"No, sir, not to my knowledge." He could not hide his astonishment.

"Ah well, perhaps when you get older."

Elton swung his chair round again. "Melissa!

36

What have we to offer this young man? Is there whiskey left?" Not waiting for an answer, he turned back to Clifford. "Sit down, young man, sit down, we have a lot to talk about. My sister will bring us all a glass of whiskey . . . and sit down too, Mercy, we have to find out more about this good young man."

Mercy said quietly: "Father, I'm sure Master Clifford is not really interested in astrology."

Her father's eyes were wide. "Oh, but he must be! Everyone is interested in astrology."

He turned to Clifford. "And you have an occupation, young man? A profession?"

"I am a deckhand on board a whaler, sir. The *Northern Wind.*"

"Ah, a sailor . . . well, it would have been better for you had you been born some three weeks earlier. In that case, your element would have been water, and your quality fixed instead of mutable, but never mind, it's not of great importance."

He fell silent for a moment and there were tears coming into his eyes again. He saw that Mercy was still clutching the shawl about her shoulders, and he said, very quietly, "Go and change your clothes, child. We will excuse you for a few moments."

"Yes, Father."

She cast a small look at Clifford and went out. When the door had chosed behind her, Elton said, sighing, "I'm a foolish and garrulous old man, Master Clifford. You must forgive me if I . . . if I run on, and on, and on, about things which must be outside the sphere of your knowledge. Sometimes, there is the need to reach out toward those to whom we are indebted, because that indebtedness makes us . . . closer to them. And in times of deep distress, we . . . we seek comfort in communication with each other." He took out his red handkerchief and blew his nose loudly. "Forgive me, sir."

Aunt Melissa had found the whiskey bottle, a mere two inches left in it, and was pouring two small drinks into the best glasses. She handed one to Clifford and he took it from her, held it up, and said politely, "I drink to your good health, sir. And to yours, Ma'am." He sipped it and said, "You were going to tell me, sir, who Sagittarius is. Or was. I'm afraid my education was cut off short when I was quite young."

Elton sighed. "Sagittarius the Archer. Perhaps he was Crotus, the son of Eupheme, who was nurse to the Muses, I don't think we'll ever know if he was or not. What we *do* know . . . Sagittarius is a constellation, Master Clifford . . ." He broke off, smiling. "If you are a sailor, you know what the constellations are."

"Yes, sir."

"Well, Sagittarius is not well seen from this country, and when you sail north for your whales, it will be even less visible, because of its southern declination."

He said, dreaming, "Before my . . . my accident, it was always my hope that I could one day travel south, so that I could see, just once, the bright arm of the Milky Way that passes through it, and perhaps stare for a while in a kind of wonder at the dark patches of nebulae which seem, quite incomprehensibly, to obscure it. Now, I never will. Do I bore you, young man?"

Clifford smiled. "I am intrigued, sir. Though I

38

must confess . . . what has the Archer to do with me?"

"Ha! It has everything to do with you, Master Clifford! When you were born, the sun was in Sagittarius. And this means that you, like the Archer, are very direct and to the point. It also means that you sometimes hold your head up in the clouds. It means that your loyalty is intense and proven. It means that you have no fear of poverty, it means that you are generous to a fault, and it means that your life will be full of change and excitement. It also means that you are prone to accidents. Particularly those concerned with the bones. I don't suppose you ever broke a leg, maybe?"

"No, sir. Not yet, at least."

"A pity. Well, time will tell . . ."

Clifford said, only faintly amused, "And all this, sir, because of the stars?"

"Yes, my boy, because of the stars." He sipped his whiskey, turned to Melissa, and said sadly, "Melissa, I fear you have been putting cold tea in the whiskey again."

She nodded, unperturbed. "It makes it last a great deal longer, Elton."

"Yes, of course."

He turned back to Clifford and said gravely, "As the earth's soil is affected by the sun, as its seas, the seas you sail on, are affected by the moon, so is Man affected by the Heavens. The Babylonians knew this, and so did the Assyrians, nearly six thousand years ago. Today, those of us who believe in a science that has lasted for sixty centuries—can you believe it? Six thousand years of accumulated knowledge!—are called *charlatans!* But one day, believe me . . . And perhaps one day *soon,* the whole world will believe in the influence of the stars on your behavior, and mine."

Clifford said politely, "I recall, sir, that when I was eight years old, I stumbled while running from one of my brothers and broke a small bone in my foot."

Elton, excited, turned to Melissa and said, "You see, sister? Sagittarius! It *has* to happen!"

"Yes, Elton."

She got up and filled their glasses again with the diluted whiskey. Mercy came in, dressed now in her best black woollen skirt, with a blouse of off-white calico bordered with chenille, and high-buttoned boots that were polished to perfection. She sat demurely on the sofa, smiling shyly at Clifford. The braids in her newly plaited hair were tight over her ears now, her face freshly scrubbed. The bruise on her cheek was the only evidence of her recent terrible experience.

Clifford caught her eye and there was a very thoughtful look on his face. He drained his drink and got to his feet. He said to Elton, "I must thank you, sir, for your hospitality. And I must beg your leave to take mine."

Elton said carefully, worrying about his choice of words, "Master Clifford, is there some way in which I can reward you for your . . . your gallantry?"

Mercy said urgently, "Father, please!"

He ignored her and went on, "We are greatly in your debt, sir. If there should be some way in which I can discharge that debt? . . ."

Mercy said again, "Father? . . ."

He sighed. "Well. There is so little that we can offer, in exchange for . . . so much."

40

Clifford said, "You are very kind, sir. But my conscience would never permit it. So, by your leave ..."

"Wait."

Elton was staring out into nothing, thinking, and he said at last, "Master Clifford ... the word of a deckhand on board a whaler must be rigorous in the extreme. Am I right?"

"You are very right, sir."

"I have a friend, a dear, close friend, a good man ..." He wanted to say more, but the whiskey had been too weak. "An old school friend whose name is Luke Doren. You may have heard of him?"

"No, sir, I fear not."

"Well, Luke Doren is a man of some consequence in the city. Part of his business enterprise, I believe, is devoted to the world of ocean-going vessels. You are a sailor, Master Clifford, and I feel ... if it would be of value to you, to move from your whaler to an ocean-going passenger ship? What do you think about that?"

There was already an excitement coursing through Clifford's veins. A passenger ship? It was the highest level on the seafaring scale, whereas the whalers were at the lowest. But he still said steadfastly, "Sir, I thank you. But I will not accept recompense for whatever service I was fortunate enough to offer your daughter."

His eyes went to Mercy and she would not accept his look.

Elton said, "No recompense, Master Clifford. A mere recommendation, no more."

"I will not accept it, sir. Though I thank you."

Mercy's eyes were on her hands, clasped discreetly in her lap. "Your horoscope for today,

41

Master Clifford," she said, "indicates that you should reach out with both hands to seize any opportunity that presents itself to you."

"My horoscope? I do not know the word, Ma'am."

Elton said clearly, "The disposition of the Heavens at this certain moment, Master Clifford."

Clifford was looking again at Mercy and she was smiling now, her eyes still cast down and refusing to meet his. She said, still not looking at him, "Sagittarians have great powers of intuition, Master Clifford. Do you not *feel* the answer you should make to my father?"

He shook his head. "No, Mistress Mercy, I feel nothing. Except, perhaps, a certain hesitation."

"It is enough. Accept, Master Clifford."

He could not believe her assurance. He turned back to Elton and said gravely, "Then I accept, sir, with great humility."

"Humility has no place in the makeup of a Sagittarian. Are you staying on board your ship?"

"No, sir. My ship, unhappily, is a wreck. I have a bed at the Angel Tavern in Limehouse."

"And you will be there for a few days?"

"For a month, at least."

"Good. Expect to hear from me."

"I will, sir, and you are most kind."

He bowed stiffly to Aunt Melissa and shook Elton's hand, went to Mercy and held her hand too. As she stood and looked up into his grave and serious eyes, she said quietly, "How can I thank . . . anyone, for what you did this day?"

"It does me honor, Mistress Mercy."

"Pray God we will meet again one day?" It was a question.

"Pray God."

"You will always be a welcome guest in this house."

"You are most kind. And for no reason."

"There was great reason."

He was still holding her hand and it was warm, vibrant, very much alive. He towered above her, a big, virile man with a barrel chest and a strong, firm jaw. He was smiling at her. "We will meet again, I am sure of it."

She said steadily, "The stars tell me that we will."

"And the stars never lie?" Was he mocking her now?

She said, "They never do, Master Clifford. Never."

"Then so be it."

Aunt Melissa saw him to the door and closed it softly behind him. When she came back into the withdrawing room, she said dreamily, "What a delightful young man. But really, all that nonsense about the stars . . . it's ridiculous, Elton. Quite ridiculous."

Elton said nothing. His eyes were on Mercy and she knew what was in his heart and went to him, crouching down beside his wheelchair and taking his hand in hers.

She said softly, "It's all right, Father. Really it is."

His head was back against the neckrest, and he was staring blankly up at the ceiling. "I saw your torn bodice, child. I know what happened."

She said fiercely, "No, Father. It didn't happen."

"Will you swear to that, Mercy?"

"I swear to it."

43

"Swear, even if it is not true."

"I swear. And it is true. Clifford came in time."

"*Master* Clifford, child."

"Yes. Master Clifford."

"Never forget your honorifics, they are important."

"Yes, Father."

"These are the trivia that distinguish us from the street people, never forget that."

"Go to your room now, child," Aunt Melissa said, "and sleep. It is late." There was a terribly leaden tone to her voice.

"Yes, all right." She looked at her father. "You had no supper tonight."

"A meal saved for another day."

"But you must be hungry."

"No. Suppertime came, and went, and my daughter had not come home. Go to bed, child."

"All right. Goodnight, Father." She kissed him on the cheek, held his hand for a moment, and when she had gone, Elton said, his voice very hard now, "Go to her, Melissa."

Melissa was clearing away the two glasses. She said, "Yes, but I think she will be all right. She's very resilient, your daughter."

"Go to her. I want to know."

Melissa stared at him.

Then, in a moment, "Elton, she told you, nothing happened."

"She told me because . . . she knew, Melissa. She knew that if what I am afraid of really did happen . . . it would kill me. I have to know."

"I can't do that, Elton. She's twenty-one years old. She's not a child anymore."

"Twenty-one is a child. Find out, and tell me."

44

There was a long, long silence. Melissa went to the kitchen, washed the glasses and polished them carefully, breathing on them to give them that extra sheen. Then she came back into the drawing room, put them in their allocated place in the cupboard, and turned to Elton and said, "All right. I will find out. I will let you know."

Mercy was weeping on her pillow.

Aunt Melissa had come and gone, the probing fingers had left their little trauma, and Mercy moved the Faenza candleholder nearer to the bed. She pulled the quilt up to make a sort of tent that would catch most of its light and found a stub of a pencil and a sheet of deckle-edged paper from her letter file, tucked away in the bottom drawer of the dresser and scented with a wisp of lavender. She began to write, licking at the pencil and purpling her tongue with it, staring into the flickering flame once in a while and seeking inspiration there.

She wrote a line, scratched it out and began again, and wrote two more and scratched those out too. When she had finished, she read the sentimental little poem over to herself:

> *Shall I recite the virtue in thine eyes?*
> *How can I? It is ever more than grace,*
> *That may, perhaps, be lauded to the skies,*
> *But crystalizes in a single face . . .*
> *That says, unspeaking, in my heart there lies*
> *A love of all the tired human race.*
> *His name is Clifford, and there never was*
> *A man so strong, so gallant, and so bold.*

CHAPTER THREE

All was quiet in the Rookery again, and there was hardly any sign left of the confusion and the mayhem that had marked the outburst from the Chartists. For the most part, they had gone to the north again, to Birmingham and Sheffield and Liverpool, and were licking their wounds and getting ready for the next time.

Of the eleven civilians killed, only four were local people; and they had been buried quietly and without fuss. The streets were as crowded as always, business was going on as usual, and no one even mentioned the name of the Chartists. It was almost as if the riot had never taken place.

And Luke Doren had come calling once again, together with his beautiful wife Genevieve, to the little house that still remained an outpost of gentility in the slum of the Rookery. He was a good man—an old school friend of Elton's who had made his way in the world with very considerable success—now the owner of a small shipping line and of no less than seven prosperous chandler's stores along the bank of the river, all the way from Waterloo Bridge to Woolwich Reach.

He had hung his gray silk hat on the tree in the hall and was standing now with his back to the empty fireplace, smoking a long clay pipe and looking quizzically at Genevieve. She was wearing one of the new dresses of moiré she had brought from Paris, of a pale amber color that set off her glorious auburn hair and green eyes to perfection. It flounced out around her, with more than sixty yards of wire in the supports, and measureless ells of the fine watered silk, that shimmered every time she moved. Her husband had said, as they set out that morning, "I wonder if you should really dress so . . . so expensively, my darling Genevieve, when we visit poor Elton?"

And she had replied, smiling, "I wear these beautiful clothes only for the sake of Mercy, my dear husband. She needs an understanding of *haute couture*, now that she is to leave that dreadful slum."

"Yes, I suppose you are right."

"Of course I am right! She must begin now to learn about clothes, and *coiffure*, and all the other appurtenances of the budding young lady. In a savage country like America, these things are of the greatest importance. Indeed, I am told that the ladies there, the ladies who have any pretensions at all to quality, are almost as fashionable as we are here."

She was inspecting herself critically in the big hall mirror, pulling the edges of the dress a little further down over her bare shoulders. "Of course," she said, "a little behind the times. But I hear they are even looking to Paris now instead of London. It's a very hopeful sign for their future, poor dears. And why are you so nervous?"

He sighed. "I face this meeting," he said, "with a certain trepidation, I would have you know."

Genevieve nodded. "Yes, I realize that," she said sympathetically. But Melissa will take good care of him, and that poor child . . . it is time for her to become a lady."

"You're right, of course, but even so . . ."

"And if you find it difficult, then let me first broach the matter."

He was greatly relieved. He put an arm around her and kissed the soft creamy flesh of her breasts, held high by the tight bodice, twin mounds of flawless ivory. He said gallantly, "You are not only the most beautiful woman in London, my dearest Genevieve . . . you are also the wisest."

Now, in the stuffy little room, the windows closed against the stench of the street outside, he was waiting for her to begin. Mercy, dressed in the patterned skirt and blouse Genevieve had given her (the bare shoulders modestly covered with a shawl), was pouring tea from the best china pot and Elton was packing his calabash with the Nosegay tobacco Luke had brought.

The small room was already filling with the deep blue smoke of their pipes and as Mercy passed the cups around (one of them very slightly chipped and kept for herself), Genevieve said brusquely,

49

"We have news for you, Elton, and for you too, Mercy. I hope you will think of it as good news."

Mercy smiled. She said quietly, "My horoscope tells me that this is a good day for news. So? . . ."

Luke sighed, determined to plunge in and get it over with. He said, "A letter arrived four days ago, from Nathan in America."

Mercy started. "From Nathan? How is he?"

"He is very well and very prosperous. In five years . . . or is it six?"

"Five years." Elton said. "Nathan left home on the tenth of October in the year 1843. I remember it well, a very propitious day."

He was chuckling to himself. "Perhaps you remember that on that day I gave you a long lecture, which you found unconscionable, on the juxtaposition of the planets and their effect on your son's probable fortune."

"Ah yes, I remember. And it seems that you were right, Elton."

"Of course . . ."

"In that short time, he has built himself a very profitable business there, buying furs for pennies, and selling them for pounds. Always a good way to make a living. President Polk is pushing the borders of the Oregon territories further and further north, and if he has his way they'll reach as far as Russian Alaska before he's through. Take my word for it, Elton, America is the place to be these days. A place with a future. A fine place for any man who knows the value of hard work. For his wife, too, I'm convinced of it."

"Dear Nathan," Mercy said. "Does it seem unkind if I say that in all these years I have scarcely ever thought of Nathan?"

Genevieve's eyes were on her, very alert. "But once," she said, "you were . . . how shall I call it? Childhood sweethearts?"

Mercy nodded. "Yes, we were very fond of each other. I will always remember him with affection. But America . . . it's so *far!* The other side of the world!"

"Not any more," Luke said ponderously. "The new steamships are cutting down the ocean-crossing time to quite unbelievable proportions now. Three weeks out and six home, it's really quite incredible. And this new country of theirs will one day become the center of the civilized world, believe me. A great place for a young man. Or for a young woman."

Both Mercy and Elton were staring at him, knowing that there was more to come. Mercy's huge eyes were wider than ever and a terrible fear was flooding over her. She said to herself: *No, it can't be. . . .*

But she knew, with a kind of prescient instinct, that it was so.

Genevieve had caught her look of alarm, and she said very gently, "Have you guessed, Mercy? Have you guessed what a lucky young girl you are?"

There was a little silence, and then Genevieve went on, easing herself in her chair and setting the crinoline just so around her ankles. "Elton, perhaps this will be hard for you to accept, but we all know that you have Mercy's well-being very close to your heart."

51

Elton nodded slowly; he too knew what was coming now. He said, "Your son wants to take a wife, is that it?"

"Yes, Elton, that is it precisely," Genevieve said. "Nathan is fast becoming a wealthy man, a man of importance in the territory, and he has asked that Mercy join him and become his bride. His long, long letter said that once these two children had sworn a kind of oath, a childhood game, no doubt. But he still remembers her with great affection, and Luke and I discussed this . . . this perhaps vexing problem at very great length before we brought you the news. We both know how much she means to you, how much, too, you depend on her. But this last raises no problem that cannot be solved, and between us, my husband and I, we have decided how to solve it. Easily, swiftly, and with great benefit to everybody."

Mercy felt she was trembling; the china cup in her hand was making little tinkling sounds, and she placed it on the table and went and put her arms around her father. She said, conscious of the tears in her eyes, "You know that I can never leave you, Father. I will *never* leave you."

He eased her arms from around his neck, and took both her hands in his, and said gently, "Sit beside me, child. This is no time for impetuosity." He looked at Genevieve and was conscious of the worn and shabby stuffing of the chair that showed itself beside the luxury of her dress.

"You are right, Genevieve," he said, "right, as always. Nothing is dearer to me than the welfare of my child. So many sleepless nights, I have wondered . . . what will ever become of her. The

52

Rookery is falling into squalor around us; even this house, in which she was born, will soon become even less desirable a place for a young girl than it is now. What future is there for her here? She must, of course, go to Nathan, there can be no doubt about that at all."

He was conscious of Mercy's tears, and she was saying still: "No, Father, no, I cannot." And he held her hand tightly and said, "No, child, you must listen to what our dear friends have to say. Perhaps . . . perhaps this is even an answer to a problem that has been vexing me for a long, long time now."

Genevieve rose and crossed to Mercy, taking her by the arms and helping her gently to her feet. She embraced her and said, "I cannot say your father will be better off by your leaving him, dear Mercy. I know that nothing will ever replace the love you have for him. But Luke and I . . . we know what has to be done. Your Aunt Melissa will come to live here and will look after your father, we will see to it. There will be money enough to provide him with the comforts that, since his accident, he has never been able to enjoy. And for yourself . . . a fine home, beautiful clothes, all the luxuries that so far have been denied you. They are your right, child! You are young, you are beautiful, and the whole world is yours! All you have to do is . . . reach out and take hold of it."

She was dabbing at Mercy's eyes with a fine lace handkerchief. "You must understand that, surely? And Nathan will make a fine husband for you; you have so much in common."

Luke was standing, in acute embarrassment, by

53

the mantleshelf, rolling finely shredded tobacco into his pipe and looking covertly at his old friend. He saw that Elton had a faraway sort of look in his eyes and said to himself: *Well, that wasn't so bad after all.* He went to the wicker basket his wife had deposited discreetly in a corner and took out a bottle and showed it to Elton, saying gruffly, "Well, is it decided, old friend? Can we drink to Mercy's new home?"

Elton, a small smile on his face now, nodded slowly. "It will not be the same without her, Luke, you know that. But I know too what is best for her. She cannot stay here forever in . . . this dreary house. Yes, it is decided."

"Splendid!"

Luke gestured with the bottle again and said, beaming, "A fine brandy from Spain. I'm thinking of buying into the house that makes it, take some of my money abroad, what do you think? And let me tell you what we have decided . . ."

Mercy had dried her eyes now, and her arm was around Genevieve, as though hanging on desperately to the loves she knew. She sighed and sat at the table that held the ornate oil lamp, her eyes cast down. She said, her voice so low they could scarcely hear it, "I will worry about you constantly, Father. I will never be sure just how well you are."

Luke said happily, "Mercy, you have failed to grasp the import of all this. Your father, bless his heart, will no longer be just a dear friend, he will be *family*! You will be my daughter-in-law, and you really believe that I can allow my family to live in anything but the greatest comfort?"

Genevieve had taken her seat again and was spreading the mass of watered silk around her, smoothing it with her long slim fingers, delighting in the sensuous touch of it.

Elton said, as Luke opened the bottle, "The glasses, child."

Mercy leaped to her feet and took two of the best glasses from the china cabinet. Luke poured the drinks and raised his glass in a toast, "To Mercy, to Nathan, to all of our new family, together!"

Mercy went over and kissed him quickly on the cheek, feeling the tears coming again, and went and sat on the floor by her father's chair. She took his hand and held it to her cheek, trying to imagine a future, in a far distant country, with a new kind of—was it obedience—taking the place of the love that was so dear to her. It was hard to control her emotions.

"Let me tell you," Genevieve said brightly, "what we think is the best course to take. In six weeks' time, the *Capricorn* sails for Boston . . ."

"The *Capricorn*?" Elton's face lit up unexpectedly. "A propitious name."

Luke stared at him, not understanding, and Genevieve said, smiling, "Elton's mania, dear husband. Capricorn is one of the signs of the Zodiac, I believe."

Elton nodded. "The tenth . . . and Mercy's birthday is January the seventh, which means . . ." He shrugged. "Well, it means that *Capricorn* is a good name for your ship. But I interrupted you, Luke."

"Well, be that as it may," Luke said. "The *Capri-*

corn, a good ship, is the vessel we have selected for Mercy's journey."

"We thought," Genevieve said, "that Melissa might accompany her, since young ladies really do not make this sort of journey alone. I am sure Melissa would relish the voyage and it would be good for her too. After something like ten weeks, the ship docks again in London, and Melissa would return to your home. While she is away, we will have someone living here to look after you—one of our own maids, a dear and devoted woman in her fifties who will cook for you, clean house for you, do all the things that Mercy has been doing and which Melissa will do in the future. This is only a question of *money*, dear Elton, and fortunately, Luke is a very, very successful man. Quite apart from the fact that . . ." she gestured modestly, "I have considerable money of my own. And nothing is too good for the father of our daughter-in-law."

Luke was filling the brandy glasses again, glad that his wife had taken over so completely. *A splendid woman, Genevieve,* he was thinking, *a wife I can trust to take over these difficult chores; and how simple she seems to make them!*

Mercy was thinking: *the decision is made, and no one has thought to ask my opinion. . . .*

But when, at last, they had gone, Elton said: "And now, perhaps a fire, child? I feel the cold creeping into my bones."

"Yes, Father." Obediently, Mercy took a Lucifer and pulled it through the glass-paper, and lit the paper under the kindling, and blew on the flames until they took hold. Then, knowing that the time had come for talk, she sat at the table and carefully tore long strips of newspaper for a while, folding them tightly into spills to be set in the little round jar that stood by the fire, spills for her father's pipe, to save the matches. She waited for him to speak, knowing that his heart was heavy at the thought of losing her; and when he did not, she took the initiative herself.

"You will miss me too, Father," she said. "It will be hard for both of us."

"Yes, it will be hard for both of us. But . . . it is the best thing that could possibly have happened. Nathan was always a very good boy. And handsome. He takes after his father. You remember how handsome he was?"

"I scarcely remember him at all, Father. I remember only . . ." She could not laugh about it, as she wanted to. "I remember that he once put three frogs in my bed."

"Three. For any other boy, one would have been enough."

"I remember sleeping on the floor all night in case there were more of them."

"You were seven years old when that happened."

"I was?"

She thought for a while about it, remembering the days when her father was still teaching, and would pick her up at her own Girls' School just around the corner from Milk Street, when they would walk home together hand in hand. The touch of his hand was so important to her! Those were the days when the Rookery was still beautiful and fresh smelling.

57

"Aunt Melissa," she said, worrying about it, "cannot cook as well as I can."

Smiling, he nodded. "But I am not really very demanding."

"She always burns the stew."

"Yes. But then, you have always spoiled me, far more than I deserve."

Her fingers were flying along the spills, the tips of them blackening from the smudged ink. The fire was beginning to burn nicely now. She banked it up with some slack from the bottom of the bucket and eased it all with the poker, letting the air come into the bottom of the grate. As she held it there for a moment, she looked at him, wondering why he looked so much older than his years. "Yes," she said, "I have always spoiled you. But not more than you deserve. I will miss you terribly."

She went and sat beside him again, sadly, listening to the relentless tick of the clock on the mantlepiece.

Aunt Melissa could not believe their good fortune when they told her.

She said, staring and stammering, "To . . . to *America!* But Good Heavens, Elton! America is . . . I might as well be going to the moon!"

She was quivering with excitement and she hugged Mercy to her, saying, "And will Nathan be there to meet you? If he is, I shall insist on a wedding while I am still there. He was always a wild boy, and we'll have no indelicacies. If you have to travel halfway across that monstrous country, full of Indians and bears and Lord knows what else . . . oh yes, we'll have a wedding the day he meets you. You must be very happy, child." She blew her long nose vigorously. "And I am very happy for you too."

"And now," Elton said slyly, "we are all members of a very wealthy family, you won't have to water down the whiskey anymore. This is a very happy day for us all, Melissa." He peered at Mercy. "The moon," he said, "is . . . what, now?"

"Entering the third quarter, Father."

"Ah . . ." He thought about it for a while. "Yes," he said. "Then this is a good day for us all."

He looked around the drab room, the faded wallpaper and the covers to the armchairs that had long lost their coloring, the big rug with its threadbare patches, and the mark on the wall where the big mahogany dresser had once stood that they had sold in a time of certain stress.

Aunt Melissa had taken the hint. She poured him a small glass of whiskey, and for almost the first time in her life she took one herself. She grimaced at it, but finished it quickly. She fussed around the house restlessly for a while and went to the kitchen and started cutting up meat and vegetables from the larder for a stew. But shortly, she called Mercy to her and said, "Mercy, I'm just too . . . too excited. Why don't you finish this for me?"

"All right, Aunt Melissa."

"You cook the meat first in a little dripping, for half an hour. And don't forget, we don't want the onions burned again, they taste terrible when they're burned."

"Aunt Melissa, I know how to make a stew."

"Yes, child, I believe you do, forgive me. It's all

59

so . . . so unexpected, I can't think how you can be so calm!"

She took hold of her niece by the shoulders, looked into her eyes and laughed, saying, "I'm trying to persuade myself that this is not all just a dream. America, can you imagine it? And I know, I'm a very foolish old woman, but do you know where I am going? Now? This very minute?"

Mercy shook her head and Aunt Melissa said, making it sound like a conspiracy, "I'm going for a carriage ride. I'm going over to the docks. I just want to . . . to *look* at a ship. Any ship. I want to imagine what it's like to spend nine or ten whole weeks . . . on the open sea . . . the middle of the Atlantic Ocean!"

She could hardly contain her excitement, but Mercy said, frowning, "Aunt Melissa . . . this is not a good day for you to go too far from the house."

"Not a good day? What on earth do you mean, child?"

"Your horoscope, Aunt Melissa, today is a very bad."

"Oh, pish-tosh, child! You know I don't believe in all that nonsense! Now let me go and gratify my silly little whims, and I will be back long before it's dark. We'll all have a very good supper and talk about the exciting days ahead of us . . ."

She put a long hatpin through her bonnet against the strong wind and left. Half an hour later, she was standing on the Adelphi Pier. The tall buildings, most of them three or four storeys high—one of them, the building of the Drapers' Guild, was as many as five—towered over the narrow

60

wharf. And the water in the Thames was muddy and dark, the tide low.

The ship she was staring at with such excitement coursing through her veins was no ocean-going vessel at all, but merely the steamboat *Cricket*, which ran between the city and the West End twice every day, a humble paddleboat of modest proportions, carrying a maximum of one hundred and eighty passengers at a paltry ha'penny a head for the twenty-five minute journey.

This was a time of intense competition for the river traffic. And though every cab and horse-drawn omnibus within the city was under the strict control of the licensing authorities, the river was still regarded as an open market, unlicensed and uncontrolled, so that the steamboat companies of the Thames were given free reign to compete with each other—a situation that gave rise to the most iniquitous practices. Even though the river was a hundred times more dangerous than the surface streets of London, the lack of adequate control over its flow of traffic inevitably meant that safety—an expensive factor at the best of times—was regarded as a luxury that the companies simply could not afford. Their piers were only too often merely ancient and worn-out barges planked over with rough-hewn timbers; and the boats themselves were frequently worse kept than their mooring places.

The *Cricket* was one hundred feet from the pier itself; and now, it was stuck in the mud. The tide was low, and on its turn the boat could, without a doubt, have been easily floated off. But the competition here was severe and to the ship's officers it seemed essential to get the paddles clear before competing boats could capture all their passengers; there were one hundred and fifty already on board, thirty of them below decks in the cabin. The great paddles were turning slowly, some of the slats splitting as they dug into the mud; but the power of the steam engines was formidable, and as the engineer pushed his levers a little too far forward, the boiler exploded.

The *Cricket* seemed to heave herself out of the water, quite slowly at first, but then with increasing speed. The whole of the center portion rose slowly, majestically, into the air, and crashed down on the Adelphi Pier. The boiler itself, reduced to shrapnel by the force of the explosion, went spinning through the air, half of it to come to rest on the bank hard by Waterloo Bridge, the other half showering down in scattered fragments of hot metal onto the Pier itself.

All of the cabin passengers, thirty of them, perished at once. Fourteen more passengers were driven deep into the river's mud by the force of the explosion and drowned there. Forty-eight injured bodies were floating in the dark water. And a few, incredibly, were still aboard the remnants of the boat, unharmed for the most part, and simply dumbfounded by what had happened.

On the Adelphi Pier, three people had been killed by falling pieces of metal. One of them was Aunt Melissa.

There was great grieving in the house that evening.

Luke Doren had heard of the tragedy first, in his

office on Vintners' Place, hard by Southwark Bridge. He had chosen this favored locale for his working quarters because of the swans on the river there. The Vintners and the Dyers were the only two guilds privileged by royal command to keep swans on the Thames; the Vintners' swans were marked by two nicks cut into the cygnet's bills. He had hurried over with the sad tidings, and after the tears had dried, the discussion of Mercy's future had continued.

"We must not allow this tragedy," Luke said firmly, "to interfere with Mercy's future. Life must go on. It is a sad and terrible calamity, but . . . yes, life must go on."

Elton, heavy-hearted, nodded. "Yes," he said quietly. "We must bear it as best we can. The funeral?"

"I will take care of the arrangements, Elton, if you will allow me to do so. As I said before . . . family, now."

"You are very kind, Luke. It is hard . . . hard for me to accept."

"Yes. Yes, I know that it must be."

"But Mercy cannot travel all the way to America alone."

"If it would make you feel more secure, I can find a suitable chaperon for her. But I think a letter to the Captain will suffice. I know him. Captain Angus MacDonald. A hard man, perhaps, but a righteous and God-fearing man. He will allow no . . . no indiscretions on board the *Capricorn*."

"And once she arrives in Boston harbor? It's a matter of grave concern to me, Luke."

63

"In Boston we have a Morse electromagnetic telegraph. Captain MacDonald can summon Nathan immediately, and he can be in Boston, let's see . . . from Oregon? A hundred days or less." He broke off, frowning. "No, I have a better idea. There is a sailing vessel leaving for Boston in three days' time. I will send Nathan a message, and Nathan can be in Boston when the *Capricorn* docks. I think that is preferable."

"Yes, yes, I'm sure it is." He sighed. "She was such a good woman, Luke."

"I know it. And now, of course, the question of your own position. The maidservant Genevieve spoke of. She will come and live here, Elton, unless . . . unless you would like to come and live with us? It can very easily be arranged. You are family now."

Elton sadly shook his head. "In this house, my wife died, my daughter was born. I will die here too, Luke, when my time comes. This is my home. I will not leave it while I can still make . . . some decisions of my own. But I thank you. You are a good friend, Luke, a generous friend."

Luke smiled. "Generous?" He said wryly, "Generosity, my dear Elton, is giving what we cannot afford to give. Unhappily, this is not the case in point."

Elton sighed. "If I did not have friends of your caliber, Luke . . ."

"Not just friends anymore," Luke said firmly. "But family."

Mercy was trimming the lamp wick, using the scissors carefully. "Father?" she said softly.

"Yes, my child?"

64

"You were going to speak to Luke about Clifford?"

He was puzzled, cocking his head a little to one side and trying to remember something he realized he ought not to have forgotten. "Clifford?"

"The young man who . . . the other night . . ."

"Ah, yes, of course. I'm glad you reminded me."

He turned to Luke and said carefully, "You have been so good, Luke, that I fear to ask more favors. And yet, I must."

"Anything, Elton. Ask."

"There is a young man," Elton said slowly, trying not to remember too clearly the shock that had been on his daughter's face. "A young man who saved Mercy from . . . well, I don't know exactly from what, but . . . in God's name, if I cannot tell you, Luke, then whom can I tell?"

He told him of Clifford's visit and that terrible night of the Chartists. Luke, his face taut with anger, listened patiently, and when he had finished, he said, "Elton, tell me where I can find this young man."

"At the Angel Tavern in Limehouse."

"I know it well. I will go there tonight."

"I do not think he will take money from you, Luke."

"Ah! A young man of sensitivity! That's a rare quality these days."

"But if you could help him to find . . . perhaps a more congenial occupation. I'm told that the work on board a whaler is very, very difficult and unrewarding."

"But the whalers make the best sailors. Yes, I'm sure I can find something for him. I have a clerk,

Mendelbaum by name, a Jew of course, but he knows of every opening on every ship in the Merchant Marine, really, quite a good man. I will send him to the Angel this very night, and I'm sure we can improve his position, one way or another."

"I take so many favors from you, Luke. But this one . . . it is very important to me. To all of us."

"Think no more of it, Elton. It is as good as done." He laughed suddenly. "They say that virtue is its own reward, but do you know? I never really believed that. Virtue must be rewarded by those of us who are able to reward it. Otherwise, we are all doomed to extinction at the hands of the worthless ones. Of whom, if you ask my opinion, there are far too many around these days. What was the name again?"

Mercy said clearly, "Clifford Hawkes."

"Clifford Hawkes," Luke echoed. "At the Angel Tavern in Limehouse. I shall send Mendelbaum to him tonight." He poured two more glasses of the good Spanish brandy and said gravely, "And now, a toast to your late sister, Melissa. May she rest in peace with the Lord."

On the street outside, the rooks were cawing loudly. There was a cat in the trees, robbing the nests, and the raucous sounds came to them, even through the closed windows. The windows had been closed to keep out the stench of the garbage that piled up in the gutter, sometimes as much as two feet high, waiting for the heavy downpour of rain that might come and carry it all away to the lower sluices leading eventually, to the fetid River Thames.

They sat together in silence, each of them knowing that the future, now, was changed inexorably for all of them. And in a short while, Mercy, leaving the two of them there to their pipes, their brandy, and their thoughts, went to her bed and cried herself to sleep.

CHAPTER FOUR

Only ten years previously, in an era when time passed slowly and the *status quo* was the order of the day, a trans-Atlantic service by the new steam vessels had been declared, with resounding emphasis, a physical impossibility.

Even when the British steamship *Great Western*, accompanied by three other paddleships of similar design, made successful crossings in the year 1838, and when the British and North American Royal Mail Steam Packet Company ships (with vessels of 1,150 tons as unwieldy as the Company's name) had emulated these startling successes, the idea of a ship driven by the power of steam was still alarming in the extreme to those who knew (and some who *feared*) that the Americas, with the march of science, were growing closer and closer to Europe.

There were even those alarming seafaring radicals who preached the frightening theory that iron was better than wood for a ship's hull. But their maritime predictions were very properly dismissed by all right-thinking seamen and the honest-to-God wooden sailing vessel was still the undisputed queen of the oceans.

The *Capricorn* was one of these. She was what was known as an "extreme clipper," built in a New York yard and promptly purchased by the Packet Company (soon to be called, more simply, *The Cunard Line*).

It was a gesture against the inexorable march of progress, a dramatic statement that a good clipper with fine American lines and a huge spread of canvas, could, given a fair wind (regardless of its direction), hold its own against any ship packed with man-made machinery. And be damned with Watts and all the other upstarts who were hoping to take over from God and Neptune with their infernal pistons and paddlewheels.

The *Capricorn*, although American in construction, had been built in close accord with the designs of the French war vessels, then the fastest afloat. She was a magnificent ship, long and slender, with no less than fifteen thousand running yards of sail on her three backward-sloping masts. She was three hundred and thirty-four feet in length, and fifty-three feet broad, and measured four thousand five hundred registered tons. Her masts were nearly two hundred feet high, and with her thirty-four sails pulling till the breaking-strain of rope, spar, and canvas was reached, she was capable of eighteen knots in fair weather and twenty-one in foul. She was a well-kept ship, and tightly disciplined; the speed of a clipper—particularly an extreme clipper—depended as much on discipline, almost, as upon its hull. One extra unwanted inch of freeway on the sheets could result in the loss of as many as four knots.

Her skipper was Captain Angus MacDonald, a Scot of somewhat chauvinistic, if not downright caricatural, proportions, and a demon with his canvas. He stood six foot three in his red woollen socks, his hair was white and close-cropped, and his face the texture of old leather that has cracked in the sun and needs the application of neats'-foot oil. He was a dour and bitter man, albeit one of the best skippers afloat.

He sat now in his tiny mahogany cabin, his huge hands wide-spread on his desk, brass-bound and gleaming, and he stared at Mercy with a touch of worry, even belligerence, on his grizzled old face. In captain's chairs of American maple, Luke and Mercy sat facing him. Genevieve, hardly finding room for her voluminous skirts, was seated in the cabin's only upholstered chair.

"Your name, sir," the Captain said to Luke, "is a greatly respected one, and I'll no' be offering ye any untoward criticism. But I'd have ye know, sir, the idea of an unaccompanied young lady on board my ship doesn'a appeal to me one whit. It's no' the proper way for a lady to travel, especially to a wild and uncivilized place like America." He grunted like a bellicose ox. "Oh, I'm no' thinkin' of the savage Indians, though the good Lord knows they're barbarous enough. I'm thinkin' more of the equally savage white men, and why would they leave their honest British homes if they had aught but mischief in their hearts? Can ye answer me that? No, of course ye canna."

71

"It's only a question," Luke said mildly, "of the ocean voyage, Captain MacDonald. Once you reach Boston harbor, my son will be there waiting. I have already arranged for this. And I am sure that on board ship, in your good hands, no difficulties will befall her."

"Well, maybe not," the Captain said grudgingly. He was trying to avoid staring too indelicately at Genevieve's deep décolleté, the upper part of her breasts gleaming softly in the lamplight. And as he was sternly controlling his anger, remembering. . . .

It was four years now since his daughter Lucy had left his home, just disappearing one day and leaving a note behind that said simply but inexplicably: "Please don't try to find me, I love you both but I cannot stay here any longer." It had sent his wife, a dour and stolid woman, into panic at first and then into a state of deep depression from which she had never recovered. The breakup of the family was bad enough, but there was worse, far worse to follow. . . .

He had stopped off at the Elephant and Castle public house (which had long since lost its original name, the *Infanta de Castille*) where the dockside touts gathered in their drunken evenings to drum up trade for the profitable Atlantic crossing—frequently on ships that were so badly equipped and ill-prepared that some of them never even reached the halfway mark before being forced to turn back.

There was fierce competition on this route. The new world was beckoning; there were no restrictions on immigration to the Americas at all; and these fly-by-night operators were accepting passen-

72

gers for whatever paltry sum could be wheedled from them. It was giving the transoceanic trade a very bad name, and the righteous Captain had decided to take matters into his own hands by turning at least some of these hired vagabonds over to the magistrates for swift and stern justice.

But to his horror, he had found his lost daughter there, a common whore for the sailors, her face painted with rouge as she mocked his repugnance. Her body had been shamelessly exposed as, at this moment, the breasts of Luke Doren's wealthy socialite wife were—an open invitation, it seemed to him, to the devil of lust that was present in all men, even the best of them.

"A passage to America," this expensively gowned woman was saying, "is all that we are really concerned with, Captain MacDonald. Once Mercy arrives there, your responsibilities are at an end. Meanwhile, I hope you will remember that she is of good family, a very modest and retiring young woman."

A sharp retort was on his lips at once. "In a long and hard life, Ma'am," he said, "I have learned to my own cost that a modest and retiring young woman can meet the Devil more than halfway, indeed on his own grounds, once she feels that the bonds of a decent and God-fearing family life ha' been loosened. I'll no' be arguin' the point with gentlefolk of your quality, but if Mistress Mercy understands that I'll allow no shenanigans on board ma vessel . . . then, as ye rightly say, no difficulties will befall her."

"And perhaps you would be kind enough," Luke Doren said, "to have her escorted, on your arrival,

73

to your company office in Boston. It is there that my son will be waiting for her."

"His name, sir?"

"Nathan Doren, Captain. He's in the fur business· and making a fine name for himself."

"I'll see to it," the Captain said, "and meanwhile, she'll have to have a cabin to herself. I've no other single ladies on board, I'm happy to say."

He got to his feet, a giant of a man in a dark blue woollen shirt under his heavy dark wool jacket. The interview was over and Mercy had not spoken a word. She had sat there like an obedient schoolgirl, listening to the Captain's doubts and not liking them at all. Once, she had been tempted to answer him back, but had refrained for Luke's sake and for Genevieve's.

Luke took out his gold half-hunter watch and wound it automatically. "We have a long ride back to Chelsea, Captain," he said. "So if you will excuse us now?"

The Captain nodded. "Have no worries, sir," he said. "Your ward is in good hands."

"I'm sure of it. And you sail tonight?"

"No sir." The Captain shook his grizzled head. "I've decided to take the morning tide instead of tonight's. The wind is playing us false and I've no wish to lie becalmed in Halfway Reach. The river's too crowded with those damnable steamships and paddleboats. No sir, we'll leave on the morning tide." He bowed stiffly to Genevieve. "Your servant, Ma'am."

He had to stoop as he escorted them out of the cabin, and up the companionway to the decks. When they had gone ashore, Mercy leaned on the taffrail and watched them drive off in the fine

74

black-painted carriage, the bay horses prancing and shaking their plumes, the top-hatted coachman in his fine red jacket cracking his whip. She thought sadly of her father, sitting there silent and alone in the little Rookery house, and she wondered if she would ever see him again.

It had been a tearful farewell. Her voyage seemed to her to be more than across the wide ocean; there was, indeed, a terrible feeling of isolation, and not only for herself. Elton had forced a smile as he embraced her, but she could feel his trembling, could see the moisture in his eyes. She wondered if he had been thinking the same thing: *shall we see each other again, ever?* The thought was more than she could bear.

When the carriage had turned from the wharf and into Stew Lane (named after the stews, or bordellos, that were still functioning there), Mercy turned away and went to her cabin, a tiny cubicle no more than six feet by seven, the roof only inches above her head. The narrow bunk ran down one wall and left space for a small dressing table with a basin and pitcher of water on it, a single chair, and a tiny cupboard.

Her steamer trunk—a fine leather one given her by Genevieve for the journey—was standing in the corridor, almost filling it. Next to it was a cheerful young steward, a brown-skinned man with a strange accent she thought might be Indian, who told her, "When you have unpacked what you need for the voyage, Mem, we will take it down to the . . . hold, isn't it?" His voice was soft and melodious, a sing-song lilt to it, and his white smile was very friendly. He had told her his name was Sharma, and he wore a starched white jacket buttoned up to the throat, with dark red trousers of a material she had never seen before. In spite of the friendly smile and the humble manner, he frightened her.

She lay down on the bunk in her clothes and stared up at the dark planks of the ceiling. She had never felt so terribly alone and she tried to think of Nathan, tried to remember him but could not define him clearly. Soon, she was weeping openly, and in a little while, she cried herself to sleep.

She did not know how long she had slept, but it was the cold that woke her, and she reached instinctively for a blanket and found, in the moments of awakening, that she was lying on top of the covers, and that there was a gentle swaying motion all around her. She could hear an alarming sound of creaking wood and shouts from somewhere above her head . . . or were they coming through the porthole, tightly closed with its heavy brass handles? She swung herself quickly off the bunk and opened the door, peering out with a strange feeling of excitement in her veins.

Were they moving?

A portly gentleman in a heavy overcoat with a muffler around his neck was easing his way past her cabin trunk, still there, and he looked at her in surprise and then raised his top hat courteously. "A fine good morning to you, Ma'am," he said.

She stared back and said, "Good . . . *morning*?"

He nodded. "Yes indeed, and a fine morning it's going to be too."

"But . . . are we moving?"

"Moving? Why, Ma'am, we've been under way for three hours or more. Were you sleeping?"

"Yes, yes I was." She could not believe that she

had slept so long. Was it the trauma of parting that had drained her so completely?

"Then a fine sight you missed when we passed the Tower," he said. "A shaft of moonlight was striking the Traitor's Gate and the ghost of Henry was standing there, beckoning to the white sails of our ship. Seeking to escape, no doubt, from his cruel captivity."

"The ghost of . . . of Henry, sir?" she asked, startled. "I do not believe I understand you."

"That most hapless of monarchs," he replied, "the sixth of his name, cruelly put to death in the Tower, like so many others. But I recognized him instantly, the founder, Ma'am, four hundred years ago, of my college at Cambridge. I with you a good day." He tapped his hat carefully back into place and strode on, and she wondered if all her fellow-passengers were as mad as he seemed to be.

She went on up the companionway to the deck, and was astonished to see so many people lining the rails and taking their last view of a country many of them would never see again. The sky ahead of them was a dark, dark gray, with just a sliver of the most brilliant red low on the calm water, and close by, so close she felt she could almost reach out and touch them, were the walls of a great fortress on the southern shore. Its long guns somehow seemed menacing in the pale light of the dawn.

There were still flares and gaslights faintly visible there and she heard someone say, excitedly, "Blue Town of Sheerness, and the Island of Sheppey."

A paddlesteamer was churning ponderously alongside them, overtaking them, and its rails were also lined with passengers, shouting at them with a kind of good-humored joviality. She heard a shout from its deck and they were close enough for her to make out the shape of a man standing there, cupping his hands to his voice, "Pour on more steam, matey, or you'll never get there."

Everyone was laughing all around her and she looked up at the huge spread of canvas billowing in the morning breeze, thinking that she had never before seen anything quite so beautiful.

There was the sound of a bell behind her, up on the bridge somewhere, and then a lighter one, a little tinkling noise. It was Sharma and he was moving among the crowd and calling out happily, "Breakfast is served, ladies and gentlemen. Breakfast is being served."

Some of the passengers, who seemed to know their way around on board this huge ship, were moving down the companionway again and Mercy followed them, wondering just what her first meal at sea would be like.

The excitement of the journey was slowly taking its irresistible hold on her.

Breakfast was a simple affair—a plate of porridge and a slice of salted bacon to each passenger—but it was strange to her too. The milk and the sugar for the porridge were combined, it seemed, in a tin can of thick, cream-colored liquid which she had never seen before, or even heard of, and after tasting the sickly syrup cautiously, she decided to eat the mess unflavored.

There was a lot of talk around her at the long bench table, but she kept very much to herself, answering the occasional questions her fellow passengers asked her with as few words as possible. She was quite unaccustomed to the company of strangers and found the experience alarming in the extreme.

She went back to her cabin after the meal was over and took her few spare dresses from her big cabin trunk so that Sharma could get it out of everyone's way, then went back on deck again to watch the sailors clambering over the rigging. High up there in the sky they seemed like flies on the tall masts.

The ship was beginning to roll now as it came into open water, though there was still land close by on the right. A town there, she realized with a little thrill, might be Margate, where she had gone once as a child with her father, when he was still working. She saw the sails dropping into place and unfurling, and the rolling was so intensified that she had to grasp the railing to keep her balance. There was one moment of acute alarm when she thought the great ship would surely turn right over. A middle-aged woman standing beside her, in an alarming dress of bright-red muslin with black flounces around the skirt, smiled at her and said, in the broad brogue of the north, "Is it your first trip, lassie?"

Mercy nodded, and the woman went on, "It's my *third*. Don't let the rolling upset you now, we're as safe as the Rock of Gibraltar, and almost as big too." She carried a tiny pink parasol and took the arm of the boy beside her and moved on.

There was a tall and handsome man striding down from the bridge and looking up at the sails with an expert eye, who cupped his hands to his mouth and called out, "Bo'sun! Watch your tops'l!"

She heard a whistle blow and a shouted command she could not understand, and then the tall man was moving toward her with an easy, swaggering sort of walk, balancing himself lightly on the balls of his feet against the movement of the deck. He wore a very heavy shirt of knitted wool with the sleeves rolled up, his forearms heavily corded with muscle, and an oilcloth hat over his long, dark hair. He had a heavy moustache which gave him a faintly foreign sort of look, and sharp, alert eyes set rather too closely together. He looked like a very hard man and perhaps a cruel one, but he was smiling now as he approached her, his dark eyes peering into hers with a somehow quizzical look in them.

"If the rolling bothers you, Ma'am," he said, "you'll be pleased to know that it will soon be over. Once we turn south we'll be driving harder, under full sail. Meanwhile, remember always to make sure there's a post, a railing, close beside you to hold onto if she takes a sudden dip, as she will once in a while."

His eyes were still on her, but he was looking her up and down now in a manner she found a little distasteful. "You are Mistress Mercy Carrol, I believe," he said. "The Captain tells me this is your first journey on board ship?"

"Yes, I am Mercy Carrol. And this is indeed my first sea voyage."

"The first can be alarming, Ma'am, but you'll soon get used to it. And my name is Butrus, Adam Butrus. I'm the First Mate and one of my responsibilities is the comfort and well-being of our passengers." He paused, and then, still smiling, "Especially those who are travelling alone and are without experience of shipboard life."

She began politely, "Mr. Butrus . . ."

"If there is anything I can do for you, all you have to do, Ma'am, is send your steward to me."

"You're very kind, sir."

His eyes were on her bust, confined under the tight bodice, and she felt the blood rushing to her face. She drew the shawl closer over her shoulders. "And if you will excuse me now, I will go to my cabin."

As she moved off, he said, quite quietly, "And Ma'am?"

She turned. "Remember, Ma'am," he said. "If you need any assistance at all, any time of the day or night, I am at your service. Just . . . send for me, and I'll be at your side as quick as a wink."

She felt he was laughing at her and she hated him for it. She made no answer as she swept off down the companionway, blushing furiously with a kind of anger she could not really account for. And as she moved along the narrow corridor to her cabin, she saw a broad-shouldered young man bending over her trunk. He was wearing a hairshirt and canvas trousers, and as she approached he turned, a look of sheer amazement on his face—it was Clifford.

She could not believe her eyes. She said, startled, "Clifford!"

His young, boyish face broke into a wide, wide grin. He stepped forward, took both her hands in his, and said, laughingly, "I could scarcely believe it. I saw your name on the labels, and still . . . I could not believe it! But it really is you?"

She was laughing suddenly with him and she threw open the door to her cabin and said quickly, "Come inside, we have so much to talk about."

But he drew back. "No, no," he said not losing the wide grin. "I am not allowed inside the cabins. I'm just a deckhand. . . ."

"But what on earth are you doing here?"

"I feel I should ask you the same question, Mistress Mercy."

"Me? Well, I'm on my way to America."

"I guessed as much, there's nowhere else this ship is going."

"Yes, of course! Well, I'm on my way to Boston, where . . ." She broke off. It suddenly occurred to her that she just did not want to talk about Nathan now, nor her coming marriage, and she said instead, "But you . . . I thought you worked on one of the whalers? What was it, the *Northern Wind*?"

"Indeed, Mistress Mercy, till a short time ago, I did. But this is your father's doing, bless his good heart." In a sudden access of alarm, he went on, "He is well? I mean . . . if you are leaving home?"

He left it hanging and Mercy said, nodding, "Yes, he is as well as he ever was, missing me badly I am sure, as much as I miss him. But what do you mean, your presence here is my father's doing?"

He still held her hands and there was great warmth in them. "You remember that night?" he said. "We talked about . . . what did you call it? My horoscope?"

"Yes, of course I remember! I told you it was time to reach out for any opportunity that came your way."

"And I did. A few days after we first met, a strange man came to see me, a man named . . . Mendlebaum, I think. He said he was clerk to a shipping company and had been instructed to bring me a letter of recommendation to the North American Mail Company, a company, you must understand, that owns very many good ships. I had no way of knowing why this should happen, but then, he told me that his employer was a gentleman named Luke Doren. I recalled then that this was the name your father mentioned."

"Yes, yes, of course, he's such a good man."

"I went to the company offices on Hanging Sword Alley, and I presented my papers. I must confess, I thought they were not much interested. But then, a little while later, a messenger came to my lodging place and told me to report on board the *Capricorn* in the West India dock. I could not believe my good fortune! You may not know this, but . . . a passenger-ship! That's the best occupation of all for a sailor, and after the *Northern Wind*. . . . On the whaler, I slept on bare boards that were always wet, and here, I have a hammock with forty other deckhands. On the whaler, there was never enough to eat, and only hard biscuits at that, while here . . . I eat like a king! And now . . . the best surprise of all is to find you here. I still cannot believe my eyes!"

"But come inside," Mercy said, urging him. "I'm sure it will be all right, for just a few moments."

He hesitated and then there was an angry roar coming from the far end of the corridor, loud and imperious and uncouth, "Hawkes! Seaman Hawkes or whatever your damned name is! Get that trunk down to the hold!"

Startled, Mercy saw a stout and bearded man with squinty eyes coming toward them, a look of fury on his face. He wore a red kerchief around his neck that made him look like a pirate, and Clifford said promptly, "Aye aye, Bo'sun Ollie."

He stooped and lifted up the trunk onto his broad shoulders, looking quickly at Mercy before moving off with it. The angry man eyed her and said gruffly, "Bo'sun Ollie, Ma'am, and if that confounded deckhand is troubling you . . ."

"Oh no," she said quickly. "He is a friend, Mr. Ollie, a friend from London town."

"A friend?" It seemed the idea gave him no pleasure at all. "Deckhands do not have friends among the paying passengers, Ma'am. Especially among the . . . the young women travelling alone."

Did everyone on board know that she was unaccompanied? It seemed such a trifling matter, and yet, in a very short space of time, both the Mate and the Bo'sun had mentioned it. She wasn't quite sure what the term *Bo'sun* meant, but she instinctively disliked this coarse and ugly man. He turned away without another word and she went into the cabin and lay on the bunk, reading her little book on astrology and trying to find out just why the stars had sent Clifford aboard this very ship.

It was a slender volume, bound in gray Morocco leather, with its title imprinted in gold leaf: "Endercroft's Prognostications." On the title page there was the annotation: "A Survey of the Probable Events, as Determined by the Planets, for the Year of Our Lord 1848." It had cost her father eightpence three farthings from his little cache of the money that Luke had provided, and it was a well-worn and well-read little book.

One of its passages in particular fascinated her. She had searched it through and through for references to her new home in America, but had found very little:

". . . a year of the most terrible violence all over the globe, with the exception of the northern parts of the New World . . . In the Austrian Empire, there is the Revolt in Lombardy and Venetia, and the war with Sardinia. In France, the outcome of the Banquet Rebellion will almost certainly mean the flight, if not the death, of the French King. In Scandinavia, which has been well-blessed by the juxtapositioning of the Planets throughout this decade, we may expect to see the beginnings of a major war, almost certainly with Prussia, which country's martial aspect is sorely affected this year by Mars itself. In Spain, the agitation towards violent revolution will continue unabated, and the trouble with the Sikhs of India will undoubtedly erupt into war. . . . In the northern quarters of the New World, however, we can expect more progress, and more enlightenment. The Mexican problem will no longer be of consequence, the territorial acquisitions of President Polk will exceed those of any other President save Jefferson, and in New York, history's first Convention for the Rights of Women will have far-reaching results, all of them excellent. . . ."

There was nothing about strangers, once-met and parted, being drawn together again, but she found great comfort in the final phrase of the passage: "A very propitious year for those fortunate enough to be born under Sagittarius, Pisces, or Capricorn."

She put the little book away, sat at the confining dressing-table, and brushed her long hair—one

85

hundred strokes with the boars'-bristle brush, as poor dear Aunt Melissa had always told her to do.

She did not see Clifford again that day, nor the next, though as she wandered around the ship's deck she kept her eyes well open for him, watching the deckhands as they scrubbed at the caulked timbers and polished the brasswork and scrambled lithely through the rigging. On the third day, she sent Sharma to Captain MacDonald to ask if she might see him.

In a short while the steward returned, beaming, and said happily, "If you will come with me, Mem, the Captain is seeing you now."

She followed him to the little cabin where she had last seen him, with Luke and Genevieve, and this time Captain MacDonald did not ask her to be seated, nor did he sit down himself. Instead, he stood behind his desk with his eyes constantly glancing at the polished brass clock on the wall as though impatient to waste time with her. But he was courteous enough, in a gruff sort of way.

"What may I do for you, young woman?" he asked.

She felt awkward standing there, but she was determined to say what she had to say. She held her head a little high, remembering his cold manner on that last occasion and not much caring for it. "One of your sailors," she said clearly, "is a young man I have met before, in London . . ."

He interrupted her brusquely, frowning, "And he has been making a nuisance of himself, is that it?"

"No, sir. Quite to the contrary. I saw him only once aboard this ship, but . . . I am greatly in his debt, and I would like to see him, if I may, and continue with him a conversation that we began and were unable to finish. We had begun to talk, but one of your . . . officers? I believe he was called the Bo'sun, whatever that means . . ."

"The officer in charge of the ship's rigging," he said, interrupting her. "Another of his duties concerns the discipline on board the ship, and had he no' interrupted your . . . your chitchat, he'd ha' been failing in his duty."

"Be that as it may," Mercy said, trying not to sound angry. "We were interrupted, rather discourteously, and I would like, if I may, to spend a few moments with this man."

"Courtesy, Ma'am," the Captain said dryly, "is hardly a quality I look for among the lower ranks of ma officers. But if he was rude to you personally, then ye have ma apologies."

"Then I may see him?"

"The seamen on board ma ship, Ma'am," he said clearly, "are not permitted to associate with the passengers. And in your own case, most certainly not."

"Because I am travelling alone, is that why, Captain MacDonald? I can assure you . . ."

He interrupted her again, sharply, "I do not need your assurances, Ma'am! I will command this vessel the way it should be commanded. I will maintain the strictest discipline among the crew, and aye, among the passengers too." He began almost to explode. "In Heaven's name, Ma'am, what kind of a ship do you think this is? I'll no' have the paying passengers treating the sailors as their equals, under any circumstances whatsoever! What manner of arrogance do you think he'd presume if I were to allow such a breach of proper conduct? Come to your senses, young woman! It's out of the question!"

She struggled to contain her anger, an anger of which she had never known she was capable. "But sir," she said, "arrogance has no part in this young man's character. He came to my rescue at a time when I sorely needed help, and he gave it unstintingly and with no thought of recompense whatsoever. And all that I ask of you is that I be allowed to spend a few moments with him . . ."

He would not let her finish. "And the ship, you believe, will run itself while the lower ranks are chatting with the passengers? Would you like me to turn her into the wind, and furl her sails, and call a halt to all the hard work that goes on day and night, unceasingly, and must go on constantly if this ship is to live up to her reputation and I am to live up to mine. Is that what you ask of me?"

He moved to the door and held it open for her, but she stood her ground and said coldly, "You are yourself aware, no doubt, that that is an exaggeration that borders on the ridiculous! I ask for a few moments with *one* man, in his spare time!"

He was as furious as she was now; and Mercy was trembling, wondering at her own fortitude against this formidable man. "Spare time?" he said. "Spare time? Ma crewmen have *no* spare time."

"A watch," she said stubbornly, "is, I am told, four hours long . . ."

He could not contain himself. "And you dare to lecture me on the rules of the sea? A slip of a girl out of the slums of the Rookery . . ."

He broke off; his face was white. There was a brief moment of silence as she stared at him, shaken and aghast, and the breath all went out of him suddenly. The color came back to his face, suffusing it, and he said, more quietly now, but very stiff and formal, "Mistress Mercy, I must beg your forgiveness. That was an unwarranted remark, and I offer you my apologies for it."

She began to speak, but he raised an imperious hand. "No," he said, "I'll ask ye to accept ma apology, and we'll forget the whole matter, it was my indignation at your . . . your romantic inclinations, the romantic inclinations of a foolish schoolgirl, that prompted my anger. Mr. Luke Doren, a gentleman for whom I have the highest respect, told me of your . . . your family, and I understand it's a genteel one in spite of your circumstances."

He paused, waiting for her to answer him, but she could not; the tears were coming into her eyes, and she fought against them, thinking of her father and his constant fight to maintain that . . . that "gentility."

He went on, less brusquely now, "I have . . . personal reasons I will not recount to you, for believing, no, not believing, *knowing*, that a young woman who frees herself from the shackles of a decent family life is easily led astray by her own weakness, and I'll not encourage it in a young girl who has been put under my protection." He paused a moment, and then, "Will ye forgive that outburst of indignation? It's no' much to ask."

She was calmer now, a tight, controlled anger inside her. "Yes," she said calmly. "I will forgive it. And may I see this young man? His name . . ."

Once again, he interrupted her. "I dinna care to know his name, Ma'am. And, no, you may not see him."

She could not credit his stubbornness. He still

89

stood at the open door, an invitation for her to leave.

She picked up her skirts and flounced out of the room.

CHAPTER FIVE

She saw him once, three days later.

She recognized the buff-colored hairshirt and the whaler's canvas trousers. He was on his hands and knees on the lower deck, swabbing at it with a gigantic brush and a pail of soapy water. She was above him, leaning on the after-rail, and watching the porpoise that curved in and out among the waves when she became aware of him; the hairshirt was a distinctive garment, and she caught her breath as she realized it was he. In a moment she called softly, "Clifford? . . ."

He swung round, looking at her, and then his eyes moved very slightly and he went back to his scrubbing. She turned round and Adam Butrus was there, close behind her, smiling down at her, a somewhat sardonic look on his face. His moustaches had been freshly curled and his dark hair was blowing in the wind.

"Mistress Mercy," he said politely. "He looked down at Clifford and back to her. "You are, I turst," he said pleasantly, "somehow finding ways to mitigate the boredom of an ocean crossing?"

She nodded. "Thank you, sir," she said. "I find it interesting enough."

He looked out at the porpoises. "They follow us always, looking for tidbits among the garbage. I suppose that's what we all do, in the sea or out of it." He was laughing quietly to himself and again it irritated her. She began to move away, but he said, still smiling, "No, please don't go. Perhaps there are things we can talk of to our mutual advantage."

She turned back. "Oh? What is it on your mind, sir?"

He turned away and gripped the railing with powerful hands, staring out across the water. "On this longitude," he said, "Spain lies five hundred miles to the south of us. To the north . . . it's nearly two thousand miles to the shores of Iceland. And ahead of us . . . an ocean that sometimes seems limitless. We are sailing at nearly seventeen knots, and yesterday we logged no less than three hundred and twenty-two miles. And yet . . . it will still take us another nine days to reach our landfall." He turned to her again. "Does it alarm you, Mistress Mercy, that we are such an infinitesimal speck on such a vast expanse of water?"

Mercy shook her head. "No, Mr. Butrus. Should it?"

"Nothing between the deepest ocean floor and the Heavens . . . except us. Sometimes the thought of it alarms even me."

"Even you?"

"I am not a man who is given to foolish fears." His eyes went briefly to Clifford and back to her, and he said easily, "Our good Captain told me that you were interested in one of our vulgar deck-hands. That is he, no doubt."

She felt the anger rising again. "Not a vulgar man, sir. A good man."

"He tells me you wanted to speak with him. Perhaps I could give him a message from you."

Her heart leaped suddenly and for a moment she was tempted to take him at his word. But the sardonic look on his face was almost a leer.

"I am sure your offer is made with the most honorable of intentions," she said coldly. "But it will not be necessary, Mr. Butrus."

He was mocking her again, blatantly. "Or perhaps," he said, "I could arrange for the meeting you so avidly desire. An hour or two together, in the privacy of your cabin? . . ."

She held his look. "I find this conversation offensive," she said quietly. "If you will excuse me." As she moved away, she felt his eyes burning into the back of her head, heard his derisive laughter following her, quiet and assured and somehow contemptuous too.

She was not to see Clifford again for another three days, search though she might. She wondered if he had been sent to work in the bowels of this great ship. Many times, she had seen Adam Butrus staring at her, that faintly quizzical smile on his handsome face, and it seemed to her at these times that he was deliberately taunting her. She turned away whenever she saw him looking at her and tried to lose herself among the other passengers as they strolled the deck, played shuffleboard on the calmer days, or sat and read in the low-ceilinged lounge below decks when the weather was wet or cold.

And then, on the tenth night out, she lay restless on her bunk, tossing and turning and finding no sleep in the stifling cabin. At last she put on a robe over her nightgown and went on deck for a breath of fresh, cold air.

The night was clear and brilliant, the moon almost full, the water calm and peaceful, the waves no higher than those of a large lake. The moonlight was making pretty patterns on the sea. She stood in the shadow of a lifeboat and stared down at them, thinking sadly about Clifford and wondering if she would see him again, even when, at last, they docked in Boston harbor and he could, perhaps, escape from the iron discipline of the clipper. The breeze was warm now, and she opened her robe a little, slid her hand under her nightdress and touched her breasts, caressing them gently.

And then, she swung round in sudden alarm. There was a shadow beside her and Adam Butrus was moving to her, almost gliding to her with a movement that seemed sinister to her. His smile was wide and he put out his strong arms and gripped the rail on either side of her, imprisoning her. He stood for a moment looking down at her as she hastily gathered the robe tighter about her.

"Mistress Mercy," he said politely. "A splendid moonlit night, a calm sea, and a fine spread of canvas . . . are you well?"

There was the smell of whiskey on his breath and she thought for a moment, incongruously, of the bottle that Aunt Melissa used to dilute with

...l and her father's patience as he poured it
...oked his battered pipe. She began to move
...but his arms imprisoned her, not even
...ng her. She looked around wildly, sure that
...was nothing but the direst trouble in store for
her now; the feeling of panic was insupportable.

Adam Butrus said, his eyes boring into hers, "Are
you frightened, Mistress Mercy? There is no cause
for alarm, I assure you." His voice was very quiet
and gentle, but his eyes seemed to be on fire, burning with an intensity that was alarming.

He was a man of enormous physical power; and
he was a cypher with a sly and secretive mind,
filled, always, with wild and ruthless schemes for
his own well-being. No one knew where he had
come from, nor where he had learned his formidable expertise at the trades of seafaring and fighting.

It was rumored that he had once been master of
his own ship, that was said to have sunk mysteriously with all hands drowned—except its Captain. It
was rumored that he had once commanded an
army of three thousand fighting men, but no one
on board this ship for dark and nefarious purposes
of his own, which had little to do with the well-
being of the *Capricorn*. It was rumored (and this
he had been heard on occasion to deny vehemently) that he had spent many years in the Americas, but doing what, or precisely where, no one
could imagine.

He had once been seen, in a Limehouse tavern, to
use his fighting expertise. Eight doughty seamen
had set upon him with murder in their hearts and
he had seized a cutlass from the wall and laid about

95

him with all the ease and assurance of the pr[o]
sional swordsman, scattering his opponents, woun[d]
ing four of them in as many seconds, and then, tossing the sword contemptuously aside, smashing two heads together with a skull-cracking force before finishing his drink and calmly walking out.

The below-decks tales about him were legendary; and no truths were known at all.

He said again, slyly, "Are you frightened, Ma'am?"

Mercy shook her head. Summoning her courage, she looked at him coldly, even disdainfully. "If you will kindly let me go, Mr. Butrus?"

He shook his head slowly. "No, Ma'am, I will not let you go. And what will you do? Will you scream?" He did not move his hands away from the railing, nor shift his eyes, nor lose the smile. "And if you scream, who will come running? The Captain, perhaps? An honest and God-fearing man, the Captain, who believes that all young women are whores."

She caug[ht] ... arouses him to righteous indignation, it gives me the greatest pleasure. Are you a whore, Mistress Mercy?"

She said savagely, "Let me go! At once, do you hear me?"

He let go of the railing now and placed his hands on her shoulders, a strong and cruel grip that dug into her soft flesh, bruising her. "Scream, Mistress Mercy," he said gently.

She found herself instinctively taking a deep breath, and his hand was over her mouth instantly, stifling any sound, as he pulled her in tightly to

96

him with his other arm around her slender waist and put his face close to hers, hissing, "We have a witness, Mistress Mercy, hiding in the shadows and enjoying the spectacle that you offer him. Shall I summon him for you?" He pursed his lips and gave a low whistle and a squat, ungainly form moved out from nearby. It was Bo'sun Ollie and he was grinning at her like a maniac.

Butrus was gripping her cheeks tightly, forcing her head back into the planking of the lifeboat till she thought it would split her head open, and she struggled against his strength to no avail at all. He held her pinned there like a rag doll, crushing her face. Now his other hand left her waist and pulled her robe open and began fondling one naked breast. She struck at him with both her fists and Butrus said to the Bo'sun, very softly, "A wildcat, Ollie . . . I fear she must be held until she understands."

The Bo'sun laughed, squinting lecherously at her exposed and cruelly mauled breasts, as he moved to her side and took hold of her wrists, twisting her arms up behind her back so that the upper part of her torso was thrust forward, painfully. Butrus's hand was sliding from one bare breast to the other and his face was very close to hers, so close that she could smell the whiskey on his breath.

He was caressing her more lightly now, fingering the nipples. Sliding the robe down off her shoulders, he said, carefully and slowly, "You were going to scream, Mistress Mercy whore, and if one sound escapes those lovely lips, let me tell you what will happen. The after-deck watch will come running and he will be sent back to his post with a flea in his ear. If your screams are loud enough to wake the Captain and he should come running too . . . can you imagine what will happen to your reputation when I tell him you tried to seduce me? For money?"

Smiling, he said, "Whores, all of you. He knows it, and I know it. But what would we do without you?" He looked at the Bo'sun and said, "The lifeboat, Ollie."

Adam Butrus's two hands were at her head now, one over the mouth and the other at the back of her neck, and Ollie was grasping her ankles and swinging her off the ground. She struggled but could not escape them, and she felt the rough planking over the lifeboat cutting into her back as they slid her over its side and under the tarpauline. She tried to kick at them but could scarcely move a limb at all. His face was close to hers again and the light in his eyes was demonic.

"Will you listen to me?" he hissed at her. "Do you think anyone will take the word of a whore against that of two ship's officers? You're going to get it, you're going to get it *now*! So lie still, for Christ's sake, and accept it! It won't be the first time and it won't be the last."

The Bo'sun, an obedient slave, was crouched above her head, holding her hands down with one of his own. The other hand he held over her mouth, forcing her head into the boards of the boat, and Butrus was lying atop of her, forcing her thighs apart with a knee, mauling her tender, creamy breasts with both hands. She felt one of them take hold of the cloth of her nightdress, pulling it up above her waist and exposing her private body. Then a hand was there too, clutching at her, a finger probing, and she bit savagely into the hand

that was at her mouth, sinking her teeth into calloused fingers and biting down with all the strength
she could muster. When Ollie, cursing, pulled his
hand away, she screamed at the top of her voice
and felt a fist descend onto her head, sending her
momentarily into oblivion and cutting off all further sound.

She heard, vaguely, a terrible obscenity from Butrus that she barely understood, and then the hand
was over her mouth again, more cruelly now.
There was the touch of flesh against her thighs and
in panic she tried to twist her body away from it.
And then there was the sound of running feet and
a movement of the boat as a lithe body leaped up
onto it, and she saw, her eyes wide with fright, that
a man was standing there, framed hugely against
the night sky. The hairshirt was a symbol to her; it
was Clifford.

He jumped down into the boat, took hold of
Adam Butrus by the collar of his jacket, hauled
him up and drove a fist into his face. Butrus went
sprawling over the side of the lifeboat to land on
the deck and then Bo'sun Ollie was on Clifford, the
two of them clenched together and struggling violently, rolling over the sides and falling heavily to
the deck beside the Mate.

Mercy stumbled to her feet, screaming, as the
three of them fought there. Bo'sun Ollie was holding Clifford from behind in a powerful grip as
Adam Butrus drove his fists repeatedly, one after
the other and with murderous force, into Clifford's
belly. There were the sounds of shouting now, and
of running men, and shadows were coming out of
the darkness . . . four, five, seven sailors, standing

there in the moonlight and watching the fight. And she still went on screaming.

Then, a stentorian bellow came out of the shadows at them: "Stop it! Stop it, I tell you!"

It was the furious voice of Captain MacDonald, standing there in his red socks and his Tartan robe. When the fighting did not immediately stop, he reached out and caught Bo'sun Ollie by the collar and drove a fist into his face, knocking him to the deck and shouting again, "Stop it, I told ye!"

Adam Butrus pulled away. He was breathing heavily. Ollie picked himself up off the deck and rubbed at his chin, and Clifford, quite unconscious now, lay there at their feet.

The Captain stood belligerently, his feet widespread, his arms akimbo, looking at the contestants. "Well?" he roared. "If ye'll tell me, Mr. Butrus, the meaning of this commotion?"

The seamen, sensing trouble, were fading into the shadows. Mercy fell and clutched at the side of the lifeboat, a little above them; she was conscious of the Captain's eyes boring into hers.

Butrus was panting, wiping the blood at the side of his mouth. "I found these two, Captain," he said, "fornicating in the lifeboat." He looked down at Clifford's unconscious body. "I ordered this seaman back to his quarters and he struck me, a savage blow that . . ."

"He *struck* you, Mr. Mate?" the Captain said.

"Aye sir. He struck me. A savage blow to the gut, like a madman. It knocked me off my feet and he leaped on me like an animal and took me by the throat . . . I was obliged to use considerable force to subdue him."

"Captain," Mercy almost screamed, "it's not true!"

He silenced her at once with a bellow, "Be quiet, woman!" He turned back to Butrus and said again, incredulously, "He *struck* you?"

"Aye sir. Bo'sun Ollie was with me. He will verify that."

The Captain's cold eyes went to Ollie. "I'll hear your report of what happened, Bo'sun Ollie," he said.

Ollie answered him, nodding eagerly, "Aye sir, it's God's own truth. They was in the boat there, fornicating their hearts out, just as Mr. Butrus says, and when he remonstrated with them, in a gentle manner you might say, Seaman Hawkes leaped to his feet and struck Mr. Butrus a blow to the stomach that I thought would have killed him. A savage, fearsome blow, Captain, and I went to his assistance, and between the two of us it was as much as we could do to restrain him. And the woman was yelling her head off at us, obscenities for the most part, sir, words I'd never expect to hear from the mouth of a woman. And Seaman Hawkes was slugging away like a prize fighter, like a man demented, and then . . . you came along, Captain, sir, and . . . you know the rest of it. In her night clothes, Captain," he said unctuously, "and all of her body was exposed, a terrible sight for a righteous man to behold . . ."

"All right, Bo'sun," the Captain said, his voice taut with anger. "You can spare me the details."

He turned back to Adam Butrus. "If there is anything further," he said clearly, "that you wish to add to what you have already told me?"

Butrus looked down at Clifford's silent body.

101

"Seaman Hawkes," he said, "and the woman, her nightdress pulled up around her waist, were coupulating in the lifeboat, as Bo'sun Ollie and I myself saw quite clearly. When, in accordance with my responsibilities, I ordered her back to her cabin, and told Seaman Hawkes I would put him on report, Seaman Hawkes got to his feet and struck me. Bo'sun Ollie is my witness, and I charge Hawkes, in accordance with the Maritime Code, with assault on a ship's officer."

"But it's not true, Captain," Mercy screamed, and there was a terrible panic in her voice. "I was alone on the deck, taking the air . . ."

"Silence, woman!" he shouted, but she would not stop.

"In God's name, Captain! . . ."

"What, you blaspheme too?"

"It is not the truth, it's a lie, a vicious lie! It was the Mate who attacked me, and Clifford came to help me. . . ."

"Silence!" He was furious with rage now. "And calumny as well as blasphemy? Be silent, woman, or I'll have you put in irons. . . ."

She bit her lip, waiting for his venom to go.

The Captain said to Butrus, "Have Seaman Hawkes confined in chains tonight. Tomorrow morning, at five bells of the morning watch, you will assemble the crew on the forward deck. Seaman Hawkes is sentenced to ten lashes for immoral behavior and twenty-five lashes for assault on a ship's officer, which, in accordance with the Code, constitutes mutiny."

Mercy was in tears of desperation. She tried to control her voice, to stifle the hysteria that was coming over her. "It is not true," she said quietly.

"You *must* believe me, Captain . . ."—she could not hold back the weeping now—"Mr. Butrus . . . attacked me . . . and Mr. Ollie helped him . . . and between them they were trying . . ."

She could not believe the contempt in his look. She put a hand to her mouth and bit into the knuckle, and he said harshly, "You will go at once to your cabin, and you will stay there till I give you permission to leave it. And tomorrow morning, at five bells . . ." He broke off and said coldly, "In your language, that is the hour of six-thirty in the morning. You will be a witness to your lover's punishment. Go to your cabin now. See to it, Mr. Butrus."

"Aye, aye, sir."

Captain MacDonald turned on his heel and stalked away. She felt the Mate's brutal hands on her shoulders again.

Mercy lay on her bunk, crying softly, knowing there there was nothing she could do but still wondering if there were perhaps some way, any way, to forestall the terrible punishment that was in store for the man to whom she owed so much. When the gently insistent knock came to her door, she said fearfully, "Who is it?"

The voice came to her, muffled: "Sharma, Mem."

"One moment, Sharma." She was lying on top of the covers in the hot night. She reached for her chenille robe and put it on, unlocked the door, and opened it . . .

Adam Butrus was there, grinning at her.

She tried to slam the door shut, but his foot was placed firmly against it and he pushed his way past

103

her and locked the door behind him. He sat down in the single armchair and stuck his long legs out in front of him, his hands clasped over his stomach. Looking at her, he said, speaking very distinctly like a teacher to a dull pupil, "I am convinced, Mistress, that you now realize that your word against mine only betrays you. I am convinced that now you will hold your silence and listen to what I have to say. Am I not right? Of course I am right."

She waited, her eyes red-rimmed with tears and wide with fright, a terrible sickness in her heart. Butrus went on, speaking calmly and even affably, a small smile on his handsome face, "He has thirty-five lashes coming to him, from a knotted rope. They usually die at twenty, or at twenty-five if they are particularly strong. But this is not regarded as being of any consequence, since his offence is technically mutiny. And we can't have mutiny at sea, can we now?"

She was trembling, unable to control herself. She drew the robe closer about her.

"But thirty-five?" Butrus said. "In all my years at sea, I've never seen a man last more than thirty, and that was only once. A Lascar, a giant of a man with muscles all over his body that . . . soaked up the lashes. He died at the thirty-first. Mutiny, it's a very serious crime on the high seas." He shrugged. "Oh yes, a man of . . . what's his name? Clifford Hawkes? Yes. A man of Seaman Hawke's apparent fortitude might survive, for a while. It's not the blood, you know. It's the pounding of the kidneys. A day or two later, we have to drop them overboard, corpses."

She knew already. Her voice was icy-cold, and

104

steady as a rock. "You did not come here, Mr. Butrus, to gloat," she said.

He nodded. "That is correct."

"And so?"

He sighed, his eyes on her. "I must confess to a small feeling of guilt in this matter. Perhaps I should not have been so . . . so reckless as to accuse him of a crime that is accepted as deserving of the death penalty. Which is what thirty-five lashes constitute, believe me."

Mercy said again, "And so?" She was trembling furiously, unable to control the frightening thoughts that were flooding over her, a young woman quite at the mercy of this terrible man.

He unclasped his hands and raised a didactic finger at her. "Let me tell you," he said, "what we can do to solve this pressing problem. After all, neither of us really wishes the death of this good young man, now do we?"

She did not answer and he went on, "We are in the middle of the Atlantic Ocean, a long way from . . . from anywhere. But a skilled sailor, like your lover, could find his way, in a small boat, to a landfall of some sort." He shrugged. "Where, I don't really know, nor do I care. We are towing a dinghy, as we always do, and with a few weeks' provisions, a man who has learned about the sea on board a whaler . . . he could find his way to some sort of salvation. And I can engineer it."

Mercy echoed him, not believing what she had heard, "Cast adrift in a small boat? In the middle of the ocean? What is it you are trying to tell me? That he can exchange one kind of death for another?"

He was smiling. "You do not know the sea, you do not know sailors. This is our world, Mistress Mercy. We are at home on the open sea, it holds no terror for us."

She said again, shaking, "A small boat, in the Atlantic Ocean?"

"Men have crossed the Atlantic in smaller boats than our dinghies. . . ." He got to his feet and sighed. "But if I cannot convince you . . . well, then he'll have to take his chances under the lash. Slim chances, but perhaps he will survive for a few days."

He went to the door, stood there with his hand on the latch, and looked at her, the mocking smile still there. She was thinking furiously, knowing that the discussion was by no means over yet.

"And how," she said at last, "will you engineer his escape, as you put it?"

He seemed very bored with the argument. "In the morning, it will be found that your lover has escaped in our hauling-dinghy. The details need not concern you. Suffice it that you know . . . yes, I can arrange it."

"Captain MacDonald said he would be in chains."

Butrus said wearily, "And he is—his wrists and ankles shackled—in a stinking cell not more than twenty feet square, with a guard on the door who is already drunk on the rum that I gave him. The decision is yours, Mistress Mercy. Either he faces certain death tomorrow . . . or an excellent chance of survival. May I sit down again?"

He had read her mind correctly. He sat down on the chair again and stroked at his moustache as he looked at her, stretching out his long legs and crossing the ankles casually. He said, smiling, "Well?"

Mercy stood there before him, trying to control her shuddering, her long hair hanging loose now down over her shoulders. "Your price, Mr. Butrus?" she asked quietly.

His eyes were devouring. "I think you already know that, do you not?"

"Yes, I know it."

"Then take off your robe and your nightdress."

For a long time she held his look. Her voice was heavy with pain. "There must be another way."

"There is no other way."

"I have a little money. Not much, but perhaps it is enough."

"It will not be enough."

She was in tears now. "If I beg you, as a gentleman? . . ."

"I am not a gentleman." He was laughing now. "Once, perhaps, I was. Now, I am a thorough rogue. In every possible respect, I find it much more rewarding. Take off your clothes."

She still could not bring herself to move.

Butrus got to his feet, a lazy, languorous movement toward her. Quite slowly, he slipped the gown off her shoulders, bared her breasts, bent down and kissed them, crushed them with his powerful hands.

"Oh my God," he said softly. His lips were crushing hers, and a hand slid down her body. She wanted to fight against him with all the strength she could muster, but she dared not. She forced herself to think of Clifford, and she tried to imag-

107

ine the darkness of his cell and the terrors that would be upon him . . . it would be down in the bowels of the ship somewhere, cold and damp and stinking, with rats crawling over his frightened body as he contemplated the terrible fate in store for him.

Her head was thrown back, her whole body rigid with fear, and her voice was a whisper, "I have . . . I have your word?" The tears were streaming uncontrollably down her face.

"You have my word," he said hoarsely; his lips were devouring her.

The robe and the nightdress were around her feet now, and she was as naked as the day she was born. She felt herself being lifted up bodily and placed on the bunk. Her eyes closed, and then it seemed he was gone, the exploring hands no longer invading her. She opened her eyes and saw him stripping off his breeches; she wanted to scream again when she saw the dreadful object there. Turning her face to the wall she forced herself to think of Clifford again, standing there on the deck in the gray light of the early morning, the powerful muscles of the man who would be wielding the knotted rope across his back. She tried to think of his handsome, boyish face, taut with pain now, the blood at the lips where he was biting them; she could hear the sound of the lash.

And then Butrus was lying on top of her, forcing her soft thighs apart and thrusting himself brutally into her. His forearm was across her throat, one hand holding her wrist, the other at her breast again. He thrust himself at her again and again and again, and the shame of it was worse than the pain

108

itself. She felt him shudder inside her, and the tears were rolling unchecked down her cheekbones, dampening the pillow under her long hair. She wished she were dead.

He pulled himself off her at last. She would not look at him, and in a little while, lying there silent and uncovered and trembling, she heard the door open and softly close, and she knew that he was gone.

She lay still for a long time, listening to the creaking of the timbers, feeling the vessel's gentle swaying. Then she rolled painfully off the bed and went to the dressing table, poured a bowl of water, and washed herself; the sight of the blood sickened her. When she was through, still feeling soiled and unclean, she dressed herself fully: the pantalettes first, then the bodice and the bust-bodice, three petticoats, the white cotton blouse that she buttoned up fully, and the heavy woollen skirt with stockings and boots. She wrapped her shawl around her and sat for the rest of the night in the chair, staring at the rumpled bunk and crying softly to herself.

She slept for a while, awoke, and slept again, and was awakened at last by a soft and somehow hesitant tapping on her door.

Slowly, she got to her feet, her legs terribly cramped, and opened it. Sharma was standing there, his brown face paler than usual, a look of terrible pain in his dark, Asian eyes. There was no wide smile now, just a look of terrible sadness on his face, and she pulled herself together with a strong effort of will and asked him what was wrong.

He was stammering. "The Captain," he said hesitantly, "the Captain has sent me, Mem, to bring you on deck. I am sorry, so sorry, a terrible day for all of us, isn't it?"

She shook her head blankly. "What is it, Sharma?" she said.

He answered her, his eyes downcast and not meeting hers, "There is a man . . . a sailor . . . he is to be flogged. I am so sorry, Mem, but the Captain . . . the Captain wishes you to be a witness. I am so sorry . . ." He was almost in tears himself.

She stared at him in shock. "A man . . . to be . . . to be *flogged?*"

She felt faint, the color draining from her face. She was falling to the ground, and Sharma's arm was there to steady her. He said urgently, seeking to comfort her and not knowing how, "I know, Mem, a terrible thing, but what can I do? I am only a steward, and the Captain . . . the Captain . . ."

She knew; but she said, as clearly as she could, "His name? You know his name?"

He nodded, still not meeting her eyes. "Yes, Mem," he said, "it is him. The young man . . . from the boat . . . last night. Your friend."

So, it was all over the ship, no doubt, the wickedly distorted version of what had happened. She felt herself falling again, but Sharma's gentle arm was around her, and he said softly, "Come, Mem. In half an hour . . . it will all be over."

She felt the pain and the fury welling up inside her, ready to explode, as she staggered with him out of the cabin, along the interminable corridor, and up the companionway to the early light of the morning.

A fine, misted rain was falling and the damp was all-pervading. The ship was rolling heavily, wallowing in the deep troughs of the waves, and the

110

sea was a deep and leaden gray, save where the white tips were curling. A lone bird was following the sails, high in an overcast sky, slipping in and out of the clouds like a lonely phantom.

CHAPTER SIX

Two seamen were stationed at the head of the companionway, and one of them was turning back an early-rising passenger, whose face was white with the fear of what he had glimpsed. The other, a wiry and gnarled old man with his head shaved, looked at her with a deep understanding in his very pale eyes. "You must have courage, Ma'am," he muttered, his voice low and filled with sympathy. Sharma was almost dragging her along now and whispering to himself in his own language. And when she came face to face with the terrible spectacle there, she felt the blood draining anew from her face.

The men who could be spared were lined up in two ranks, facing each other. In the center, his hands lashed above his head to one of the masts, his hairshirt removed and his broad back exposed, Clif-

113

ford was standing wih his feet wide-spaced and a thin, taut line to his mouth.

He caught her eye as she stumbled past him. She was shaking so violently she could barely keep her feet and she raised her eyes and saw Captain MacDonald standing there on the lower deck, his Mate Adam Butrus beside him. A thin, wiry sailor, also stripped to the waist, was standing by, holding a length of knotted Manilla rope. She heard the Captain say, very calmly, "Over here, Mistress Mercy."

Sharma led her to where he was standing; she looked into his cold, passionless eyes and said desperately, "I must talk to you, Captain, before you do this terrible thing."

"You will watch," he said, his voice very hard. "The price a man pays for his lust, the price a woman pays for her evil ways . . . you will watch."

And now, the explosion came. "Listen to me!" she shrieked. She broke free from Sharma and ran to him, beating at his chest with her fists and shouting at the top of her voice, "Lies, lies, lies! Can't you understand? What kind of a devil are you? You've been told lies . . . lies! . . ."

He did not deign to move. He said quietly, "Mr. Butrus, restrain her."

Her arms were grasped from behind and she was dragged away in a firm grip. She struggled against it and found herself powerless, but she shouted at the Captain again, desperately, "Lies, Captain, in God's name listen to me . . . listen to me . . . Give me one, just one moment to tell you the truth . . . one moment . . . I beg of you!" She tried to sink to her knees but could not. Struggling harder, she threw her head from side to side and shrieked out, "In God's name, Captain, I swear, I swear on all that is holy . . . in the name of God Almighty! . . ."

His head was turned away. He swung round to look at her now and he shouted back at her, "Haven't you done enough of the Devil's work on this ship, woman? I'll have no more of your blasphemy!" Without changing the tone of his voice he shouted, "Carry out the sentence, Mr. Ollie!"

She screamed and fought, and when the first blow fell, a sharp, incisive sound, she heard Clifford call out once, and then no more. There was only the sound of the rope and Bo'sun Ollie's coarse voice as he called the strokes; and at the count of four, she fainted away.

She was in her cabin when she recovered and Sharma was bending over her solicitiously, his delicate, feminine hands undoing the buttons at the top of her blouse, around her throat. She felt no offense at the light touch and knew he was trying to help her. When he saw her eyes were opening, he brought her a glass of water from the jug and cradled the back of her head with his hand so that she could more easily drink it.

Her heart was heavy with anguish. "He's dead, isn't he?" she said, but Sharma shook his head and even managed a smile.

"No, Mem," he told her. "I think Mr. Hawkes is a very strong gentleman, isn't he? He did not even lose his sense, his . . . his consciousness, and when they had finished and they cut him down, he would not even let them pour seawater over his wounds. He put on his shirt, pulling it over his head with no help at all, and walked away and

115

went below decks. He is a very brave gentleman, your Mr. Hawkes."

The relief was flooding over her. She lay back on the pillow and let Sharma smooth the blankets around her. She reached out and touched his hand and said, "You are a very good friend, Mr. Sharma."

"Not *Mister* Sharma, Mem," he said gently. "Just ... Sharma."

"Will you see him this day?"

"Yes, Mem, of course. Soon, when the watch is changed, I will take him a little rum. Secretly, you understand, because the Captain does not allow drinking on board this ship, but I have a friend on the watch now who will give me some. And if you would like me to take him a message, Mem?"

"Oh yes, please! Tell him . . . tell him how much I suffer for him, and tell him . . ." She hesitated, and then made up her mind, knowing that she could trust this gentle servant. "Tell him," she said slowly, "that if he can come to my cabin tonight . . . I will be waiting for him."

Instinctively, Sharma lowered his voice. "If he is discovered, Mem . . . it will mean more terrible things for him. But perhaps there is a better way. . . ."

"Any way," she said eagerly, "any way at all, Mr. Sharma, just so that I can speak with him?"

He was whispering now, and there was a touch of anxiety in his dark eyes. "Tomorrow morning," he said, "at six bells of the morning watch, he will go to work in the number three hold, which is where your cabin trunk is stored, isn't it? He has to clean out the bilges there, and at eight bells, when we serve breakfast, I can take you there to him. I will let it be known that you are not well, and will have only tea in your cabin. And in the hold there will be no one coming, just the two of you, and if you are not longer than half an hour, I think there will be no difficulties at all."

"You are sure of that, Mr. Sharma?"

"Yes, I am sure of it. I will ascertain myself that no one will go there. I will have a friend at the hatch outside, and I will tell Mr. Hawkes to find a place for you there to hide, just in case someone should come. A matter only of moving a few trunks around, isn't it? But no one will come, it will be safe, I promise you." He hesitated. "And always, Mem," he said at last, "if I can help you . . . you must call on me."

She felt like embracing him. He saw the beginnings of the movement and bowed quickly, touched his fingers together, and smiled. "I must go now," he said. "Tomorrow morning, at breakfast time, I will take you where you have to go."

"And Mr. Sharma," she said, "will you also please tell the Captain that I would like to see him as soon as possible?" She saw the surprise on his face and went on, "Tell him, if you will, that I am no longer . . . hysterical. Tell him that I would like a few moments of quiet conversation with him at his earliest convenience. A matter, perhaps you can say, of a very serious complaint."

He nodded, not relishing the idea, and left her. He came back later in the morning and shook his head. "I sent your message to the Captain, Mem," he said slowly, "but he will not see you. He told me to say . . . if it is indeed a serious matter, then you can discuss it with Mr. Adam Butrus, the First Mate."

117

She was very calm now. "Thank you, Mr. Sharma."

He smiled at her and left her to her own devices.

She spent most of the day below decks; the rain was heavier now and there were the beginnings of a storm coming up. She toyed disconsolately with her food at lunch, decided to miss supper altogether, and went to bed at nine o'clock. She did not even bother to light the oil lamp, but undressed and washed herself by the light of the candle that swung in its little holder over the dressing table. She snuffed it out and curled up under the covers, awaking—how much later was it?—to find that the candle was alight again, and that a man was in her room, the glass shade of the lamp in one hand, a lighted Lucifer in the other. He was touching it to the wick, firing it as he scraped off the accumulation of carbon.

It was Adam Butrus. She stared at him in shock, in horror, and in loathing. She took a deep breath and opened her mouth to scream out, but he was on her in a flash, a hand over her mouth and a knee pinning her down to the bed.

"You fool!" he whispered furiously. "Are you insane?"

Her fury was almost uncontrollable, but her struggles were to no avail, and when she had ceased them, he said, holding her tightly still, "You will bring them running to your cabin and tell them I broke into it, is that what you have in mind? At the first sound out of that pretty mouth . . . you know what I will do? A sharp blow on the side of the head to silence you, and then . . . then I will drag Sharma's unconscious body in here . . . you want to hear the rest of it? You take me for an idiot?"

She could not believe the venom in his voice. "The Captain already knows you're a whore. What do you think he will do when he finds you with a naked savage in your bed? Is that what you want? Is it?"

She closed her eyes and waited. In a moment he released her cautiously, getting to his feet when she made no further move. He began to pace the tiny cabin, recovering his habitual equanimity, and he said at last, a twisted smile on his face now, "And the wick on your lamp is burned. Perhaps I should put your steward on biscuits and water for a few days." Without changing the tone of his voice, he went on, "Will you listen to me now? Or do you wish more violence?"

She was tight with fury. "How did you get in here?" she asked. "And how can you . . . how can you *dare* face me now?"

There was a dry, mocking laugh. "I am beginning," he said mildly, "to believe that I am not truly welcome. Is that so?"

"Will you get out of my cabin? At once?"

He shook his head and that detestable smile was still there. "No," he said. "Not till you have heard what I have to say to you. A matter of the greatest interest, not only to you, but also to a certain vulgar deckhand whom we both know."

She was trembling again as she always was it seemed, in the presence of this hateful man, and quite unable to control her anger. There were no tears now, only a deep and unchecked loathing. "I will not listen," she said furiously, "to anything you have to say. I have nothing but the utmost

119

contempt for you, so leave my cabin at once, or I will indeed scream . . . and we will find out if your falsehoods, your filthy lies can save you again."

His manner was so pleasant and courteous that she could not credit it. The hand was raised again, seeking to calm her. "You can imagine," he said affably, "how much your attitude distresses me. And yet, I must confess, perhaps I deserve it."

"Deserve it? We made a bitter pact last night, to my own undying shame, and you did not keep your word."

"I never intended to keep it," he said casually. "And if you remember, I told you I was no gentleman, but a rogue. In the excitement of your passion for me, perhaps you forget that?"

She stared at him. "You never intended . . . You *admit* your villainy?"

His smile broadened. "Of course, dear lady. I told you, I remember, how much more rewarding roguery can be. And the reward was very great, let me assure you. I scarcely remember the last time I loved a virgin."

He took off his heavy oilskin coat and hung it there on the maplewood peg as though this were his own home, then sat down and said cheerfully, "But enough of the past, it is the future—Seaman Hawkes' future, and yours, and mine—that we must discuss now. And I am afraid that I have some very unpalatable news for you, Ma'am."

She was trying to imagine what more could befall her and her eyes were wide. Her hand was at her throat, hugging the blankets there, protecting her modesty. She tried to make her voice sound strong and confident, but it was only a whisper. "What news is that?"

Butrus said dryly, "It seems that your young man is not quite prepared to learn his place, nor to submit to the rigid discipline which is so necessary aboard a great ship like the *Capricorn*. I fear he was heard this day muttering threats against my life, the life of the First Mate, the man who really runs the ship. Bo'sun Ollie heard him, quite distinctly, and so that we should not have to use poor Ollie all the time, there were three or four other amenable members of the crew who heard him too."

He reached into the pocket of his heavy woollen jacket, withdrew a sheet of crumpled paper, held it up and said, "Of course, poor Ollie cannot read or write, but he had one of his cronies, a seaman who went to school for a year or two, write it all down for him. Personally, I find the phraseology illiterate in the extreme, but Captain MacDonald does not expect erudition from the ranks. Let me read it to you . . ."

He flipped the folded paper to open it up and read, very seriously,

"*I was going about my duties with my usual perseverance, when I came upon Seaman Hawkes, a troublemaker if there ever was one, caulking the third quarter of the foredeck and making a very bad job of it, and when I remonstrated with him . . .*" He looked up and laughed. "*Remonstrated?* Poor Ollie doesn't even know the word, but he has a capable scribe." He went on reading.

"*When I remonstrated with him, he said to me, and these were his exact words, to the best of my good rememberance: 'Bosun Ollie, I ain't going to*

121

forget what you and Mr. Bloody Butrus done to me today. We don't have no witnesses here, so I can tell you, Bo'sun Ollie, that you and Mr. Bloody Butrus are going to wake up one morning soon, and find that you are both dead, your throats cut from ear to ear. And when you both cry out "Who done this to me?" the answer is going to come to you out of Hell: "I done it." And the voice will be my voice, the voice of Seaman Clifford Hawkes.' I was tempted to strike him down there and then, but with admirable forbearance . . ."

He broke off again, laughing. "You like the phrase "admirable forbearance," Mistress Mercy? I find it quite charming. Poor fellow, he has pretensions of his own, but a stout man both in belly and heart."

He went on reading, *"But I decided that I should make this report to Mr. Butrus instead. Therefore, I have engaged for the sum of three pence the services of Seaman Second Class Matthew Ellis to write it for me, since the unhappy circumstances of my lowly birth did not allow me the benefit, which, I assure you sir, is deeply regretted, of an education. Signed with a mark this day, September 27, on board the good ship* Capricorn."

He slipped the paper back into his pocket and said happily, "Well, there it is, Ma'am. A documented promise of mutiny. Do you know what they will do to him for a threat against the lives of two ship's officers? They will hang him from the yard-arm, without any doubt at all. Flogging is too palatable a punishment for a threat of this sort. Documented and sworn to, by a ship's officer? Of course they will hang him! A hanging is very good

122

for discipline and Captain MacDonald is a very stern disciplinarian, as you may have learned."

She knew what was to happen now and was steeling herself against it. She said, anguished, "And his report, this tissue of lies, has not yet been delivered to Captain MacDonald, is that correct?"

"A man's life is at stake," Butrus said piously, "and I could not bring myself to pursue this unfortunate affair without first consulting you. After all, who will be weeping if Clifford Hawkes is hanged? Only you, dear lady."

She could not bring herself to speak. The Mate got to his feet, and slowly, quite slowly, began stripping off his clothes, all of them. She quickly turned her face away in disgust from his pulsating manhood as he stood above her, and then he leaned down and pulled the blankets away from her, and took hold of the nightdress at the throat. Undoing the buttons one by one, the back of his hard hands rubbed against her nipples and he slid the nightdress down over her smooth shoulders, down past her slim waist and over her hips, leaning down to kiss her as he smoothed it over her thighs and calves and her ankles and then tossed it aside. As he stood over her, tall and straight and powerful and throbbing, he looked down at her naked, vulnerable body and said hoarsely, "I never saw anyone so beautiful in all my life. And you are *mine*! A chattel, nothing more! To service me, woman, whenever I desire it! It will be quite often, I assure you."

He took both her wrists in his powerful hands, held them over her head, and pushed them down into the softness of the pillows. He lay between her thighs and spread her knees apart with his own, grinding himself against her. He released her wrists and pawed at her tender breasts, then plunged suddenly and brutally into her. She bit her lip and suffered as he ground his teeth into her shoulder, like an animal, in the throes of a deep and selfish passion; and she thought it would never end.

There was a warm and frightening sensation she had not been conscious of before, and he lay there for a few moments on top of her, her legs straightening out now of their own volition, her face turned to the planks of the wall. She thought: Is this the act of love? This coarse and brutal thing?

He eased himself from her in a moment and smiled at her gently as though they were truly lovers. Caressing her cheek lightly, he said, "In the course of time, dearest Mercy, you will learn to love me as you should. With an endearing and reciprocal passion to equal my own." His voice hardened. "In the course of time, the course of many nightly visits to your bed. Your young friend's life depends on it, believe me."

"It's not over yet, is it?" she asked. Her voice was dulled and expressionless.

"Over?" He was laughing again now. He rolled off the bunk and began climbing into his breeches, his white torso glistening in the lamplight. "No, it is not over. Every night, perhaps, at about this time. Don't bother to lie awake awaiting me, I have a key. And it may happen one night that you will find I do not really like an unresponsive partner."

He sighed. "I must confess, unhappily, that it is true that I tire of my mistresses very quickly. And in your case . . . with a life at stake? You don't have to enjoy my ravishing you, Mercy. All you have to do, really, is *pretend*. I don't in all conscience, give a damn whether it pleases you or not. But the next time . . . pretend."

"The next time?" It was more than she could bear.

"Yes. The next time. Then, perhaps, I will like it better. Your skin is smooth, your breasts are firm, your thighs are long and slender, and there's passion in that body if only I could find it. Make use of them, Mercy, before I tire of you too and hang your lover by the yardarm. It's a small enough price to pay, so pay it . . . willingly."

He was dressed now. He stood above her, looking down and mocking her. "Next time, hold out your arms to me and tell me . . . tell me that you *want* my love. I'll like it better, even if you don't mean it."

She still lay naked and motionless on the bed, and he leaned over her and ran his hands over her breasts again, continued down her taut stomach to the crevice of her thighs. He kissed a nipple and said again, "Next time . . . enjoy it. Or Clifford Hawkes will hang. Goodnight, my love."

He pulled up the blankets solicitously, tucked them under her chin, and he was gone.

She did not sleep for the rest of the night, but lay still under the coarse blankets, listening to the susurration of the waves as they lapped against the wooden hull. The ship was rolling more violently now, seeming to climb steeply up and then thud down into the troughs with a heavy, pounding sort of sound. Three times in a rhythmic sequence and then more forcibly on the fourth, a steady progression that was repeated over and over and over again, but broken on occasion with a sudden sideways motion accompanied by a fearsome shuddering as though the hull were about to split in two. She found it no longer frightened her.

When the first light of the morning streaked through the closed porthole, she got up and dressed herself carefully in her best skirt and blouse, plaited her hair and rolled it into buns over her ears, and put on her shawl and her bonnet as though she were going calling on a dear friend. Then she waited patiently for Sharma.

He came shortly after the breakfast gong sounded, carrying a cup of tea for her on a wooden tray, and whispering, "First, Mem, a nice cup of tea, drink it while it's hot, there is time."

She took a small sip of the strong, steaming liquid, and put the cup down on the dressingtable. She said, "When I come back . . ."

"All right. Just follow me. If anyone should ask you, Mem, where you are going, you will say, please, that you need something from your trunk and that I am taking you to get it." He smiled brightly. "No one will, but it is better to be prepared, isn't it?"

She followed him out into the corridor, and he opened a locked door and took her down a short flight of three wooden stairs. They led to a second corridor so narrow there was barely room to pass along it, and through another door and into a tiny passage where they had to stoop low to move on, then through another door to a dark and damp little cubicle where a seaman stood, grinning at her. He touched his forelock politely and said, whispering, "You must be quiet down there, Ma'am."

She nodded.

Sharma whispered a word or two with him, and the seaman lifted off a heavy wooden hatch and said, "A ladder, Ma'am, seven rungs, there will be a light down there when I close it again."

"And I will be here," Sharma whispered to her conspiratorially, "when you return. About half an hour, no longer please, because at one bell the Bo'sun begins his round below decks, and we must avoid him at all costs. A very evil man, Bo'sun Ollie, isn't it?"

She nodded, and gathered her skirts around her and made the careful descent into the darkness. The hatch cover slid quietly into place as she reached the bottom, and as a yellow light flared, she saw Clifford there, turning up the wick of his lamp and then hurrying across the packed trunks and boxes toward her.

He showed no signs of the terrible ordeal he had been through, and there was laughter on his frank and open face as he held out his hands for her. She threw her arms around his powerful chest and clasped him tightly, not even surprised by her own forwardness. He held her tight for a moment and then whispered, "Over here, Mistress Mercy. . . ."

He led her carefully to a tiny place he had made among the cases, touched a long crate he had placed there, and whispered, "Here, we can sit here together for a while." He reached up and turned the lamp down very low, then looked at her, smiling. "How very good it is to see you," he said. "I think about you every day, and every night . . ."

"Oh Clifford . . ."

"Are you well?"

"Yes. Yes, only . . . yesterday, when they . . ."
The tears were flooding back at the awful memory

of it and she rested her head on his shoulder, saying, "I was so afraid for you."

"Yes, I could see it in your face. It is all over now."

She knew it was not. "Yes, it is all over," she said. "And it must never happen again."

"It will not. And I do not think Adam Butrus will bother you anymore."

"No, I am sure of it." *If only it were true!* she thought.

His arm was tight around her shoulder as they sat there in the darkness, and he went on, seeking to comfort her. "He is a vile and evil man, but even he will not dare to arouse the Captain's suspicions a second time."

How wrong he was!

But how comforting to feel his arm about her too! She wished she could stay here with him forever, in this dark and tiny prison that lay, she was sure, far below the level of the waves that pounded against the hull. She eased herself closely to him and he winced when she inadvertently touched his back. "Will it be long," she asked, "before . . . before you recover?"

"I have recovered already," he said simply. "You bring me . . . comfort, and pleasure . . . and everything is all right again."

"And when we get to America," she said, "what will you do? Will you stay on board the *Capricorn*?"

He shook his head and he was laughing quietly. "You told me once, you remember, what your stars had indicated to you? That I must . . . how did you put it? Reach out with both hands for? . . ."

"For opportunity. Yes, you must!"

128

"Then perhaps there will be better opportunities in the New World, who knows? And you? What will you do there?"

For a long while she did not answer him. She wondered if she should hide from him the true reasons for her journey, but he was so close to her now that she could not.

"What I must do there, Clifford," she said, "troubles me deeply . . ."

She broke off, hesitant, and he said to her very seriously, "If it pains you to talk about it, Mistress Mercy . . ."

She shook her head. "No," she said fiercely, "I must tell you! There is a young man there, waiting for me in Boston."

Was it her imagination, or did she feel a certain tenseness on him? She went on quickly, "His name is Nathan Doren, Luke Doren's son, and . . . well, we grew up together, and my father . . . my father would like me to marry him now."

She could feel his eyes on her. "And you, Mistress Mercy? Is it your wish too?"

"No," she said emphatically. "It is not my wish. And yet, if it is what my father wants for me . . ."

"But the days are long gone," he said gently, "when parents arranged their daughters' marriages."

. "I know." She sighed. "I can hardly remember what Nathan Doren looks like. I remember most of all a ten-year-old boy who used to pull my pigtails, and sometimes put lizards in my boots. He went to America when he was sixteen years old, and for the life of me I cannot even remember what he looked like then."

"A wedding," he said quietly, "to someone you hardly know?"

129

"Yes. It doesn't seem, now, to make very much sense."

She could feel his discomfort and she said earnestly, "I have lived a very sheltered life, Clifford. When this matter was first broached, my father was there, and Luke Doren, and his wife Genevieve, who is very, very beautiful, and . . . and, how shall I put it? She may not even be aware of it, and I will not hold it against her, a good and generous friend, but . . . she is very *demanding*, without, I think, even being aware of it."

"And so, this demanding woman persuaded you of what *she* considers your duty? Is that what you are saying?"

Mercy shook her head vehemently. "No, no, no! She is thinking only of . . . what is good for me, I swear it! She is a dear, dear friend, and I love her truly. But now, don't you see, I no longer have those . . . those tight restrictions around me, I am alone now . . ."

"Not alone," Clifford said earnestly.

"No, not alone." She was abashed. She went on, "But now, so far from those I have always loved, I am learning to make my own decisions, to go the way I feel I *must* go. Genevieve, and Luke, and my father . . . and I love my father so dearly!" She dabbed at her eyes with a lawn handkerchief. "These are people I *love*, Clifford. But they no longer control my destiny. *I* control it. And in spite of the pain I know it must cause to my loved ones, I feel that Nathan Doren has no part of that destiny."

He held her hand tightly, and they sat together in silence for a while. "We have very little time left," he said at last.

She nodded. "Can we meet again? Like this, perhaps?" She felt his hand tighten on hers. "Perhaps we can, though it will not be easy. The Bo'sun watches me like a hawk. And Adam Butrus . . . every time I see him, he looks at me in silence with a . . . a sort of mockery on his face, as though he is planning more trouble for me."

He shook his head. "I don't know, it's just a feeling. But neither Butrus nor Ollie is the kind of man to be satisfied with paying back . . . just once. They are both cruel, vindictive men."

She remembered Butrus's harsh words of last night: *Your young friend's life depends upon it* . . . and there was nothing she could tell him. She said instead, knowing the answer already, "What more can they do to you, Clifford? They've done enough already, surely?"

"I don't know. And perhaps I am wrong."

He brightened up a little and touched her hair lovingly. "But the only thing that matters is that he leave you alone. As long as I am confident of that, nothing else is of any importance."

She was in deep distress, worrying about him. "If you were to speak with the Captain? Perhaps he would . . . I don't know, but . . ."

He laughed softly. "On board a clipper like this, Mistress Mercy, the Captain is . . . a kind of God. A lowly deckhand only sees him at a distance, prowling the bridge. Between him and the likes of me, there is the First Mate, the Second Mate, and half a dozen other officers, right down to the man who is really responsible for the crew. And that man is Bo'sun Jake Ollie. No, I could never hope to get the Captain's ear. Never mind, a few more days

131

now and we'll be in the New World, and then . . . then we will see what happens."

"How long?" she asked.

"Five more days. Unless we run into heavy weather, we shall be docking on the second of October. It will be a record run."

"The second? I will look it up in my little book."

He seemed puzzled. "What book is that, Mistress Mercy?"

She smiled shyly. "My little book about the planets."

"Ah yes, of course."

"They never lie, Cifford. I will find out what the second day of the month has to offer us. Both of us."

He was caressing her hair now, and he pulled away at the sound of a slight tapping on the hatch-cover. He got quickly to his feet and pulled her to him in a modest embrace. "The signal," he said, "you must go now."

She was careful not to touch his sorely bruised back. "And soon? . . ."

"One way or the other, soon. We can talk through Sharma, your steward, he is a very good man."

The faint gray light came streaming down as the cover was removed, and he took her to the ladder and waited till she had gone, then went back and got on with his work.

Sharma was there waiting for her, as he had promised, and he took her back to her cabin without incident. Her tea was cold now, and he said, as though this were all that mattered to him, "I bring you another cup, Mem, isn't it?"

She took off her shawl and bonnet, lay down on the bunk in her clothes, and thought about Clifford. She searched around in her reticule for the little poem she had written to him so long ago and so far away. She licked a stub of pencil and began adding more lines to it, forcing behind her all thought of that lascivious and evil man Adam Butrus.

She thought about what her dear Aunt Melissa had called, in her stern and dutiful lectures, her "most prized possession," cruelly stolen from her by a vile debaucher, and she wrote on the paper quickly, "If only it could have been saved for you, dear Clifford."

And then, shocked by her own indelicacy, not knowing what had come over her, she scratched it out vigorously, the words a reproach to her sensitivities even though, in a moment of carelessness, she had written them herself.

She felt that she was blushing furiously, and she tucked the paper away again and knelt down by the bed and said her prayers, although it was the middle of the morning now:

> Gentle Jesus, meek and mild,
> Look upon a little child,
> Pity my simplicity,
> Suffer me to come to Thee . . .

She added, "And please . . . take care of Clifford too, he needs you so badly now. . . ."

CHAPTER SEVEN

In this year of our Lord 1848, the race for the huge profits culled by the ocean-going clippers was reaching its peak. Spurred on by the trade in slaves, opium, and tea, the companies were building ever faster and faster ships, slimming down their lines, lightening their oak hulls, and designing more and more canvas into them.

And that trade was flourishing. In this single year, eighty new clippers had been built—Baltimores, mediums, and extremes—and most of them were crossing the Atlantic. By October, they had already carried a total of forty-two thousand passengers to the New World, where immigration was still quite unrestricted. (A year later, with the discovery of gold in California, those numbers were to be more than doubled.)

The salient features of the clippers—the narrow

beam and the enormous spread of canvas—made it possible for them to attain speeds as yet only dreamed of. In fair weather, they could comfortably cruise at a steady eighteen knots. When the weather was less than admirable, driving the passengers below decks, where they tried hard both to put on a show of nonchalance and also to keep their balance at the heaving cardtables . . . when the wind sprang up and drove them ferociously forward with all sails billowing splendidly . . . when, sometimes, the aft strains on the backstays and the shrouds shifted unexpectedly to athwartship, then only instant and concerted teamwork by the highly skilled rigging men could avert disaster.

The key word was "teamwork." The men were trained to work together so closely that each man was aware, almost by a kind of telepathy, of what his neighbors in the rigging were doing and just how quickly they could do it. (Even in calm weather, a misunderstanding in this area could lead, in a few moments, to a loss of an hour or more in sailing time, which could never be permitted.)

And this teamwork, in turn, led to a kind of camaraderie among the sailors whose understanding, each of the other's temperament, weaknesses and strengths too, took on, in foul weather, a tremendous importance.

Seaman Hawkes was on the grass-rope yard of the mizzen royal, reefing the sail, and far below him he heard the Bo'sun's furious voice calling, "Watch that spanker, Hawkes!"

He yelled back, "Spanker pulling out now, Bo'sun," and looked up to see the royal billowing gracefully out.

But the man above him, on the skys'l yard, was yelling down at him, "Cliff! I need a hand here!"

Clifford swarmed quickly up the mast to the skysail yard, and saw that the reefing of the driver had become knotted. He pulled his knife out of its sheath and sliced quickly through the knot, and the man said, "Jesus Christ, if the Bo'sun sees you doing that . . ."

His name was Dred Manners, a grizzled old seaman in his sixties, with very pale blue eyes and a shaven head. He pulled the ends of the cut sheet together, took out his knife with the splicer on it, and said, grinning broadly, "Holy Christ, I haven't seen a trick like that since I was fifteen years old, on board the *Wayward Spirit* in the China Sea."

Clifford was already splicing the rope ends, repairing the cut. He laughed. "On the whalers," he said, "we do it all the time. At the end of a good six months' whaling, there's not a ten-foot length of sheet without a splice in it."

He looked down and saw Bo'sun Ollie staring up at him, and he called down, "Fore upper tops'l's in trouble, Bo'sun!"

He was too high in the sky to hear the obscenities he knew that Ollie was muttering, but he saw him run forward and heard the shouted orders he was giving the men on the yards there. He heard one of them, a young man named Enderby, yelling down, "Driver won't come free, Bo'sun." And he looked at Dred and laughed, saying softly, "That'll keep the bastard occupied for half an hour or more."

They went on splicing together, letting out the skysail as the wind took its hold on it. The ship was rolling heavily now, and the mast was moving through an angle of more than forty degrees. Manners looked up at the filling sail and said, "There she is . . . Do you know what the Bo'sun has in store for you, Cliff?"

Clifford, holding on tightly to the spar against the ship's rolling, stared at him. "The Bo'sun? In store for *me*? No, I don't, Dred. And maybe you'd better tell me if you've news I should have heard."

"You'll be the last man to hear it, boy, if not from your friends."

"It's a friend I'm listening to now, Dred," Clifford said.

Dred Manners nodded. "That's a fine lady you have there. She had to watch you take a beating that could have killed you. And how you survived it, I'll never know. I've seen men killed, good men too, at the tenth, twelfth stroke of the rope. But the bastard Butrus, and the bastard Ollie, are planning new trials for you, boy. The talk among some of the crew—what you might call the Butrus faction, the men who'll sell whatever honor they may have for an extra mess of oatmeal—is that once we hit the Sargasso Sea, Butrus is going to deliver a report to the Captain, bless his demented soul, that says you're planning more mutiny."

Clifford could not understand it. "But they've had their revenge," he said. "God knows, they paid me back in good measure."

"Listen to me, boy," Manners said fiercely. "When we dock in Boston, there's a strong likelihood that your young lady will go straight to the magistrate's court and tell them what was done. And if it's not a likelihood, then it's a fear that will certainly be haunting Adam Butrus every moment of the day. You know her well, boy, so tell me. Is

138

that something she just might do? Or will she choose to forget all about it? If she has any spirit in her at all . . ."

He left it hanging and Clifford nodded. "Aye, I think she might do that, Dred."

"And if she does . . . the court will call you in to give evidence, and between the two of you, it's at least possible that Adam Butrus will find it hard to convince them that he and Ollie are telling the truth, and that you and the lady are lying. I'm told she has a . . . a guardian, is it? back in England, a man of some importance in the maritime world. It's a risk they dare not take, Cliff. They dare not let you reach Boston alive."

The top of the mast was sweeping back and forth past scudding clouds; only the horizon was dark. Dred Manners went on, his nimble fingers at work on the sheets:

"They've now got themselves four witnesses who heard you threaten to cut Adam Butrus's throat from ear to ear. This is my seventh tour on the *Capricorn*, boy, and we've never had a hanging yet, unless we count that Lascar back in 1842. He was just a savage and deserved it anyways."

"Dred," Clifford said quietly. "You're an old man, and maybe you listen to too much gossip."

Dred nodded. "Maybe."

"But you've the wisdom of your years too."

"Aye. I have that, boy."

"So tell me what's on your mind."

Dred waited till the motion of the mast was at its extreme, and spat formidably into the sea; a stream of tobacco-colored spittle sailing out there. "There's only one thing you can do, boy," he said slowly.

"Between now and then, you have to leave this ship before it becomes your coffin."

"Leave it?" Clifford asked incredulously. "In the middle of the Atlantic Ocean? You have lost your senses, old man."

"It's my age," Dred said placidly, "that has given me the judgment to advise you. When we reach the terrible Sargasso we'll be becalmed, without a doubt. You must have observed that we're sailing a long way to the south, to take advantage of the Gulf Stream and the unseasonable winds . . . And when we run into the Sargasso, we'll be trailing a dinghy behind us, in case we have to be towed out of the Doldrums. If you take my advice, boy, the moment that dinghy is trailed out there . . . you'll steal it. You'll hoist the sail, and with luck you'll hit land almost before we do. But even if you don't, your chances on the open sea are a very considerable mite better than they'll be aboard the *Capricorn*."

He had finished his splicing, and he shook out the sheet and let it run free. "We'll miss you, boy," he said sadly. "But I, for one, have no great desire to see your dead body fed to the sharks."

Bo'sun Ollie was back, yelling at them again, "Get down to the upper tops'l, damn your eyes! The wind is changing, can't you feel it? Get down there, fast!"

Clifford shouted down, "Aye, aye, Bo'sun!"

The two of them swarmed down the rigging and Clifford said, very quietly, "I thank you, Dred, for what you have told me."

"It's your only salvation, Cliff," Dred said urgently. "Between the two of them, else . . . you'll be a dead man, before the week is out. Get together enough biscuits and water, maybe a fishing line, enough to last you a week or two, and take your chances with the ocean. It'll not be a great problem for you, you're a good sailor, with salt-water in your veins."

Clifford was worried. He was thinking: How can I jump ship, how can I run away? . . .

The ship was trimmed to perfection, and they began the descent together.

Two days later, they hit the borders of the Sargasso Sea.

This fearsome stretch of seaweed, encompassing an area of the Atlantic Ocean from forty to seventy degrees west, and from twenty-five to thirty-one north—more than four thousand square miles of it in all—had long been the dread of the mariners.

Christopher Columbus had been becalmed there, standing with dead sails, for eight days, surrounded by limitless vistas of the round, berry-like bladders of the gulf weed packed tightly upon the surface of the water. It was a morass that was widely believed—indeed, *known* with absolute certainty—to be capable of dragging even the greatest ships to the ocean depths.

Captain MacDonald, staunch sailor that he was, would have no part of this belief, (even though it was not to be disproved till more than half a century later), and he had run before the favorable winds far to the south, defying the bloated demons of the sea to do their damndest, knowing that he could force the *Capricorn* through it, even if there were only the whisper of a breeze. And that if there were not, the strong arms of his men at the dinghy's oars would haul them till Kingdom Come if need be.

And as they entered the densely packed mass of brown weed, the hauling-dinghy was lowered and towed behind them, and Captain MacDonald looked up at the sails and saw them losing their wind one by one. As they began flapping, they were quickly furled by forty-seven sailors swarming over the rigging, and soon, only the three skys'ls, the fore top gallant sail, and—inexplicably—the crossjack, were holding any wind at all. She was making three and a quarter knots now and holding her own.

Captain MacDonald, standing on the bridge and watching the skysails, said, "Mr. Butrus. Tomorrow morning, if we've dropped below two knots, we start hauling. See to it."

Butrus, worried more than he liked to be, nodded. "Aye, aye, sir," he said. "A course of two seventy, I presume?"

"No sir. A course of one hundred and ninety."

Butrus stared. "Dead into the Gulf Stream, sir? With due respect . . ."

"One hundred and ninety, Mr. Mate," the Captain said emphatically. "Ninety miles from here, a hundred and twenty if our luck is against us, we'll pick up the winds of the Corner Seamounts."

"A hundred and twenty miles . . ." Butrus was trying to hide his very considerable agitation. "Sir, I repeat," he said, "with much respect, that's a three-knot current we'll be fighting with eight oars and the heaviest ship of the line to tow . . ."

"Then you'll change the rowers every hour, Mr. Butrus. They'll row their damnedest until they drop, and then, you will relieve them with another crew to row until they drop too. In three days we'll find wind, believe me. And if we fail to find it, which I strongly doubt, then we'll turn and haul due south."

Butrus did not wish to show his anxiety; due south meant deeper into the dreaded sea, and there would be trouble with the men. "Of course, Captain," he said nonchalantly, "the crew knows that Boston lies almost due north of us now. It knows, too, that few ships have ever escaped the Sargasso and been seen again. But, of course, a fine clipper like the *Capricorn* . . ."

"Precisely," the Captain said; he was getting angry now. "West of the Bermuda Islands, Mr. Mate, the stream changes direction and runs due nor'west also, you should know that. With the stream and the Seamounts' winds helping us along, we'll be up to twelve or fourteen knots within no time at all."

"Aye, aye, sir."

The Captain's eyes were cold as steel. "And I'll have no talk of what the crew thinks, Mr. Mate. The crew does not run this ship. I do. And if my First Mate is fearful of implementing my orders, then our imminent arrival in Boston will see a change in *Capricorn*'s officers."

"Aye, aye, sir."

Butrus was thinking: We'll haul ourselves deeper and deeper into that terrible morass, and we'll be swallowed up like so many other fine ships, doomed to perdition with the rest of them, good ships all. . . . He moved off to prepare the hauling roster.

And as Seaman Clifford Hawkes strained at the afterstays of the mizzen mast, tightening them after the buffeting they had recently taken, he looked down into the water, calm now with the beginnings of the brown weed covering the surface, and saw the hauling-dinghy bobbing along behind them.

Manners was moving towards him, a great coil of cordage slung over his bowed shoulders, his battered briar pipe clenched between his broken teeth. "A new sail aboard her, boy," he said, as he tossed the cordage down. "I helped them fit a dipping lug on her last night, a good one."

Clifford shook his head. "You're a good friend, Dred Manners," he said. "But I don't think I want to jump ship, even this one. I've been at sea for nine years now, starting out as a cabin boy, and I never left a voyage uncompleted yet."

"They're plotting to kill you," Manners said. "And if you need it, I'll give you all the proof you need. Talk to Edmund or to Hays, or to Blackwell. We were all on the same watch when we heard it."

"Heard what, old man?" Clifford asked, insisting.

Dred Manners spat a stream of amber juice out into the ocean, and looked up to the heights of the mizzen. "The lower tops'l's in need of a reef. Give me a hand, boy."

Clifford stared up at it, frowning. "No," he said, "we're turning a degree or more. She'll fill out in a moment."

"Well, maybe you're right, at that."

"So tell me what you heard, Dred."

Manners sighed. "It's all over the ship now. And a dozen of the men have begged me to persuade you, knowing that I'm the only man who can. Butrus was in his cups, just a trifle, and he was telling the Bo'sun . . ."

He dropped his voice and looked over his shoulder. "He was telling the Bo'sun that a day or two

144

out of Boston, he'd have no more use for you, whatever that means. And that he was going to report you to the Skipper for mutiny. You know what that means, don't you?" Clifford was expertly slipping a double sheet bend over the great hook of the stay, and Manners grimaced at it. "All you need, Cliff, is a cat's paw . . ."

Clifford changed the knot and said, worrying, "A day or two out of harbor? Yes, I know what it means, Dred. It means that I'll stand trial ashore, before a Maritime Jury. A jury of honest men, they'll never convict me."

"But if a day or two means three or four . . ." Manners scratched at his bold head. "Adam Butrus is no fool, Cliff. If he starts to think of a Maritime Jury too, then he won't wait till we're close enough to land for their jurisdiction. They're *smouldering*, Cliff, the both of them. They'll never regard what they did to you as payment in full . . . for what you did to Butrus. The way I heard it, what you did was take a woman out from under him, and that's something he'll never forgive you for, flogging or no flogging. And tomorrow, we start hauling south into the Sargasso . . ."

"*South*?" Clifford could not believe his ears. "We're hauling *south*? It makes no sense, Dred!"

"Aye. I know it, and you know it. But the Captain, it seems, is convinced we'll find wind there. And the point is, boy, that if you delay till there's a hundred miles of gulfweed around you . . . you'll never be seen again. Slip away tonight, this very night, there's good cloud cover over the moon and you'll not be seen . . ."

He turned back to his work; Bo'sun Ollie was approaching, squinting at them as they talked together. He took hold of a shroud and hauled on it, heaving it back and forth, and he said angrily, "A foot or more of play! If you want to get out of this sea alive you'll tighten them up, all of them!"

"The spanker's tight as a drum, Bo'sun," Manners said mildly, "and the crossjack too."

Bo'sun Ollie was looking up to the sails high above him, searching out faults in their set and finding none. "Get up there," he shouted, "Seaman, and let it out!"

Manners sighed. "Aye, aye, Bo'sun," he said, "but she'll be in danger of spilling if we find a mite more breeze."

"Get aloft!" Ollie yelled and Manners slipped up the rigging, hand over hand like a youngster a quarter of his age. Ollie studied the bracing, a sour and angry look on his face. "Get rid of that cat's paw," he said, "and put in a double sheet. You think you're still on a whaler?"

Clifford changed the knot again, holding his silence. "And tomorrow morning," Ollie said, "you'll be on the first shift in the hauling-dinghy."

"Aye, aye, Bo'sun."

"And the second too."

He turned on his heel and stalked away. Looking back as he stooped to enter the after-cabin, he laughed sardonically and then he was gone.

Clifford looked down at the dinghy again. Soon, there would be eight sweating men at the oars there, bending their backs to near the breaking point, hauling the great ship slowly through the weed and the eerie stillness of the sea, and Bo'sun Ollie would be in the stern above them, shouting out his orders: "Give way there! . . . Lay out on your oars! . . . Give way! . . ."

146

Towing a ship of more than five thousand tonnage was fearsome work, but in a day they could cover as much as twenty miles, the sharp bow parting the bladders of the weed and clearing a path that seemed to close behind the stern relentlessly. It was like trying to haul a ship through four hundred thousand square miles of porridge.

Clifford thought about Manners's warning, and knew that the old man was right. Alone, in a thirty-foot dinghy, he could plough his way through seven, eight, perhaps ten miles in a single night. But still. . . .

He had his doubts and he swarmed up the rigging again to join Manners on the top gallant yard. He said quietly, looking out over the vast expanse of the brown sea, "Do they still have hangings on board passenger ships, Dred?"

"Aye, they do." The old man was nodding vigorously as he let out the reefs. "At four bells of the morning watch. They put a guard at the companionway to turn back any passengers who might be up early, seeking out the fresh air of the morning, and it's all over in twenty minutes, the body cut down and fed to the sharks. This very night, boy. It's your only chance."

Clifford did not answer for a while. He was thinking of Mercy. "All right," he said at last. "This night it shall be."

"Good," Manners said. "The moon rises at two in the morning. At two bells I take over the stern watch, and Edmund will be in the crow's nest, so there'll be no one to watch you sliding down the towrope."

"You'll be in dire trouble, both of you."

"No. A pitch-black night . . . we'll not be ex-

147

pected to see a yard beyond our noses. And if we are . . ." He shrugged. "A day or two in the brig will do neither of us any great harm. It's a small price to pay for saving a man from his own murder."

Clifford reached out and took his hand in a warm, firm grip. "I'll make for Boston direct," he said. "You know a tavern there where we can meet again?"

"The Mermaid," Dred said promptly. "Look for the Mermaid Tavern on Lipton Road. For as long as we're in harbor, I'll have some of the boys there every night, waiting for you. If you're not there long before us. If we ever get out of this damned sea under sail, which I doubt."

"The Mermaid," Clifford echoed, grinning. "And we'll drink the place dry . . ."

"I'll have a word with the cook before I go on watch," Manners said happily, "and there'll be a haversack of bacon and biscuits in the lee of the winch-housing, look for it, there'll be enough to last you for ten days, though if you use your muscles well, you'll hit the coast in five or six."

He looked out to the northwestern horizon. "The stream will be against you, boy," he said gravely. "You'll have to keep rowing day and night. Or you'll slip back in your sleep, a mile for every yard you make."

"I know it."

"You'd best not sleep until you're clear of the weed, but that shouldn't take you more than thirty or forty hours. You'll just have to . . . keep at it."

They looked down on the crowded deck at the passengers lining the rails, staring down into the dark water, like marionettes way below them. This

148

was their first sight of the terrible Sargasso, and many of them were frightened by it; its reputation was a fearful one.

Sharma was moving among them with two other stewards, passing around mugs of steaming broth for the midmorning snack. One of the passengers, taking two mugs and passing one to his lady, said nonchalantly, "The Sargasso Sea, I believe, Steward? Is this not it?"

Sharma nodded, smiling to mask his own worries. "Yes, Sahib, the Sargasso Sea." He was about to hurry off, but the man stopped him. He was short and plump and affluent-looking, dressed in a frock-coat and black trousers, his top hat set just so on his bald head as though he were strolling down the Mall on his morning constitutional. The girl with him was young and sweet, with a widely flounced skirt below a tiny waist, her shoulders and the upper part of her breasts bared to the hot sun and beginning to show signs of sunburn. He said carelessly, "I've always heard that the Sargasso was a place of great danger, but . . . apparently the Captain does not share that opinion."

Sharma was acutely conscious of the worry underlying the nonchalance. His smile widened and he said, "Old wives' tales, Sahib. We enter the sea a little bit to catch the wind, isn't it? And in a few days now, we shall be in Boston . . . Excuse me, Sahib."

He moved off among the gaily dressed passengers, and high up in the rigging, Clifford was watching him. He was thinking: I must see Mistress Mercy before I go. . . .

He was confused about her and worried. It

149

seemed to him that a strange kind of destiny was forever bringing them closer. Was it the influence of the planets and the stars she so fervently believed in? A kind of destiny plotted for him by the Heavens, over which he had no control at all? Was he, then, just a cypher? To be guided, perhaps against his own volition, by the power of the stars?

He worried about it and he thought long and earnestly about the man she was to meet, the son of the gentleman through whose efforts he was travelling—just as Mercy's stars had told her he would—to the wide-open new world of the Americas.

Could he find her again in Boston? And if so, what should be his attitude? She was, after all, a lady in spite of her poverty, and he himself was nothing more than a deck hand, seeking out a living on a few shillings a month (which he would forfeit now if he jumped ship, with no paymaster to greet him at the end of the long voyage).

He thought he would wait till the eight bells that signified the hour of midnight, when the Bo'sun would be busy changing the first watch for the middle, and then, somehow, go to her.

He could not forget their little tryst in the hold, and the comfort of her warm hand in his. He was sure that she felt a very considerable affection for him and he brooded for a while, miserably, on the differences between their social stations in life.

As the noon hour, and the afternoon and evening passed, the slight breeze that held the sails still taut was dropping even more, and the *Capricorn* was making less than two and a half knots. The great spread of canvas was beginning its ominous flapping sound, like individual gunshots cracking out up there in the skies. Bonnets and drabblers had been added to the sails under the Bo'sun's watchful eye, and still the trifling speed was slackening; and all on board knew that by three bells of the morning wach, the burdensome task of hauling would begin.

No one could regard it with anything but anxiety. The physical effort itself required almost superhuman strength and would reduce them, long before their turns at the oars were over, to a state of the most terrible exhaustion; but worse, far worse, was the thought that they were hauling their ship, because of a stubborn Captain's recklessness, deeper and deeper into a part of the great ocean that terrified them all.

Clifford finished his turn at the watch at five bells, and went to the tiny, cramped quarters where no fewer than twelve of the crew slept in, quarters scarcely larger than a cupboard. There were six men of the middle watch there sleeping in their hammocks, and two others were playing cards by the light of a tallow candle. One of them was a man called Hays, and the flickering light of the flame was reflected, exaggeratedly, in his staring, exopthalmic eyes.

He beckoned Clifford over, and made room for him on the boxes they were sitting on, saying quietly, "I have a package for you, Cliff."

He was a tall and gangling man in his forties, with an untidy shock of iron-gray hair, and a great hooked nose that seemed to proceed him mightily wherever he went. He reached into the pocket of his oilskin blouse and brought out a small bundle,

151

tied in canvas and bound with cord. "Fishhooks and line, Cliff, you'll need them."

The other man was grinning at him, part of the conspiracy, a youngster not yet out of his teens and already on his seventh crossing. His name was Becker, a freckle-faced boy whose face seemed permanently burned by sun and wind. He said happily, whispering, "You're mad, Cliff Hawkes. You'll die in the sea with the rest of us, but you'll be alone, and that's worse, a lot worse . . ."

He too reached into his pouch and pulled out a canvas package. "Jam," he said, laughing to himself. "I filched it from the kitchen this evening. I reasoned that if a man's about to die, it might as well be with his belly full."

"The secret of the Sargasso," Hays whispered, "is to sit well back in the stern, you know that? Get your bow up as high as you can."

Clifford nodded. "Yes, I know it. We used to do the same with broken ice."

"It's a terror to look at," Hays said, "especially if you've never seen it before. But I've been three times through the Sargasso, and I've lost the fear of it I used to have. The weed is a bladder, a million million bladders, with naught but air in them, and they try to keep a light boat out of the water. It's as though you can never find any underneath it. But it's there, Cliff, it's there, no more than half a fathom down, so you dip your oars deep, and keep the bow high as you can."

"I was planning," Clifford said, "on standing in the stern and pushing instead of pulling. You agree with me?"

Hays nodded wisely. "Aye," he said. "It's more tiring, so try pulling first. And if you can't get your oars deep enough, you're right, it's a good plan, stand aft and push. How much water will you be carrying?"

"I'll have my billy, that'll last me for four days, I'll make a landfall by then. And if I don't . . ." He gestured with the little canvas bundle. "This will be mighty useful, friend. I'll catch fish and squeeze the water out of them, and if you know the Sargasso . . . tell me how deep my line should be?"

"No more than a fathom," Hays said promptly. "There's a lot of fish down there, feeding on the slugs that live off the weed."

"Good, good . . ."

"On one crossing," Hays said, "we had a skipper who was mad to find out what the sea was made of. Right at its edge he put out a net and hauled in half a ton of the muck. And with it, we found enough sea bass to feed the whole crew for two days, and they were delicious."

Clifford shook hands with both of them. "You'll say goodbye to my mates for me?"

"Aye, I will do that. And we're all waiting to see you again in Boston, all of us."

"Aye. At the Mermaid Tavern. I'll be there before you even start turning north."

"Just watch out," Hays said gravely, "for any dark clouds low in the sky. If you see them, Cliff, turn away from them, whichever course you have to take. Turn *away* from them, and row like a maniac till you can't row another mile, and then row twenty more. Because they mean a storm is coming up, and a storm over the Sargasso . . . it's enough to scare the bejabers out of any man, good sailor or not. The wind lifts up the weed, and dries it, and it falls like . . . oatmeal all around you. And dried out or not, it hits you in the face like ice-cold potage being hurled at you. And it piles up on top of the water till the sea's so far down below it that you're high and dry and feel you can get out and walk. But don't try that, Cliff, it's the quick way to find a wet grave. Aye, three times I've crossed the sea, and when I tell you I lost my fear of it . . . I'm lying. It's an unholy place."

"Well, it'll not be worse than the ice I've been used to all my seafaring life. What time is it now?"

"Seven bells struck," Becker said, "a little while ago."

"Then soon, they'll be changing the watch. I'd best be going. There's a thing I have to do."

"Aye," Hays said slyly. "You'd best see her before you go, or she'll be worrying they threw you overboard."

He felt his face was coloring; but these were good friends. "You know about that?" he asked, and Hays nodded vigorously. "Every man jack of 'em below decks knows about it, and it's strange . . ."

He was peering into Clifford's eyes, smiling to himself. "Not a man among them has spoken . . . how shall I put it?" he asked. "No one has said a single word you might take offense at. When you met her in the hold the other day, we were all . . . well, I suppose *covetous* is the word. But then, somehow, the way it will, a different idea began finding its way into the talk, and everyone agreed . . . well, they agreed that it was a fine and . . . a chaste thing that was going on between you. Maybe it's hard to understand in a sailing man, especially when he's at sea, but . . ." He grinned

154

cheerfully. "Just make sure Bo'sun Ollie doesn't know what you're up to."

In a little while, Clifford tapped at the door of Mercy's cabin.

CHAPTER EIGHT

It was past midnight, but Mercy lay awake in her bed, in a darkness that was complete and silence that somehow seemed unreal. Even the gentle lap of water at the ship's hull outside her porthole was no longer there, and she knew that the dreaded Sargasso, of which Sharma, with feigned nonchalance, had told her, was all around them now. She had heard some of the other passengers discussing it and had been very much aware that even the hardiest of the men, joking about it, were merely disguising their own worries.

She had heard the distant bells that sounded the half hours, and she was learning to interpret them, some of the time at least, correctly. Midnight was approaching, and she still could not sleep, and she knew well the reason why....

Soon, without a doubt, Adam Butrus would be there again, to defile her and to mock her. And the mockery was almost as bad as the defilement—that contemptuous scorn with which he used her body, as an object of his physical lust and nothing more, knowing that the life of her "young man" (she had already begun to think of Clifford in this way) depended not only on her acquiescence but now, it seemed, on her simulated pleasure in the disgusting act of rape.

An unresponsive partner, he had called her, with hate in his voice. And he had said: All you have to do is *pretend*. . . .

How could she hide her loathing for him?

When the tapping came at the door, it startled her. In the first dulled moment of apprehension, she knew that it was Butrus. And then, the thought came to her quickly: *He has a key, he does not do me the courtesy of knocking.*

She was on her feet in a flash, opening the door in the darkness. In the faint light of the swinging candle in the corridor, she saw him there, the young man of her dreams, and her relief was overwhelming but tempered terribly by her fears. But before she could say a word he had slipped inside the cabin and had closed the door behind him. She said urgently, "Clifford, no!"

He was already pulling a Lucifer through its little piece of sandpaper and lighting the lamp, and he said to her, whispering as he removed the glass funnel and touched the match to the wick, "No, Mistress Mercy, I must . . . I *must*!"

He replaced the funnel and turned to her. She threw her arms around him and whispered, "Clifford, it's not safe! . . ."

There was a strange excitement on him, a burning light in his eyes that was almost feverish. "It is safe," he said, holding onto her tightly, "no one saw me come here, and no one will see me leave, I will not compromise you, I promise you that."

"No, that's not the question . . ." How could she tell him of her great fear?

"I *must* talk to you," he said fiercely. "I must! For the moment, nothing else matters."

"Oh, yes, yes . . . but you must be brief, Clifford." He could feel her heart pounding against his chest.

"I leave this ship tonight," he whispered.

She stared at him, dismayed and uncomprehending.

"In a very short time," he went on, "as soon as the watch is changed. And more than anything in the world, I want . . . promise me that I may see you again in Boston. Promise me!"

She could only stare at him blankly. "Leave the ship?" she echoed. "But dear Clifford, I don't understand . . ."

Her arms were still around him, and he was holding her pressed tightly to him, his tall, straight body as strong as the oak from which the ship had been built.

"Butrus and Ollie," he said, "the First Mate and the Bo'sun, between them they are planning to kill me. Everyone on board knows it . . . I am twenty-four years old, Mistress Mercy, and still . . . I have faced death many times, with resignation, in waters far worse than these. But now . . ." His voice softened. "Now there is a fierce desire in me to live, and to keep on living, and you are part of that desire."

"Oh, Clifford . . ."

"And tonight, as soon as the watch is being changed, I will steal the dinghy that we are towing, and I will row my way to Boston. All I want now . . . I want your promise that once there, you will at least agree to listen to me."

"But Clifford . . ."

"No buts, Mistress Mercy," he said firmly. "There is a hard and punishing time ahead of me, and I will need all the willpower I can muster. If I know . . ." How gentle his voice was! "If I know that you will at least hear my plea . . . this will give me the strength that I need."

"Yes, yes," she said fervently. "But you must go now! If they find you here . . ."

"What more can they do to me? And who will find me here in the privacy of your cabin?" He held her hands tenderly, but with great strength; she fancied she could feel the blood coursing through his veins, vibrant and comforting.

"Yes," she said urgently, "you will find me, you will find me. I will not leave Boston till I have word from you, at the office of the company, and if you cannot get there, then send me a message and I will come to you."

His eyes were boring into hers. "And the man you are to marry?"

"I will not think of him now. I will not!"

She was surprised by her own assurance. "But you must go now, you must, if you only knew the danger you run here . . ." She could say no more; indeed, she wondered if she had already said too much.

And then, there was the ominous sound of the

160

key in the lock. And as they stared in shock, Adam Butrus was there.

He too stared at them for a moment of silence, his hand on the latch of the open door; and then he kicked it shut, and the cold, sardonic tone of his voice was tempered with a well-restrained anger. "By all the devils of the night that come to plague us," he said, "I never expected this."

He was even smiling, his strong white teeth showing in the yellow light of the lamp. "Your bed, Ma'am," he said, "seems to be a very busy place. And this, no doubt, is the reason for the dull and boring frigidity of what would otherwise be a very satisfying body . . . I should have guessed it. The reason for which no passion throbs in your miserable loins when I invade them, the reason for which . . ."

He could say no more. Clifford's hands were at his throat, cutting off further insult. Butrus's head was thrust down to contain the threat and he brought his two arms up in a wide, swinging motion to break the hold, an expert in fights without number, and smashed a powerful fist into Clifford's throat, knocking him to the ground. Instantly they were rolling over and over together in the tight confines of the miniscule cabin, over the bed, the chair, and up against the dressing table. Butrus held a practiced hand over Clifford's throat, forcing his head down, and he was pounding his other fist repeatedly into his chest—savage, punishing blows over the heart, the quickest way to kill a man, he had long since learned.

She saw Clifford's eyes bulging, his face darkening, and she threw herself on top of Butrus's back

161

and tried to hold back the driving arm, but could not. There was a fury in him now that was like an animal's, a bull gone wild. Clifford's leg was twisted under the low bed, and he was trying to free it, but he could not move and Mercy, gasping, fell back onto the bare boards of the floor and slashed at Butrus's face with her fingernails. But he merely broke the rhythm of his pounding once and knocked her away savagely with a blow to the side of her head.

She heard the washbasin break as their bodies crashed into the dressingtable. The water jug tumbled over, and the cold cascade over her head seemed to revive her. She struggled to her feet and took the heavy jug in both hands, bringing it down on the back of Butrus's head with all the strength she could find in her. It shattered into shards as the Mate collapsed to the ground and lay still. Her hand went to her mouth and her voice was hushed. "I killed him . . ." she whispered.

Clifford was struggling to his feet, his face deathly pale now, and he put his arms round her and held her for a moment. She could feel the pounding of his heart. He broke away in a moment, and crouched beside Butrus's silent body and lifted an eyelid, felt for the heartbeat. He shook his head at last and said grimly, "No, he is not dead."

He raised himself up again and put an arm around her, and they stood like lost children looking down at him. "What now?" she whispered.

They sat together on the edge of the bed, and he was very calm and competent now, as though some kind of Rubicon had been passed and they were now committed to a definite course of action.

"Now," he said quietly, "we have some very important decisions to make, and we must make them quickly. If he were dead, it would be simple. But he is not."

She gasped and he held her hand tightly. "Yes," he said softly, "I know. If he were dead, it would have been at least partly your doing and you would never forgive yourself for it, even though he richly deserves to die. But he is alive, and we must face the inevitable now."

"If we can discover what it is . . ."

"Yes, if we can reason it out. You know what he will say, do you not?"

"Yes," she said steadily. "I know it. The same as he did before."

"And this time, they will hang me, without a doubt, except that they will not find me, I will be far away in an open boat. But this is of no matter, Mistress Mercy. The question is . . . what will happen to *you*?"

"I will tell the Captain the truth," she said vehemently, "and this time . . . I will *make* him believe me!"

"And perhaps, this time, he will. But I think not. The risk is too great."

He was talking rationally, quietly, and with great assurance now. Mercy was hanging onto every word he said. Staring at the recumbent body as though seeking inspiration there, he went on, "How can we guess what a man like that will do? He's a ruthless and evil man and he may light upon the simplest of all the answers to his predicament. Your death. It would mean nothing to him."

She was trembling violently. "But if I were to go

163

to the Captain," she whispered, "now, this very minute, go to his cabin and tell him that Butrus forced his way in here . . ."

"And he would learn," Clifford said steadily, "that you were receiving me in your cabin? A vulgar seaman from below decks? No, I will not permit it."

She was silent for a moment, her eyes cast down; he had not even asked her why Butrus was there, and she felt a terrible color rising to her cheeks. "I must tell you," she said at last, her voice so low that he could hardly make out the words, "why Butrus came here . . ."

She felt his hand tighten on hers, almost painfully. "No!" he said quickly. "There is nothing you have to tell me."

"But I must, Clifford!"

"No! I will not listen!"

He took both her hands and looked steadily into her eyes. "I know," he said carefully, "that whatever the reasons were, they were honorable reasons. Perhaps I can even guess what they are, and the weight of them on my heart . . ." He shook his head. "No, we must not think of them now, we must put them behind us."

"How can we?"

"We must!"

"I will live with those . . . those terrible memories forever."

"No! You must forget them!"

The bell was sounding on the deck above them, eight sonorous notes, and he said urgently, "There is only one thing that we can do."

There was a great understanding between them.

164

Her heart had missed a beat. "Yes," she said eagerly, "Only one thing now . . . I must come with you."

He wanted her to be sure. "It will not be easy for you," he said gravely. "A small boat, on the open sea, for as many as five or six days, many more perhaps."

"Will it be easier for me if I remain on board?"

"I think not. But can we be certain, Mercy? . . ."

"Only one thing is certain," she said impetuously, "and that is that I will not remain another day or night on this terrible ship."

Butrus was stirring, and Clifford took a blanket from the bunk and tore it quickly into strips, binding his arms and ankles and wrapping a thickness of it around his mouth. His mind was racing and he knew that what they were planning was filled with the most awesome dangers, dangers that she could not even begin to understand. It scared him, and yet . . . *there was so little time for irresolution.

Mercy was already packing a few prized items into her reticule—her little almanac of astrology, the tortoise shell-backed little mirror her dear father had diven her, the diary that was a present from Aunt Melissa, the scented sachet she had made from lemon verbena and lavender . . . She found it hard to believe that she could embark on such a hazardous adventure with so little thought or anxiety, and when she pulled herself up short to think about it for a moment, it astonished her that she had made up her mind to do this the moment Clifford had said "*I will leave this ship tonight . . .*"

She looked down at Butrus. His eyes were open now, and he was staring at her in the lamplight with a look of venom in his eyes that made her shudder. "Look at his eyes," she said to Clifford, speaking clearly and distinctly, "and know what evil looks like."

Clifford stooped down and made the knots of his improvised bindings more secure.

"If I had any doubts at all," she said, "about what we are doing now . . . one look at that loathsome creature's face would dispel them forever."

He took her arm and said simply, "Come."

He turned the wick in the lamp down fully before they went out into the deserted corridor together. They slipped quickly through the door that led to the crew's quarters, and three of the sailors were there, waiting, and they looked at Mercy in huge surprise. Then one of them was grinning broadly, a man with a hooked nose so large it was almost a caricature. He thrust out a hand to Clifford and shook his, saying warmly, "Good luck to you, shipmate. When you've gone, I'll see she gets back to her cabin safely."

"She's coming with me," Clifford whispered, and the broad smile disappeared momentarily, then was back again, broader and more msichievous now. "Good, good," he said, "and good luck then to the both o' ye."

One of the others, a freckle-faced young boy still in his teens, was staring at them in shock. "She's going with you?" he said hoarsely. "In an open boat on the Sargasso? . . ."

The older man said quickly, "With anyone else, Clifford, I'd be worrying too, and perhaps you're the only man aboard who can carry it off, as I know ye will. Come, come quickly. Bo'sun Ollie is forward, the Captain's in his bed, and the only enemy we've lost track of is Adam Butrus, he should by rights be in his cabin, but he's not, so we have to keep our eyes skinned for him."

"He's in the lady's cabin," Clifford said quietly. "He went there with evil in his foul mind, and he's trussed up like a chicken for his pains. Just let him lie there till they find him in the morning."

"Good. Come then!"

There were no less than five other seamen posted there, friendly sentries along the way, beckoning them from cover to cover as they went down a short flight of steps and up another, and one of them, almost the last, was holding up a warning hand as he lounged against the bulwark picking his teeth. Clifford pulled her back into the shadows, and they saw a cook's helper go by and toss a pail of swill over the side, and when he was gone again, the sentry signalled and they hurried to the shadowy bulk of the windlass housing. A tall, grizzled old man rose up out of the darkness and Clifford whispered to him, "She's coming with me, Dred." He peered over the side to the dark sea and turned back to them. "Dred Manners," he said quietly, "the best friend a man could have, this is Mistress Mercy, who'll be in dire trouble if she stays another day aboard the *Capricorn*."

The old man had taken off his oilskin hat. He took her outstretched hand and shook it, saying quietly, "Have no fear down there, Mistress. Your Clifford is the best of all the men aboard this ship, you'll be in good hands. But wait . . ." He found a coil of rope and slipped the end of it through a wythe at the end of the spanker boom. "By your leave, Ma'am," he said, and tied the end of it around her waist, knotting it firmly. "Ye'll simply slide down the rope there, Ma'am," he said, his voice as low as a zephyr. "Ye're not likely to fall if your arms are strong, but if ye should, this'll hold you till I lower you down to the dinghy." He picked up a haversack and Clifford slung it over his shoulders. They held a whispered consultation for a moment:

"There are life preservers aboard, Dred?"

"Aye, eight of them."

"And how many oars?"

"Eight oars too, and there's a spread of good canvas in the aft locker, it'll give you shelter from the sun if you should need it. It's my thinking the lady will . . ."

"And ropes enough if we need them?"

"Aye, all you'll ever need. Ten gallons of water in the main container, four in the small one, enough to last you to Kingdom Come and back, there'll be no need to stint yourselves on water. You've a compass?"

"Aye, in my pouch, if I need it. But we'll have the sun and the stars to steer by."

"The Mermaid Tavern," Dred Manners said, grinning. "With luck and the strength of your arms, you'll be there ahead of us. So, good luck to you both." He doffed his oilskin hat again respectfully. "May God be with you, Ma'am."

There was another rapid handshake and then Clifford was over the taffrail, gripping the heavy rope with both hands, swinging a leg over it below him. He looked back at Mercy, no more than an indistinct blur in the dark of the moonless night. She heard his whisper come to her, "Very slowly, or you'll burn yourself on the rope . . . Just follow me down. One leg, behind your knee, over the rope . . ."

She was grateful for the darkness that hid the terrifying sight from her. She felt the rope about her waist tighten as the old man took the strain on it. She clung to the unaccustomed hawser for dear life, her heart pounding, her light body seeming to weigh far more than she had imagined as she felt the terrible strain on her arms.

The rope at her waist was a comfort to her, and soon, she felt Clifford's strong grasp on her ankles and then around her body, helping her into the dinghy. He untied the safety rope and let it fall free, and cast off the painter quickly. Indicating a seat for her, he took one behind her and she swung round and watched him winding rags around the rowlocks to silence them; then he had set the oars and was heaving on them mightily.

The *Capricorn* was a dark shadow looming over them, towering out of the dark water, and she could not believe that she had come down so easily and so quickly from such a dizzying height. It seemed an incredibly short space of time before it was swallowed up in the darkness and she turned again to ask eagerly, "Are we free? Are we really free?"

"Sshhh . . ." She could see his eyes gleaming now. "You must keep your voice down," he whispered. "Our voices carry well in the night . . . just for a few more minutes . . ."

She felt abashed, knowing that she should have realized this, but the unbearable excitement of the moment was overpowering her. She felt that she was trembling, and to occupy her mind in these frightening moments she undid the plaits of her long hair and shook it loose. It was somehow an obscure symbol for her.

She felt the boat rocking gently and Clifford was shipping the oars and moving to her. He took her hand and whispered, "Now you sit here." He guided her to one more seat aft, and helped her clamber over it to sit facing the rear. Then he took a life preserver from a locker and slipped it over her shoulders. "Your arms through here," he whispered. "Yes . . . and the cords, you tie them like so. . . . You wear this always, all the time until we reach our destination."

He placed his feet as wide apart as the planking of the chimes would allow and took up the oars again, pushing rhythmically on them, his tall strong body moving in a tireless cadence as he swung the craft around through a half-circle. She watched him with wonder in her eyes, thinking how easy he made it seem.

She was startled to hear the sound of the ship's bell coming to them across the water, three clear notes, and he saw her surprise and laughed softly. "Aye," he said, whispering still, "she's still there. But with luck, that's the last bell we'll hear."

"Three bells," Mercy said hesitantly. "That's . . . half-past one in the morning?"

He nodded. "Three bells of the middle watch, half past one. By the time they sound the four, we'll be well away."

"And when daylight comes?"

The rhythm of his body was fascinating and she wished that somehow she could help.

"By daylight?" he said, echoing her. "At this latitude, daylight will be shortly before four bells, that's? . . ." He waited.

"Six o'clock?"

"Aye, six o'clock." His voice was still very low, and she knew that he was talking, even while he strained at the oars, just to comfort her. He whispered, "You're an educated lady, Mistress Mercy. Do you know about mathematics?"

She grimaced. "I can set up minor arcs and major progressions, but not much more," she said, delighted at the look of puzzlement on his face. "Astrological calculations," she whispered.

"Ah . . . well . . ."

He was happy with her contentment. "Perhaps ours is not as complicated as that," he said, "but in navigation . . . the distance of the horizon, in nautical miles, is one point seven times the square root of your height in feet. The deck of the *Capricorn* is sixteen feet above the waterline . . . and one point seven times the square root of that is six point eight, or a little under seven miles. We're moving now, I'd say, at three knots, which means that by daylight, give or take a few hundred yards, we'll be twelve miles away from them. In other words, we'll be out of sight of their deck. From the crow's nest, the horizon is twenty-five miles away, but a man can't see that far even with a good glass, and we're a tiny speck on a very big ocean. And what all that means is . . ." He was laughing openly now. "It means," he went on, "that we shall still see

171

the tops of their masts, but they won't see us. Are you hungry?"

She shook her head. "No, I'm too . . . too excited. And you?"

"When daylight comes, we'll have a bite of bacon and some biscuits. And if you want to sleep . . . in that locker there you'll find a roll of canvas. It won't make much of a bed, but it's better than the bare boards of the dinghy."

"And I won't sleep either," she said, "until you do."

"Then you've many a sleepless night ahead of you," he said, smiling.

The night was cool and there was no breeze at all. When the moon came up Clifford looked at it and searched the horizon all around them. The *Capricorn* was still there, two miles or more behind them now. And when the moon rose higher and shed its silvery light on the sea—a silver tinged with a strange burnt umber now where the wet bladders of the weed reflected its sheen—the ship was more than four miles off, her sails still full-rigged, not yet hove to, and Clifford said, wondering, "Our Skipper's a hard man, and maybe an unjust man, but I'll give him his due. If there's a breath of wind anywhere on the ocean . . . he'll find it.

It startled her. "Does that mean," she asked, "that they can catch up with us?"

"No. They're running with it, slight as it is. And we're rowing into it. Every square foot of his canvas is taking him away from us. They'll never catch us now, Mistress Mercy. All we have to worry about . . . is the sea. But we'll fight it, and we'll win."

172

When daylight came, it was just as he had promised. They could make out, very faintly, the tops of the *Capricorn*'s masts and no more of her; and all around them the brown morass was spread out like a heaving amber-colored carpet, as far as they could see.

He put down the oars now and shipped them. Sitting down heavily, he looked at her thoughtfully for a moment. "And now," he said at last, "I have to start asking myself if this was a foolish thing we did."

"No," she said impetuously. "I'm sure it was not. We're safe, Clifford, both of us. While a few hours ago . . ." She could not bear to think of it.

"And you have no regrets?"

"None. None at all."

He opened up the haversack Manners had given him, and took out his clasp-knife, cutting off two pieces of bacon. He handed her one with a rock-hard water biscuit, and then set about counting the others carefully and exploring the depths of the bag. He laughed when he found a small stone bottle of rum and laid out all the provisions on the seats, enumerating them as he did so.

"We have bacon to last us a lifetime," he said, "and beef jerky, a pound or more of crystalized sugar, enough dried apple to feed an army, a score of onions . . . more cheese than a hungry man could eat in a month, and limes to keep away the scurvy. How long does he think we'll be taking for this journey? We'll have enough left over when we get there to feed a whole tribe of painted Indians."

He unwrapped the bundles they had given him in the crew's quarters, checked over the fish-hooks, and slipped them back into his pouch. "And Becker's jam too," he said laughing.

"Becker?"

"The boy with the freckles on his face." He was uncorking the small stone crock and dipping a finger there, licking it appreciatively. "Hmm," he said happily, "plum, I hope you like plum jam, Ma'am?"

She nodded eagerly. "I love it!"

They were like two youngsters on a picnic, quite oblivious of the mortal dangers ahead of them.

"You've good friends on board," she said, and he nodded. "They're all with us in spirit, Mistress Mercy, and if you listen well, you'll hear their good wishes coming to us over the ocean. It'll be a great comfort to us in the long days ahead."

She had never tasted the seamen's biscuits before. She spread jam on one of them and bit into it hopelessly till he showed her how to break it into pieces by striking it hard on the gunwhale and then scraping at it with the teeth. "Not the choicest food in the world," he said, "but soon, we'll catch some fish, and we'll live like kings. Have you ever eaten raw fish?"

"*Raw?*" The idea startled her, and he held up one of the limes and explained, "You sprinkle the white flesh with lime juice, you'll find it delicious. And now . . . there are other things to talk about."

They were munching on the bacon and sipping on the water together; and he moved over to the locker, took out the spread of canvas and lashed it to the sides of the boat. "When the sun gets high," he said, "it might become insupportable for you, and we don't want you burning up with the heat of it. So this will be your shelter. You can sleep un-

174

der this in the heat of the day, and when you're out of the shade, keep your shawl about your shoulders and your face turned away as much as you can, it will be more comfortable for you. Drink when you're thirsty, we've plenty of water, and if you hold a pellet of sugar in your mouth it will give you more energy than you'll ever need. We're about three hundred and fifty miles off the coast now, and though I don't know too much about the American coastline, I'd say our nearest landfall would be somewhere along the coast of Pennsylvania. That's a long way south from Boston, but I've studied the charts well, and the Gulf Stream flows north along the coast there. So we can land as soon as we see the coast and make our way north overland . . . or we can stay aboard the dinghy if we've found it comfortable enough—which is to say if we've become hardened to it—and let the stream and the oars take us all the way to Boston."

He fell silent for a moment. "That's where we both have to go," he said at last. "You to find your . . . your young man, and me . . . my mates will be waiting there to be assured that we're not both dead. And I owe it to them not to disappoint them."

She was smiling softly to herself. "Poor Nathan," she said. "I don't believe I will ever see him, and I must confess . . ." She broke off, frowning. "No," she said at last. "I was going to say that I don't really care a hoot about that, but I do. Only for my father's sake." She shrugged. "Well, we shall see."

Clifford said nothing. He put away the supplies

carefully, took up his oars again, and began rowing. The sun rose high in a blinding blue sky and she crept under the crude shelter and lay there watching him, wishing there was some way she could be more than just a useless passenger.

"If I were to take one of the oars?" she asked. "You could teach me, and I'm sure I would learn fast."

He laughed. "We'd be going round in circles," he said. "No, this is something I do well, a whaler's the best training in the world for an oarsman. We have to tow our ships through broken ice once in a while, and that's not easy. No, Mistress Mercy, though I thank you for the offer. You had no rest last night, and the best thing for you now . . . is sleep."

"I cannot sleep while you have to work so hard."

"Sleep."

"No, I will not."

"Sleep."

He was smiling still and the sweat was pouring from his forehead now. She shook her head stubbornly, but soon her eyes closed against her will, and she drifted off for a while. She woke up with a start and he was still straining vigorously, tirelessly, at the oars, his hairshirt soaked through with perspiration. It seemed to her that the sun was on the wrong side of them and she looked around, startled. "But . . . have we changed direction?" she asked.

"No," he answered her cheerfully. "But the sun has. You were sleeping there like a baby, and I'm glad of it."

"Oh no . . . for how long?"

He glanced at the sun. "Three hours, perhaps a little more."

"And all this time you have not stopped rowing?"

He gestured with his head. "Look there, Mistress Mercy," he said. "If you stand up carefully, you can see it. Open water."

She got to her feet and looked. Ahead of her the dark brown of the weed stretched on and on and on . . . and beyond it, there was a streak of the most brilliant blue below the dark clouds that seemed to hug the horizon. "Is that . . . open sea?" she asked.

He nodded. "Aye," he said. "We're leaving the Sargasso behind us. And you see? There's no terror in it at all. When the weed is no longer clutching at us, we'll make better time. I'm going to try for a landfall in seven days."

He redoubled his efforts, and in an hour or less the great brown mass of the weed seemed to part a way for them. The blue-gray water was a welcome relief, even though the little dinghy was rocking now, climbing up the crests of the waves and slipping down the other side of them, so that she had to steady herself by holding on to the gunwhale with both hands. It was not an unpleasant sensation, but there was an urgent problem facing her now, and she worried about it for a long time, then thought: Well, the open sea is no place for overly genteel modesty, and there's no shame in it at all. . . .

But her inhibitions were still strong and she could not meet his eyes. "If we were to stop for a little while," she said hesitantly, "you could rest, and I could perhaps . . . slip into the water and . . . and freshen up a little? I feel . . ." She was blushing furiously. "I feel I could derive a great deal of benefit from contact with clean water."

"Ah, yes, of course."

He shipped the oars and sat down, and reached out to take her hand. "We'll both do this two or three times a day," he said gently. "You'll use the stern, where it's easier to climb aboard again. If you feel you have to remove your outer garments . . . I'll straighten out the forward locker, and there'll be no embarrassment to you at all. But first . . ."

He found a coil of rope and started tying knots along it, fastening it to the cleat set in the stern post. He held up its end and told her, "This goes around your waist every time you take a dip in the ocean. We don't know what the currents are here, and we don't want you swept away while you're making your ablutions. And once you're safely in the water, you'll call out to me and let me know, because I have to keep watch. I don't know whether or not there are sharks in these waters; perhaps there are. But if so, believe me, I'll see them long before they see you, and I'll have you aboard, naked or not, before you can bat an eyelid." He was smiling broadly and she felt the blush suffusing her face.

He went forward to the locker and started tying a hook to the end of a length of line. She took off her skirt and her petticoats, and eased the blouse carefully from the confinement of the life preserver. Looking to see that he was carefully turned away from her, she slipped the pantalettes down over her ankles and straightened her shift and her bodice. Tying the long rope around her waist as he had told her, she slipped over the side.

The water was surprisingly cold and she held on tightly to the weaving rudder. "Master Clifford," she called out primly.

He came and stood above her, looking down at her and laughing. "I should have checked the knot you made in the rope," he said. "I'll be bound it was a granny."

"A granny? What's that?"

The water was lapping against her body, lifting her up with the boat and dropping her down again with a strangely exciting motion. She had bathed in seawater before, at Brighton Beach and at Margate, when she had worn a special dress of colored calico, decorated with frills, and long black bathing stockings. There, the sand had always been firm under her feet, the waves cresting with little rills of surf. But here the ocean was bottomless and the movement of the water caressed her near-naked loins, the unaccustomed bulk of the cork preserver forcing her chin up. She tried to hold the shift down to her knees, modestly, but it kept riding up around her waist.

Clifford was staring out to the north of them, and there was a worried frown on his face. She followed his look and saw the dark, swirling cloud there, a long way off and low on the horizon. Even as she watched it, it seemed that it was growing in size or getting nearer, perhaps both. Clifford said calmly, "Best get back on board as soon as you can, Mistress Mercy. We have to start rowing again."

He began to turn away, but then he turned back and held out a hand for her. "It's a high sea," he said. "You'll not find it easy. I'll help you."

She clutched at the gunwhale with both hands and struggled to lift herself up. Everytime the waves receded they dragged her down again and he said at last, "One knee on the gun'l, as soon as the wave takes you there."

She swung a leg over on the next upward sweep and found herself half-aboard. He took her by the shoulders and pulled her over as she struggled with the shift, trying to cover up her thighs and saying gruffly, "Get dressed as fast as you can, Mistress Mercy, I don't like the looks of that squall there."

He took up the oars as she started putting her petticoats on, but she used only one, and slipped her skirt over it and then struggled into the pantalettes, and now the wind was whipping up the water around them, slicing white tops of spray off the tops of the waves and rocking the little craft with a violence that was alarming in the extreme. He shouted at her over the noise of the wind, "That rope there! Slip a half-hitch over that pin, any kind of a knot, wrap it around your waist and tighten it, she's going to hit us any minute now ... Quickly!"

The dark squall was almost on them. The wind drove them with unbelievable force as he turned the dinghy head-on into the wind and held it there, using his back more than his arms now. The boat swept up high and dropped down with a sickening lurch into the troughs again. He looked at the rope she was winding around herself and shouted, "A slippery-hitch now . . ." He saw her look of uncomprehension and said, "Pull just a loop of rope through, not the end of it, hang on to the end! And if you have to get free . . . give a strong pull on it. Hold on now, it's on us! And there's nothing to be afraid of . . ."

The funnel of the wind hit them, hard.

For a moment, it seemed to pick the boat up out of the water altogether, and send it scudding across the tops of the waves, then she saw Clifford hurl the two oars down under the slats of the seats and throw himself forward on top of her. One arm was over her shoulder, the other gripping the rope she had tied around the seat. He shouted, "Now, we just hold on! We ride it out! . . ."

She felt she wanted to scream, so she bit her lip to hold it back. His face was close to hers, and he shouted in her ear, "There's nothing . . . nothing to worry about! We've a stout boat under us, and we'll be out of it in a few minutes. Just hold on tight to me!"

It was tossing around like a cork in the water, slamming down into the depths with a terrible sound of finality, then being lifted up again and twisted around and slammed down once more. A wave broke over them and filled the dinghy with swirling water. A moment later it emptied itself out as it was up-ended again and it twisted around and drove on at a terrifying speed. It seemed to dive stern-first into a thick mass of the gulfweed they had so recently left behind them, and then they weed was all around them again, and they were cutting a way through it on the wind, on an even keel now.

Instead of waves now, there were great stretches of the sea that seemed infinitely higher than others, and the boat would slide relentlessly up them for interminable lengths of time, then slide down, faster still, to the lower levels, and then up, up, up again, inexorably.

He was winding a rope around her and he handed her the loose end of it, shouting. "Hold on to this. If we overturn, haul on it. But don't let go, it's your lifeline, you understand? You don't let go of it whatever happens! There, wrap it around your waist, so . . ."

She was too frightened to answer him. He sat close by her now with a single oar, alternately rowing and backpaddling as he tried to keep the boat turned into the swell. The sun was sinking lower and lower in the sky, and still the wind drove them on, then the clouds came and obscured it completely, and the rain was lashing at them. When night came, Clifford was still straining at the oar and she was still lashed to the seat, sure now that they were both going to die.

And then, with startling suddenness, a roar came to them out of the west, and a dark funnel of air, so powerful that she could not believe it, picked up the little craft and sent it spinning once more across the top of the sludge as though it were a stone slung from a catapult. It skimmed along the top of the morass for more than a minute on its side, as they held on desperately.

And then, quite slowly, it tipped over and crashed down on top of them.

The last thing Mercy felt was Clifford's arm reaching around her waist with a force that almost squashed the life out of her. A thought flashed through her mind that she was in his arms and that they were dying together. Then, she lost consciousness. . . .

CHAPTER NINE

When she awoke at last, it was quite dark and she was terrified. She just did not know where she was. There was a rope around her waist, there were bare, wet boards under her back; and she was freezing cold.

She heard herself groan, and as she tried to move her painful limbs, a hand took hold of her arm and a dear and friendly voice said urgently, "No, don't move, Mercy. Are you hurt badly?"

She could see almost nothing in the darkness, though the moon was bright, almost as bright as day. She wondered if she had lost her sight. But then the clarity came, and she saw Clifford perched on one elbow above her, his hand under her head. "Are you badly hurt?" he asked again and she shook her head, not knowing what had happened. "No, I don't think so . . . and you?"

185

The morass of the weed was all around them, brown bloated bladders that shone strangely under the moon. Their hull was swaying with a strange and eerie movement, sometimes turning itself quite around and slipping sideways, as though being dragged around by a giant hand down under the heavy wet carpet somewhere.

Clifford eased the rope that lay across her, and she saw now that she was covered over with his wet hairshirt; his chest was bare, pale and muscular.

"I'm sick at heart, Mercy," he said, "but that's all. I lost control of the boat. We were in the eye of a hurricane, it picked us up like a toy, and hurled us. Are you sure you're all right?"

There was a great bloodied gash on his forehead and she touched it with her fingertips lightly. "But you're wounded."

"A small cut, nothing worse than that. The boat up-ended itself, and it came down on top of us. I thought . . . Oh God, I feared you were dead."

The cords of the life preserver were cutting into her and she tried to undo their knots. He said, "Wait, let me help you." He undid the fastenings for her and loosened up the front part of it. "Sit up for a moment," he said. He helped her raise her shoulders and opened up the preserver completely, easing it under her head and shoulders. When she lay back, it was a cushion under her against the rough boards of the hull.

He lay his head down on her breast and in a moment he moved his hand there too; she felt no more than the infinitesimal pressure of his fingertips, and she stroked his hair. "But we are both alive," she said. "That awful storm . . . has it gone?"

"Not quite. We're on the edge of it and it's veer-

186

ing away from us, but we're still being driven, at God knows how many knots, far to the southwest."

Her hands were exploring the slatted boards under her. "And this is . . . the underside of the dinghy?"

"Yes." He almost smiled. "We still have the dinghy," he said. "True, it can't be rowed, it can't be steered, we're at the mercy of the winds and the currents, and only Neptune himself knows where they might take us. But we are still afloat. And yes, we are still alive."

She was silent for a moment, staring up at the stars and the planets. Her voice was very quiet, and calm too. "Are we going to die, Clifford?"

She felt his hand tighten, almost involuntarily, over her breast, and then he pulled it away sharply, as though conscious of the intimacy and shamed by it. He sat up suddenly and said, "No, by God! We are not going to die, Mistress Mercy, not while I have any strength left at all in this . . . this miserable body."

She pulled the hairshirt free from under the rope at her waist and said, "You're freezing, take it . . ."

"No." He shook his head. "It will help to keep you warmer than you might otherwise be. The night is cold for someone who is not accustomed to it."

"Cold for you too. Take your shirt."

"I am used to the waters of the Arctic, remember? No, use it as a blanket, it's a good warm shirt."

There were goose pimples all over his upper arms, and she could even feel them with her fingers. She eased herself out from under the restraining rope.

187

As she slipped the shirt over his head, she said, "You tied us down like this? Together?"

"You were unconscious, and I was afraid I'd lose my senses too, so . . ." He grimaced. "Yes," he said. "I lashed us together to the boat. If either one of us should be swept away . . . better we both should die."

The moon was very bright now and the clouds were scudding by. There was an eerie feeling of motion that was more than the rise and fall of the boat beneath them.

"But . . . we are still moving?" she asked, puzzled about it.

"Yes," he said. "We are moving fast. There are strange currents here, currents the like of which I've never seen before. And there is no way we can control where we are going."

He was easing the rope that ran around the hull, slipping a new knot along it. "Keep your legs always under the rope," he said. "Else, a sudden swell, a twist of the wind even, and you can slip into that morass there." He was smiling at her now. "And I have no wish," he said, "to finish this long journey alone."

She clutched him to her tightly. "Oh Clifford," she whispered. He kissed her gently on the lips, drawing back at once, as though knowing he had overstepped the bounds of modesty. "Tomorrow," he said abruptly, "when the sun is high, and not before, I'm going to try to turn the boat right side up. It will not be easy, but . . . perhaps I can do it."

She felt somehow that he was talking just to comfort her, telling her things he would do that could not be done, to give her hope.

188

She lay silent and still on the cushions of the preserver and he went on, "We have two hundred pounds of cork sealed into the hull below us and two watertight compartments, so we cannot sink. This kind of boat never can. There's an age-old system of righting an upturned dinghy, and for one this size, four men are enough."

He grinned at her, his boyish face alive again. "Well," he said cheerfully, "I don't have three strong shipmates to help me, but . . . there's also a lot of trapped air in the boat, and the sun will expand it, and if we can somehow get to open sea, and use the force of the waves instead of those good strong arms . . . I don't know. Perhaps it can be done. We'll never find out unless we try."

"And if we can't?"

"Then at least we can open up the lockers down there, and get food and water, and even like this, upside down and drifting, we can hold out for a very long time. Never give up hope, Mistress Mercy, it's the sailor's first command."

"As long as you are with me."

"I will be with you for . . . for as long as you wish."

She felt weak and she sighed. "I'm so tired," she whispered.

"Then sleep. It's not a good bed, but . . . sleep."

She lay back on her cushion and he readjusted the rope across her waist, then lay down beside her, his head close to her shoulder. He put his hand at her waist, very lightly, and in a moment he moved it up until he was almost, but not quite, touching her breast. She waited, excited by his touch, and there was the barest pressure there, the side of his hand against the lower part of the soft swelling.

189

She still waited, but he would move it no further, and she eased her own hand to cover his, and moved it gently till it was grasping her breast fully. She lay still and looked up at the bright stars, her mind racing, the blood pounding through her veins. He did not move; there was just the slightest pressure of his hand, an almost imperceptible caress. A fingertip found the hardening nipple and lingered there, just touching.

"Venus," she whispered and he started. "Venus?"

"Up there, looking down on us," she said quietly, and his eyes followed her look. The sky was brightly lit with a million stars, and he stared up at it, wondering. His hand had ceased its exploration. "Venus," she said again, her voice a soft sibilant in the darkness. "Love, affection, desire . . . they all stem from that one planet."

"Desire . . ." he mumbled, and it seemed to disturb him. The hand had gone from her breast, and she took it gently in hers and laid it back there. Now, he slid it under her damp blouse and her bust-bodice, and felt the soft resilience; she could feel his trembling.

She waited; and in a little while she knew that, exhausted, he had fallen asleep. She lay quite still, and soon he stirred in his sleep and thrust a thigh over her loins. She felt—or was it only fancy?—a faint throbbing there against her hip, and she was trembling, shuddering, wanting desperately the warmth of his body in her arms.

And then, the oblivion came over her too and sleep took its insidious hold on her. They slept together like children in each other's arms.

When the violent rocking of her bed awoke her, the sun was already in the sky, still low on the horizon and burning with a brilliant red-gold. Clifford was standing above her, his feet wide-spaced on the hull of the upturned boat and all around her the sea was free of the brown weed, rising and falling in a steady, almost monotonous rhythm.

He saw her eyes opening, and he threw his arms wide, saying happily, "You see, Mistress Mercy? Another day, and we are still alive, and I feel . . ." He gestured broadly. "I feel . . . on top of the world! Did you sleep well? Don't answer me! I know that you did."

She stretched her cramped limbs and answered his laugh. "You do? And pray how do you know that, sir?"

"Because you were snoring, and a good snore is an indication of a sound sleep."

"I was not, Master Clifford," she said indignantly. He bent down to pull away the confining rope and helped her with the life preserver, fastening it loosely around her once more. She looked around at the limitless horizon, wondering. "We left the Sargasso Sea?" she asked incredulously.

He nodded. "We left it behind us. I awoke an hour or so ago, awakened, you must understand, by your snoring . . ."

"I do not snore, sir."

"And the sea was calm and bright, a deep and glorious blue, just look at it. And where we are . . . I do not have the faintest idea. In three, four hours, you and I between us will right this boat, and then we will continue on our way, to whatever our destinies have in store for us. Meanwhile, I am famished. You want some bacon? Some of those quite inedible biscuits? Jerky? Sugar? Dried rings

191

of fine English Newton apples? What is your wish, Mistress Mercy?"

His mood was contagious. She stood up, and balanced herself precariously on the upturned hull. "We have all those delights?" she asked and he nodded gravely.

"Only a few feet below us," he said. "Can you swim, perhaps?"

She laughed. "How would I know how to swim, sir?"

"Never mind. You have your lifejacket and a rope to hang on to. It's very easy, really it is."

"Just tell me what I have to do, Clifford."

"Remember the pocket of air," he said, "inside the boat. We slip down into the water. We take a deep breath and ease ourselves under the gun'l, then we come up inside the boat with its bottom over our heads. Does it frighten you?"

"No, it does not. Not if you are beside me."

"I will be," he said emphatically. "Keep your eyes open, and if you close them, I will tap you twice. On the face, like so . . ." He touched her cheek, and went on. "When you can open your eyes and breathe again, then we will find what stores there are left in the two lockers. We need water, we need food, and perhaps we can even bring the canvas up to give us some shelter. Then, when the sun is high, and the air contained there is at its maximum, we will try to turn the dinghy right side up. It may be hopeless, but let us try."

She began, with no sense of immodesty at all, to remove her skirt, but he stopped her. "No," he said. "Your skirt will hold air . . . it will help you to surface quickly, you must keep it on. Now . . . we slide gently over the side. We take a deep breath, we go under the surface of the water, and we come up under the boat. Are you ready?"

"Yes, I am ready. But hold my hand, Clifford."

"When we surface there, reach up and hold onto one of the seats, all right?"

"I am ready."

They sat down close to each other on the wet hull of the boat. He held her hand and said, "Go!"

They slid down into the dark water, and she felt him pulling at her, and then the gentle slap on her cheek, and she opened her eyes and saw that the bottom of the dinghy was an arch over their heads, enclosing them in a kind of wooden cavern. She reached up and took hold of one of the seats, and eased her way forward, hand over hand, with Clifford close beside her, his arm always ready to support her.

There was a strange and somehow frightening light under the dinghy, as though they were in a world of their own, quite cut off from the rest of the universe. She shook her wet hair away from her face and groped at Clifford; his hand found hers. And in the semidarkness they moved to the forward locker.

It was already open, the door hanging loose. It was empty. She saw Clifford scowl at it—blaming himself, she thought—and they moved slowly aft together, holding hands, and found that the aft locker had broken open too, its door twisted off the hinges and gone. There was a roll of canvas jammed in there, with some ropes and the bailing-bucket wedged in the opening, and they found a sorry packet of cheese and nothing else. The two containers with their water supply had gone.

He reached up and thumped on the bottom of

the boat, listened to the hollow sound of it, and said, "The watertight compartments have held up, at least . . ."

"But . . . the drinking water, Clifford?" she whispered.

He saw the look of alarm on her face. "Aye, it will not be easy, but . . . there's water enough in the sea if you know how to find it. I still have the fish-hooks and line in my pocket. Come, we'll start getting some supplies of our own."

She held her breath and squeezed her eyes shut, swooping down under the gunwhale with him, and a few moments later they were sitting on the slatted hull again.

He squinted up at the sun, burning hot now, blinding them, blasting down and roasting them. He pulled out the hooks and the line, and broke off a small piece of cheese for bait. He trailed the line in the water and they waited in silence while the sun climbed higher and higher.

She watched him jerk the line as it tightened suddenly, then his open clasp-knife was in his hand and he was stabbing with it into the water. Using it as a gaff he hauled aboard a fine, speckled fish nearly two feet long, with a projecting chin and very formidable-looking teeth. He said happily, "A barracuda, enough food and water there to last us all day . . ."

He hacked off its cruel head with his knife. He scraped off the scales, cut out a hunk of white meat and said, grinning, "Now, if you've a piece of cloth the size of a handkerchief? . . ." She lifted her skirt, ripped off a length of calico from her petticoat, and gave it to him. He wrapped the piece of flesh in it and handed it to her. "Now bite on this,"

194

he said, "chew on the meat, and suck the water out of it. There'll be a fishlike taste to it, but it's all food and water, and I'm sorry we have no lime to go with it. Just keep chewing, there's all the nourishment and the liquid you'll need there."

They gnawed on the fish for a while and Mercy found it surprisingly good. Perhaps because she was so hungry. She could not recall how long ago it was that they had last eaten.

When the sun was high above them, Clifford wrapped the rest of the fish up and carefully stored it away in his pouch. Standing up precariously on the hull, he watched the heavy swell of the waves around them, calculating, wondering if the task that was ahead of them could be done at all.

He said at last, "You'd best leave this to me, Mistress Mercy. You'll take hold of the painter and float close by, and you must try to keep on the windward side of the boat at all times. Let me show you what I plan to do."

He helped her to her feet and put an arm about her to steady her, waiting a while till she became accustomed to the rise and fall of the dinghy and was aware of the pattern of the waves.

"You'll notice," he said, indicating, "it's the third wave which is always the big one. Now, if I can maneuver the stern around, as I think I can, so that we're broadside on to a third wave . . . as we begin to drop down, I'm going to get under the windward gun'l and tip her over as we go down. Make sure you stay well to the side, and above us if you can manage it, at the far end of your rope. All right?"

"All right."

195

She slipped over the side and he followed her. She was losing her fear of the water now and she watched him grasp the stern-post and kick out strongly. In a little while he called out, "She's coming round fine!"

The hull was broadside on to the crest of the wave, and as it went over the top and began to slide down, she saw him duck under the gunwale and disappear from her sight. Her painter tightened, and she hung on grimly as it pulled her fast down into the trough, then it was rising again, more slowly on the upswing, and Clifford was there, muttering under his breath. He looked back over his shoulder and checked the motion of the water, and suddenly dove down deep again as the boat went hurtling into the trough once more.

For more than three hours, he tried tirelessly, bracing himself under the windward chime and kicking out furiously as the downward sweep began, then resting for a while and trying again, and again, and again.

Looking back, he yelled out, "Now!" and as the wave picked them up she saw the flurry of the water that was his thrashing body. As the boat swept down she saw one end come up, the stern where her painter was fastened, and she let go of it and held her breath in fear. The dingy hung there motionless on its side for a moment before it turned over and crashed down again right side up.

She heard his yell of triumph, then he was swimming furiously towards her, grabbing hold of the ropes of her preserver and swimming with her strongly back to the boat.

For a brief moment of terror, it disappeared over

the high crest of a wave and there was a fearful panic on her.

"Kick your legs!" he yelled and the wave took them together high up and then down again, and he reached out and grabbed at the trailing painter and wrapped it quickly around her arm. He was aboard in seconds, leaning over the stern and dragging her over. They collapsed on the bottom and lay there, exhausted, breathing heavily and knowing that once more another danger was behind them.

His face was very close to hers, his arm around her shoulders, a hand at her hip; she could feel the strong beat of his heart, and it comforted her. "We have a dinghy again," he said at last. "And now, now there's a little wind, and we have a good sail I can rig when it strengthens, as it will when the sun goes down . . . and all is well again, Mercy."

She pushed the wet hair away from her face and looked at him. "You are quite . . . indomitable, Clifford," she said. "Is that the right word, indomitable?"

He was smiling. "With the life of a sweet young girl in his hand, any man is indomitable. But I thank you for it."

"And are you not exhausted?"

"No. I will allow myself the pleasure of exhaustion only when we find a beach to land on."

There was so much of comfort in his arms! But in a few moments he eased himself gently away from her and got heavily to his feet. He dragged out the wet canvas and spread it out to dry in the evening sun. He unfastened two of the oars from their housing and almost mechanically sat down to start rowing again. She watched him for a moment, knowing that the awesome weariness was at last coming over both of them; she could hardly bring herself to move.

"Clifford?" she said at last.

Was it her fancy or was he actually sleeping while he rowed? He jerked his head up, not stopping the insistent movement of his arms, and looked at her. "We must sleep," she said. "Both of us."

He nodded. "In a little while. When the sun has gone down, and the night is cold . . . Yes, we'll sleep. We'll use the canvas for a bed, and in an hour or two . . . in the morning, I'll use the sail, and we'll make better time. I don't know where we are, Mercy. We were driven south, a long way south, and a landfall now . . . I don't know. Perhaps the coast of Florida. Wherever it might be, it will be to the west of us, and I'll row into the sun until it's gone. The wind is still freshening, and soon it will be strong enough to carry us along faster than I can row, it will be easy then." He looked up at the sky. "We need just a little more of it."

"Sleep now, Clifford?"

"Lie down in the last rays of the sun, Mercy, dry out as best you can."

She ran a hand through her tangled hair. She was in a terrible mess now, her skirt torn and still sodden, her blouse ripped at the shoulder, even her bust-bodice gaping open. She began trying to untangle the knots so that she could at least braid her hair and she said, muttering, "What I wouldn't give for a comb . . ."

He was suddenly laughing again. "A comb?" he

said. "In the morning, when I've rigged the sail, you shall have one."

She stared at him, not understanding. "The backbone of a fish," he said, "it's a fragile thing, but will be strong enough for your lovely hair."

She felt that she wanted to laugh too, but there were tears in her eyes that would not go away. "We're in a sorry state," she whispered. "And Heaven alone knows if it will ever improve."

"Heaven knows and we know," he said stolidly. "It will improve. What do your stars have to say about it?"

She brightened at once, remembering. "The stars," she said. "Yes, they tell us . . . it is a propitious year for both of us. You are Sagittarius, I am Capricorn, and everything is just right for us. And I still have to use a fishbone for a comb."

He would not stop rowing, and when the sun went down, he said, "Drag the canvas into the bottom, Mercy, and make your bed."

It was heavy and parts of it were still wet, but she placed it just so and knelt down on it, looking up at him. "And will you come lie beside me too, Clifford?" she asked.

He nodded gravely. "Yes, I will rest for a short while now. And there's great comfort when I know you are close beside me."

She lay down and stripped off the heavy skirt, using it as a still-sodden blanket, and watched him while he shipped the oars carefully. Then he lay down with her, an arm around her shoulder, one hand on her soft breast again, and she snuggled closer and pulled the ends of the canvas over them. Soon, they were both fast asleep, lost in a kind of exhaustion that was close to coma, and she did not wake up until the first streaks of red-gold light were long in the sky behind them.

Clifford was already at work.

He had raised the slender mast and was rigging the white canvas sail to the boom. He saw her stirring as the sleep dropped from her and his grin was broad and cheerful.

"Another good day," he said happily. "Did you sleep well?"

She could not believe the night had passed so quickly. She stretched her cramped limbs and fancied she could hear the joints in them creaking. "Yes," she said, "I slept like a baby. And you?"

"Well indeed."

"But for how long, Clifford?"

"For most of the night. And now, we have a good sail. The rest is easy now."

He was hauling it up and when it was fastened in place, he took the rope from the boom and said, "Now, hold the sheet, the rope, while I make us a rudder. Ours is gone. Just keep it taut and when it catches the wind, play it out gently. All right?"

"All right."

"I'll make a sailor out of you yet. . . ."

He thrust an oar over the stern and lashed it to the stern-post, working it vigorously, his eyes on the sail. When it began to billow and the dinghy keeled over a little, he said: "Good, good . . . now take a single turn over that belaying pin and bring the end of the sheet back here to me. Come and sit with me, and we'll go sailing . . ."

She took it to him and he hauled on it to correct the improvised rudder a trifle as she sat beside him.

They were skimming over the water now and the sea was calm, its color a strange gray-blue, with only the slightest of swells. He reached under his seat and brought out a comb for her. He said, smiling, "You see? Now you can do your toilet. But gently, if you please, it's not as strong as tortoise-shell."

She could not help laughing at his eagerness. It was the backbone of the barracuda, the bone ends trimmed to precise equality, their sharp edges shaved off. She ran it carefully through her hair, sitting beside him in her pantalettes and her torn petticoat and doing her toilet just as if she were in her room in her house—so long ago now?—in the Rookery. She thought of her father and wondered if the new servant Luke had provided was feeding him properly. It worried her that the arrangement was really in exchange for a marriage that she knew now would never come to pass.

She sat combing her hair slowly. "As soon as we reach land," she said, "I must write to him."

He was startled. "Write . . . to whom?"

"To Luke Doren. He's such a good man, I'm sure he'll understand."

He did not know what she was talking about. "Understand what?"

"That I will never marry his son," she said calmly. "Do you find that . . . wrong of me?"

"No, I do not." He was very decisive about it.

"Even though I made a kind of bargain with him?"

For a long time, he did not answer. "I owe Luke Doren a great deal too," he said at last. "And yet . . ." He sighed. "If we were both older and wiser, we could find excuses, no doubt. Will he be angry?"

"Who, Luke? No, of course not. He's a kind and gentle man and he will worry for a short while, then . . . he will shrug it all off, I'm sure of it."

She wished she could believe what she was saying; but with the insouciance of her years, she thrust the idea firmly to the back of her mind. *First,* she was thinking, *we will get ourselves out of the mess we are in now, and then . . . then, we will see.*

All day, they ran before a strong wind, which rose sharply when the night came and quieted down a little at sunrise. The next day and the next and the next after that, they held their course, with only chewed fish-meat to live on.

Their lips were beginning to swell and blister with the exposure, but he kept his good spirits and they were infectious. It was only when she was sleeping that Mercy dreamed of disasters ahead of them.

Clifford said, one morning—was it the seventh, the eighth day in the dinghy?—"The *Capricorn* has long since docked, I fear. I had hoped to beat it into harbor. But here we are, still on the high seas. Are you worried, Mercy?"

She had determined desperately, days ago, never to show the fear that was in her. She shook her head. "No," she said. "Not worried, not discouraged, not even . . . alarmed."

"Good. There is truly nothing to fear. It's taking us a long time, but sooner or later, I promise you, we'll find land."

He looked exhausted, she thought, after nights

and more nights of no sleep at all, not even a cat-nap. His face was burned, his new growth of beard bristling; but there was always, she saw, that fierce determined light in his eyes.

Only once did he rest for a while, and it was quite against his own volition. She was sitting beside him at the improvised tiller, more than half-asleep herself. He had long been silent, his eyes drooping. She was conscious that every few moments he jerked his head up, fighting the onslaught of complete exhaustion, and leaned a little tighter into the oar. She was watching the sail, and she saw how it billowed and caught the wind every time he swung the boat over a trifle. She took over the oar and held it steady and, lifting up his head, he smiled at her. "All right," he whispered. "A few moments only. A steady pressure on the oar . . . the sail as it is now . . . the sun . . . the sun . . ."

He was asleep. It must have been an hour before he suddenly awoke with a start. He looked at the sail and then at her, murmuring, "Perfect . . ."

He hauled in their fishing line and brought another fish aboard. He wrapped a piece of the meat in cloth for her again and touched her lips very delicately, worrying about the blisters there. "Keep your lips as moist as you can," he said. "It's not easy, I know."

He took over the tiller again, as she slowly bit down on the food that was keeping them both alive. There had scarcely been a cloud in the bright sky all day long, and when the evening came there were birds flying high in the sky above them wheeling in a wide arrow formation. Clifford stared at them, his young face alight with excitement.

"Geese," he said at last. "Perhaps it means we are near land. I think it does."

There was a new and frantic excitement on them now. "We'll hold this course," Clifford said. "We're running well, almost due west-so'-west, two-forty degrees, give or take an inch or two."

The evening came, then the dark of the night, and they were still running fast, though the seas were choppier now and the boat was being tossed about violently. The crests of the waves slapped against the gunwales, a strong wind following now.

Then the moon came up and the sky was soon bright with its glory. They saw ahead of them and a little to one side, the dark outline of a land mass on the horizon. Clifford hauled in the sheet of the sail and forced the rudder over. The craft swung round and headed toward it, keeling over under the strain till the water was coming over the side.

They watched its approach, the excitement of it tingling their nerve ends. There was the stark outline of a mountain against the sky, purple-black in the moonlight, and soon they could see trees there, tall palms that seemed to lean out over the water.

A huge black rock flashed past them, very close off their bow, and Clifford quickly turned into the wind, and staring at other rocks that lay low in the water all around them.

He dropped the sail and took to the oars. There was white surf pounding furiously everywhere and Clifford yelled, "Hold on tight, Mercy, we're crossing a reef! Lie down in the bottom! Hang on tight! . . ."

She threw herself down instantly and flung her arms around a seat. A wave picked them up and held them on its crest. Slowly, as though drawn up into the skies by some mysterious force, the boat rose up above the level of the water and hung there momentarily. Mercy screamed as she lost her hold, then Clifford's arm was around her and they were falling free. They hit the water together and heard, rather than saw, the dinghy crash down onto rocks beside them with a fearful splintering sound. A broken spar, up-ended like a jagged spear, went hurtling past her head.

Mercy found herself in churning water, sharp rocks scraping at her body, and she screamed again. Clifford was there beside her, his arm around her, striking out furiously against the surf. A new wave came along and lifted them both up, breaking his hold and smashing her down again with a force that drove the breath from her. She gulped in great quantities of strong salt water, and feeling that she was turning over and over, she tried to find the surface blindly. She knew that she was dying.

A receding wave sucked her back and she clutched at rocks that tore the flesh from her hands. Then Clifford was there close beside her again, reaching out for her, standing waist-deep in swirling, pounding water, and lifting her bodily up. There was a terrible pain in her head and she felt that unconsciousness was coming and she fought hard to maintain her senses, knowing that this, now, was the final challenge. . . .

He was walking, carrying her cradled in his arms, swinging his body against the force of the water that tried to suck them under the rocks. In a few moments—had she lost her senses for a while?—she knew that there was dry, hard ground under his feet.

He collapsed with her to the sand, then began dragging her up the beach to safety, and she found herself on her stomach, his hands at her back, tearing away the life preserver and then pressing gently, firmly, rhythmically as he drove the water out of her lungs.

She choked water out of her mouth and felt him rolling her over. He pressed his ear to her breast to listen for the heartbeat, and she heard him say softly, "Oh God, help me now . . ."

She felt him tearing at her bodice, and then his hands on her bare flesh, pressing down once again with a quick, almost cruel, jerking motion, and she felt herself coughing uncontrollably. He said, whispering, "Thank God, thank God . . ."

She opened her eyes and he was on his knees, straddling her waist, gasping to gulp in great deep breaths of air, his hands hanging down at his side. Almost mechanically, he fumbled with the strings of her bodice, bringing the sides of it together over her nakedness, tying the fastening with clumsy, trembling fingers. She heard the desperation in his voice, "Speak to me . . . speak to me, Mercy . . ."

She coughed once more, then reached up her arms to him, and he fell beside her and held her tightly.

"Oh, Clifford . . ." she whispered.

There was grass under her back now, sweetly smelling grass, and the sound of the sea was no longer a frightening thing but a gentle, sibilant cadence of water swirling among the rocks and surf breaking on the sand.

His hand was on her hair, stroking it, then

touching her cheek. As she felt the consciousness slipping away from her, she heard his labored breathing quieting down and knew that he was at last letting go of everything too.

CHAPTER TEN

She could not, at first, remember where she was, nor how she came to be there. The warmth of the sun was all over her body and the strange sensation of a touch on her forehead. She awoke with a start and opened her eyes to find Clifford crouched on his haunches beside her, the back of his hand at her temple. He was looking down into her eyes and smiling that boyish, open smile she had come to love so much. She took his hand and held it to her cheek, lay there till she was fully awake, and said at last, very softly, "Clifford . . . my Clifford."

"How do you feel?" he asked; there was so much sympathy in his eyes. She eased herself into a sitting position and looked around her at the palm trees leaning toward the waterline, at the dense mass of the forest behind them, at the surf breaking on the beach.

"So we found land," she said at last. "Beautiful land."

"Yes. Though where we might be . . ." He grimaced. "Somewhere, I imagine, in America. A New World for us, anyway. How do you feel?"

"Well, I think . . . yes, surprisingly well. And you?"

"Your poor hands are torn and lacerated, there's a cut across your shoulders. Sea water, perhaps, will cure them. I tried to find out if you had any broken bones, and I could feel none, but . . . can you stand? Can you walk?"

He helped her to her feet, and she almost fell. She put her arms around his neck and hung on to him. "Yes," she said. "No broken bones."

"Walk a few steps, let us be sure."

She nodded and walked around him, saying, "A little stiffness, it will pass."

"Good. We have some exploring to do and we must start at once."

"All right."

"We must find water, first of all. There's food here in plenty, and there will be water too. But we must find it. Are you thirsty?"

"Not intolerably so."

"Then let me show you what I found."

He produced a huge green nut he had balanced just so in the sand there and held it out for her. She stared at it, puzzled. It was crudely cut open at one end and was half-full of a pale, creamy-white liquid.

"What is it?" she asked and he answered her, grinning broadly, "I'm not sure, but I think it's a coconut. Or something like it, anyway."

"A coconut? No, I've seen coconuts at the fairs

in England. We used to throw little wooden balls at them to knock them off their perches, did you ever do that?"

"Aye," he said laughing. "The coconut shies, and I was very good with them. But all this green fiber, it seems to be the husk, and it's so tough. . . thank Heavens I have a good strong knife. Taste it, it's good."

She peered into the exotic nut suspiciously, sniffed at the liquid there, and said hesitantly, "You don't suppose it might be . . . poisonous?"

"I'm sure there must be many poisonous fruits here," he said gravely, "and you are right. We will never try any of them unless we are sure. But these . . ." He gestured broadly. "They're all around us, fallen from the trees, and early this morning . . ." He laughed at the memory of it. "I nearly woke you up to show you! I heard a noise in the forest behind us, and went to find out what it was. There were two pigs there, wild boars, I think, and they were rooting around with these nuts and tearing them apart to get at the food inside them. So no, they're not poisonous. I found a fresh one, and cut it open with my clasp-knife, and the flesh inside is soft and tender, not a bit like the ones from the fairgrounds. And there's enough juice in them . . . go on, try one."

He watched her drink, spilling half of the juice down the front of her blouse. She laughed and said, "Delicious."

"We still have to find water, the first rule for survival. And we have to find out where we are, because . . . I have no idea at all."

She had finished drinking the juice, and he used his knife-blade to ease out the soft white meat for her to eat. He said, "I have a line in the water for fish, there are so many kinds of them swimming around. Lobsters too, which I can catch with my hands. So . . . we won't starve here. And I think . . ." He broke off, unsure of himself.

"You think what, Clifford?" she asked.

He folded up his knife and slipped it back into his pouch. "Let us go for a little walk along the beach," he said, "and we'll decide together what we have to do."

She nodded and he took her hand. They walked slowly along the hard-packed yellow sand that lay between the forest and the sea.

He said slowly, "We don't know where we are, Mercy. All we know is that it is somewhere in the Americas. We're a long way to the south, I'm sure of it, or we wouldn't have this sun, but where? . . . I don't know. Now, there may be people living within a mile or two of us, perhaps even closer, a settlement, a colony, a trading-post, who knows? There may be white men nearby, or Indians, or perhaps . . . savages of some sort, we just don't know."

He heard her little gasp of anxiety and said quickly, "It's not likely that we're in any danger. It's even probable that there's complete safety for us quite close by. But that is what we have to find out."

He found some lengths of cord from the wrecked boat and wound them around his waist, pulling out some broken spars from among the rocks and tossing them up onto the beach.

He said slowly, "It's part of . . . part of our human condition that we all need a home. We had one that was a dinghy and now we have one that is

212

a patch of green grass near a gentle beach. That's all it is, but it's . . . our home. I think we should stay where we are for just a few days, where we know there is enough food and drink. I will build us a shelter of branches, and we can rest for a while. Then . . . only then, when we both feel strong again, we can move on and see what lies ahead of us."

He stopped and took her shoulders and looked into her eyes. "What do you think?"

"I think . . . I think I want to do whatever you think is best, Clifford."

He shook his head. "No. Tell me what you really feel, Mercy."

They turned back and continued their strolling, and she said, smiling gently, "Before his accident, my father used to teach history, at a fine old school . . ." She stopped, remembering, and then, "A school on Milk Street, in London. You know where it is?"

He shook his head, puzzled by the digression.

"Hard by London Wall," she said, "in what we have to call, henceforth, 'the Old World,' because ours, now, is the New. And one of the theories he had—a deep-thinking man, you understand—was that wars are fought, empires are built, and the whole world, indeed, turns on what he called 'the territorial imperative.' Do you follow me, Clifford?"

"Just like the whales," he murmured. "A patch of deep water like any other, but . . . their home."

Mercy nodded eagerly. "So let's stay in our territory until we know it better. Perhaps in the forest, or on the beach, or high on the mountain there?

Let's look around for a while. As you say, we already have everything we really need."

They moved on again, slowly, like lovers strolling. "And we will have each other," she said. She was trembling; she felt his hand tighten on hers.

They had reached the little patch of scented grasses that he had pulled for her bed, and he stood for a moment looking down on it with a faintly quizzical look in his eyes. "Our territory. And now we will begin to expand it."

They walked together in the forest. Very soon, it appeared that they could proceed no further, so closely knit were the trees, the bushes, and the giant vines which closed around them. There were cedars, pine, and rubber trees; dense bushes of cassava, and tamarind, wild bananas, breadfruit, mangoes and lemons, pomegranates; and ebony, mahogany, rosewood, Brazilwood, logwood and *ranie*, trees that they had never seen before and could only stare at in wonder. Some of the trees were sixty feet high or more, and others twined around with creeping liana-vines. It was an alien world of wonder and excitement, and Clifford, forcing a way through it all with the utmost confidence, was leading her on a zig-zag path. When she asked him why, he told her, "I am looking for a path, a track, which will mean there are people here. Perhaps there are none. Perhaps there are only the two of us for hundreds of miles. Does it alarm you?"

"No. I feel safer here than on the streets of London. Certainly safer than in that terrible Sargasso Sea. There, yes, I was frightened."

"I know. And I was aware that you were trying to hide it from me."

214

They stopped in a little while, and Mercy said, "Listen! Do you hear it?"

He strained his ears. "Water running?"

"More than water running. A fall, by the sound of it."

He listened again. "Yes . . . over there."

They fought their way through the jungle together, guided by the comforting sound. Soon the undergrowth parted miraculously ahead of them and a great gray mountain of granite towered there, with immense vines, brightly flowered, creeping up its massive flank. A thin sliver of waterfall, no more than six feet or so across, was pouring down from a tremendous height, foaming as it fell free down the mountainside, a pencil of white spume that poured into a crystal-clear pool at its bottom. It was a splendid sight, and they stared at it breathlessly for a moment, then ran to the pool together. Clifford dropped to the ground and cupped the water to his lips, tasted it, and shouted delightedly, "I never tasted such water! Try it, Mercy!"

She followed his example, lay on her stomach by the pool, and cupped the water into her mouth. Then she turned over to lie on her back and looked up at him. His eyes, bright and alert, were on the forest around them, searching out the advantages of it.

He turned back to her and his boyish face was filled with pleasure. He moved over and crouched beside her, his hands dangling, one of them lightly touching her tangled hair. "Our new territory?" he asked softly. She held his look, suddenly aware of a tightening of her muscles, almost a shuddering.

"We have water here," he said, "and a very short

distance away there is the sea with all its fish . . . and the coconuts . . . and we will watch the birds and see what berries they eat so that we can do the same. I can build a shelter here, a few cut branches to lean against the rocks there, where the sun strikes them . . . our new territory!"

She rolled over on to her stomach and propped herself up on her elbows. Dangling a hand in the water, she said, "And I will take a bath here."

It seemed to her that he hesitated before he answered. "Not here," he said. "The water is too deep. Let us follow the stream along and find a better place."

"All right."

She got to her feet and he took her hand. They walked along the bank for no more than a hundred paces, where they found a glorious pool of still water, no more than three or four feet deep. She saw a bird with the most brilliant plumage perched on an overhanging limb and knew that she had never before seen anything quite so lovely.

"Here," she said, "it's beautiful . . ."

There was filtered sunlight striking the surface and two huge butterflies, with blue opalescent wings more than six inches across, were fluttering there, chasing each other, seeking to mate, perhaps. There were huge water lilies everywhere, their creamy-white petals as smooth as the best French velvet; and a tiny, sharp-beaked bird with shining feathers of green, blue, and yellow, flitted past them.

She looked up at Clifford. "If you will turn your back for a moment?" she asked shyly.

She saw the reddening of his cheeks. "Of course," he said. "I will . . . look around and see what our

216

new territory has to offer us. Call me when . . . when I may return."

"Don't go far?" she pleaded and he nodded gravely. "Only far enough, Mercy, for your privacy."

He moved off and looked at boughs that he might cut with his clasp-knife. He worried about her and in a little while she called to him and he hurried back to the brink of the pool. He saw her, as he dropped to his knees there, modestly half-hidden behind a rock on which a tiny yellow flower was growing. He saw her clothes there, neatly folded and laid out on the bank, the heavy wollen skirt, the single petticoat, the bodice and bust-bodice, the torn stockings and the shoes, and an article of white calico he thought might be called pantalettes, though he was not too sure about this. He knew that she was naked in the water, and he felt a strong stirring in his loins which he tried desperately to subdue, but could not.

She came out from behind the rock, crouched low in the water that was up to her neck, water so clear that he could clearly see her white limbs there, and he could not take his eyes off her.

Mercy said steadily, "Join me, Clifford. The water is good."

He hesitated, knowing with certainty that a course was opened to him now that was opposed to all that he had been brought up to believe in. But he got to his feet and said, "If you will turn your face away, Mercy . . ."

She disappeared behind her sheltering rock and he stripped off all his clothes and laid them neatly beside hers, a kind of symbol for him, and stepped naked into the water.

He crouched down quickly as she showed herself again and moved toward him, very slowly, a strange light in her eyes. She stopped when she was a few feet from him and sat down in the clear water. He did the same and they stared at each other for a little while, each of them knowing what was in the other's mind. She was trembling violently and could not control it, nor even find her voice.

She said at last, hesitantly, "It's so fresh and clean, the water."

He nodded vigorously. "Yes. After the salt of the sea . . ."

"Cold . . . and refreshing . . ."

"Yes, very cold. And yes, refreshing too."

"There were many occasions there, on the sea, I mean, when I thought I would never again want to . . . to feel the taste of salt in my mouth."

"I know. I know what you mean."

"When we dropped down over the side of the upturned dinghy, before you righted it . . . I thought I would die with the taste of it."

"Yes, I know . . . saltwater is something you have to become accustomed to. I remember once . . ." He broke off, swallowing hard.

She asked, "Remember what, Clifford?"

He took a deep, deep breath, and said quickly, the words pouring out with a rush, "There was a time once when the *Northern Wind*, my ship you understand, she only measured in at three hundred and eighty-five tons, a hundred and sixty feet in length. A good ship, but a small one . . . she was rammed by a huge sperm whale. He charged us three times in a row, trying to sink us, and on the third charge I was one of the four seamen in the rigging who went overboard. They had the grappling-nets out in no time at all, good shipmates all of them, a man will freeze to death in two minutes in those waters . . . and yet, do you know? It's not the cold that I remember; it's the taste of salt in my mouth. Yes, I know what you mean."

There was a long, long silence as he searched desperately for new words. He said at last, nodding wisely, "Yes, the taste of salt in your mouth. You remember when you climbed down the hauser to the dinghy? From the after-deck of the *Capricorn*? I was so worried about you."

"Yes, I remember. I was frightened too."

"I was sure, once, that you were going to fall."

"I nearly lost my grip on the rope. But your friend, Dred Manners, had another rope around my waist, and I felt . . . safe in spite of everything. I remember thinking that it was dark. If I had been able to see the water down there . . ."

"Yes, I know. Sometimes it's good to be . . . quite oblivious of the dangers."

"Yes. Quite oblivious, that describes it exactly."

"Yes, exactly. I think so . . ."

There was another long silence and then Mercy said, uncertainly, "If we stay in too long . . . will we catch cold, do you think? Aunt Melissa always told me . . . never to stay in the water for more than a few minutes."

He plucked up his courage and moved toward her, taking her two hands in his and still making sure that their bodies were not touching. He said, almost desperately, "Oh, Mercy . . ."

"Oh, Clifford . . ."

They were suddenly clutching at each other, his arms tight around her, hers about his neck. She could feel, now, his erected manhood throbbing against her, a strange and quite terrifying experience for her that none the less filled her with an overpowering sensation of a sensuality she did not know she possessed. She was trembling, shaking violently. He held her tightly to him, crushing her lips with his, his hands probing, searching, exploring, even between her thighs.

In a moment, he picked her up bodily, just as he had done on the reef back there, but they were both naked now, and the touch of flesh was irresistible. He strode with her to the shore, putting her down very gently on the dark green moss, and crouched beside her and looked into her eyes with a great tenderness. She lay quite still as his hands moved over her and there was a heating of the blood. She wanted to writhe and dared not.

She said at last, with a terrible contained quietness, "Clifford? There is something I must tell you . . ."

He shook his head. "No. You told me that once before, I remember. I would not listen then, and I will not now."

"But you *must*, Clifford. Please?"

"No, Mercy. Be silent. Let me love you."

The tears were beginning to swell in her eyes now. "I am . . . *despoiled*, Clifford," she said. She could feel the salt moisture rolling down her cheeks.

"Sshhh, be silent."

"No, no, no! How can I? I am not . . ." She took a long, deep, shuddering breath, and contained herself by a strong and deliberate effort of will, though she could not contain the tears.

"Clifford, listen to me," she whispered. "Adam Butrus came to me . . . and he said you would die,

220

unless I . . . unless I . . . oh, Clifford, the shame of it!"

She was weeping uncontrollably now. He kissed the dampness on her cheeks and said quietly, "I was sure . . . that something like that had happened. That you made this sacrifice . . . to save my life . . . should I love you the less for it?"

"But despoiled, Clifford! Violated! No longer the . . . the virgin I would wish to be for you! A shamed and despicable woman!"

His lips were close to hers. "Sshhh . . . be quiet. If you love me . . . as I love you . . . as I believe perhaps you do . . ."

"Oh, Clifford! But . . . you deserve so much more."

"More? What more is there in the whole wide world? I love you, Mercy. I love you so dearly. So very dearly . . ."

She could fight against her own volition no longer.

She reached up hungrily for him, and he moved a strong thigh over hers and rolled on top of her. He kissed her lips, her neck, her breasts, and when she opened her thighs to receive him, he entered her gently—so very gently—and then lay still for a while. Feeling the warmth of her surrounding him, he stroked her hair, her tear-stained cheeks, her shoulders and her delicate breasts, and then began, so slowly, to move his hips back and forth, a movement of infinite temperance. He waited for her passion to rise and burst forth, in a gasping paroxysm before he allowed his own to come to its climax.

His face was nestled in her neck as he lay there, quite exhausted, for a very long while. And then, at last, he stirred and eased himself up onto his elbows, not moving his loins. He looked into her eyes, and kissed them both one after the other, and cradled her head in his strong hand, and brushed his cheek against hers, and made no further movement.

He would not move himself from her and she stretched her legs, containing him tightly, a powerful feeling of enchantment enfolding her. They lay quite still together for a long, long time, in a silence that needed nothing to make it perfect.

There was the sound of a myriad birds around them, the sweet scent of honeysuckle in the air, and the susurration of the waterfall plunging into its depths. In a little while, he began to move his hips again, gently at first and then with a rising passion, plunging into her deeper and ever deeper, and the Heavens exploded for her once again. She clutched at him tearfully and could not find the words to tell of her ecstasy.

He collapsed atop her and took a long, deep breath. Kissing her again, his lips lingering on her eyes, her cheeks, her breasts. He still would not move from her, and he looked into her eyes, and there was the old, stern and courteous Clifford there again. He said, slowly and very carefully, "We will not easily find a preacher on this barren beach, Mercy. But in the eyes of God . . . you are my wife now."

"Oh, my darling Clifford . . ."

"Does it alarm you?"

"Oh, Clifford . . ."

"I have nothing to offer you except a great, great love."

"My darling."

"No property, no money, no goods, no future

222

except that which we can find together. It is a terrible prospect for you, I fear, is it not?"

"No. It is all that I could desire, Clifford! I want nothing else in the world!"

"Nothing shall come between us. Nothing! Ever!"

"And I am so happy, so . . . so deliriously happy!"

She began to ease her leg to one side a trifle, and he said urgently, "No . . . do not move, my love. Let me sleep, like this, for just a little while. I want to sleep . . . and dream of you, and of all that lies ahead for both of us . . . and to know that I am still joined to you, part of you. Lie quite still . . ."

"I will."

She enfolded him in her arms and he lay quietly on her, murmuring softly, "My own beloved Mercy . . . my love, my wife . . ."

She let him sleep, suffering the heavy weight of his strong body on her, still feeling the unconscious warmth of him and knowing that she had never been happier in her whole life.

By nightfall, he had cut a dozen long boughs with his knife, and had placed them carefully against the big gray rock that lay to the side of the waterfall. He bound them in place with cut vines (some of which, though he could not know it in this strange new world, were of the wrong kind and would quickly decay), and had covered the whole structure with closely packed palm-fronds.

He had spent nearly three hours on it and when it was finished, he stood back so that he could admire it, saying excitedly, "There! Did you ever see better architecture, better design, better construction in all your days?"

He had draped some trailing flowers that he thought might be orchids around its tiny entrance, and had covered its floor with long, soft grasses. Setting smooth round stones in an open patch between the shelter and the stream, he laughed and said, "All we need now is a fire, a house has to have a good fire."

"A fire?" she echoed. "You still have Lucifers?"

"There may be some in my pouch," he said carelessly, "and if there are, they may even be dry and still serviceable. But I choose not to look for them. Whoever heard of Lucifers in the jungle? We need a bundle of very dry grass now, if you would kindly pull some for me?"

There was great delight for her in his pleasure. He found a piece of hard, dead wood, and wedged it carefully between two heavy granite rocks. He took a rope from around his waist and dropped it over the stick, pulling it rapidly back and forth with both hands in a sawing motion, and in a moment he said excitedly, "Now, the grass, there, where it is smouldering! . . ."

She took her tuft of dried grass and held it there. In a moment it began to smoulder too, then suddenly burst into flame, and she placed it delightedly in the stone grate he had made. He dropped some small pieces of wood on it and blew on them furiously, crouching down on his hands and knees. When they were burning nicely he put on heavier pieces of wood and said with the great satisfaction of a child, "There! I told you! Why should we need Lucifers, or any of the other . . . appurtenances of civilization? Everything we will ever need is here in this forest. And now . . . I believe there is a mandatory formality to be observed."

She wondered what he meant, but he picked her up bodily, and cradled her in his arms for a moment, then stooped low and carried her over the threshold of their new home.

He laid her down gently on the bed there, slowly stripped off her clothes, and his too, and made love to her once more. They lay back in great contentment afterwards and watched the flames in the twilight. They whispered together, as though not wanting to disturb the natural sounds of the friendly forest.

"Happy?"

"So happy, my love. And you?"

"More than ever before. I do not think I ever knew true happiness until this day."

"If you are hungry, we can go and find a fat lobster and cook it on our fire," Clifford said, remembering. "And I left a line in the water, didn't I? There'll be a dead fish on the end of it by now. Shall we go and see?"

"Let's stay here, Clifford. It's so good to lie beside you, like this."

She was stroking his body gently and in a little while she murmured, "Clifford?"

"Uh-huh?"

"Where do you come from? In all the long . . . years?—it seems like years that we have known each other—you have never told me. Where were you born?"

"I was born in Portsmouth. Have you ever been there?"

"No. And when did you first go to sea?"

He sighed. "A long, long story, Mercy. I used to

225

think of it as an unhappy one, but when I began to make my own way in the world, I realized how lucky I was to have shed so early all the trappings of . . . I think you once called it 'gentility.' "

"And we tried so desperately to hang on to ours!"

"Yours, I am sure, was of a different kind. My father was a . . . well, a very rambunctious sort of man, I'm afraid, and my mother a kind and gentle lady who spent a great deal of her time weeping. I was the youngest of five boys. When I was ten years old, I discovered that she was not my mother at all. I don't know who my real mother was, some . . . serving-maid, I believe, who had long since been discharged. There had always been obscure taunts from my older brothers which I had never understood. And when, at last, I fully realized that I was . . . well, a bastard, and not really liked at all by any of my family, I ran away from home and went to sea."

"At ten years old?"

"Yes. I was already man enough to know that the fine old house on the heights of Hampstead Heath, with more servants than I could count, and tutors who came every day of the week to make a perfect little gentleman of me . . . with its three carriages and eight beautiful horses . . . even at ten years old, these things meant nothing to me any more. I first became a cabin boy on board the *Blue Dolphin*, the oldest and most decrepit whaler you ever saw. But I met a lot of good shipmates there, and they taught me . . . by the time I was fourteen I could climb the rigging with the best of them, I could navigate a ship if need be in the most treacherous waters of the Arctic, and I knew tides, and winds, and currents as well as any seaman aboard. At eighteen, I moved to the *Northern Wind*, and that is where, six years later, your father and Luke Doren found me."

She snuggled closer to him. "And you don't, sometimes, long for that fine old house? With all its comforts and luxuries?"

"No, not one jot."

He was very emphatic about it. "There was no great future there for me, just a life of . . . idleness. I would have been a spoiled brat by the time I was fifteen if I had stayed. My eldest brother will take over the title in the course of time, and all the estates with it. He's better suited to it than I am."

"The title?"

She was old-fashioned enough to feel a little thrill of excitement, and he was very conscious of it.

He said, laughing, "My grandfather died four years ago, and so my father became the Duke of Haddingsworth. And when he drinks himself to death, as he surely will, the eldest son will become the next Duke and inherit a fortune. Well, I wish him all the joys of it, he's not a bad fellow, really. As for myself, I would not change my present condition for all the tea in China."

He held her tightly and smiled into her eyes, saying, "I always felt that. But now, I feel it more strongly than ever. If I had never run away to sea . . . there would have been no Mercy Carrol in my life. And that, my love, would be a tragedy too sad to contemplate."

The darkness had fallen, and soon, suffering still from a lingering exhaustion, they slept in each other's arms all night, till the morning sounds of the forest woke them to a new and different day.

Life was very good to them now; and they knew that here, with their own little piece of a beautiful forest and with each other, there was nothing else in the world that they could possibly want.

It was in the evening of the following day that they learned, quite by chance, just where their destiny had brought them.

They were exploring their territory together, a few miles along the beach in each direction, and they saw in the distance a tall pile of stones, a cairn. They ran to it excitedly and crouched beside it.

It was a grave, a six-foot length of broken limestone laid out in the sand. Into a taller pile at its head a crue cross had been forced, a cross made of dark and time worn timbers, the broken spars of a wrecked ship. The spars were fastened together with four stout nails that had become so rusted that when they touched it, the cross-piece fell to the sand. There was a long and crudely lettered inscription laboriously burned into it.

Clifford picked it up and looked at it, and there was astonishment in his eyes. He looked at Mercy and said, "Cuba. We have reached Cuba."

She stared at him, and he looked back to the inscription and read to her slowly:

"On this wretched island of Cuba, in December of the year 1757, my shipmate Jed Besom died of his wounds and berried here in Peace. Our ship, the good ship

*Explorer, broke up on them rocks, and
only me and Jed made it to the shore.*"

The hot iron had burned out, and had been re-
heated, and the etching was deeper again:

"*I berried him, and who will berrie me, for
I am all that is left now. My name is Dan
Brent, Second Mate.*"

Mercy was staring at the sand at her feet. Her
voice was a hollow echo. "Clifford . . . oh God . . ."
He crouched down beside her. There was a bone
there, bleached white by the sun, and he scraped
away the sand carefully and found the ribcage, and
the pelvis, and then the legbones. He found the
skull and lifted it, put it gently down again, and
looked up at Mercy.

" 'Who will bury me?' " he said. "Ninety-one
years later, we will bury him."

Together they scraped a deep hole in the sand,
and placed the skeleton there and covered it up
again. Clifford brought heavy stones and placed
them there, side by side with the first grave, and
searched the beach for more than an hour before
he found the piece of wood he wanted.

He took his clasp-knife and carved an inscription
on it, placing it at the head of the grave. He read it
to her slowly:

"*Dan Brent, Second Mate, and friend to
Jed Besom beside me.*"

He took her arm at last and led her gently back
into the forest that was their home.

CHAPTER ELEVEN

Cuba was an island in torment.

The primary turmoil, perhaps, was caused by conflicts between the Creoles who were locally born, frequently of mixed parentage, and their Spanish overlords who came and went from the Iberian peninsula at the whim of the government in Madrid, and who were referred to, somewhat contemptuously, as "Peninsulars."

But it was by no means the only battle.

Slavery had indeed long been outlawed over most of the civilized world; but it was still rife. Treaties were signed, promises made, noble intentions spouted forth in a thousand pompous speeches. But the import of these grand designs, it seemed, would never filter down to those who actually kept slaves—or worse, to those who still slipped their slaveships past the watchful Abolitionists, to those who sold them, to those who still kept them in the old state of absolute servitude.

It was to the European Danes that the honor fell of first abolishing slavery completely; a Royal order had been issued fifty-six years previously to the effect that slavery in Danish possessions should cease by the year 1802. By an Act of 1807 (to come into effect in 1808) the United States had forbidden the *import* of slaves. Even so, it was not until the Ashburton Treaty of 1842 that America took an active part in the trade's suppression by joining the British and French Naval squadrons off the west coast of Africa to inhibit the slavers' operations.

Even so, there was still a "Fugitive Slave Law" passed in the United States as late as 1850, the Kansas-Nebraska Bill of 1854; and the Scott Decision could still bring the pro-slave faction considerable comfort as late as 1857.

Cuba was still under the iron hand of the slavers. But it was widely known there that the Congress of Vienna, already thirty-five years old, had declared that slavery in general should be abolished "as soon as possible." The French had abolished it in 1848, the Portuguese in 1830 (but only north of the equator). The Cubans knew that the British had taken the final steps during the Ministry of Earl Grey with a measure that received the Royal assent of His Majesty King William IV in 1833. It was a measure by which a system of apprenticeship was established as a preparation for complete freedom.

The slaves, during this period, were bound to work for their masters for three-quarters of a twenty-four hour day, (and were liable to corporal punishment if they failed in their duties). Children under six years of age were to be set free at once, and arrangements, however nebulous, were to be made for the slaves' "religious and moral instruction." In this year of 1848, the French Provisional Government ordered immediate and effective emancipation of all slaves in the French colonies.

Such a giant step forward could scarcely be a secret for long. All over the colonies, the slaves who had not yet been freed quickly learned of it on that extraordinary grapevine by which the oppressed survive. They began formulating demands, and when those demands were met only with the lash, they began collecting their crude weapons together.

They were not, however, one cohesive force. Every group of slaves had its own petty tyrants, its rogues, its would-be "strong man" whose interests in freedom meant merely more enslavement for others under their own terms. Had the slaves been able to oust the self-seekers and the natural villains among their number, slavery would have ended more than half a century earlier, but the endemic evil that is part of Man's character was as rife among the blacks as it was among their masters. It was never a simple division of good from evil in accord with the dictates of oppressor and oppressed.

And so, in Cuba, the slaves were in revolt all over the island. They rallied round new-found leaders and left them at trifling whims. They fought, and killed, and gave up, and hid in the mountains while they looked vaguely for their next self-appointed leader. The tribal heritage of the African jungle could not easily be erased; perhaps it never would be.

But there was yet a third conflict being fought on very different terms—the obverse side of the coin that was the slaves' disjunction. The Spaniards themselves, the Peninsulars, were only too well aware that the iron chains that bound their Colony together, this "Island of the Sea" as the name meant in its local language, were falling apart. They knew that the island was up for grabs and they wanted to be among the grabbers.

Both Mexico and—most importantly—Colombia, were scheming with the various local and warring factions to acquire control of this profitable island paradise. Cuba had become a prize covetted by almost every state that could find the funds for an expedition. Even the President of the United States, James Polk, had offered the Spanish Government the sum of one hundred million dollars for it. (Polk's abiding passion had been the acquisition of more and yet more territory to bring under the American flag; but the Spaniards had indignantly refused this liberal offer.)

Every Governor, every petty *alcaide*, regarded himself as the potential new master of this fruitful territory. Every minor official from Pinar del Rio to Punta Maisi was preparing himself in anticipation of the day on which he would become the island's new ruler, scheming against the corrupt and decadent government in Spain, and sometimes—if they could find the money—raising armies of mercenaries to bolster their positions.

Spain had troubles of her own: Mexico was knocking at the door; the United States had not given up entirely; and President Marquez of Colombia (that "President of the Gallows") was about to mount an invasion to end the Cuban problem once and for all in accordance with his own maniacal ideas.

It was a time of conspiracy and of turbulence. (Here, perhaps, the planets were wrong. They had ordained, for the New World, a period of progress and of prosperity, though admittedly only above the Tropic of Cancer; and Cuba lay a little below it.) There were conspirators in every candle-lit cellar, brigands who called themselves Freedom Fighters on every mountain, and just plain murderers behind every bush. Everyone, it seemed, was at everyone else's throat, either openly or clandestinely.

The most deadly of all these schemers, by virtue of their sophistication, were the provincial Governors. They were men of education, daring, and great wealth. While professing the strongest loyalty to their home government on the peninsula, they spent their waking hours scheming against it; and they spent their monies—the result of the labor of their slaves—gathering well-paid soldiers of every nationality into units of palace guards that rapidly became small armies.

Havana, founded three hundred and thirty-four years earlier by Diego Velasquez (though he discovered he had placed his capital in the wrong place and felt constrained to move it, lock, stock and barrel, a few years later, thirty miles north to the other shore of the island), was a city and a port that rivalled not only in commercial importance but in population as well, the trading centers of Buenos Aires, Rio de Janeiro, and even New York itself. Its enormous significance as the key to the Spanish colonies of the New World had been made official by a Royal decree which named it the

"*Llave del Nuevo Mundo y Antemural de las Indias Occidentales.*" That "key" had been incorporated into the city's coat of arms, together with a depiction of its two fortresses, which had been built in the seventeenth century to hold the English, French, and Dutch pirates at bay, as well as the navies of any other covetous state that wanted to get their thieving hands on the island; and these, it seemed, were legion.

Havana was the seat of government, housing the greater part of Cuba's garrison, and it was growing richer day by day with the still-flourishing slave trade. But it was cut off from the rest of the territory because of a system of communications that was less than satisfactory.

And so, in the provinces, the power of the provincial Governors grew as they began to learn that Havana was unable to control their excesses, even if it heard of them. In the eastern province, the trade in coffee and sugar, bolstered by the immigration of many thousands of Frenchmen who were escaping the depredations of the Negroes in Santo Domingo, had reached such great proportions that there was open talk of secession. "Why," the Governor of Oriente Province was asking, "should we have to share the fruits of our labors with Spain, and with their lackeys in Havana?"

He had long dreamed of autonomy for the Oriente. And he could think of no better man than himself to rule it.

He was a Spanish grandee named Manuel Alphonso Canovas Castelar y Figueras de Aguilar, an imposing figure of a man in his fifties. Shrewd, ambitious, and forceful, he was a man of ancient line-

236

age and of great culture. His spies were in every corner of the island, in the Dominican Republic (a country now only four years old), and in its sister nation Haiti, in Colombia, Honduras, Mexico, Florida (where the American pro-slavery faction was stronger than anywhere else in the United States), and as far afield as New York.

His palace, built one hundred and fifty years before, stood on the eastern cliffs of Santiago's bay, two hundred feet above the sea portal that gave access to the harbor, a point from which he could prudently watch all the maritime activity and still enjoy the sight of the low hills, climbing gradually up the spectacle of the Sierra Maestra to the west.

It was a palace of splendid luxury. Almost every wall in the main rooms was hung with great floor-to-ceiling tapestries from all over Europe, most notably from Arras, Brussels, (including two magnificent Leyniers and a Pannemakers of truly great merit), and even from Tournai. There were more than a score from the Santa Barbara factory in Madrid, mostly with panels after Goya designs. And in the Great Hall itself there was one single hanging of enormous proportions that was virtually priceless—a design executed by the great painter Bayeu y Sabias and by unknown students of the Academy of Santa Florina.

There were great chandeliers everywhere with brightly shining faceted drops of rock crystal, and not one of them contained less than six candles (many of them with twelve; and one, in the Great Hall, with fourteen—a display of light that was wont to make the guests who had not seen it before gasp in astonished delight).

The carpets underfoot were of the deepest, most

luxurious wool, some of them brought—at great personal expense by the Governor—from as far afield as India, Tibet, or Chinese Turkistan. There were drapes of heavy Spanish velvet over most of the windows. Almost all of the furniture here had been shipped from Spain—chairs and sofas in gilt and scarlet silk; brocaded divans in heavy velvet from England and Hungary; and settees, couches, ottomans and daybeds from all over the civilized world.

The Governor had come here more than fifteen years ago, already a rich man from the benefits of his estates in Catalonia. But in Cuba, his more than forty thousand acres of sugar, coffee, tobacco and forest hardwood, worked by an average of three thousand slaves, had multiplied his fortune ten, twenty, perhaps even a hundred times.

In those long years, grinding his way upward through the ranks of the peninsular bureaucracy, he had learned above all one vital fact: that the bonds which bound the island to Spain were crumbling. Every state within a thousand miles of Havana, it seemed, was ready to pour in money, troops, and arms without number, to bribe one local faction against another, to seduce those who already held a limited power into seizing more and more of it. Even Havana itself was not exempt from the general corruption; there were factions there too that, while loudly proclaiming their steadfast loyalty to Queen Isabella, were plotting among themselves. They knew that absolute power, and its attendant riches, could be theirs if they were ruthless enough.

And Governor Aguilar was not only a very rich man; he was a very shrewd man too.

He was striding in the Great Hall now, a silver goblet of wine in his hand, as he listened to the reports of his two most favored aides, Colonel Tebaldo Manteras and Captain Galisteo.

"The French in Guantanamo," Galisteo said, "are demanding military protection from the raiders, Excellency."

Aguilar said sharply, "Demanding? Or requesting?"

"Their word, Excellency, not mine," Galisteo said. "I took the liberty of suggesting they rephrase their note into more courteous terms."

"Good."

"It seems that a group of fugitive slaves broke into one of their outposts this night and killed three of their sentries."

"A sentry who allows himself to be killed by slaves deserves no better fate. What do you hear from Havana?"

"All seems well in Havana, Excellency. Our men there are waiting for any signs of activity that might be directed toward us."

"The pigeons?"

"Twenty-eight of them should have arrived there this morning."

"The handlers?"

"Excellent, sir. And I'm setting up an auxiliary loft on the Medio River. It should speed up our communications by as much as six hours."

Aguilar pulled the embroidered bellrope and said absently, "It's not of much importance, but how many of the Alcaides do we have now?"

"Twenty-two, Excellency," Galisteo said promptly. "There are three others who we feel can be per-

239

suaded to join our camp, and only two about whom we need worry. Cueto and Jiguani."

"Ha! Creole blood in both of them!"

A young serving-girl came in, in answer to his summons. She was a pleasingly plump, dark-skinned Creole with bright, alert eyes that seemed to take in everything around her and jot it all down in the recesses of a fertile mind. She wore a long black skirt and a white blouse that was cut very low, and her dark hair hung in ringlets about an oval face. It was neatly tied with colored ribbons in the fashion of the *Peninsulare* women, a style that the Governor always thought was a little above her menial station.

He said, "Wine, Gabriella," and she curtsied. He patted her behind as she filled their goblets again. He watched her go out, a slight smile on his aristocratic face. He turned to Manteras. "She's new," he said. "What do you think of her, Tebaldo?"

The Colonel left his gilt-and-scarlet chair and stretched his pudgy legs. A short, pot-bellied and cheerful man, he went to the window and looked down over the harbor. "For me," he said grimacing, "a little too plump, but a good firm bust. I like that."

"And the warmest thighs in the island. And I sometimes wonder why we ever bother with our own *Peninsulare* women. These Creole girls . . . undo a single drawstring and they've got their clothes off before you can sneeze."

He threw open a window to let the cool breeze in and stood with his good friend Manteras, watching the ships in the harbor. A coastal vessel was loading sugar there for transport to Havana and he scowled at it. "A fourth part of its value is

240

what they're paying us now," he said angrily. "And *we* pay for the shipment! I can't wait for the day we throw those robbers in Havana out of the island . . ."

There was a quick knock at the door. In answer to his "Enter!" a stooped and elderly man hurried in, dressed in knee-length breeches of brown sailcloth, white stockings, a shirt and lackluster shoes. He was clutching a pigeon in his hands, and stammering, "Excellency . . . word from New York. But late, I fear. Very, very late."

Aguilar took the bird from him and examined it carefully. "The gullet," he said, "sliced open by a hawk. And she still found her way here?"

"Yes, Excellency, three weeks late . . . she found her way home."

He peered at the wound with deep concern in his eyes, and gently touched the black markings at the side of her head. "And she is . . . Mina, I think, Pedro?"

The old servant nodded. "Yes, Excellency, she is Mina. One of our best."

"And you can nurse her back to health?"

"I will do so, Excellency."

"Good. The letter?"

Pedro extracted a tiny sheet of parchment from his pouch and unrolled it. Aguilar took his glass from the desk and studied the parchment intently, carrying it over to the window for better light. The writing was miniscule, in fine Spanish penmanship with India ink, and he read to them slowly:

" *'Transcribed this day of November seventeen by Carlos Velez, Scribe.'* "

He looked up and said wryly, "Velez, in loft

twenty-seven, he could copy out the whole of the Bible on the head of a pin."

He went on reading, squinting through the heavy glass: "*To His Excellency Governor Manuel Alphonso Canovas et cetera et cetera,*' (and, by God it's all here, every title and decoration)." He sighed and took a sip of wine. Then: "*'I have the honor to inform your Excellency that my ship, the 'Capricorn' docked in Boston Harbor only one day and a half behind schedule. I have secured passage south on board the 'Alice Grey', one of the new, pernicious propeller-driven craft which I find offensive to both nose and ear, but which is, however, probably the fastest ship afloat in these waters. In spite of the infernal engine on board, she does carry excellent square sails on her foremast, with fore and aft canvas on her main and mizzen, with two very large jibs forward. She was built as a Mexican war transport . . .'*" He broke off and rubbed at his eyes, and took another drink of wine. "He does run on, doesn't he?" he said.

He read on: "*'Her lines are good, her speed more than satisfactory, and she will reach Havana on the twelfth day of December or shortly thereafter.'*" He stared at the Captain. "The twelfth? We'll have to move fast, Calisteo! And give Pedro here a goblet of wine, this is splendid news."

Galisteo poured the old man a goblet of wine and gave it to him, and Pedro dipped a finger in it and touched the pigeon's beak with it, cooing softly like a pigeon himself.

Aguilar read aloud, continuing: "*'. . . whence I will make my way with all possible speed to Santiago de Cuba, to place my services, as we have arranged, and for promised recompense, at your*

242

*Excellency's disposal. My chosen second-in-com-
mand, Captain Jake Ollie, a man I have recently re-
cruited but in whom I have the greatest confidence,
is with me, and begs to offer your Excellency his
respects. I have the honor to be your Excellency's
most faithful and devoted servant, et cetera and et
cetera . . . Adam Butrus.'* "

He put down the magnifying glass, and locked
the little roll of parchment away in a drawer, and
said: "Very well, Pedro. Wait nearby, you will be
needed soon."

"Yes, Excellency."

"And take good care of Mina. She has done me a
very great service this day."

The servant bowed himself out, and the Governor turned to Manteras, smiling happily, enjoying a
secret joke. "And now," he said, "you will no
doubt ask me who the devil Adam Butrus might be.
And *devil*, I assure you both, is exactly the right
word."

"I must confess," Manteras murmured. "The
name is not known to me."

But Captain Galisteo said sharply: "Not
. . . *Colonel Adam*?"

The Governor nodded. "Colonel Adam, of Haiti,
a man of formidable reputation."

Manteras's eyes were bulging. "*Mi Dios!*" he said.
"That's the man who drove Boyer out of the country!"

"Exactly!"

The Governor stabbed a finger at him. "General
Jean Pierre Boyer, one of the finest soldiers France
ever produced. He was barricaded in Christophe's
Citadel, an impregnable fortress if ever there was
one! And Colonel Adam led a thousand ragged,

243

ill-armed slaves up the mountain side, and in a single moonless night broke in and massacred nearly twice that number of highly trained, disciplined troops. Before Boyer could rally his men to defend themselves . . . the raiders had gone. I'm told that Adam lost less than a score of men in the whole operation. In my opinion, that exploit alone is an indication of his worth, but there were others, many others. In Venezuela, it took him less than three months to organize the forces that sooner or later are going to drive Paez to perdition, he's already on his way there . . . . In New Granada, he became a legend almost overnight. In Mexico they tremble when they hear the name Colonel Adam."

"And he's on his way here?" Manteras asked.

"He is indeed."

"To join our mercenaries?"

"To command them, Tebaldo."

Manteras returned to his seat; he was smiling gently now. "I heard of an episode in Venezuela," he said softly. "A small raid of no great importance at all. But he had fourteen officers dragged from their beds in the middle of the night, and executed. Just the *officers*. The men, it seems, promptly joined forces with him."

"I believe that is correct," Aguilar said casually.

"And in most of those legendary episodes, Colonel Adam was fighting with slaves. Or at least with what the people themselves call . . . the people."

"That is true too."

Aguilar was beginning to laugh now at Manteras's discomfort, and he went on, gesticulating, "But don't allow yourself to be persuaded, my friend, that Butrus's philosophy is anything other than our own. He has one guiding dictum in life: *pay me, and pay me well.* It's all that matters to him, believe me."

He could sense a certain hostility there. A man of Colonel Adam's reputation could mean only the disruption of the lives they led, perhaps even an end—a curtailment, certainly—to their privileges.

The Governor said, seeking to ease their doubts, "I am not engaging Colonel Adam on the strength of his reputation alone, outstanding as that may be. I have used him before. When I was merely a lackey of Spain, and the Governor of the province was seeking my arrest on charges—quite groundless charges, I assure you—of treason . . . what was his abominable name?"

"Fantero," Manteras said, his eyes gleaming, and Aguilar nodded.

"Yes, Fantero, a man of no merit at all. Poor fellow, he fell from this very room one night, the verandah there . . . two hundred feet down to a watery grave. Colonel Adam, at that time, was already a dear friend of mine, and I have heard it said . . . he was present at the time of Fantero's untimely death. What a shame! Cut off in the prime of life, a great future ahead of him too. But it was at that time that I discovered the force that drives this strange man Adam Butrus on toward his destiny—which will undoubtedly be a knife in the back one day. That force, gentlemen, is money. Every cause he has fought for . . . it's the money to line his pockets that makes him the good soldier he is. The side that can pay him . . . is the side that employs him. The side that wins. Even with no troops behind him, merely unarmed slaves, barefoot

245

and in rags, he wins and lines his pockets with every endeavor."

"Paid by slaves?" Manteras said skeptically, and Aguilar shook his head. "No. By the anti-slavers in the United States. They've plenty of money and they know how to spend it. Or perhaps I should say, Butrus knows how to wheedle it out of them. He's not only a good soldier, he knows how to argue persuasively. Expecially when it's his own interest he has at heart."

He looked at his empty goblet and said, "Where's that damned girl?" He pulled the bell-rope, and when she came in he watched her pouring from the heavy silver pitcher and said to her, "Gabriella . . . you sleep with Colonel Manteras tonight."

There was bright laughter in her huge round eyes as she threw the Colonel a look and curtsied. "*Si, Execelencia*," she said, "*con mucho gusto, mucho mucho gusto . . .*"

She pulled the wide neck of her blouse down a little lower over her bare shoulders as she bent over the Colonel's goblet, and he touched her breasts, the gently swelling sides of them, with both hands. He said, questioning, "Your name is Gabriella?"

She curtsied, "*Si, señor Colonello.*"

"You are very beautiful, child."

"*Muchas gracias, Señor Colonello.*"

"And have you had many lovers, Gabriella?"

"No, *Señor Colonello*. You will be the first." She threw a look at the Governor and looked into Manteras's eyes and said again, "The first . . ."

He threw back his head and laughed. "If you love as expertly as you lie, I will be a very happy man, Gabriella."

The curtsy again. "Far better, *Señor Colonello...*"

His hand slid to her hip and stroked it and he wondered what precisely it was that made these Creoles so much more desirable than the Spanish women from the mainland.

She straightened up, her shoulders pulled back, her fine bosom out-thrust. She was thinking: this old man is a fool, I can make him do anything I want....

The Governor was frowning thoughtfully. He looked at Captain Galisteo and said, "His ship arrives in Havana on the twelfth, so it behoves us to move with a certain expedition. Have Pedro send a message to our people there at once."

"Yes, of course," the Captain said. "And I'll set up a relay of horses."

"No. He's a first-rate sailor, so have them take him over to the south side of the island as soon as he docks. Let them have a good boat waiting there, a sloop or a cutter with a great deal of sail on it, let him handle it himself and he'll be here in a little over two days. And have them give him, Galisteo, a good-sized pouch of gold coins. There's never any harm in keeping a good servant happy."

"Very well, sir."

"If this man," Manteras said, "really deserves his reputation ... then I think you've just taken a very big step forward. We've a lot of good soldiers now, and if Colonel Adam can whip them into shape ..."

"The moment they learn he's coming," Aguilar said happily, "you'll see a change in them. There'll be scarcely a man among them who hasn't heard of him. I'll give him three months to clean up Oriente,

247

and then we'll march on Havana and to the devil with all of them."

Gabriella was still poised there, a hand on her hip, waiting to be dismissed, and the Governor said irritably, "That is all, Gabriella. You will be summoned when you are needed."

She made a little gesture of obeisance again and swept out. Manteras said, relishing his secret thoughts, "What a delight! What would we ever do without the charming Creole girls? I can't wait to get to bed tonight."

As soon as the door closed behind her, Aguilar raised his goblet in a toast. "Let's drink to it, my friends," he said. "Within the year, I will be master of all Cuba!"

Manteras and Galisteo echoed his sentiment. "To the master of all Cuba . . . Your health, Excellency!"

CHAPTER TWELVE

It seemed to Mercy and to Clifford that the long, thin pencil of water that was the fall, was growing a little wider and a little stronger; even the muted roar of it was changing. There was rain falling now in the distant mountains high above them.

The myriad colors of the flowers around them changed too, from reds to yellows to a dark, dark purple, and back to red again. The shelter was growing, both in size and density as he found with an almost childlike pleasure, new vines to use, new fronds to make into its roof. They had neither of them ever been so happy.

Their life was one of idyllic perfection new, carried to heights of happiness that bordered on the delirium of absolute bliss. It was the kind of perfection that, historically, cannot last in an imperfect world where there are people enough, in all conscience, to spoil it. It was the kind of happiness that seems axiomatically to be doomed to a sudden and dreadful termination.

They ate regally. There was lobster or crab or barracuda whenever they fancied it, and there were wild oranges and bananas (which they tried cooking once, on sticks over the fire, and found it to be very satisfying indeed), and coconuts in abundance to eat and to drink. They experimented with a large, round, pendulous greenish-brown fruit (they did not know it, but it was breadfruit), found it unappetizing, and went back to the foods they knew.

Once, Clifford almost fell onto a young boar. He wrestled it to the ground, though it had gashed his leg deeply with its tusks, and killed it with his knife. They ate a whole haunch of it, roasted, in one meal, and the next day, after hours of unaccustomed and inexpert scraping with his knife, he made her a pair of moccasins to replace her sadly ruined shoes, taking enormous pride in his accomplishment.

Her lacerated hands had healed with constant applications of seawater, and Clifford's beard now had grown fiercely. They were both in the peak of perfect health, and their happiness was complete.

He swam in the pool every day and tried to teach Mercy, with only limited success, how to swim too. As they lay naked together on the grassy bank one day, he picked up the knotted rope that had become his belt, fingered the knots, and said, "Tell me, Mercy . . . how long have we been here?"

She shook her head. "No. I don't want to count

days. They are all too perfect. I want them to last forever, and if I start counting . . ."

He said, insisting, "Tell me how many."

She lay on her back and enjoyed his caresses as she looked up at the high canopy of the foliage above them; a shaft of sunlight was striking a deep-red orchid up there, its long trailing vine fingering its way out of the dark-green shadows, and she said: "Look! Did you ever see a more beautiful flower?"

He followed her gaze and saw it, and said, getting to his feet, "If I am to climb trees, I will at least put my breeches on." He put them on, and examined the huge tree carefully, looking for handholds, and muttering, "No rigging, how can I climb with no rigging?"

But he went quickly up there, hand over hand, and came down again a few moments later. He twined the orchid carefully in her long brown hair and took off his breeches again before he lay beside her. He kissed her lips and said, "Now tell me . . . how long have we been here?"

She sighed. "Did you ever hear of a man named John Donne?" she asked.

"I have never known," he said, "of a woman who could be so . . . so inconsequential. Who, in Heaven's name, is John Donne?"

"A great English poet. Two hundred and fifty years ago he wrote a line I feel constrained to quote for you. He wrote: *'For God's sake hold your tongue, and let me love.'* I will not talk about days that we have been here, nor how many days of . . ." She could feel the tears of happiness coming into her eyes. "Oh, Clifford," she whispered, "I need your love so much, so very much . . ."

251

"Sshhh . . . be silent, woman. So hold your tongue and let me love."

He loved her then, long and gently, and rested atop her for a while as he always liked to; and in a little while he raised himself up on his elbows and said, laughing, "All right . . . now tell me. How long have we been here?"

"Clifford, you are quite impossible! We have been here for . . . oh, three weeks? No, more. About a month."

He reached out carefully to where his clothes were, and gave her the knotted rope, saying, "Count the knots on it."

"Then let me get comfortable."

"No. We are both very comfortable like this."

"I'm sure," she murmured, "that mathematics and love are quite incompatible." But she fingered the knots and counted them, saying at last, startled, "Forty-seven days?"

"I will tie the forty-eighth knot when the sun goes down."

There was a sudden, indefinable panic on her. "Are you tiring of . . . of our territory, Clifford?" she asked.

"No!" he said vehemently. "How could I ever tire of a home we built with our hands, you and I? How can I tire of anything if you are with me?"

He kissed her eyes and said, "My first great love, the sea, is close by. My last and final love is in my arms. How could I wish for more contentment?"

"And yet?"

"What is it that lies on the other side of the mountain? On the other side of the mountain beyond that? And beyond and beyond? Are there people? Cattle? Horses, sheep, goats? A settlement, perhaps? I feel we have to know, Mercy."

She said quietly, "Then let us go and find out, Clifford."

He sighed. "There is another 'and yet.'"

"And that is?"

"And yet I could happily spend all the rest of my days here with you. Do I sound confused?"

She said, smiling, "A little."

"It's very hard to be in love, and to be wise."

"Yes. I know that too."

"It's just that . . . we are in Cuba, a country I scarcely ever heard of. I want to know . . . I feel we *must* know what this strange new land is really like."

He eased himself gently from her and lay on his back, staring up at the sky. She rolled a long and slender thigh over his loins, propped herself up to look into his eyes, and kissed him. She said, "Then let us move on, my Clifford. Let us find out what else this new country has to offer us. He also wrote . . ."

"Who?"

"John Donne. He wrote: '*I wonder, by my troth, what thou and I did till we loved.*' And yes, our love has indeed begun a new life for both of us. So let us explore it together."

"And now that I hear you say: *move on* . . . I realize what a foolish idea it is."

"We will go to the top of the mountain and see what there is to be seen from there."

"No."

He shook his head. How sure he was again!

"No," he said, "we will stay here forever, and we will let that other world come to us if it wishes to. And if it does, we will tell them: go and leave us in peace, ours is the most perfect of all worlds, and we will share it with no one."

"And this must be what, then? The middle of November?"

"Yes, I think so."

She was brushing his body with her long hair, and it was hard for him to think in such prosaic terms.

She said, "If only I had been able to save my book. But if I remember rightly, Taurus, an earth sign, is in opposition to Scorpio, which is a water sign. And Leo, which is fire, is in opposition to Aquarius, which is air. Are you following me?"

"Not in the least, but go on."

"Then what all this means is that we should stay here for about twenty more days. After that, we can start our long explorations; everything will be just right for them." She said slyly, knowing that he did not really believe her, "It's about what we call quadratures. They're very complicated, and very important too."

"Even when you talk such nonsense, I love you dearly."

Her hands were caressing him, feeling the newly aroused strength of his manhood, and she whispered, "Then take me again, Clifford. I need you so badly. . . ."

He reached for the soft protuberance of her excited breasts, moulding them strongly, moved to her again, entering her completely, fusing his body with hers and knowing that nothing, ever, could separate them or shatter the great love they had for each other.

But the twenty days ordained by the juxtaposition of the planets were not to be. (Had she been able to consult her little almanac, she would have learned that her quadratures were wrong; but the book was lost, rotting in the gulfweed somewhere.)

It was only seven days later that a man strode out of the forest to confront them, while they were eating their midday meal. They rose to their feet and looked at him in surprise, a surprise not unmixed with alarm.

He was huge, standing well over six and a half feet tall, with powerful, bulging muscles, and a skin as black as coal. He was almost the first Negro Mercy had ever seen. There had been a black man at the chandler's shop on Carrier Street in the Rookery, a sailor who had left his ship many years ago; but he was a slight and wizened man with a courteous, friendly manner. He had a mischievous look in his eyes and a quip always ready on his lips, not at all like this angry, malevolent-looking giant. He had only one arm, the other cut off at the elbow. He wore a ragged shirt of torn blue wool with tight breeches to the lower part of his calves, and he was barefoot. In his left hand, he dangled a machete, with the easy grip of a man who is accustomed to its constant use.

There was venom in his eyes, a kind of suppressed fury, as he stared at them. He said, his voice filled with anger and loathing, *"Que estan haciendo aqui? Quien son ustedes? De adonde vienen?"*

Clifford stared back at him, conscious of Mercy's fright beside him. He moved in front of her and said, "Friends, we are friends, you understand?"

255

The giant's eyes went to Mercy and back to Clifford. "*Americanos*," he said angrily.

Clifford shook his head. "Not Americans. English."

"*Ingleses?*"

"Er . . . yes. *Ingleses*. Do you understand English?"

The Negro held his look and they had the impression that he was searching for words and phrases. He said at last, "Yes, am speaking English good, of course! So you tell me, what you doing here, where you come from? You tell me!"

"Our boat was wrecked," Clifford said, and the huge man interrupted him angrily. "Reck? What is reck?"

"*Wrecked*. Our boat, our ship, on the reef, the rocks . . ."

"Ah, shipwreck . . . where are other people? How many, you tell me!"

"No other people, just the two of us. We came here in a small boat, driven here by the wind."

"And where you go?"

Clifford shrugged. "We will go nowhere, for the moment. This is our home."

"Your home!" The anger went from the dark face suddenly, and a huge grin of sardonic pleasure took its place; and then he was laughing, bellowing out his laughter, doubling up with the gusto of it. He flipped the machete point down into the forest floor, slapped at his thigh and shouted, "Your home! White man go any place, he don' care who live there, is *his* home!"

The pleasure went again, as quickly as it had come, and he said more quietly, "This *my* home,

256

friend, and I don' like too much white folks in my home."

"I'm sure," Clifford said calmly, "that there's room enough for all of us. My name is Clifford Hawkes, if I may know yours, sir?"

The anger was in the eyes again, more sullen now. "My name . . . Juan Theophilus, you hear tell of me?"

"No, I fear not."

"Everybody heard tell of me. Everybody know Juan Theophilus."

"If I sound remiss, I ask you to forgive me. But no, I have not heard the name before."

"The slave Juan Theophilus."

"A *slave*?" Clifford asked puzzled. "But surely, slavery has long been outlawed?"

"England, yes, I know, we learn these things. But America . . ."

He wiggled a huge hand at them. "In America, half and half. Some say keeping slaves bad, some say is good, very good. In Cuba, they still got slavery, they don' want to free slaves here. You know Christophe?"

"Christophe? No, I think not."

"Henri Christophe," Mercy said. "In Haiti. The Emperor Christophe, he led a slave revolt twenty years ago, a very famous man."

His eyes were on her, a great deal of distaste in them. "Famous," he said, "and *mad*! He kill himself. But they don' got slaves now in Haiti. Soon they don' got slaves in Cuba too!"

He plucked his machete out of the ground with a movement so fast they scarcely saw it. He waved it at them and shouted, "Now Juan Theophilus make rebellion too! I free my people now! I make

257

them free men! And nobody don' stop me!" He pointed the machete at Clifford, only inches from his nose, and shouted, "You *Inglese*! So you tell me . . . you don' ship slaves no more! How long? How long, *friend*, you don' carry slaves in your ships?"

The bright steel of the machete was glinting under his eyes and Clifford said hesitantly, "Well, some years now, I believe . . ."

Mercy said swiftly, "Since the year 1842, six years ago, British ships have been guarding the African coast and hunting down the slavers, Mr. Theophilus."

He lowered his weapon slowly and looked at her carefully. "A woman," he said. "How come a woman know all those things, the man don' know?"

"My father," Mercy said clearly, "was a teacher of history at a London school. The progress of the anti-slavery factions all over the world was of great interest to him."

"Why?" He would not take his eyes off her.

"Because it was abhorrent to him. He hated slavery with all his heart, Mr. Theophilus. And even in Cuba, which is Spanish territory . . . there was a treaty between England and Spain that outlawed slavery thirteen years ago! How can there still be slavery here?"

He scowled. "Treaties? Treaties don' mean nothing! So you tell my poor brothers they got a treaty! They don' got food on their plates! They don' work good, they still get whipped!"

He lifted up the stump of his arm and shook it obscenely, shouting, "You see that? You know why they do that to me? *Who* do it to me? *Slave-*

master do it! And why? He take young slavegirl, virgin slavegirl, only he find out someone take her first, before he get her, and he know it was Juan Theophilus!" His fury subsided very quickly. "But it don' matter none," he said. "We got a treaty now."

"Very many of us," Mercy said quietly, "believe your condition should be improved, Mr. Theophilus. By freedom."

He was squinting at her now. "You call me Mister. I am a slave."

"My father insisted on the honorifics too."

"I don' know what you talking about," he said, glaring.

She answered him steadily, "Then I will tell you something that you will perhaps understand. This year of 1848 has seen a great deal of violence all over the world. In England, France, Austria, Scandinavia, everywhere. A year of turmoil greater than any in the past four centuries. And not without reason. For those of us who understand the Heavens, it was . . . inevitable."

The black man was fast losing his patience with her. He thrust his machete into its ragged leather scabbard and picked up the hot lobster from the fire, tearing it apart with his teeth and wolfing the flesh down.

"Your woman talk too much," he said to Clifford, but Mercy went on.

"And most of this movement is an expression . . . of people's need for freedom. And the planets . . . their position now indicates . . ."

He interrupted her bursquely. "I don' know planets," and went on eating.

Mercy said, "The stars then! They indicate very

259

clearly . . . that any drive toward freedom for the people *must* succeed. According to the stars, Mr. Theophilus, your revolt will be a successful one."

He was staring at her wide-eyed, the food half-way to his mouth. He seemed suddenly frightened. He said hoarsely, "The . . . the stars?"

"The planets. Yes, if you like, the stars."

For a moment he just glared at her, his eyes wide with an emotion she could not understand. And then, with a lightning movement, he thrust out his hand and took her by the throat, a grip so strong that it paralyzed her.

Clifford was there in a flash. He pushed one hand into the giant's face, took hold of his wrist with the other, and swung him around so violently that he lost the firm grip and fell to the ground. Mercy stifled a scream and saw that Clifford was crouched, ready to do battle. But this huge, quite unpredictable man was staring at Mercy still.

His voice was a whisper, "You . . . a witch."

She pulled herself together quickly. "Not a witch," she said, trying to control her shaking. "An astrologer."

"I don' know this word neither. We got witch-woman my camp. She tell me . . . she say this year, the stars . . . they kill me."

Mercy shuddered. She was very conscious of Clifford's arm around her now. The Negro was getting slowly to his feet, and she said to him, "If I could know the day, the hour of your birth . . . without that, all I can say is that your movement will probably succeed."

He took a long, deep breath and held her look for a while, then suddenly thrust a bare, splayed foot into the fire and scattered its ashes. He drew a

260

crude circle in them with his big toe and said angrily, "So you tell me what you see there!"

"No. I do not read ashes. I study the stars."

He squatted on his haunches by the circle he had drawn. He traced a cross in them with his finger, making a smaller circle to encompass it, and stared at the design for a long, long time. He said eventually, shaking his head, "I don' know. Ashes tell me . . ." He pressed them with the back of his hand in three places and said, "We got trouble here . . . and here . . . and here. Over here, maybe don' look too bad. Jus' . . . maybe."

He looked up at her, squinting, his head cocked to one side, a deep frown on his face. All the anger had gone now completely. "But you tell me," he said, "I gonna win, is that what you telling me?"

Mercy was fast recovering from her shock. She shook her head. "I say only that . . . if yours is truly a movement toward freedom, then the stars predict that it cannot fail. That is all I say."

She felt Clifford's warning pressure on her side; had she gone too far? She fell silent.

Theophilus looked at them from one to the other, and nodded his head slowly. "*Ingleses*," he said, "good people, you don' ship slaves no more. Come, you come with me. I take you to better place now."

Clifford shook his head. "No sir," he said politely. "We will stay here, if you don't mind. This is our home now. Our . . . territory."

He looked at Clifford for a long moment, a sour, malevolent expression on his face, and then he cupped his hand to his mouth and made a low, muted sound like the cry of a bird.

Mercy gasped.

261

All around them, ten, fifteen, twenty men were moving stealthily out of the forest. They were dressed in rags, some of them more than half naked, and they were all armed. Some of them had machetes, some knives, some clubs. Two of them had ancient rifles; and one of them carried a carpenter's saw, hefting it like a weapon.

Theophilus said again, "You come with me."

He turned without further ado and Clifford took Mercy's arm in his strong hand and tried to still her alarm.

He said to her gently, his handsome bearded face quite without fear, "When the odds are against us, Mercy my love, we run with the wind, wherever it may take us."

She was sure only of the comfort of his touch and she whispered, "I'm frightened, Clifford."

How strong and assuring his voice was! He was even smiling. "Don't be," he said. "We run before a sudden unexpected wind. And when the wind changes, as it will, we will trim our sails and still run with it . . . until it becomes unacceptable. And then . . . no longer. Believe me, Mercy, no longer than that. Trust me."

The slaves were gathering round them, an escort of lithe and angry barefooted fighting-men, armed with the weapons of the dispossessed.

The episode in their lives that had brought them together was coming to its inexorable end; and another was just beginning.

For all of the afternoon, they marched through the forest. In a few hours they came to a well-defined trail that led across their path and turned west on it, climbing steeply up the mountain. In a little

262

while they crossed over a shallow but fast-flowing stream, where the water, cold as snow, swirled about their legs as they walked unsteadily through it.

Some of the men had gone on ahead and some were far to the rear. Theophilus walked in the center in silence with the two of them, casting a surreptitious and somehow worried look at Mercy once in a while and saying nothing.

But when the sun went down, he called a halt and said to Clifford, frowning, "Your woman tired, white woman don' walk too good, got no . . . no strength like black woman."

Mercy had found a seat on a granite boulder, wanting so badly to lie down on the warm earth but knowing that this would not be a good thing to do just now. She said, protesting, "No, I'm all right. If you could just tell us where we are going? How much further?"

Theophilus did not answer her. He shouted an order and some of the men started cutting bamboo poles with their machetes. He came back to Mercy and offered her a metal cannister from his belt and said roughly: "You thirsty, you drink."

She smelled the contents surreptitiously and barely touched it to her lips, burning her tongue, and handed it back to him and said politely: "I thank you, but I'm not really thirsty."

He grinned, and shouted an order, and handed the canister to Clifford. Clifford took a long, deep drink and grimaced. Theophilus said, laughing, "What, you don' like good rum?"

"That is *rum*? Well . . ."

"You never taste it before? Is good."

"Oh yes, I've tasted it. Not quite the same as

263

yours, perhaps . . . on the whalers we have a ration every day, to keep out the cold."

"Whalers? What is whalers? I don' know this word."

"Ships that catch whales. Very large fish that give us oil for our lamps. I used to hunt them once. And will you tell me where we are going?"

"I tell you," Theophilus said. "We go my camp. I got witch-woman, you got witch-woman. Now we find out for sure."

"Find out . . . exactly what, Mr. Theophilus?"

He said awkwardly, "I tell you, Mister . . . Mister . . . you tell me your name again?"

"Hawkes. Clifford Hawkes."

"Yes, yes, I know that. So I tell you, Mister Clifford." He crouched down and smoothed a section of sand with a broad hand and drew a small circle in it, half surrounded by a larger semicircle. He touched the inner circle and said, "Guantanamo is French town, they got sugar fields . . ."

His hand moved to the outer circle and sliced little incisions in it. "Here, they got a line of forts. Not big. Small. We don' got enough guns, and we need more guns. So . . . I take three, four hundred men, we make attack, here, here, here. We get guns. Three forts, we got maybe fifty, sixty, good rifles. Next, we go here, here, here. We got maybe fifty more. Time we finish, they don' have no more guns, we got all the guns we want. What you think, Mister Clifford?"

One of the slaves was running to Mercy with a tin cup full of water and she drank it gratefully. Clifford rubbed at his beard and said, "What I think is . . . is there a better way of achieving

264

what you want to achieve? Instead of fighting with machetes against men armed with rifles?"

Theophilus laughed out loud. "We don' *fight*, Mister Clifford," he said. "We just cut their throats."

Clifford said nothing and in a little while the men who had been working with their machetes produced poles and criss-crossed vines for Mercy to be carried on. In spite of her protestations, Theophilus insisted. "A long way to go," he said. "We carry you, you don' walk no more."

"I don't need it," she said weakly, knowing it was no good at all, and Theophilus grunted. "You ride," he said. He crouched down beside her and his voice was surprisingly gentle now. He was gesticulating with his huge hand, scarred and calloused and powerful, saying quietly, "You know about stars, and this very important for me. It mean that you are my friend. Your man hit me back there, and anybody hit Juan Theophilus, I kill him, one-two I kill him. But he your man, and you my friend, is why I don' take his head off and throw it in fire. Never forget . . . you my friend now."

He stood up and gestured at the litter. "You ride," he said. He turned away and shouted orders in his own language to the men. Clifford helped her aboard the crude stretcher, whispering to her, "A symbol, a symbol of your importance to them. And you must save your strength, I fear we will need all of our energies soon."

He walked beside her as the column moved steadily onward. They came to the edge of a tall cliff and walked along its edge for an hour or more, watching the sun go down over the sea, incredibly far below them. It was a vista of extraordinary beauty, with huge and dark green trees, spotted here and there with brilliant red and purple orchids, falling like a dense carpet all the way down to the wide swathe of yellow sand that was the beach, curling in and out among the rocks, the white surf breaking lazily over it. They could not believe that they had climbed so high and so far.

The sky was blue above them, then gold further down, and a brilliant red along the horizon where the clouds lay in soft layers of scarlet tinged with mauve; it was breathtaking.

They left the cliff and penetrated deep into the dark forest again. Now, as they started moving slowly down into a hidden valley, a dozen more men and women joined them, some of them carrying flares that pinpointed the darkness with flickering, smoking yellow light. They bore with them, on a long pole carried by two men, the biggest pig Mercy had ever seen; it must have weighed close to three hundred pounds. It was roasted and blackened on the outside, the pole thrust through it from end to end.

Theophilus called a halt and the men gathered round, tearing the flesh apart with their bare hands. Theophilus, an angry man again, shouted furiously, "Stop! I gonna kill somebody!"

They fell back from his anger, and he glowered at them muttering, "You always gonna be slaves, you don' got no manners at all. We got white lady here, you don' know about her. Is a *witch*."

Mercy was conscious of their eyes staring at her. Theophilus took his machete from its scabbard and carved off a huge slice of meat from the haunch, handed it to her and said gravely: "You eat good . . . only you remember please—my poor brothers in the field, they don' eat like this, all they getting is corn. Here, we free, we eat good. Soon they gonna eat good too."

She took the meat from him, still warm, and waited. Nobody moved. There were thirty or forty pairs of eyes on her now and she felt acutely embarrassed. There were old men there, waiting; and children, waiting. A score of hungry men and a few women with their eyes fastened on her waited for her to begin eating. She took a hesitant bite and immediately they were at the pig, tearing at its flesh with their hands. A fight broke out and Theophilus knocked the two contestants to the ground with one mighty blow. In less than half an hour, there was nothing left of the carcass but bones, that were sucked noisily as they finished it off.

By the light of the flares, the column moved on. And it was dawn before they came to the camp.

It was hidden deep in the forest of the valley, a camp of bamboo shelters covered over with fronds, some of them brown and dying, others freshly green where the newcomers had built their own little pieces of territory.

There were women and children wandering about, most of them in rags, and a dozen men prowling with ancient flintlock muskets. There were flares everywhere, casting a strangely-warm glow over the men and women, a few children among them, who were gathering to watch their arrival, and beyond the yellow lights the forest looked even blacker and more dense, giving the little compound an air of lonely isolation, a feeling, even, of improbability. There were mutterings among the people and there was the thunderous sound of a waterfall coming to them—quite unlike the friendly sound, Mercy was thinking, of their own waterfall—as it pounded its way down the cliff somewhere in the hidden vastness of the jungle. It was a loud, insistent roar that seemed somehow ominous, as though the very magnitude of it were stressing their own frailty.

There was an elderly, hollow-chested black man there, quite naked, tied to a tree, his wrists bound high above his head, a rope around his throat that fastened him securely to the trunk. His head drooped, his eyes were closed, and he could have been dead.

Theophilus stopped beside him and said to Clifford very quietly, "This man . . . his name Hosannah. He try to tell Spaniards where we hiding, he send them message, long letter. Only letter don' get there, we find it, we got a man here who read good, and so . . ."

He lifted up the man's head and the weary eyes opened with nothing but despair in them. Theophilus said, "He try to tell them . . . how many men we got, how many guns, how many machetes. He tell them we got eight sentries every night, he tell them where we are . . . and for what?"

He turned to Mercy, his eyes alight with fury. "For gold! They promise him gold coins and he sell us."

The movement was the lightning motion of a fighting animal. He whipped the machete out of the scabbard and drove it through the bound man's chest so strongly that it embedded itself in the tree trunk behind him. Mercy screamed and Clifford clutched her to him, burying her face against his

268

shoulder. Theophilus, his anger gone again, said to them nonchalantly, "Better he is dead, he don' sell us no more. Now, I show you where you gonna live."

Mercy was in shock. She let Clifford guide her and the huge Negro led them to a palm-frond shelter. He shouted at the occupants inside and when they had scurried away, he said, more quietly now, "You sleep here two, three hours. Soon, I come for you. You don' try to run away, you don' get too far."

He turned on his heel and stalked away and Clifford led Mercy into the shelter. There was a tiny flame there, a length of string tied around a piece of fat, spitting and sputtering on its scrap of broken pottery, a pile of rushes on the floor for a bed, and nothing else.

He crouched beside her on the trampled-earth floor as she lay there weeping, and he whispered to her, "We will leave this terrible place as soon as we can, Mercy. Keep up your courage, it will not be long, I promise you. Try to sleep for a while. In the hours to come . . . we will need all of our strength and our wits."

He held her tightly and lay beside her for a while. When he knew that she had cried herself into the sleep of utter exhaustion, he eased himself carefully out of her arms and crept to the entrance of the shelter to see what was around them.

There were three men there, one of them carrying a huge pistol, the others armed with machetes. The pistoleer gestured with his weapon. "You stay," he said roughly. "You stay!"

He crept back into the hut and sat down beside his sleeping lover, worried about the damp on her cheeks. He moved around the confines of the little hut, inspecting its flimsy walls carefully, walls made of long dried fronds wedged in among sticks. They rustled when he touched them, but he found that if he moved with infinite care he could pull them apart almost in silence. There would be a sentry at the back there, he was sure. He sat down beside Mercy and began planning just how they would make their escape as soon as she' had rested for a while.

Theophilus came for Mercy a few hours later. Clifford woke her up and got to his feet, but the Negro said brusquely, "Not you. You stay!"

Clifford held his look and said clearly, "No. I will not leave my wife. Where she goes, I go."

"No!"

"Yes!"

"You gonna fight me? You gonna fight my whole camp?"

"I am going where my wife goes. I will not leave her side."

The dark eyebrows shot up, crinkling the wide, intelligent forehead, and he said at last, shrugging, "All right, you come too. Only you don' talk none. The woman got the brains, not you."

"I will accept that," Clifford said calmly.

They were led together to a small clearing in the center of the camp and an ancient woman was seated there: a Creole, with heavily wrinkled, ol-ive-colored skin, and long white hair that fell to her waist. Her eyes were sharp and alert, the palest of pale grays, her mouth a thin line of discontent and suspicion. She wore a loose, voluminous dress of cheap cotton, a tent to hide her shrivelled body.

270

There were three small fires in front of her and a live chicken, its feet trussed, was fluttering in the dust at her feet. She looked at Mercy and began to speak in her own dialect, her hands fluttering like the hands of a ballet dancer. Theophilus, his eyes alight with emotion now, translated:

"She say . . . you sit down . . . she know what you believe in . . . is nothing matter, only what you believe in . . . she know the stars too . . . she tell you what gonna happen now . . . we all sit down . . . we listen to what she say . . ."

The droning voice stopped and the pale eyes were clouded over, unseeing. They sat on the sand around her and Theophilus said urgently to Mercy, "Now . . . you tell her . . . what you tell me."

There was a strange feeling of unreality in the air. Mercy said hesitantly, "I can tell you very little . . . I cannot foresee events. I can only tell you . . . of tendencies."

"Then tell."

"My book," she muttered. "I need my book, and I don't have it . . ."

"I find it for you, you tell me where is."

"Somewhere in the Sargasso Sea . . ."

The old woman was droning on again and Theophilus translated as she spoke:

"She say: 'This man, he gonna die soon.' Now *you* tell me."

Mercy herself was almost in a trance, seduced by a strong and uncanny sense of the unreal. Theophilus's voice was low and quiet and hesitant, as he interpreted between them. There was the heavy scent of incense in the air.

Mercy said slowly, "Uranus is moving through the first House. It means restlessness . . . and

271

change. It means . . . a period of freedom is approaching . . . perhaps a limited period . . . There is a drive toward new endeavor . . ."

The old woman said, "We have trouble in the camp . . . We move soon, maybe . . . Brother fight against brother . . ."

Mercy said urgently, "No, not till later . . . in the fourth House, yes. Not now . . ."

"And this man die. He die soon." Theophilus was trembling visibly as he spoke.

And then, Mercy felt the hair at the back of her head tingling: the old woman's staring eyes were changing color, from gray to green to hazel . . . and then to the darkest brown. There was a terrible wildness in them now. She reached forward, picked up the trussed chicken, and bit through its neck with her ancient, yellowed teeth. She plucked its feathers while it was still struggling and tossed them on the three little fires, filling the air with their blue smoke.

The men and women crouched around the fires were staring, their bright eyes reflected in the flames. She began to speak again in a low, singsong, and Theophilus translated, trying to contain his emotions but not succeeding.

"There is water . . . strong water . . . and white woman . . . there is blood, much blood . . . There are bullets, and men die . . . I see fire, much fire . . . I see man with one arm, he lie dead . . . and woman with him . . . this is time to run away . . . run away . . . better you hide . . ."

The old woman fell silent, her dark eyes staring now. As Mercy watched, incredulous, the eyes began changing their color again, and she was sitting there on her haunches, swaying to and fro and moaning slightly. Theophilus said at last, his voice hoarse and frightened, "What you say, white witch-woman?"

Mercy was desperate. "I do not know!" she said, and she was almost in tears. "Burned chicken feathers . . . and . . . and . . . and . . . I don't *know!*"

He was very calm and controlled now. "You say I win?"

"I don't know!"

"Before . . . you tell me I win."

She made a gesture of complete helplessness. "Yes, and I say it again. The time . . . the time is good. If you can succeed ever . . . yes, perhaps now."

He looked at her for a long, long time, and got to his feet heavily. He turned his gaze on the old woman, swaying now and mumbling to herself, and he said at last, "This crazy old woman . . . what she know?" He sounded very unsure as he turned to Clifford. "You take your woman," he said, "you take her to your hut. We talk again soon. I want to think now."

He stalked off and left them there, and their guards were waiting. Clifford helped Mercy to her feet and took her back, under their watchful eyes, to the shelter. He sat down beside her as she lay back on the rushes. Taking her hand, he said quietly, "We leave this dreadful place tonight, Mercy. As soon as the moon goes down."

She nodded miserably.

But neither of them could guess at the circumstances of their leaving.

273

CHAPTER THIRTEEN

There were three hundred men lined up, most of them fearfully, in the stone-paved square of the palace's inner courtyard.

They were clothed, more or less uniformly, in the dress of the governor's palace guard, with short green jackets decorated by scarlet epaulettes and broad crossed bands of white leather, long baggy trousers of gray serge and calf-length black leather boots. They wore the peaked, truncated cone cap, each set with a single short red plume of scarlet in a round patch of green cloth, that was called a *shako*. (The Spanish had copied it from the French who had, in turn, taken it from the *scako* of the Hungarian armies.)

They carried, quite indiscriminately, an assortment of weapons: flintlock rifles with ring-lock bayonettes, pistols, swords, and twelve-foot long lances. In spite of their brilliant colors, they were a sorry lot.

The four turreted towers loomed high above them in the heat of this sunny day, and along the castellated walls the guards were pacing, aware also of a change that was coming about in their condition.

Most of the troopers, by far, were Spanish, but there was a smattering among them of Frenchmen, recent immigrants from Haiti escaping the troubles there, and of Dutchmen who had jumped ship here. There were a handful of English renegades and a few Portuguese too. This was an army of mercenaries who had sworn allegiance to their temporary master, the Governor of Oriente Province, and to hell with Spain and even Havana.

Adam Butrus, with Jake Ollie by his side, was inspecting them; or rather, it might be better said that he was looking them over with a great deal of contempt on his handsome features. He wore a resplendent uniform now, a scarlet coat with breeches of brilliant green wool, a white silk sash across one shoulder, a white leather strap for his sword over the other, with gold and scarlet patches everywhere, knee-high boots of polished black leather, and a red-and-green *shako* decorated with red-and-white pompoms. The hilt of the sword was richly decorated in gold and silver, its scabbard covered with red velvet into which an intricate design had been woven with gold wire.

Beside him, Jake Ollie was dressed in the standard dark green of the Governor's officers: a turkey waddling beside a strutting (but very dangerous) peacock.

Butrus strolled up and down the six ranks of the

276

soldiers in silence, letting them see what a splendidly martial figure he cut, as they wondered why he did not deign to correct, once in a while, the slope of their arms or even the set of their uniforms.

He strode up and down, twirling his fine moustaches (waxed now to peaks of perfection), for a full fifteen minutes, saying not a word while they fidgeted nervously. He marched out in front of them, Captain Jake Ollie by his side, looked them over for a moment, then bellowed,

"Scum! Listen to me, scum! You all know who I am, and in my long and honorable career as a soldier and a sailor, I never set eyes on such a useless-looking, bootless, inept and worthless rabble! You know my reputation too. But you may not know what that reputation is built on. So listen to me, you vermin, and I will tell you! It is built on discipline, on training, and on an ability I seem to have for finding the cowards among my troops and hanging them! Because, cowardice is like the plague, it's catching, and I won't have the good men among you, and I'm sure there are many, infected with it. I look into those dull, unseeing eyes, and I search in vain for the fire that says you are *soldiers*! You are not! But by the time I've finished with you, by God, that's what you will be. You will be proud of the uniform you wear, and prouder still that you once served under Colonel Adam! You'll boast of it to your children and your grandchildren—if you ever survive, which I doubt. You'll learn, or you'll die in the effort of it, what it is to be fighting-men. Under *my* command!"

He paced back and forth for a moment and looked at a group of workmen who were erecting a high platform with a ship's boom lashed into

277

place above it. They were stringing three ropes to the cross-piece, and he pointed to it and yelled at the men: "You know what that is? It's a gallows! Because before this week is out, there'll be the need, as God is my witness, to hang a few of you as a salutary lesson to the others! It's ready for you! It's waiting for you! So listen now to something I will tell you once and never again."

He lowered his voice and said more quietly, "I demand instant . . . and unquestioning obedience. If I tell one of you to take out his dagger and drive it into the gut of the man beside him . . . then, by God, that's what he'll do. And he'll do it at once, or he'll feel the rope around his own neck. And under my command, those of you who already know how to fight will learn how to fight better. And you'll become rich. Rich, you scum! Because I reward courage with gold, as I reward cowardice with the noose. His Excellency, on my insistence, has placed a store of gold coins at my disposal, and they'll be paid out, unstintingly, for your bravery."

He thrust out a finger at the scaffold and shouted: "While the brave get rich . . . the faint hearts will hang there, high, till the crows have picked their eyes out! Remember that! Now . . . I want each of the three captains to give me his best sergeant. I want each of those sergeants to select ten of his best men. Tonight, I plan to test your mettle. I want to see what kind of men you are, I want to see the spirit you're made of. This night, thirty-three men, with Captain Ollie and myself . . . we march thirty miles up into the mountain, the Sierra Maestra. The next night we march another thirty, and every night from then on yet another thirty, five nights in all. At the end of five nights, believe me, you will have learned how to move in the forest like animals, in stealth, in silence, in secrecy. And then . . . then, I will find out what you are made of. There is an armed camp of slaves deep in the mountains under the so-called command of a slave named Juan Theophilus, a giant of a man with only one arm, and there's ten gold coins for the man who brings me his head. He has, by all reports, a hundred and eighty men, perhaps two hundred. They are armed with machetes, with daggers, with clubs. It may be that they have a handful of guns. If they were soldiers, then I'd take along a dozen more of you, but they're not, they're slaves! We destroy them, we destroy their camp, and we bring back the head of Theophilus in a sack as a present for His Excellency! We leave at sundown, and we return in ten days. Three sergeants, thirty men. Riflemen, all of them. I have no wish to be encumbered with lances in the forest. They will all present themselves on the watchtower in the west wall one hour from now, at which time they will learn, down to the smallest detail, exactly how we will proceed on the march, and in the attack. See to it, Ollie."

Jake Ollie, preening himself in his fine new clothes, saluted. "Aye aye, Mister Mate," he said.

Butrus looked at him coldly and Ollie said, mumbling: "Yes sir, Colonel Adam, sir."

Butrus strode off to find himself something to drink.

The camp was silent and lit by more than a score of flares. They were stuck in the ground, tied to trees, wedged in between limestone rocks. There were a number of sentries prowling, most of them weary and half-asleep, a few of them were quite drunk. There were three more around the crude hut that had been given to Mercy and Clifford for their shelter, two of them in front, chatting together and surreptitiously drinking once in a while from a gourd of rum, and the other fast asleep on the ground at the rear.

Clifford, as soon as the silencing of the camp noises had told him that it was asleep, had already left the little prison once. He had carefully pulled a hole in the frond-wall at the back, stepping gingerly over the recumbent form of the guard there, and had spent more than an hour exploring his surroundings.

What he had found worried him.

The tiny clearing where the camp had been set up was no more than half an acre or so in size, surrounded by forest so dense that it was almost impenetrable. Easing his way around the perimeter on his belly, he found that it was reinforced almost everywhere by heavy branches of vicious thornwood, with curved spikes more than an inch long, closely set together and sharp as needles. He had found three openings in the formidable fence—the trail by which they had entered the camp—with two flares there to illuminate it now, another which seemed to be unguarded . . .

He saw the sentry there in the nick of time, a black shadow in the darkness of the tree that stood hard by it, crouched in the lower branches. He drew back and continued his reconnaisance.

The third exit was more promising. It lay only fifty paces from their little hut, behind it, and there was a trail with a single man leaning against the trunk of a tall tree that towered up into the dark sky, immense and overshadowing, a giant among the other trees. He found an overhanging rock nearby, a great slab of granite only a few feet off the ground, and he crawled below it and lay in a small cave there, ripe with the stench of bats. With only his head exposed, he watched the opening to the trail and its solitary guard for a long, long time, waiting for the clouds to pass from over the moon, watching the skies carefully and estimating just how long it would be before the darkness became absolute.

Not long, he thought; the bank of heavy cloud was moving forward inexorably. He turned his eyes back to the sentry as the moon came out. He was very tall and thin, with a blanket draped over his shoulders that made him look like a ghoul; there was a cutlass thrust into the belt that held the blanket around his skeletal waist.

And then the moon was covered up again, and he crept carefully back to the shelter and squeezed his way silently inside again.

Mercy threw her arms around his neck and hugged him tightly. He kissed her, holding her against his chest and feeling the furious beat of her heart.

"Are you all right?" he whispered. "No one came?"

"No, no one . . . I was so worried for you."

They sat down together on the dirt floor, and he held her hands in his and whispered, "We will leave here now. You must pay very careful attention to what I have to tell you."

"All right." Her eyes were on his, bright in the tallow-lit darkness.

He said very quietly, "It will not be too difficult,

281

but we must be very, very careful, and absolutely quiet. We lie on our bellies . . . if you will forgive the word, and we use our elbows, like this . . ."

He lay down on his stomach and used his elbows like oars, a few slow strokes. If not for the tension she felt, she would have laughed.

"This is the way," he said, whispering, "that we used to stalk seals on the ice. The secret is to move very, very slowly. Try it," he said, urgingly, and he watched her critically as she copied his movements. He was smiling now and he nodded eagerly. "Yes, like that, only not so fast. Each time you put an elbow on the ground, you must make sure there is no dried twig under it that will snap and betray our presence. Infinitely slowly . . . I will be ahead of you and when I stop, you stop . . ."

They sat down together again and he said, "Now, we have to crawl about fifty paces and that will take us ten or fifteen minutes, no less, very, very slowly. If anyone should see us, then we jump up and we *run*. You grab hold of my hand and we run. But I do not really expect this if we are careful. The grass is long, the moon will be clouded over in a few moments, and I do not think this will be necessary." He broke off and frowned. "The danger you are in, dear Mercy," he whispered, "I cannot bear to think of it . . ."

"As long as you are close beside me."

"No, you are not listening! I will be *ahead* of you!"

"But close."

"Yes. Very close, all the time. Now, the second step. The way out of the perimeter, about fifty paces away, is a trail through the jungle, which seems, just here, to be otherwise almost impenetrable without a machete and a lot of noise. Close by there is a small cave. That is where we go first. You will lie down inside it . . ."

He broke off and she could see that he was grinning. "It smells formidably," he said, "but that's a small price to pay for safety. You wait there, hidden, while I go incapacitate the sentry."

He felt her hands tighten their grip on his and he whispered gently, "No, I will not have to kill him. A blow over the head . . . it's not the first time I've knocked a man out, and it probably won't be the last, so there's no cause for alarm. He has a cutlass and this will be very useful to us. Then, when I come back for you, we crawl out of the camp into the trail. And then . . . we move as fast as we can, as quietly as we can, and as far as we can. Where the trail leads, I cannot guess. But the clouds are breaking from time to time, there will be stars to guide us, and if we make our way, however slowly, south and *down*—then sooner or later we will come to the beach."

"And the sea. Your first great love."

He was laughing softly. "But not my last and final . . . yes, we find the sea. We should not go back to our old home. We'll spend a day or two exploring and we'll find another place . . ."

"A better one."

"No. Nothing can ever be better than the days I spent with you there, nothing! But we will build a new home, and live together for the rest of our lives, and Mercy . . . oh, Mercy, I love you so very much."

"Clifford, Clifford . . ."

His hands were all over her body, exploring. He pulled away from her in a moment and whispered, "All right. Are we ready?"

"If you are, I am."

"Then let us go. Remember . . . very slowly, and with no sound at all."

"All right."

He pulled the woven palm-fronds aside and peered out into the absolute darkness. He could dimly make out the shadow on the grass that was the sleeping guard. He was snoring loudly, grumbling and muttering to himself alternately in a drunken stupor. They waited for him to settle down, eased their way through the opening together, and crept toward the welcoming safety of the forest.

They had only gone a few yards, when she saw him roll to one side quickly, under the cover of a bush of tiny yellow flowers, and she followed him breathlessly and lay silent as he pulled her under its foliage. They held their breaths, frozen into immobility.

A squat, bare-chested black man was moving toward them, weaving unsteadily on his feet. He had an old rifle slung across his back and he was drinking from a metal flask. They saw him stumble and fall, so close to them that they could have reached out and touched him. He picked himself up again laboriously, mumbling to himself in a language they could not understand. He stood there as they lay silent under the heavy bush, and fumbled at his breeches, and urinated long and loudly. Clifford's firm hand was on Mercy's wrist, holding it tightly, and she scarcely dared breathe.

At last he moved, humming a tune and doing a little jig. They waited till he had gone and eased themselves slowly out from under the bush, crawling on to the tiny cave.

The granite slab was close above their heads, so closely confining that Clifford could hardly weave his shoulders in there, and through the narrow gap they watched the guard, studying his every movement, trying, even, to insinuate themselves into his thoughts.

What was he thinking as he stared unseeing around him, his mouth a little open, his eyes infinitely sad and filled with something that looked like pain? Was he dreaming of that freedom that his leader had promised him? A freedom, surely, that would not easily come to him? There was a lassitude, a hopelessness even in the way he moved.

He wandered away now to a flare that was wedged into a crevice close by their hiding place, lit a *sheroot* from it, the flame illuminating his dark, squat-nosed features, outlining them in yellow as he sucked in the blue smoke and exhaled it again. There was a fringe of black beard around his chin and a scar ran down his cheek from close to the eye almost to the lobe of the ear.

At that moment, the first shot of the battle rang out. Startled, they saw the guard hurled sideways as a ball took him in the shoulder and he spun round and fell to the ground. There was a sudden shriek of pain, perhaps of surprise too, and he writhed his body in the dirt for an instant, then lay still.

And immediately, as though the first shot had been a signal, the firing started in earnest. It was all around them. Much of it coming from down the trail that was their only avenue of escape.

Adam Butrus had brought his men in near silence to within a hundred feet of the camp. His four scouts, all of them Frenchmen, were deserters from General Boyer's Haitian army, who had settled here after leaving their Guantanamo sugar fields to throw in their lot with Governor Aguilar, and had quickly found the three ways into the compound.

Butrus had split his men up, therefore, into three natural groups, each under a single sergeant, one each on the north, east, and west. He himself, with Jake Ollie, and two men, had scouted the camp's perimeter and easily found its weaknesses. (One of those men, by the name of Fernand D'Estes, who suffered with bronchial troubles, had almost betrayed them with a fit of coughing; Jake Ollie had promptly "arrested" him, and had him bound and gagged and tied to a tree; after the battle, he was to be taken back to the palace to be flogged, ceremonially, in front of the assembled troops.)

The three-pronged strike force had been there for more than an hour before Butrus gave the signal to open fire.

They were using the new elongated bullets of surprising accuracy, the lead balls being rammed into position against the explosive cage by a ramrod which was ended in a cup-shaped receptable (a French invention) that pounded the missile into a shape by which it would readily engage the rifling of the weapon's barrel. They were also using the greased patch and wooden wad (the "sabot") between the powder and their balls. The result was a

286

bullet that flew, not only with an unusual velocity, but also (perhaps for the first time in history) where it was aimed. So that in the first three volleys, every man in the camp who happened to be out in the open, and visible in the light of the flares, had been hit. And a dozen others had been struck by bullets that were aimed elsewhere.

Theophilus was one of these who had been wounded by the purest chance. He had been in his hut with his scribe, writing out a laborious speech for himself by the light of a tallow candle, when a stray lead ball had richocheted off a tree and buried itself in his chest.

For a moment, he had lain there in bewilderment and shock; then, giant that he was, he had struggled to his feet and bellowed, "To arms! Slaves! To arms!"

He had run out into the compound, gripping his machete and looking for a head to split open with it, and found nothing put panic and chaos. Screaming men and women, and a few children, were running in all directions across the camp. Those who had weapons throwing them away as they tried to force a way out through the thorn-fence that lacerated their bodies as they died from the constant, regular volleys of gunfire.

Theophilus raised his machete high and screamed again, "To arms!" And then he too dropped his weapon as he fell and crawled on his hands and knees under the bushes by the perimeter, laboriously pulling his way under the fence.

At the sound of the first shot, Clifford had thrust Mercy bodily into the recesses of the cave. He whispered fiercely, "In God's Holy name . . . what happened?"

He wormed his way back to the entrance and watched the flashes of fire coming from the entrance to the camp that was to have been their salvation. Mercy was beside him again, clutching at him fearfully. Three men in uniform were running across their front, one of them forcing a ramrod down the barrel of his rifle as he ran, and she whispered excitedly, "Soldiers? Are they soldiers, Clifford? We are saved . . ."

"No, not soldiers, ssshhh . . ."

Butrus's men had discarded their *shakos* before they had begun the long climb up the mountain, covering over their brilliant medley of uniforms with loose *ponchos* to serve as camouflage, a device which caused them to regard their devious new commander with a great deal of respect. A soldier always went into battle in all his colorful glory. Now their Colonel was telling them, "You will hide yourselves in cloth that is the color of the forest, and you will not be such good targets if they have guns." It was an artifice they had never heard of, and could only marvel at.

They saw two ranks of seven or eight men each, moving from the trail and advancing into the compound itself, the first rank firing and falling back to reload in a very orderly manner, as the second rank advanced to take their places.

Yes, they were soldiers then . . . or perhaps skilled brigands, trained like soldiers?

Clifford was worrying about it and a screaming slave was charging forward, machete raised high, One of the riflemen fired at him pointblank, and

288

when he fell to the ground, two others moved in and drove their ring-bayonettes repeatedly into his body. They were little more than fifty paces away, lit by flares and the flames of a hut that was burning now, and the screaming went on and on intolerably. Mercy had closed her eyes and buried her face in Clifford's shoulder, trying to drive the terrible sight and sound away. Clifford whispered, "No we have changed one vile enemy for another . . ."

They waited. The lines of men moved on and were lost to them, dim shadows now on the far side of the compound, and in the silence that followed, they saw the shadow of a huge man, crawling painfully across the ground before them. They saw him stagger to his feet, and move on a few paces before falling again. He was clutching at his stomach with one good arm and Clifford whispered, "Theophilus!"

They stared at him for a moment from their safe hideout, listening to the sound of richocheting bullets that whined through the camp and to the sound of shouted orders in Spanish. Clifford touched her briefly on the shoulder and said, "Wait here."

"No, Clifford, no . . ."

"He's hurt badly, I must help him. Wait here . . ."

He was gone, bent low and running toward the wounded Negro. When he reached him, he threw an arm around his shoulder and pulled him down to the ground. Theophilus said weakly, "*Inglese* . . . where your . . . your witch-woman?"

Clifford began to drag him toward the cave, but the huge Negro shook off his hold and found his feet again. He began stumbling toward the forest. Clifford stumbled after him, caught him by the arm, and said, whispering savagely, "No, this way, a cave . . . there may be more of them out there, you must hide . . ." He clutched at him and Theophilus, his eyes glazed and almost sightless, shook him off and ran on. He fell onto the forest floor close by the trail and lay there, thrashing his huge body around in agony.

Clifford bent over him and a bullet caught him in the side with a sudden, sharp, unbearable pain. He spun around and fell to the ground, trying to staunch the blood that flowed from his chest. Dizziness swept over him and he thought, "Mercy, oh Mercy . . ." Then he lost consciousness completely. His last conscious thought was that Theophilus was driving a furious fist repeatedly into his face and screaming at him, "She lie to me, your witch-woman . . .", then was staggering off into the forest, a man dying on his feet and kept alive only by the formidable power of his will.

The roar of the waterfall seemed to be shattering his eardrums. There was a fierce and terrifying pain in his side, just above the waist. Worse, there was a tight constriction at his throat, a heavy weight grinding into it and stifling his breath. He opened his eyes, looked up, and saw an evil face leering down into his. He thought for a moment of insanity: But . . . that is Jake Ollie, Bo'sun of the *Capricorn*; we are a thousand miles away now, why is he holding his boot at my throat?

Unconsciousness came again and in it he heard distant voices fading in and out of the pounding purgatory of his awareness. They faded away, came again, multiplied a thousandfold, and faded into oblivion again.

". . . Georgia," a voice said, "the coast of Georgia, that's where the winds should've taken them. Or Carolina, maybe . . ."

"Florida, the stream should have carried him there . . ."

"Mebbe. But they were in the Sargasso, it should have swallowed them up, the way it nearly did us."

"The Sargasso . . ."

". . . and a lug sail, he couldn't have got this far . . ."

He felt the sudden pain of a heavy boot in his groin and heard a coarse laugh. The void was there again, and when it had partly gone, sweeping down on him and coming back, with all the exploding stars, ". . . aye, they were late."

". . . and he got away. I got ten men looking for him . . ."

". . . an if they don't, Jake Ollie . . ."

Was it Ollie then?

And why was the topgallant flapping so miserably? Clifford mumbled, "Dred? Dred Manners? She's losing the wind up there . . ."

He could not understand why his words sounded so remote and far away. The strange, disembodied voices came to him again out of the oblivion.

Why could he not move his arms?

". . . a bullet on him? Just a waste, Ollie . . ."

". . . more than a couple of hundred feet down there . . ."

"Jesus, he's heavy . . ."

He opened his eyes and saw Jake Ollie's round

and bearded face close to his. He was being cradled in his arms like a baby, and the sound of the waterfall was tremendous now, searing its way into his mind. How long since he had been hit? Where were they taking him? Where was Mercy? Was she in the dinghy still, or down there under the waves, slowly drowning?

And suddenly, in a moment of acute consciousness, he felt himself being hurled bodily into space, and there was nothing around him but free air, and he was tumbling, tumbling, tumbling . . .

There was wind rushing at him everywhere and he thought desperately: The topgallant will need another reef . . . *Dred, where are you? The To'gallant!*

The water hit him with a blow that drove every iota of breath from his shattered body and he felt himself being turned over and over and over by the force of unexpected water. There was no taste of salt to it at all . . .

He tried to flail his arms and could not move them, and he could not make up his mind whether he were still truly alive or if this, perhaps, was some delirium of an afterdeath he knew nothing of. He felt himself crash into a rock, driven against it by the power of the water. As he clutched at it he felt his hands slipping and the water took him again, turning him over and over. His leg was tangled in a branch, but the branch was being swept along at speed too, the fallen limb of a mighty tree. He threw his arms over it and let it carry him, as he began to lose consciousness again, to wherever the force of the mountain river might take him. The only thought in his mind now was of Mercy.

And then, there was nothing but the darkness of oblivion all around him. The river swept his unconscious body along with its powerful, surging current.

CHAPTER FOURTEEN

The troops had marched twice through the confines of the camp, shooting and stabbing as they moved with a cold, mechanical precision. A handful of them had returned now to the trail where the tall tree was. They stood there waiting, talking together quietly. One of them had a wounded comrade slung over his shoulder like a sack of coals.

Flames were leaping up all around the camp now as they fired the pathetic huts. Mercy heard orders shouted and there was still the sound of screaming, dying now as the sounds were abruptly cut off one by one. She felt great fear, both for herself and for Clifford. She had seen him stumble off after Theophilus and then the forest had swallowed him up in its shadows. She could only pray that he too was hidden there somewhere....

For a short while, when he did not come to her,

she wondered if she should, after all, disclose herself to the intruders and ask for their help. But the memory of those cruel faces as they had driven their bayonettes into the wounded slave was enough to hold her in check. So she lay there, silent and motionless, holding herself pressed into the furthest wall of the tiny aperture.

There was the sound of shouted orders again and the men who stood by the trail ran back into camp. In a moment she heard, quite clearly, a shouted roll call as they answered their names. She heard them marching off, on the other side of the enclosure, a strange shuffling sound to their pounding feet on the leaves of the forest floor. It died away and she lay still for a long, long time till there was almost no sound at all save the crackling of the flames, a frighteningly terminal sort of sound. She came out from her cover cautiously and stood silently in the shadows for a while, then moved cautiously back into the camp.

She trembled violently at what she saw there, unable to control her emotions. Once, she had seen a dead man, his lifeless eyes staring into hers as she lay on a London street under the boots of the fleeing Chartists. But there were untold numbers of them, there, lying still where they had fallen. She saw a burning timber lying across the body of a child and steeled herself to drag him away, but he too was dead. She could not believe the scope of the tragedy and the tears were streaming down her face.

A shadow was moving, close beside her. Gasping she swung round to face it. It was the old witch-woman, hobbling on a stick, her pale eyes seeming paler than ever. The two women stood there facing each other and Mercy said at last, shaking: "My man . . . where is my man?"

She could remember none of her few words of Spanish and she repeated desperately, "My man . . . *Inglese? Inglese?*"

The old woman did not answer. She reached out a bony hand, clutching, and took Mercy's wrist in a strong grip. She pulled her away and they went together across the camp to the trail, till they heard the roaring sound of falling water and still they stumbled on. When they came to the brink of the fall, the old woman let go of her wrist and pointed, speaking in her own language. Mercy said hopelessly, "I don't . . . no . . . *no comprendo* . . . where? Where?"

The old woman held out her arms as though cradling a baby, swinging it to and fro for a moment, then making a motion of hurling it over the fall. She pointed again to the rushing water and Mercy gasped. "Down there?"

The bony hand was tight on her wrist again, dragging Mercy to the very edge of the precipice, and now the old woman said, somehow making it sound like a mockery, *"El Ingles esta alli . . . Alli!"*

Suddenly she was laughing, a high-pitched, frightening, maniacal laugh. She turned abruptly and hobbled off. When she paused and looked back she was still laughing, her eyes wild and staring now, the laugh becoming a scream of torment. And then, she disappeared, almost as though she had walked into the flames and been devoured by them.

Mercy looked fearfully down over the edge of the cliff. The waterfall was more than fifty feet across and pounding down to the depths for perhaps as much as two hundred feet, great clouds of mist rising from the bottom and obscuring the pool she knew would be there. She wondered how, in the darkness, she could find her way down there. One of the most terrifying experiences of her life was about to begin. . . .

She was certain that in the light of day she would never have found the courage. There was a great tangle of bushes, creepers, the roots and branches of long-fallen trees, with twisted vines woven among them, and great jagged slabs of granite everywhere. She lowered herself fearfully over the edge, easing her way carefully through the dense, wet vegetation. A vine she was clutching came out of the mud, and she fell and rolled for more than a hundred feet before she found herself wedged, at the edge of a frightening drop, under the trunk of a fallen conifer. The rough bark of it tore at her flesh.

She lay there for a moment, recovering from her fright, and found a ledge that led to one side, closer to the waterfall. She followed it warily till she was close beside it, and clambered down over shining rocks for more than half an hour, the sound of the falls drumming painfully in her ears. She found she could go no further and crawled back onto the wet land again, sliding on her behind in the mud, grasping the vegetation all around her to slow down her progress.

She found a great tunnel under the pounding water itself and crossed on slabs of rock over to the other side. It was an eerie feeling, as though she were cut off from the rest of the world by a great wall of rushing water that roared mightily and sent up a powerful spray to drench her. There was blood pumping out of a cut in her arm, so she tore

298

a piece of cloth from the hem of her blouse and bound it to staunch the flow. She reached the opposite bank and found a narrow path there, leading steeply down. She ran on down it, fast, falling in the darkness and dragging herself to her feet again.

When at last she reached the bottom, she stood by the huge pool and stared at it in dismay. The deep water was swirling savagely in a great whirlpool, rushing off in two separate branches into a jungle so black that she could see no more than a few paces anywhere.

At first, it was all so silent and oppressive that she was afraid even to whisper. Then she raised her voice and called out loudly, "Clifford? Clifford?"

The answering silence was a mockery. A great bird fluttered in the foliage beside her and she gasped as it flew out with a raucous, cackling sound. She shouted again, and again, cupping her hands to her mouth and listening to the sound of her own voice, over the roar of the falls, bouncing back at her from the rock wall.

She moved off slowly along the bank and picked up the narrow trail once more. She stumbled on along it, knowing there was almost no chance at all that she would ever find him, but thinking of him lying there and waiting for her to come to his help. The thought of it drove her on.

The path came to the water's edge in deep black mud, to a crossing that seemed to have been built up by human hands, with logs and branches and tree stumps wedged in to make a sort of dam. There was even a rope there to assist in the crossing.

A slave trail? A track made by the soldiers who had attacked the camp? A path for whatever denizens of the jungle might be silently moving around here? She could not even guess. She took hold of the rope and moved carefully over, in kneedeep water that swirled blackly about her legs.

A long, low reptile moved out from the bank, thrashing at the water with its enormous tail. She screamed and ran on, collapsing once and forcing herself to her feet again to find the bank, stumbling up it and falling to the ground again. She was scarcely conscious of the passage of time, nor of how far she had come, nor even precisely why. She knew only that she had found a path and had followed it, that perhaps Clifford—if he was still alive, if he was truly down here somewhere, if, if, if, and God help us both now!—might have done the same.

But why should he? Was he dead? Was he lying alone deep in the hidden recesses of the forest, bleeding to death, perhaps? It was a blind unreasoning that drove her on and nothing else. The path ran close to the river's edge now, and the water was clean and rushing fast. She thought: *He will have been carried this way on it.* And the thought gave her courage.

There was a sound in the bushes ahead of her, a sound that was like the fearsome grunting of some strange animal. She stared into the darkness and saw a dark shadow there, no more than twenty feet away from her. It was moving, a great animal of some sort lumbering slowly out from the cover of a black mass of vines. She froze, unable to move. Her throat was dry. A bear? A lion? What kind of savage wild beasts did they have here in this strange land?

Her hand was at her throat and she began to back off, then the shadow rose up unsteadily and a harsh voice said, "You!" She stumbled and fell to the ground. The shadow seemed to be towering over her suddenly, the white eyes staring down at her.

It was the giant Theophilus. He was swaying on his wide-spread feet, his one arm clutching at his side. He said again, his voice thick and heavy with pain, "You . . . *Inglese* witch-woman . . ."

She saw him fall and heard his moaning. He was propping his upper body against the trunk of a tree and staring at her, his breathing terribly labored.

She whispered, "Theophilus . . ."

Was he an enemy? Or was he not? "*Your friend,*" he had said, "*never forget that . . .*"

She said hoarsely, "I saw them kill your people, a hundred of your people, more . . ."

He could scarcely speak. "Yes . . . they kill them all, Spanish soldiers . . ." There was a dry, rattling sound in his throat.

She said: "Clifford . . . please, where is he?" He did not answer and she said again, urgently, "Clifford, my man, my husband . . . he went to help you."

His head was rolling from side to side. "Help me? No, nobody help me . . . only . . . only Theophilus help me." He lifted up his head and took in a great gulp of air. Lumbering to his feet again, he stood above her, his eyes on fire. He said, almost shouting now, "Juan Theophilus, the Leader, he help me only!"

"Please," she whispered. "If you know . . . where he is?"

He was almost himself again, a dead man kept alive only by an invincible strength of will. She could see blood on his mouth now and on his chest

301

where the blue shirt had been ripped open. He was driving himself to speak, almost dispassionately, his eyes beginning to glaze over.

He raised his hand and pointed it at her, saying slowly, haltingly, "You tell me . . . you say this a good day for me, you say I gonna win. The soldiers come . . . they kill my army . . . they kill me . . . they kill my brothers, my people. . . . You tell me, a good time you say . . . your movement a good time now . . . but no. I don' mind they kill me. But they kill my dream too, my dream. You lie to me, witch-woman. You tell me lie."

"No . . ." she whispered. "No . . ."

He seemed to be searching the dark ground with frenzied eyes and she could not imagine what it was he was looking for. Then, suddenly, he stopped and picked up a long, thin stick and struck at her savagely with it. She screamed as it slashed across her shoulders, falling over onto her back, and he began raining blows down on her in a paroxysm of rage.

He screamed again, "You lie to me!" and he struck her again and again, across her thighs, her stomach, her breasts. When she rolled over onto her back to avoid them, she could feel it tearing into her flesh. She could not control her screaming. Then he was falling to his knees, straddling her and turning her over. He dropped the stick and hit her savagely across the face, twice, knocking the breath out of her with the shock of it. The huge hand was ripping at her skirt and her underclothes, and she struggled and fought the arm that was across her body.

She knew that her loins were bare. In sudden, terrified shock she felt him drive into her with a

302

rending, searing pain that seemed to explode into her fragile body, a monstrous power that horrified her beyond all understanding. She was aware of a sudden, crushing weight on her chest as he collapsed on top of her, and then, she lost consciousness completely.

Mercy's intuition had been correct.

Clifford had indeed been carried this way by the force of the river. The turbulence of the pool spewed out into two distinct branches: the first a mighty river that went on to other falls, thundering down to the gorge that led between the mountains to the sea; and the other, a gentler stream that wound its way through a deep tunnel of overhanging foliage and fed a wide and spongy marsh that nestled there in its own little valley. It was here that the stream had brought him. Where the stream left the trees and entered the swamp itself, it had deposited him gently on a broad mud bank on which tall yellow reeds were growing.

Here a *cocodrillo* had crawled out of the swamp to investigate this new arrival in its domain, and had watched him a while, unblinking. It had even dragged its scaly body over the unconscious form; but satiated with a fat young boar it had recently taken, it had left him alone and returned to the marsh.

In a little while, a vagary of the swelling current had lifted him up once more and carried him to a wide and pleasant clearing of long grasses where the stream almost meandered along peacefully. There was a huge silk-cotton tree there, towering more than a hundred and fifty feet high. To one side of it there were cedars, dark against a lightening sky, and tamarinds, mangoes, and wild lemon trees.

The water was lapping at his legs, and there was a searing pain in his side. In a moment of consciousness, he dragged himself further up the bank with infinite slowness, a single thought driving him, to find the cave where he had left Mercy, knowing that she would be frightened if he were away too long. He could not understand why the water was there. Had there been a stream running through the camp? And where were the soldiers? And yes, where was the giant Negro who had been their captor . . . what was his name?

The clarity was coming back and he thought with sudden shock of Bo'sun Ollie, hauling him to his feet and lifting him bodily in his arms as though he were nothing more than a small child. The sound of the water came to him again. Where had it gone now?

Bo'sun Ollie?

No, he knew it could not be. He wondered if the terrible pains in his side and in his head were driving him out of his mind. He was trying to turn the dinghy right-side up, but where was Mercy? Was she in the water behind him? Was her life preserver safely tied around her? He found it was not the dinghy that he was struggling with, but the gnarled and twisted stump of a long-dead tree. He was battling it mightily, closing his eyes to drive away the fearful pain, and he heard himself calling weakly, *"Mercy . . . stay clear . . . I'll roll her over now . . ."*

He wedged his shoulder under the trunk, and kicked out with his legs against waves that were no longer there. The sudden pain seemed to split him in two. He found himself biting his lip to stifle the scream that came to his throat and there was the taste of blood there now. The heavy trunk rolled over with his effort and he rolled with it, up and over through the air, reaching out for Mercy to drag her aboard again....

The oblivion swept over him. When he opened his eyes again he was lying on his back in the grass, a great weight across his stomach. One leg was strangely twisted, over his head and caught in a branch, and he eased his hips around to free it. Lying still on his back for a while, he wondered how he had come to be under this massive treetrunk that was pinning him down so firmly and so painfully.

I left the cave, he was thinking, quite clearly now, and ran for a ... a hundred or so paces, was it? And Theophilus was there ... and he was badly hurt ... yes, and that is why I left the cave, to help him. He was thrashing around on the ground and he was dying, I'm sure of it ... no, he ran again. He ran further before he fell ... and I was helping him to his feet ... two, perhaps three hundred paces then. And if I can crawl back to the cave ... she will be waiting for me, wondering why I did not come back to her at once, and how long is it now? Ten minutes, perhaps? Or fifteen? Then why is there that gray light in the sky? The east? No, it cannot be the east ... and there was the sound of, what was it, a waterfall? And why was Bo'sun Ollie at the cave? I was fighting with him and we fell from the lifeboat onto the deck. Mistress Mercy was screaming ... and the other man, who was it, the Mate? What was his name? Two hundred paces then, back along the trail, and I can crawl on my belly, and if the soldiers are still there, as they must be, and whose soldiers are they? What are they doing there? They were using their bayonettes on wounded men, and if they find the cave . . . No, I must hurry back. But first I must turn the dinghy over. He made a mighty effort to shift the huge trunk, and the pain exploded inside him. He screamed "Mercy!" at the top of his voice as he rolled over with it, his legs flailing helplessly as he lay across it. Then, mercifully, oblivion drove him into its black and peaceful void.

Mercy was conscious only, at first, of a fearsome weight on her chest that was crushing her ribs and making it hard for her to breathe. There was a terrible stench in her nostrils and an icy coldness between her thighs that both puzzled and frightened her. In a gasp of sudden realization she screamed and twisted herself around, pushing out strongly with both hands, seizing the massive shoulders and forcing them away from her in sudden violence. The body was cold to her touch and she could not stop her screaming as she felt, rather than saw, that Theophilus was dead.

She bit her lip and cut off the screaming as the horror of it came upon her. She lay there for a moment shuddering uncontrollably. She heard herself whimpering, *dear God, dear God* . . . and she eased herself out from under him, pulling herself free and knowing that she was going to vomit. She choked as she rolled away, took a hold on herself and tried to stop the trembling that convulsed her. She lay on her side in the wet humus and drew her knees up to her chin. She tried to pull the torn skirt around her. She wept uncontrollably, thinking her heart must be bursting, and turned onto her back,

306

gasping and staring blindly up at the treetops, try-ing to force away the nausea of it.

In a little while she got to her feet and leaned into a tree. She let her mind go blank, deliberately pulling down a veil over what had happened. But she could not so easily hide it, and she walked steadily to the edge of the river. She stood there looking down into its dark and swirling water.

The roar of the falls was muted now, a dull, in-sistent sound, almost mesmerizing, and there were early morning rays of the sun streaming down through the foliage, with butterflies dancing in them, very beautifully, a tiny ballet.

She sat down on the bank, then stretched herself out on her stomach and drew herself closer to the water, watching the little swirling pools and their strange, elusive patterns.

How easy a thing it is! she was thinking.

She thought of Clifford and knew that she did not want to die; yet, what was there left for her now?

She trailed a hand in the water. It was icy cold, colder than the dead body back there. She watched the turbulence of the water about her fingers. A cream-colored flower was trailing there on a flat green leaf and she plucked it from the water and stared at it, counting the velvet petals, twelve of them. Each had a pretty reddish-brown at its cen-ter, where long purple stamens were sprouting. In-finitesimal cups on slender stalks, they were dusted with a bright powder that came off on her fingertip when she touched them. A huge frog was sitting on a flat wet rock, very close to her face, staring at her, the lower part of its throat heaving. As she watched, it leaped suddenly, its legs spreadeagled,

307

and landed with a plop in the water and disappeared.

She thought: *A few deep breaths, and it will all be over . . . Have I the courage? And Clifford? If he still lives? . . .*

There was another sound coming to her ears over the thunder of the falls. She was not alarmed anymore.

Scarcely caring to look, knowing that nothing more could possibly befall her (and if it did, no matter now) she merely eased herself round and looked casually over her shoulder. Two men were breaking out of the forest where the track was. They were soldiers, dressed in red and green uniforms with tall peaked caps of black leather, and carrying their rifles slung over their shoulders. They pulled up and stared at her as she got to her feet slowly, not caring what might happen now.

One of them looked back and called "*Señor Capitano!*" A moment later a tall, distinguished-looking man was there, parting the foliage with a sword. He, too, stared at her in considerable surprise, saying sharply, "*Mas . . . que haces aqui? Da donde vienes? Quien eres?*

She shook her head and he peered at her, puzzled. He said in English, "But . . . you are not a Peninsular girl, I think? American, no?"

She said listlessly, "I am English, if it matters."

"English?" His eyes were sweeping over her, seeking to understand what she might be doing here. He raised his hand in a slow and uncertain salute. "Would you tell me, Mistress, who are you? How you came to be here?" His English was good, the slightest trace of an accent here and there.

She said again, "Does it matter? I was in the

308

camp . . . I saw your soldiers killing the slaves . . ." Even the memory of it sickened her, and she felt she was close to collapse.

"My soldiers?" he asked, puzzled. "*My* soldiers? I think not, Mistress."

He gave a sharp order in Spanish to one of the men, who saluted smartly and hurried off into the forest. The other soldier was staring at the body of Theophilus, half-hidden by the shrubbery, a ray of sunlight that seemed somehow mystical striking it now. He moved to it and turned it over, made a sudden exclamation, and said sharply, "Capitano!"

The Captain moved to them and looked down at the black giant for a moment, then back to Mercy as the soldier rolled it face down again. He said sharply, "And this man, Mistress?"

She could scarcely hear her own voice. "A slave . . . a leader of the slaves . . ."

"And a friend?"

She could hardly summon the energy to answer him; there was a terrible sickness on her, a weakening of her legs, and she felt that she was falling. As she collapsed to the ground he was suddenly beside her, supporting her.

"No . . . not a friend," she whispered. "He . . . he . . . oh God, dear God . . ."

She was sobbing uncontrollably, and through her tears she saw that a dozen or more other soldiers had disclosed themselves from the forest. One of them, a grizzled sergeant, was unbuckling his canteen and handing it to the Captain. The Captain held it to her lips and said, "Here, drink this, you will feel better."

It was a strong and heavy wine, and as she drank, the Captain said gently, "I am Captain Cordoba, *señorita*, in the service of Her Gracious Majesty Queen Isabella of Spain and the Spanish Dominions. I will not ask you now how this came about . . . what happened with this . . . this dead slave. Perhaps, when you feel stronger, we will speak of that too. But now I ask you only what is both urgent and important. The soldiers you spoke of. Where are they?"

The wine was warming her, bringing her a kind of hope. "You are not . . . they are not your soldiers?"

"No, *señorita*. They are renegade troops of a man who has turned traitor to his country and to his Queen. And I am on my way to Santiago to arrest that man and to bring him to justice. If you can tell me where they are, perhaps even how many of them?"

"How many? I do not know. Even where, I am no longer sure. A long way from here, a long time ago . . . Last night, I think. Yes, last night. A camp above the waterfall . . ."

"How many, *señorita?*" he asked, insisting. "How many did you see? How were they armed? Forgive me that I must question you at such a time, but . . . perhaps all our lives depend on your answers."

She took a long, deep breath. She was slowly coming back to reality, aware that this quiet and courteous man was not an enemy. She said, "I saw, perhaps, about twenty men? I heard . . . I think, more than that. They killed all the slaves in the camp and then they marched off in the other direction, away from here. And I am not even sure that they were soldiers."

He was frowning. "Not soldiers? But their uniforms, *señorita?*"

310

"No . . . they were wearing . . . sacks, almost like robes."

"But boots?"

"Yes, I think boots."

"And trousers?"

"Yes."

"And caps on their heads?"

"No caps."

"But carrying rifles?"

"Yes. It was not easy to see them, their clothes seemed . . . almost invisible against the forest."

"And that, no doubt, is why they were dressed like that. I find this very helpful, Mistress."

"I have a friend . . . no, my husband . . ." She was in tears again. "He was with me, but he disappeared and I learned . . . I learned that . . . I don't know, I don't know whether he is alive . . . or dead . . ."

He gestured helplessly. "We have seen no Englishman, Mistress. I will send men to find the camp, and perhaps. . . . We will see."

"Oh please . . ."

"But first I will take you to our wagontrain, and I will put you in the care of . . . of a woman who will look after you. And then . . . then, we will see."

He was helping her to her feet. "Can you walk? It is not far, but if you cannot, then I will have the men prepare a litter for you."

"You are very kind. No, Captain, I can walk."

"And your name, Mistress?"

"I am Mercy . . . Hawkes. My husband is Clifford Hawkes, a ship's officer."

"We will try to find him for you, Ma'am. If you will excuse me for a few small moments?"

311

He spoke to the Sergeant rapidly in Spanish, and turned back to her, smiling. "We can go now, if you are ready, Ma'am."

The Sergeant was gathering some of the others about him, sending them off into the forest, and the Captain said, smiling, "The question of the other soldiers. We are not strong, but against twenty or thirty mercenaries, yes, we can defend ourselves. If they should be nearby, I wish to know, and I am sending out scouts. They will also look for signs of your husband. This is a very large forest, Ma'am, but . . . who knows? Perhaps fortune is on our side." He sighed. "In truth, we need her."

She walked with him for a little way along the track and she heard the sound of the soldiers on the flanks cutting their way through the heavy undergrowth with their swords. When she fell once (or would have fallen, but for his support), he said courteously, "Then by your leave, Ma'am," and picked her up in his arms and carried her.

She objected faintly, but he would not listen to her. He said, a smile on his handsome, aristocratic face, "Soon, *señora*, you can rest, and sleep, and perhaps even forget the troubles that plague you. We have made camp for a few days and when we move on, you will ride in a wagon and be comfortable and secure. Meanwhile, I will carry you."

She fought against sleep for a little while, but it came over her at last. When she opened her eyes again, faintly ashamed of her weakness, the Captain was setting her gently on her feet.

They were in a wide clearing in the forest, a place of gently undulating grasses with a huge banyan tree in its center. There were some wagons drawn up there, a dozen or more tents pitched under smaller trees, a long line of mules tethered to three horizontal poles. More than a hundred soldiers were moving around, seated on logs and cleaning their weapons, polishing their leather, crouched over small fires and cooking their food. There were two young women walking through the camp, dressed in extravagant clothes, and engaged in earnest conversation together. Mercy wondered what they could be doing here.

The Captain led her to a tent, somewhat larger than the others, outside which a table had been set up, a single canvas chair by it. An orderly was already running in with a second chair and placing it there. The Captain indicated it and said, "Please, Ma'am . . . if you would be seated?"

They sat down and he took off his gold-braided cap and set it down, ruffled his long hair with his fingertips, and looked at her. He said courteously, "Now that you can feel safe, Ma'am, can you tell me more of the recent events you have experienced? If it would not pain you to do so? But first . . . are you hungry? Our food, I fear, is simple soldiers' fare, but perhaps . . ."

She shook her head. "No, I thank you, sir . . ."

"Some maté, perhaps?"

"Maté?"

"Paraguayan tea. It is good for the stomach, if you forgive the indelicacy, Ma'am. It also calms the nerves."

"Then maybe a little, sir. You are very kind."

He gave an order to the waiting servant and said, "You saw, you told me, some thirty soldiers. Can you tell me about their weapons?"

"They carried guns, Captain. Rifles, I think, though I cannot be sure."

313

"Were they, would you say, well disciplined?"

"If disciplined means restrained . . . no, they were not."

"Efficient?"

"I cannot tell, sir."

"No cannon, I presume?"

"I saw none, sir."

"Swords?"

"Not exactly swords, I think," she said hesitantly. "But . . . long knives of a kind I think are called . . . *machetes*?

"Machetes, then. And their commander? A Spaniard? A Frenchman?"

"I do not know, sir."

"And no more than twenty or thirty of them?"

"I saw no more than that number."

"Well . . . my scouts will find the tracks they made. And I think we must find you some new clothes, Ma'am."

There had been no change to his tone at all and when the orderly came with the steaming drink in two silver-mounted gourds, with thin reeds in them also decorated with silver strainers, he gave him an order and turned back to Mercy.

"There is a woman here," he said carefully. "I am tempted to use the word *lady*, in spite of her profession." He was fidgeting awkwardly, unsure of himself now.

He stood up abruptly and began pacing to and fro, gesticulating broadly. "Please try to understand, with sympathy if you can find it in your heart . . . We have marched and driven our wagons all the way from Havana, on an expedition that may last three, four months, perhaps even more. My troops are the best in the Spanish Possessions,

314

and they are granted, on occasion, the services . . ."

He would not meet her eye. He went on quietly, "They are allowed the services of women, whom we carry with us. Forgive me that I speak so frankly, but I too am a soldier. Perhaps I have lost the delicacies of polite conversation. These women, six in all, are under the care of a seventh, whose name is Estrellita. Estrellita, in spite of her profession, is . . . yes, a lady of great quality, and indeed of education, to whom every man in this camp, from myself down to the humblest soldier-orderly, is deeply devoted."

He was groping for the words now. He said, embarrassed, "It may perhaps be hard for an English lady of quality to understand the . . . the needs of soldiery. There is a small camp of Creole women who follow us as we march, our camp-followers. I do not allow my officers and my warrant-officers to visit them, a question . . . how shall I put it? Too much rum quickly loosens a soldier's tongue, and I am not anxious for those in authority . . . for those who know what might be called the secrets of a military expedition, to be put in close contact with people whose loyalty is most certainly not to us. Therefore, it seems incumbent upon me to provide the higher ranks with . . . with equivalent comforts. And to maintain adequate decorum, I have placed those . . . comforts in the care of a knowledgeable woman who . . . who . . ." He broke off, gesturing wildly, and said at last, "It is not easy to speak of those things to a lady, Ma'am."

"Do not concern yourself on my account, Captain," Mercy said. "I am at least aware of the needs that must . . . please, speak as freely as you wish."

"Very well, Ma'am, with your permission. Estrel-

315

lita was once the madam of a brothel in Havana. She is a woman of fine character. She speaks Spanish, French and English with equal fluency, and she is . . . yes, indeed, a *lady*." He was smiling gently, and he went on, "I make the point, and belabor it perhaps, because I want you to be assured that even in a wagontrain of a hundred and seventy-five rude soldiers, I would never hand you over to the care of the woman in charge of our . . . our young ladies . . . unless I had the greatest confidence in her. The greatest possible confidence."

"I know, sir," Mercy said, "that you are concerned for my well-being. And I thank you for it."

"Good. She will find new clothes for you, of which, it seems to me, you are sorely in need."

"I am indeed."

"She will see to your food and your bed, since I myself, unhappily, will be greatly concerned with more prosaic matters."

"I am grateful to you, Captain."

"And let me assure you," he said earnestly, "that though you will be in the company of . . . of *women*, you yourself will be regarded as a *lady*. I will see to it that no embarrassment will come your way, none whatsoever. You had best stay with us till we reach Santiago, in a few weeks' time. Then, according to your desires, I can have you taken to Havana, the only place in Cuba these days that is safe. And if we are fortunate enough," he added gravely, "to find your husband . . . then I will see that he goes with you."

Dear Clifford! Where was he now? Was he searching for her in the forest? Had he given her up for dead? She refused to admit to herself the possibility that he had perished.

316

"Meanwhile, dear lady, be assured that . . ." He broke off, a delighted smile on his face. A woman in a gorgeous gown of deep blue taffeta was approaching them, the orderly by her side.

And she was the most startlingly beautiful woman Mercy had ever seen.

The gown was partly covered by a silver redingote, cut away at the front as was the fashion, to display the tightly fitting, very high corsage with a single *bouillon* around it (displaying remarkably fine, upstanding breasts). Plain sleeves swelled out at the shoulders to a fullness at the wrists. The full skirt was widely flared and decorated with flowers and ribbons. Her jet-black hair was falling to her very white shoulders in ringlets, set off with small slips of tight ribbon.

But it was her eyes that caught Mercy's attention. They were very, very dark and huge, perhaps the slightest bit slanted with a strange and disconcertingly distant look in them, as though they were not quite sure what to fasten their interest on. Her nose was fine and delicate, her lips full and well-curved, her white skin flawless. She held herself straight and very proudly, the shoulders back, the fine white bosom outthrust. She carried a fan of bone engraved with a floral design and small operatic figures posing, a printed score of music around its edges—a work of exquisite design and execution. Mercy thought of the Captain's phrase: *"A lady, in spite of her profession . . ."*

Her hand was out and Mercy took it and waited, until the Captain said easily, "My dearest Estrellita . . . may I present Madam Mercy Hawkes, from England, whom I am placing in your care. She has lost her husband, she herself has been sorely abused,

317

and she needs the comfort that I know you will give her."

Estrellita said, her voice soft and low and very melodious, "Señora Hawkes. Welcome to an abode that you may find a little primitive. I will do my best to see that you are comfortable here." She turned to the Captain. "And will she be with us long, Juan?"

It seemed to Mercy that she was not looking directly at him, but a little over his shoulder. She followed the look and saw three young ladies standing there, a little way off, watching them and giggling together.

"As far as Santiago," the Captain said. "After that . . . who knows? Meanwhile, I would like her to ride in your wagon, where she will, I am sure, be safe."

"Of course."

"And you could find her some clothing, don't you think? Hers is a little the worse for wear, I fear."

"Yes, a very simple matter. Your favorite color, Madam?"

Mercy grimaced. Those wonderfully expressive eyes! They were cast down, as though not wanting to meet hers.

"I am not as well versed in fashion as I might be," she said. "But, if I could borrow something to replace this torn skirt and blouse. Really, anything will do, anything at all."

"Anything at all will *never* do!" Estrellita said emphatically. "You are very young, I think. So . . . bright colors, perhaps. A woman has so few years of youth and she must make the most of them while they last. They are soon, soon gone."

318

"Yes, yes . . . I am almost twenty-two years old now."

"And as slender as a twenty-two-year-old girl should be."

She put out a hand and touched Mercy on the shoulder. The hand slid down to her breast and followed its contour, and on to the waist and even down to the hip, just touching lightly and moving on again. Startled, Mercy caught her breath; the hand stopped its movement instantly.

Estrellita said quietly, "He did not tell you, my dear Captain? He did not tell you?"

Captain Cordoba turned away. "No," he said. "I did not."

Mercy said, faltering, the realization coming over her with a sense of shock: "Tell me *what*, Madame Estrellita?"

She answered quietly, and with infinite sadness. "I am blind, dear child. Quite blind."

The hand was suddenly at her eyes, touching her cheek so softly that it was like the kiss of a butterfly. "No," she said, "there is no need for tears. I have long since become resigned to it."

The delicate hand continued its vision again and she murmured, "Yes, very slender. I have a girl named Francesca who is your size exactly. And she has a splendid wardrobe."

Mercy reached out and touched her. "No," she whispered. "I did not know."

Estrellita turned to the Captain. "If you have finished with her, Juan?"

"Yes, Estrellita, for the time being."

"Then I will take her to my wagon and I will call Francesca. We will see what we can find for her. Shall we see you again soon?"

319

He was smiling at Mercy, aware of the distressed, quite uncomprehending look in her eyes. He said, "Let us all have dinner tonight, the three of us, what do you say?"

Estrellita inclined her head. "Dinner it is, then. If you will excuse us now?"

He took Mercy's hand and kissed it. He said gravely, "At nine o'clock, Ma'am. And by then my scouts will have returned. Perhaps we will have news of your husband. Pray God we have news of him."

Estrellita took Mercy's arm. She said, "Come, I will show you the way. The ground is very broken here, you must watch where you place your feet. But have no fear, I will guide you."

As they moved off together, Mercy stole a look at Estrellita's proud and lovely face. She could not believe that a woman could be so sorely afflicted, yet still be so serenely beautiful.

CHAPTER FIFTEEN

The two Creole girls were searching the river banks for foodstuffs to take back to their village—plantain, sago, okra, mangoes, bananas, paw-paws, pomegranates, avocadoes, or whatever else a bountiful Nature might provide them with. They had already come across a lush growth of sweet cassava, dense and nearly five feet high, and were pulling up the long fleshy roots and storing them in the burlap sacks they had brought with them.

They were twins and very beautiful, with huge, lustrous dark eyes and skin that was almost the color of the finest maté. Their bodies were very slender, narrow waisted, with firm, high bosoms and long jet-black hair that hung loosely over their shoulders and always seemed to tangle with the undergrowth as they used their machetes to carve themselves a way through it.

They wore simple shifts of printed cotton, which they had made for themselves in the few private hours their father, the wily keeper of the tavern in Sagua de Palmirito, allowed them. They were seventeen years old and this, for them, was always the best day of the week—Wednesday, the day they were invariably sent out to scour the jungle and replenish the tavern's larder.

Wednesday was a day of delight for them, a time when the tavern floors could be left unscrubbed—their father did all the serving with the help of the bad-tempered crone who had been helping him ever since his wife died, eight years ago now—a day when they could wander at will through the richness of the forest, searching out its recondite pleasures, and forget their abject poverty.

Their names were Almira and Alvira—or, as their father called them, Vira and Mira.

He had named them himself, with a kind of perverse enthusiasm, when he had seen, even in their first few days of life, that they were truly identical. Even today, he could never tell one from the other. For their own part, they always took a malicious delight in confusing him. "No, Father," Alvira would say, "I am Almira . . ."

They had taken off their simple dresses and were swimming now in a gentle reach of the river, where its overhanging boughs were festooned with brilliant flowers. The sun was hot, the water cold, and one of them, Almira—or was it Alvira?—had draped her naked body over a slab of gray rock and was lowering her hand gently into the water. There was a long, fat, silver-speckled fish there, hovering. She moved her fingers to it carefully and began tickling its underside. Then, with a rapid

322

movement of her arm, she flipped it onto the bank, and called out happily, "A fine fat fish for supper tonight, I caught him . . ."

Her twin was crouched in shallow water close to the opposite bank, her fingers frozen in the act of entwining a yellow flower in her lovely black hair, and she was staring in a kind of startled surprise a little way down the river. There was no shock or fear there at all, but only a sudden, intense excitement. She said, bewildered, "*Un muerte*, a dead man . . ."

The other twin swam quickly across and stood with her sister for a few moments, watching, standing up to her waist in the water. Then the two of them moved together very slowly down to the flat patch of black mud where Clifford's silent body lay. The slime sucked at their legs as they forced a way through it and clung to their calves as they freed their limbs with slow, squelching sounds.

He lay on his back with his arms outflung and his head was held up in the fork of a dead and half-submerged branch for all the empty world of the jungle to see. His eyes were closed, his mouth open, and he was deathly still.

It was a strange sight for them, one which they could not fully comprehend. It was not their first brush with death. A dozen times or more in their young lives they had seen dead men lying on the tavern floor, the victims of knife-fights that seemed always to be breaking out on Saturday nights there. But this, by the looks of him, was no Creole. There was a whispered consultation between them.

"Are you sure he's dead?"

"He must be . . ." She touched the body and withdrew her hand quickly, "Cold . . ."

"Where did he come from? An American?"

"He must be . . ."

"But there aren't any Americans around here . . ."

"Yes there are, we had one the other night, you remember? The old man who asked all those questions?"

"He wasn't old, silly . . . what shall we do with him?"

"What do you mean, what shall we do with him? You want to carry him home and tell Papa: Look, we found a dead man?"

"No, I mean . . . look at those beautiful boots."

"Yes, and the shirt too. What's it made of?"

They were fingering the hairshirt, puzzling over the material.

"I don't know . . . it's not wool or cotton. I never saw anything like that before."

"Well, we'll take the boots and the shirt . . ."

She rolled the body over, and said suddenly, "A pouch! It must be full of gold coins!"

They opened the pouch up and found in it a fine clasp-knife and a length of rope, also a piece of rag in which, they were sure, something of great value must be wrapped. But it contained only a lock of brown hair tied with a short piece of cotton thread. Disappointed, they discarded it and one of them said philosophically, accepting the disappointment as the natural course of things, "Well, never mind. Here, help me with the boots."

They fumbled with the laces, trying to untangle the knots, and dragged the boots off and admired them. Almira said, "Pull his arms up, over his head. Yes, like that." They eased the shirt over his shoulders and Alvira said, "Look how white he is!"

"Yes, I know, all Americans are white. But you

324

know, without that awful beard . . . he must have been a very handsome young man."

"Yes, I think so. What about the trousers? That's very good canvas."

"We have to take everything, a pity to waste such fine clothes. We can wash them in the river and take them home to Papa. He'll be delighted."

"The drawers too? They're calico . . ."

"Yes, the drawers too, what does a dead man want with drawers? If he goes to Heaven, he'll look ridiculous wearing drawers and a halo and nothing else. And if he goes to . . . to the other place, they'll be burned up anyway."

They thought it was a hilarious idea and tried to stifle their laughter. At last one of them said, forcing herself to be serious, "Yes, We'll take the drawers too, they'll make fine sacks."

They stripped him quite naked and stood for a moment looking down at him and giggling. Almira said, "He was very large, wasn't he?"

"Almira! Please! You have to show respect for the dead."

"He was very large, that *is* respect . . ."

"I wonder if we should bury him, what do you think?"

"Whatever for?"

"Well, I don't know. A decent Christian burial?"

The other twin said, gesticulating, "How do we know he was a Christian? He might have been Protestant, all the *Americanos* are Protestant."

"Yes, that's true."

"And why should we bury a man we don't even know? It doesn't make any sense at all. Besides, we should be going home soon, or Papa will be very angry with us."

"Not when he sees the good things we're bringing him." She picked up one of the boots and examined it critically. "Look at that leather! It's beautiful! They must have cost a great deal of money."

"An American, they're all rich. Don't you remember the old man?"

"What old man?"

"The one who came the other night, silly, the one with the green coat and leather breeches. I saw the bag of coins he was carrying. It was so big! And they were *gold* coins! He must have had a hundred of them. What was his name?"

They had gathered the clothes together and were squelching off through the mud again, the body there quite forgotten.

"Amos," one of them said. "I remember it well. I asked him: 'How can a man be called Amos, it's not even a name.' "

"Yes, that's right, Amos."

They thought it was hysterically funny. They were still laughing when they reached the other bank and set about washing the hairshirt and the trousers and the drawers. They laid them out in the long grasses to dry, slipped into their dresses again, and wandered off, deeper in the forest, looking for wild okra now. They found very little of it, but they came across a splendid mango tree, and climbed into its high branches to pick as much of the fruit as they could carry, clambering expertly over the branches and dropping the fruit into their sacks. It was a game for them to see who could climb the highest. It was late in the afternoon before they realized that if they did not hurry now, it would be dark before they got back to the little village. Their father would be furious with them, in spite of the fine new clothes they had found for him.

They hurried back to get them and rolled them up. Putting them in the sacks, Almira said suddenly, "You know . . . we should have buried him. I'm sure of it."

Her sister shrugged. "Well, if it makes you feel better, perhaps we can drag him away from the water so that the *cocodrillos* won't eat him."

"Yes, I hate to think of that, he really was quite handsome. And all we have to do, really is cover him up with a few inches of soil. As you say, away from the river. No, I'd hate to think of the *cocodrillos* eating him, it's really not very nice."

"Then let's hurry, or Papa *will* be angry. All I want is another beating."

"It won't take long, a few minutes . . ."

They left the sacks there and hurried over to the water's edge. When they were halfway across Almira reached out and grabbed her sister's wrist and said, in sudden shock, "But . . . what happened?"

They stared at the twisted branch where he had been and the body was no longer there.

One of them whispered: "They took him already . . ."

"The *cocodrillos?* At this time of day? How could they?"

"So where is he?"

They stood there uncertainly for a moment, then waded slowly over, and stood in the slime, open-mouthed and staring. There were clearly visible signs there, a deep imprint in the mud where a body had been dragged.

"Somebody came? . . ." Almira whispered, and

Alvira shook her head. "There would be footprints, there are none."

"Then?"

"Yes, he wasn't dead. He dragged himself away, you can see clearly . . . look, here, here . . . he went into the forest there."

"He wasn't . . . wasn't dead?"

They found at last the imprint of naked feet in soft earth, then a deep impression and the mark of two hands where, it seemed, he had fallen.

One of them whispered hoarsely, "Shall we . . . shall we follow?"

The other shook her head vehemently. "Follow him? You're crazy! He might kill us. An *Americano*, you never know what they're going to do next."

"Then let's get away from here before he comes back!"

"Yes, let's do that."

They hurried back to the opposite bank again, slung their sacks over their shoulders, and walked quickly down the trail that led, eventually, to the village. In a little while they were both giggling uncontrollably, taken at the same moment with the same thought.

One of them said, laughing, "But he's naked!"

"I know! It's *funny*. . ."

"No boots, and no clothes at all. What will he do in the jungle?"

"Well, he can make himself a skirt, out of leaves, if he knows how."

She nearly collapsed with laughter as they hurried on. The sun was well over the tops of the trees and the twilight rapidly fading before they reached the village. They almost ran along its tiny mud street to the adobe shack that was the Tavern.

Their father was standing at the door, waiting for them, the four-foot swish he used for beating them already in his hand. But he relented when he saw the boots and the fine hairshirt they had brought him, and gave them each only a couple of cuts across their behinds.

"We have ten, twelve people here tonight," he growled. "You expect me to serve them all? And some ruffian stole three of my cups. First thing in the morning, get some over-ripe coconuts and make us some more, half a dozen of them."

They followed him inside and set about their chores.

It was a single room, quite large, with a door on one side that led to a tiny lean-to that was the kitchen. Another door facing it led to the storeroom where the kegs of rum were stored, together with the two casks of whitish, foaming beer that their father made from crushed maize fermented with crusts of underbaked bread.

There were three tables there, made from adze-hewn slabs of mahogany (which he had also cut himself in the forest), each with benches around it. There was a long counter of the same material along one wall on which the jugs were stored, together with all the tin plates, knives, and the drinking vessels—these last made from gourds, coconut shells, or tin.

The roof of the building was made from closely thatched coconut fronds. From its long palm-trunk rafters, strings of onions, red peppers and garlic were hanging, together with a dozen or so different kinds of sausage, made from hog blood, pork meat, onions, fennel and chili.

In spite of the poverty here, it was a warm and homely place with a big charcoal fire in one corner at which there would usually be a chicken or two turning on a spit, and sometimes a whole young porker, with a big iron trivet in front of it on which the bread was baked.

There were a dozen customers here tonight, men from the village itself who mostly cut *ocuje, granadillo, guayacan, yaya,* and other decorative woods from the forest, for transportation by mule and donkey on the long, long haul to Santiago, where the Spaniards paid high prices for them. A few of them grew tobacco and sold it locally. Two of them had been cattlefarmers, owning four or five cows each, from which their wives would make cheese for sale. But the last party of Spaniards to pass through here on one of their frequent scourings of the jungle for dissidents, had driven the cows off for their own use and now these two men had no further source of income. They would sit here each evening, staring glumly into space and hoping that some less unlucky fellow would offer them rum or at the very least a jug of beer to drown their misery in.

Almira was sweeping up the floor with a long rush broom, and Alvira went round filling cups for those who had money. Their father crouched by the fire with one of the boots in his hands, working the leather carefully to keep it soft while he dried it out.

The two girls were still giggling; they were thinking of the dead man, who had got up and walked away stark naked into a forest that stretched into the distant mountains for as far as their imaginations would take them.

Clifford could not understand what had happened.

Knowing nothing of the country, knowing only the tales he had heard of the New World, he could only imagine that some kind of jungle savage had taken all his clothes. But if so, then why had he not been killed? Or scalped?

He knew only that at every step he took, the jungle floor, soft though it seemed, was lacerating the soles of his feet. The wound in his side had stopped throbbing now and was no more than a dull, insistent pain that he could bear.

A bullet there somewhere? If so, it had to come out, he was sure, before the lead could spread its poison all over him. Had it done so already?

He found a moss-covered stump and sat down heavily on it, trying to assess his position, trying to decide what he should best do now.

And most of all, where was Mercy?

He touched the wound in his side delicately, his fingers probing. It was just below his ribcage, a small round hole no more than a finger's breadth across. But there was another, a larger one a little behind it, far more painful than the first. The flesh there was torn and jagged.

What had she done after he had left her in the cave?

Had the soldiers found her? He shuddered at the thought of it. Or would she have waited, securely hidden, till all apparent danger was past?

And there was the rub, *apparent* danger. They had come, it was obvious, to attack the camp, and

331

they would have reduced it, without any doubt, to rubble. And what then? Would they leave guards on it? Perhaps not. And so, in the course of time she would have left the shelter. . . .

But *how much* time? He stared up through the treetops at the moon, and knew that a whole day had gone by since the attack, knew too that there was only one thing left for him to do now.

He rested for a while, knowing that he would need all the strength he could muster for the arduous task that lay ahead of him. He found a thin dead branch that would serve as a stick to lean on. When it snapped under his weight he found another, larger and stronger, strong enough to serve as a weapon if need be.

Slowly, painfully, he hobbled along the bank of the river, back along the way it must have carried him. When he fell on his face in the long grasses there, he lay still for a while till his strength came back, and pushed on again, driving himself with the thought of her. Every time he fell, he rolled over onto his back and waited patiently for yet a little more strength. There was a kind of relief sweeping over him when he heard at long last, in the remote distance, the sound of the waterfall.

He plowed doggedly on, and the thunder of it was growing inexorably nearer. He lay down on his belly at the water's edge and drank deeply, rested again, looking up at the moon and learning from it that five, perhaps six hours had passed since he had started moving back.

The land began to rise and the undergrowth was thicker, but he found a trail and followed it, a wider trail in which he fancied he could make out, here and there, where there were patches of hard-caked mud, the ruts of wagonwheels. The path began twisting away after a few miles, in quite the wrong direction. He cursed and moved back into the forest and found the river's edge once more, the water swirling fast and furiously now.

The moon set and the darkness was almost absolute. There were thorn-branches tearing at his flesh. He stumbled into the shallow water and fought his way upstream. Cold now and throbbing all over with deep pain, he drove himself on doggedly toward the sound of the roaring.

Soon there was mist all around him and he saw a streak of pale light in the sky, low on the horizon, and knew that he had been stumbling on in a state of complete torpor, for how many hours now?

The water was getting deeper, and he moved to the bank and crawled along it on his hands and knees, using his stick to propel himself along.

And there it was at last, the fall, towering high above him, a monstrous height. He made a deliberate decision and lay down again. He let the sleep come over him, knowing that with a little rest would come the strength he would need now. When he awoke, the pale gray had turned to a brilliant crimson and he began the arduous ascent.

He pulled himself slowly up, hand over hand, grasping at roots, grasses, vines, bushes, anything that would support his weight. Three times he fell back, once slipping almost to the bottom again. Twice he stopped to rest, then drove himself fiercely on again. A steep overhang blocked his progress and he worked his way slowly round it. When the sun was almost overhead, he pulled himself painfully over the lip of the edge and onto the plateau.

In the daylight, it took on quite a different aspect, the density of the forest not as formidable as it had seemed during the night. He hobbled quickly along the narrow trail until he came to the cave, praying that she might, by some remarkable miracle, still be there.

He fell by the granite slab and crawled inside. He found there the scratchings in the damp sand they had made together, the imprint of her body where she had lain tight against the furthermost corner.

He crawled out again and stood listening to the silence for a while, then moved slowly, from tree to tree, from cover to cover, into the camp itself.

He was appalled by what he saw there. The charred remnants of the slaves' huts were mute testimony to the terrible things that had happened there, as fearful as the bodies that lay sprawled over the compound, the flies buzzing furiously about them now.

He walked from one side of the compound to the other, then twice around its perimeter, but could find no sign of any life at all. He stripped a dead man of a pair of canvas trousers, took a heavy woolen shirt from another and a pair of old but solid sandals from a third, found a sharp knife and a good machete and a broad leather belt with a scabbard for it. Only then, standing in the middle of the clearing and cupping his hands to his mouth, did he call, strongly, throwing the sound of his voice as far as he could,

"Mercy! Mercy! Mercy!"

The silence of the forest was a mockery to him.

He called again and again and again, a terrible

desperation overpowering him. There was no sound at all, except . . .

There was a stirring in the forest behind him, the sound of someone moving clumsily through the undergrowth, and he swung round, knowing that it could be no one else but his beloved Mercy. She was coming to him with her arms outstretched, seeking the comfort and the safety that only he could give her . . .

Instead, he saw a strange and almost ludicrous sight.

A man was coming out from among the trees—a thin and wiry sort of man, in his forties perhaps—dressed in a remarkable green coat of wool that came down below his knees and seemed to have pockets over every inch of its surface, with baggy leather breeches and high laced-up boots. He was leading a donkey, loaded down with a sack on each side of a rough wood-and-canvas saddle. His face was sharply aquiline, having a long thin nose and sunken cheekbones. He had heavy black eyebrows over dark intelligent eyes that seemed, just now, to be very wary indeed. He was clutching the donkey's halter in one hand and in the other he carried a cutlass with a very heavy handle, but it did not seem to be held threateningly.

He stopped a little ways off, and looked Clifford up and down, very carefully. He said at last, "A fellow-American, I do believe . . . in spite of the extraordinary clothes you chose to wear."

Clifford stared at him, wonderingly. There was a look there he did not trust, but he said at last, "Not an American, sir, but I am glad to see you, nonetheless."

He began to move toward him, but there was a

sudden gesture with the cutlass—not with the blade, but with the handle, held out in front of him in a strange and bewildering way. The stranger said in the voice of an educated man, "You may not know this weapon, sir. A cutlass pistol?"

His head was jerking from side to side. "It carries a charge and one very large ball in the handle. The Elgin percussion cutlass pistol, sir, much in favor in the United States Army these days."

"You have no need, sir," Clifford said steadily, "of any weapon."

"Then if you would kindly drop that fearsome machete to the ground and tell me who you might be?"

He let the machete fall. "My name is Clifford Hawkes and I was shipwrecked on the coast here some time ago."

"But not an American, I think you said?"

"An Englishman, sir."

"Ah . . . what a relief . . ."

He slid the cutlass into its scabbard, dropped the donkey's halter, and came forward, his hand outstretched. "Then let me take your hand, sir, and beg your forgiveness for suspecting your intentions."

Clifford took his hand, albeit warily, and the strange, green-coated man said simply, "My name is Amos Woodchuck. I am employed by a timber company of Mexico to count trees, a dull and tiring occupation. But these days . . . anything to make a living."

He said again, still gripping Clifford's hand, "Amos Woodchuck, Mr. Hawkes. And I cannot tell you what a pleasure it is to meet someone in this accursed forest who is not patently a savage, or an enemy, or both."

But there was still a wary, suspicious look in those bright eyes, in spite of the wide, friendly smile. He said, beaming, "Shall we sit down, sir, and eat, and talk, and find out what common causes bind us together in this benighted land? What say you, sir? Perhaps your undoubted knowledge, and mine, can be brought together and give us comfort. It is a hard and tiresome world, and if we gentlemen of quality do not stick together, and aid each other where we can? . . . Then what is to become of us?"

He was already unstrapping the saddlebags. He hesitated, looked around him, and said, "But there is the stench of death here, an offensive stench in the nostrils of gentlemen. Let us see if perhaps we can find more pleasing surroundings."

A little bewildered and quite unsure about this garrulous and quite untrustworthy man, Clifford followed him into the forest.

her, and see how she reacts. Perhaps, ... at best I
can simply send her back to her village."

One hour after her arrest, when he had already

CHAPTER SIXTEEN

One of the wagons had been given over entirely to the young ladies and one of them to Estrellita herself. The other seven, it seemed, carried the expedition's supplies.

Mercy could not believe that a mere wagon could be so inordinately comfortable and luxurious.

It was an ordinary military supply-wagon, with high wooden sides of adze-hewn planking, and high bows of bent beechwood over which a heavy, dull-gray canvas was stretched and tied down. But inside, the canvas had been lined with a soft cotton material that had been dyed a pale emerald green, cunningly draped at the front and at the rear to form prettily pleated drapes. Its plank floor was covered over with a carpet of fine wool in a pleasing shade of beige, decorated with small green leaves and pink flowers, a big wardrobe of carved oak filled with dresses, each more beautiful than the other, and a full-length mirror on the inside of its door. There were two shiny brass beds (the second one newly brought in by soldiers), and a very low divan at one end, covered over with a delicate tapestry of fine wool which had come, Estrellita told her, from the factory of the Fleming Vandergoten in Madrid.

She had said gently, "I am told that it is the most beautiful piece of artistry that a woman could set eyes on. They tell me that the running brook, and the autumn colors, are particularly satisfying. Is it true?"

Mercy nodded. "Yes, it is true."

Estrellita was moving easily about in the confined space, quite at ease, setting out three glasses on a little table of polished wood and fingering a silver decanter. The tips of her fingers were on the glasses as she poured the wine.

There was a third young woman there, a dark and slender girl with flashing, very dark eyes, whose name was Francesca. She was laying dresses on one of the beds, four, five, six of them, in brilliant or subdued colors, with a selection of petticoats, three white sateen corsets of the flared, tight-waisted type called "sylphides," a few aprons in browns and purples, a few bonnets, some combs for the hair . . .

She said, holding up a dress of white muslin with a half-high decollete and deep flounces on the skirt, "This one, I think. What do you say? With perhaps an apron of broche silk? Or, if you like a lower neckline, this one, a chemisette. It's very flattering to a figure like ours . . . but you must wear

340

your hair pulled back tighter, I think. I can show you how to do it."

Mercy was dressed only in the new short pantalettes that Francesca had produced for her. *Very* short, Mercy thought—they were of the new new style, joined at the center. The ordinary divided pantalettes, which consisted of two thigh-pieces attached to a kind of belt and left the crotch entirely open, had gone out of fashion just a few years previously. These were very modern indeed, with notched edges covered over with pretty embroidery. Mercy held the taffeta chemisette up against her body in front of the mirror. Its front was fold-over and deeply cut and there were three layers of the prettiest flounces on the skirt.

"Do you think I can wear this?" she asked. "It will show a great deal of . . . of *me*, won't it? But it's so pretty . . ."

Estrellita said, as though examining it herself, "It will be perfect on you, my dear Mercy." Then, to Francesca, "Is that the gray one?"

"*Si, Señora* . . . the gray with the blue decoration."

"Ah . . . then the black Morocco boots, the ones with the tassels on them. And what do you have for a comb?"

"I thought . . . the German tortoiseshell. Or, if you prefer it, the gilt one with the ruby glass beads."

"No, the tortoiseshell is better."

"*Si, señora.*" Francesca gasped and said suddenly, "*O mi Dios*, I forgot! Lieutenant Cantera is waiting for me!"

"No," Estrellita said calmly. "I told him you

341

would be busy this evening. Querida has gone to him."

"Oh, good . . ."

They spent more than three hours fussing over her. When they had all finished, Mercy was dressed as fashionably and as elegantly as any lady strolling the Mall on a summer evening. She had never before worn such fine clothes. But suddenly there were tears in her eyes, and she was biting her lip to drive them away. She sat down on the divan and wept bitterly, feeling Estrellita's arm over her shoulder, comforting her.

Francesca was staring at her in surprise, not knowing what was happening, but Estrellita said gently, "There, there . . . perhaps they will find him, after all."

She said through her tears. "You know about my husband? About . . . dear Clifford?"

"Of course I know! Juan told me, our Captain. He has a dozen scouts out searching the forest, and if your man is alive, and we pray to God that he is, then they will find . . . some sign of him. If he is dead . . . then you must face that too, with courage. It is a hard world for any woman, Mercy. And without courage . . . we are nothing without courage."

"Yes, yes . . . I'm sorry."

"Never despair, Mercy. Never, *ever*, despair."

Mercy found a fine lacy handkerchief tucked into the tiny pocket of her skirt and dabbed at her eyes with it. In a little while, when the darkness had fallen, Estrellita took her over to the Captain's tent.

A table had been set up there lit by a flare that was flickering close by and casting a saffron light

342

over his aristocratic features. He bowed to them both, very formally. When they sat down to dine, he waited till the two serving-orderlies had moved back into the shadows, then said quietly, "I fear, Ma'am, that I have no news of any sort for you. My scouts have returned, and . . . well, let me tell you what they found."

He was pouring wine into slim metal goblets and it was hard to imagine they were in the middle of a Cuban jungle.

He said, "First, they found the camp you spoke of, and told me of the massacre there. You must understand . . . these scouts are the best in the Island, two Creoles among them, men who have learned to read the language left in the earth by people who move over it. They read the signs there in a manner that you and I would find . . . disconcerting. They can look at the imprint of a woman's foot and say if she was pregnant or merely carrying a load on her back. They can look at the footprint of a man and say, with reasonable accuracy, how old he is. They found there the tracks of thirty or forty men, the soldiers you spoke of. But not . . . not soldiers, Ma'am, as I understand the word. Some wore boots, some shoes, some skins wrapped around their feet . . . a rabble. Armed, yes, with rifles, and with bayonettes, and with swords and knives; there was very considerable evidence of that, I fear. I am led to believe that these are the mercenaries hired by the man I have been sent to arrest, the renegade governor of the Eastern Province, what we call here the *Oriente*."

"And could they tell . . . is it possible that, for one reason or another, my husband went with them? A prisoner?"

343

He sighed. "There is no way I can answer that, Ma'am. Is there a reason for which you suggest that?"

She shook her head miserably. "I just don't know. He went into the forest to help . . . to help a wounded slave. I saw the slave get up and run, and my husband ran after him, and they disappeared from my sight. It was very dark . . . but a little while later, I saw a line of soldiers coming from the same direction. I think . . . I fear they may have taken him. Or killed him." It was hard to fight back the tears.

The Captain said slowly, "They found only the bodies of slaves, black men all of them. It is indeed conceivable that they may have taken him prisoner."

He was watching her shrewdly. "But when we found you, Ma'am, you were below the falls and a very long way from the camp. Were you searching for him there?"

"Yes. There was a woman in the camp, a witch, and she told me . . . *I think* she told me . . . that he had been thrown, by whom I do not know, over the edge of the falls. I could not speak with her, the language . . . but I thought I understood. Now I do not know. I think that had he in truth fallen there, I would have found him. I followed the river for a very long way before . . . before I could follow it no longer. My mind was . . . vexed, confused. It still is. I just . . . don't know."

Estrellita said quietly, "I can take her to Rosita, Juan."

The Captain snorted, "Rosita! How can she help her? Rosita is a monster!"

344

Mercy reached out urgently and touched Estrellita's hand. "Rosita?" she asked.

The Captain said, deprecatingly, "There is a girl in the camp here, a gypsy. She came here all the way from Spain, and before that, from Romany. When you have finished drinking your maté, she will take the gourd and empty out the leaves onto a plate. Then she will tell you how many children you will have, how tall or short your husband will be, how he will prosper or suffer, how there is great wealth or abject poverty awaiting you . . ."

Mercy's hand tightened on Estrellita's. "Oh, please . . ." she whispered.

Estrellita said calmly, "Tonight I will bring her to our wagon. And we shall learn what she has to say."

The Captain looked at Mercy and grimaced. "She once told that I would never reach Santiago de Cuba alive, that I would walk into a trap to be sprung by an Englishman. There are almost no Englishmen in Cuba! Your husband, perhaps? I think not. She said, with great conviction, that I would be killed by a sailor? A sailor? Between here and Santiago there is nothing but mountain, forest, and jungle. No sea anywhere. And I have to tell you that I have an abiding loathing of the sea. I will move Heaven and Earth never to go near it. So there is Estrellita's gypsy-girl for you. But if you think she might comfort you . . ."

He looked at Estrellita and said, "But I will not have Mercy still further confused, my love. So . . . a little discretion?"

Mercy was convinced that the blind woman was looking straight into her eyes; it was a strange and even frightening sensation.

"Tonight," Estrellita said, "when we have finished our dinner, we will take our maté to my wagon and summon Rosita to us. We will listen to what she has to say."

"Yes, oh, yes . . ."

Mercy could not contain her excitement. She also experienced a terrible feeling of guilt that she was sitting here in such excellent company, enjoying a dinner of roast pork stuffed with chicken, and sweet potatoes and beetroot, and Spanish wine in delicate goblets . . . and who could imagine where Clifford might be, what agonies he might be enduring?

When they had finished their meal, one of the orderlies brought them maté in silver-mounted gourds, with the hollow reeds, silver-tipped, that they called *bombillas* to sip it through. Estrellita said, "With your permission, Juan, we will retire with our maté to my wagon?"

The Captain leaped to his feet. He kissed both their hands, bowing deeply over them, and said to Mercy gravely, "Your sleeping arrangements . . . they are satisfactory?"

"Thank you, Captain, they are more than comfortable."

"You are in good and competent hands, but if there is anything else I can do to make your stay with us more endurable?"

"You are most kind. And I am so very grateful."

He hesitated. Then, "May I, without undue presumption, compliment you on . . . the change in your appearance? But a few hours ago, it seemed to be, you were . . . a ragged waif at the water's edge. And now, a lady again. A beautiful English lady. A good night to you, Ma'am. Early in the

346

morning, we wll be on our way, but it need not disturb you. Perhaps you will hear the shouts of the muleteers. If they wake you, please accept my apologies in advance. A very good night to you, Estrellita ..."

She took Mercy's arm and led her off, with superb confidence in the darkness. A girl was hurrying across their path, and Estrellita stopped short, saying, "Florinda?"

"No, *señora*," the girl answered. "I am Inez."

"Inez ..." She said impatiently, "Well, I wish you would learn not to stumble in the dark like Florinda. Find Rosita for me. Where is she tonight?"

"With Sergeant Garcia, *señora*."

"Well, wait for her, and when she is finished, tell her to come to me. And where are you going?"

Inez, a young, plump and sprightly girl in a dark chemisette, with hair brushed high over her forehead, cast a quick look at Mercy and dropped her eyes. "To the Captain," she said.

"Ah, good. Then tell one of the soldiers ... when Rosita is free, not before, I want to see her."

"*Si, señora.*"

The girl swept off, stumbling again, and Mercy said awkwardly, "Estrellita ... I feel guilty over another matter too."

"Oh? And what is that?"

They carefully circumvented a pile of stored boxes in the darkness and Mercy said, not knowing quite how to phrase it, "If I am ... an embarrassment ... if you have ... other things you should do?"

Estrellita laughed and squeezed her arm tightly. "No," she said. "I do not have other things to do."

347

They were walking arm in arm together, like very old friends, and she went on, very quietly and confidentially, "Once, yes, I was a whore, and a very good one. But not any more. Do I shock you, Mercy?"

"No, I am, perhaps, a little . . . naive. But not without understanding, Estrellita."

"I am sure of it. And I am glad of it too. Well, I was working, so many years ago, in a brothel in Havana, and one day . . . something happened, and I never knew why or what it was. I woke up in the morning and it was quite dark, so I turned over and went to sleep again. When I woke up once more it was still dark and I slept again. And again, and again . . . and then, I felt my maid shaking my shoulders, and I heard her say, 'Estrellita, wake up, wake up, it's the middle of the afternoon, you have to get ready.' And it was still dark. I knew, then, that I was blind, and I did not know how this could have come about. I was in the most terrible panic and I wanted to kill myself, but . . ."

They had reached the wagon and Estrellita was leading her up its ladder unfalteringly. They went inside where a small oil lamp was burning and sat down together on a divan. Estrellita reached behind her under her voluminous dress to loosen the laces of her corselette, and said, a long, drawn-out sigh, "Ah . . . whoever invented this infernal binding? It's the death of all of us."

She got to her feet, went to the wardrobe and opened it. Reaching in she counted the clothing hanging there with the tips of her fingers, took out a long blue robe and laid it to one side, and started stripping off her clothes, hanging them meticulously on counted hangers.

348

She went on as she undressed, "There was a doctor, a client of mine, a dear and good man, and I sent him a message and he came to me at once. Poor man! He was weeping when he told me: 'Estrellita, you will never see again . . .' I went to live with him for more then a year. Then he died and I rode in a carriage to the funeral, and wept for him at the graveside, a good and kindly man who had helped me so very much . . ."

It was the first time Mercy had ever seen another woman's naked body. Estrellita was slim, and very straight, with small, pointed breasts with a beautiful curve to the underside of them, rounded hips and long, slender thighs. Her skin, from shoulder to ankle, was pale ivory-colored, and flawless, her stomach taut and very firm.

She reached out a hand to the shelf in the wardrobe, and lighted without any hesitation at all on a slim bottle of oil there, knowing precisely where it was, poured a little into the palm of her hand and began massaging it into her shoulders, her fine breasts, her stomach, her thighs. She turned, and her eyes were just a trifle to one side of Mercy's. She said slowly:

"I walked back to where the carriage was waiting. There was no one to help me, and I discovered that I did not *need* any help. There was the smell of the horses, and I could even hear the coachman stirring in his seat and know what it was. From that day on, I never needed any help at all. My dear, good friend was gone, and I went back to his house, and entered it, and climbed the stairs unaided, and I slept in our bed and wept for him. The next day, a woman came who said she was his wife. There was a terrible scene, but . . . when it was over, and I left the house, I realized that she had never known she was shrieking at a blind woman. I found my way, really quite easily, back to the brothel where I had stayed for so long and worked so hard. I told them, 'I will never use my body again, ever; but if you can find work for me, for enough money to live on. Give me a broom and I will sweep your floors. I have been happy here, and it is the only home I know'. The owner, a fat and tired old woman who had always been very kind to me, her name was Madame Walevski I remember . . . said nothing, but I heard her go to the door that I knew led to the kitchen. When she came back she said to me, 'What do I have in my hand, Estrellita?' And I said, 'A broom, Madam.' She gave it to me and said, 'Then let me see how a blind woman can sweep a floor.' I swept up every trace of dust, knelt down in the corner and swept it all into a little piece of paper, then put the paper into the fire that was burning there, and I told her, 'Madame Walevski, it is Friday, and you will need more logs for your fire tonight. A *sheroot* in the ashtray that has been only half-smoked, means that you had a client this night who was not satisfied with the service you gave him.' I heard her gasp. In a moment she said, 'Estrellita, will you manage this place for me?' "

She corked the bottle of oil, placed it just so on the shelf, reached for the robe and slipped into it. She came and sat down beside Mercy as though she knew precisely where she was, and went on.

"There was a young lieutenant of the Army who came to us one evening. The girl he had chosen was named, I remember, Ursalina—we used to call her Lina—a young slip of a girl hardly sixteen years

350

old. When he had finished, he asked me, very courteously, if I would join him in a glass of wine. 'If you would do me the honor,' he said, a nice young boy. He told me that his captain wanted the services of a Madam, to engage a few young ladies for his officers and his senior ranks, and if the proposition were of interest to me. . . . I was wearing, I remember, a long red dress with no less than seven petticoats, and a wine-colored *redingote* that exposed almost all of my bosom, of which I have always been proud. He laid his hand on my breast and I slapped his young face so hard . . . how I which I could have seen the expression on it! He stammered an apology, handed me a card, and said, 'Madam, if you would be so good as to present yourself at this address tomorrow? . . .' I could not believe that he had not realized I could not see. I said to him, and I must admit I was mocking him, 'How can I serve your captain, sir? I am blind.' He must have been staring at me in some desperate kind of confusion, for he scuttled away like a rabbit, and I never heard his voice again. But two days later, a Captain Juan de Cordova presented himself. Yes, our dear Captain, a fine and honorable gentleman. That was more than three years ago, and . . . I know, I feel it, that he needs me so badly, and yet . . . I told him then that I would find for him all the girls he needed for his men, but that I myself . . . he has never said an immodest word to me, nor touched me. When we dine together, once or twice a week, I always wear my most beautiful gowns, and I am sure that his eyes are constantly on me. I know that he desperately wants to bed me . . . but he always says, at the end of the evening, 'Good night, Estrellita. Sleep well.' And then he calls one of the girls to his bed, which is not really the proper way to behave. He is supposed to tell me whom he wants, but he is, after all, the Captain. I like to think that when he is lying between Inez's thighs, or Ramona's, or Bonita's, he is thinking of me. Tell me, Mercy, is he truly as handsome as they say he is?"

"Yes, a beautiful man."

"Tall, yes, I know, I hear his voice. But straight?"

"As an arrow."

"And those moustaches . . . gray, they tell me. Or are they white?"

"A whitish-gray."

"And the lines of his face . . . deeply etched?"

"Not too deeply, no."

"His eyes . . . they say they are very, very dark."

"A dark brown. And very gentle and understanding."

"And his chin?"

"Firm. Very firm. As a strong man's chin should be."

"And does he look, would you say, an old man?"

"No, most definitely not. He is what? Fifty, perhaps? He looks much younger, and very . . . virile. A man a woman can admire."

"Ah . . . I know all these things. Of course I know, I have asked all the girls, and sometimes I think they mock me for it. It is good to hear it from you, who will not mock me, I am sure."

"Never, Estrellita!"

A hand was reaching out, touching her face, and Estrellita said, whispering, "Your eyebrows . . . a prefect curve."

352

They talked together quietly like old friends far into the night, until Rosita came, a plump and somehow oddly shaped woman in her early thirties. She had an enormous bust and very thin arms, with a mass of dark, untidy hair that was almost black. Her skin was very smooth and dark. There was a wild, untamed sort of look in her gypsy eyes.

She took Mercy's gourd and peered into it and spoke a few words in her own language.

Estrellita said, translating, "She tells you to drink all the maté, and then to empty the leaves onto a plate. Here, I will give you one . . ."

Mercy sucked up the rest of the drink through the *bombilla* and emptied out the leaves. Rosita crouched on her haunches, stared at them for a long, long while, and Mercy waited anxiously. Estrellita spoke for her again, interpreting in little sentences, phrases, words.

"There is no doubt . . . your man is alive. There are many, many years ahead for you both. I see him clearly, a tall young man . . . very strong and muscular . . . he wears . . . clothes that are not his . . ."

"Where is he?" Mercy asked eagerly, "can you tell me where he is?"

"A long way from here . . . in twelve, fourteen days . . . you will meet . . . and soon . . you will be parted again. I see a man with a donkey . . . an evil man . . . and there is a woman, no, two women . . . they are very young, I think, and they have something in common . . . very much alike, almost . . . identical. Yes, quite identical, I cannot tell one from the other."

Mercy said desperately, "And is he well?"

353

"Yes, he is well. But there is something troubling him. I do not know what it is."

"And happy?"

"No. He is not happy. He is searching for something . . ."

"For me?"

"Perhaps. I cannot tell. There is a leaf here which is his, and it is curled up more than it should be. It means . . . yes, he is searching, toward this other leaf here . . . I think this is yours, but I cannot be sure. Yes, it is yours. One is inclining toward the other, and it means that he is searching . . ."

"And will he find me? Will I find him?"

Rosita held the plate out for her and said, "Shake it for me, once only, and very gently."

Mercy took the plate and did as she was bid, and Rosita stared at it again and said, "Yes, you are coming together. The two young women are coming closer to him too, but he is turning away from them now . . . and the man with the donkey, he has gone, perhaps he is dead. I am not sure."

"And Clifford, my husband," Mercy said urgently, "can you tell me where, where he is?"

"Not far away," Rosita said. "And yet . . . still a long way. The path he is taking . . . yes, it is still two weeks, perhaps a little longer, before he finds you."

"But he will, in the end?"

"In the end, undoubtedly. And I see for you many children, fine strong children, all surrounded, as you both are, by troubles. But you are fighting against the troubles . . ."

She shook her head, her eyes flashing. "In a few days . . . when you have been with us longer . . . I will tell you more. And now . . . you must cross my palm."

She held out her open hand and Estrellita traced three lines on it with the edge of a tiny silver charm, laying the charm carefully in the center of her hand. Rosita closed her fist, holding it out for Mercy to see, and when she opened it again, the silver charm was gone. She gathered up her skirts and swept out without another word.

Mercy said, her voice hushed, "We will meet again in twelve or fourteen days . . . but be parted again?"

Estrellita said, smiling, "Perhaps she was right in the first and wrong in the second. Who knows?"

"And two young women?" She was frowning, unsure. "And an evil man? Does that mean danger to him?"

"If he is strong, then danger will mean nothing to him. Shall we sleep now? It is late."

"Yes, maybe we should."

"There is a nightshirt for you on the left-hand side of the wardrobe, and a very pretty bedjacket. When you have taken off all your clothes, Mercy, come and stand by me for a very brief moment. I wish to see what you look like."

"All right."

Mercy took off the beautiful dress. There was a slight rustling sound of taffeta as she stepped out of it and laid it carefully over the divan. She removed the three petticoats, the tightly laced corselette, and the stockings and the pantalettes, she moved to the wardrobe for the nightshirt and Estrellita said quietly, "Wait, Mercy. Come over here."

Quite naked and trembling a little, Mercy moved to her and stood by the low divan. Estrellita

355

reached out very gently and laid her white hands on her hips, traced the curve of her thighs down to her knees and up again on the inside of them, and over her stomach and up to her breasts, lingering there for a moment. Then she carefully fingered her shoulders, her chin, and her face, delineating the cheekbones, the nose, the eyebrows, even the lobes of her ears. And then the body again, infinitely slowly, all the way down to the thighs. She was quivering under the gentle touch, and Estrellita murmured at last, her voice a whisper, "You are a very beautiful woman, Mercy . . ."

The fingertips were at the eyebrows again, exploring. "Those eyes . . . are they brown?"

"Yes, they are brown."

"And so huge . . . yes, a very beautiful woman."

"I don't really know how you can be sure of that, Estrellita."

"I can be sure. My hands are my eyes and I see you very clearly, in all of your beauty."

Those hands, soft and delicate, dropped to her breasts again, the fingers brushing the hardening nipples. "Go to bed, Mercy," she whispered, "and sleep well. We will talk together again in the morning. Kiss me first."

Mercy leaned down and kissed her lightly on the cheek. The slight shaking was there again and almost mechanically she opened the wardrobe door and took out the nightshirt and the lovely embroidered bedjacket, slipping them on.

She lay down on the bed and pulled the coverlet over her and saw that Estrellita was turning out the lamp. She heard the sounds, a faint creaking of wood, the whisper of linen, as the blind woman climbed into bed, and she thought: her hands . . .

356

her ears too, to tell her all that is happening all around her . . .

"Goodnight, Estrellita," she whispered. "And thank you . . ."

"Goodnight, Mercy." How soft and comforting her voice was! "May your dreams be beautiful dreams. And may tomorrow be a good day for all of us."

She lay and worried about Clifford for a while, a deep sense of fatigue sweeping over her.

Where was he now? Alone out there in a vast and endless forest? No, not alone . . . there was an evil man with him. Or perhaps two young woman? Who could they be? Did they really exist?

She fell asleep, the sleep of utter exhaustion, the deep feather mattress engulfing her.

She awoke in a little while, drowsily, not really awake but still more than half-asleep, and she was aware that she was no longer alone. Estrellita's light and slender body was beside her in the bed, one arm across her waist, the hand tucked warmly between her thighs. There was just the slightest rhythmic movement in her hips.

She murmured, " 'strellita?"

"Sshhh . . . sleep."

"Will I ever . . . ever see him again, 'strellita?" Her voice trailed off into a sigh.

The blind woman's murmur, even, was in itself a caress. "Sshhh . . . it is a time for sleep, a time for dreams."

"Dear 'strellita . . ."

The infinitesimal, insistent, and persuasive motion of the hips that were moulded so closely to her own, the gentle stirring of that warm hand, were a great comfort to her. She fancied that they were

Clifford's arms about her, and she sighed contentedly.

But they were not Clifford's. They were, instead, the delicate hands of a very beautiful woman who was loving her now, slowly bringing her to a state of exquisite ecstasy, almost as he might. She did not at first quite understand what was happening to her; and when she did, there was a tiny sense of shock that stirred in her consciousness, a sudden feeling of trepidation that made her catch her breath.

The subtle urging of the motion at her back increased its tempo, and in few moments, in spite of herself, her own orgasm took hold of her and swept her away in its pleasurable excitation. She dared not move and she allowed the euphoria to overcome her.

She fell into a deep and utterly peaceful sleep.

CHAPTER SEVENTEEN

The cool night breezes were blowing through the great hall of the fine palace, and down below the rugged cliffs, the surf was pounding against a dark and rocky shore.

The night was warm and humid, a storm brewing out at sea, and the windows that overlooked the harbor were open.

Governor Aguilar was at the huge oak table, staring thoughtfully down at the map spread out on it, a map all covered over with crayon marks that had been drawn with a firm, incisive hand. Adam Butrus, dressed now in his uniform boots and breeches but with his jacket discarded, was lounging on a damask-upholstered chair, his long legs up on a high stool while he sipped at his goblet of wine. His fine silk shirt, elaborately ruffled and immensely elegant, was open at the neck. The

Governor never insisted on formality among his close friends, and he enjoyed the company of this competent and ambitious man. *As shrewd and determined as I am myself,* he was thinking, *and my future is in his hands entirely.*

He said, frowning, "Cordoba, Captain Juan Alonzo de Cordoba, I know him well. He's a fine soldier, Adam."

Butrus said dryly, "A fine soldier with only a hundred men . . . is no longer a fine soldier. He's a man whose defeat is imminent. A dead soldier is not a fine soldier."

"Three hundred and forty men," the Governor said imperturbably. "With twelve pieces of ordance and an almost unlimited supply of ammunition. He can give us the devil of a time with those cannon."

Butrus got languidly to his feet and helped himself to more wine. He moved over to the table and stabbed at the map with a broad and powerful hand. "We meet him here," he said, "before he reaches Sagua de Palmirito. And with due respect, Excellency, your spies in Havana need a good flogging, all of them. They get their information from the enemy . . . by listening to everything the enemy tells them and believing it. I have more faith in my Creoles."

"Yes, your Creoles." The Governor sighed. "Not the most responsible of people. A little over one hundred men, they say. I choose not to believe them."

"Cordoba has four lieutenants, fourteen sergeants or warrant officers, and one hundred and seventy troopers, of whom eleven are currently incapacitated by sickness. He has three cannon, which are

360

being carried in a single wagon. That means they are small. They are probably the Rodman water-cooled cannon, the most inefficient piece of ordnance ever delivered to an army. It's cumbersome, it's slow to use, and it has far too much recoil for rapid realigning. But to the devil with his cannon, he won't have a chance to use them."

"You are thinking then in terms of an ambush, I take it?"

"Of course. We can't afford to let him march into Santigo. We stop him in the mountains."

"And we are aware, are we not, that this will be our first overt move against Havana? Once committed, there can be no withdrawing. We will have shown our colors."

"No, sir." Butrus was smiling gently. "That is why I want to meet him in the mountains."

He began pacing, formulating his thoughts carefully. He said, gesticulating, "If he should reach Santiago, then obviously, only Santiago can oppose him, and it would indeed be an overt act of treason. But up in the Sierra, long before he reaches what Havana might think of as our sensitive areas . . . there are a dozen armies of rebel slaves up there, one or two of them well enough armed to offer resistance to Cordoba's trifling force. There are gangs of so-called Liberators roaming the hills who are no more than bandits, and they too are well enough armed. There are at least three administrators between here and Havana who have fairly strong forces of their own . . . Cordoba will be annihilated, and there will be no survivors to carry tales of just who the attackers were. If need be, and I doubt it, we can still protest our loyalty to

361

Havana long after Cordoba's pathetic little patrol has ceased to exist."

"Good, good. It's always wise to keep our options open." He stared down at the map again. "It should take him, what? Ten days to reach this valley here?"

"Longer. His wagons slow him down. I would say fifteen days at least. Provided, of course, that he doesn't change his line or march, which he well might."

"Yes, he probably will ... and your own men?"

"We still need more training, but they're getting better."

"I hear you hanged three of them yesterday. Was that necessary?"

"If it had not been, I would not have done it, Excellency. Cowards, all of them. You'd be surprised what the sight of a coward hanging on the gallows does to other men."

"Well . . . will you be ready to move out in time?"

Butrus shrugged. "I myself take the main force out at the end of twelve days. Meanwhile, I have thirty men here, here, and here, along the Cordillera." He thumped a hand on the map and said, "Thirty men I know I can trust, with fast horses, they're scouting out the land. Meanwhile I'm doing some exploration of my own. Your maps, I fear, are not very good. In fact, they are useless."

He swung round as the door opened and stared at the apparition there. It was a gross and obese young man in his twenties, with slack, wet lips and hideous, bulging eyes. There was saliva on his chin and he was sniggering. He was wearing an elaborate woman's evening gown, slit open at the sides to give room to his girth, with rags stuffed into the bodice to simulate bulging breasts. He shuffled into the room and said, "Papa . . . I'm hungry."

The Governor sighed. "Fernando," he said sternly, "there is a bellrope in your room. Pull it. Someone will come. Say you are hungry. You will be fed. Now leave us, please. I am busy."

"And can I have wine too?"

"You can have what you damned well like, boy, you know that. Now leave us, please."

"Very well, Papa. I just wanted you to know that I am hungry." He turned and shuffled his way to the door. Giggling, he said, "But you didn't mention my dress, Papa. It's new."

"It's very beautiful, Fernando," Aguilar said. "Now go to your room."

When he had gone, Aguilar sank into a chair and put his head in his hands, saying bitterly, "My son, Adam. In God's name. I get sick every time I look at him. Pour me another drink, there's a good fellow."

Butrus silently refilled his goblet and handed it to him. Aguilar looked up into the sardonic eyes and said, "Yes, you're right. There's nothing you can say." He drained his wine at a gulp and said suspiciously, "You didn't know?"

"No, sir."

Aguilar snorted. "Oh come, Adam, what do you take me for?" He leaned back and half smiled, a twisted, rueful sort of smile. "One of the things I most admire in you, dear friend . . . there's *nothing* you don't know about what goes on around you. And this is hardly a secret."

"Well," Butrus said carefully, "I had indeed heard of your concern for the future of your noble lineage. It's none of my business, so . . . I paid no heed to it."

"My only son," Aguilar said. "And look at him!"

He leaped to his feet and said, "Dammit, Adam, I can read your mind like a book! You're about to tell me that I'm still a vigorous man, that I can have more sons to my name! Admit it, isn't that what you were thinking?"

"Something like that, sir," Butrus said, smiling.

The Governor was pacing, his bearded chin sunk into the silk ruffles at the top of his coat. "I wish it were true. Vigorous, yes, thank God! But . . . his mother died when she gave birth to that . . . that monster. And in the long years since, I've bedded a hundred women, promised 'em marriage if they'd produce a son for me. Not one of them could. Something in me, no doubt, I can hardly blame so many of them . . . did I say a hundred? It must be a thousand. The doctors—and what do they know?—tell me there's still hope for me, but I don't believe it, God knows I've tried hard enough, fornicated myself into the grave, almost . . . and so . . . my only hope of perpetuating what you call my noble lineage—and I thank you for that—lies in that sordid creature. Oh, give him his due, he's ripe enough, he goes at it like a rabbit. But only with the slave-women, and I don't want any taint of the damned tarbrush in my grandchildren."

"A question, surely, of money?" Butrus murmured.

Aguilar sighed. "Yes, you'd think so, wouldn't you? But not a single one of our decent *Peninsulare* women will even go near him, in spite of the huge sums of money I've offered them. They're all too damned rich already. I brought a woman all the

364

way from Havana once, a young girl of good family, with seven brothers, sons in the blood, exactly what I need. I told her . . . I swear, Adam, that I told her all about him. I even said: 'You can spend your time with him blindfold.' I offered her a box," he spread his hands wide, "a box this size, filled with gold coins and emeralds, and I told her: 'There's another like it when my first grandson is born.' And she agreed. She played with those emeralds as though they were baubles, and she said, her exact words, Adam! She said: 'I don't really care what he looks like in the least, toys like these will buy all the sons you want, a dozen of them if need be.' But she lost that equanimity when she got here, Adam. She made just one comment when she saw him. She said: *'Holy Mother of Christ,'* and she fled. Took the bribe with her too, damn her eyes. Never saw or heard from her since. And I have a standing offer . . . you must have heard of that too?"

"Five thousand gold coins, I believe," Butrus said.

"Yes. To any of our Spanish ladies who'll allow herself to be impregnated by that . . . that ape. And we'll all pray to God that his kind of idiocy is not hereditary, or we'll all be in a fine pickle, won't we?"

"Then you'll just have to go on trying to breed more sons yourself. It could be that the doctors are right. They are, sometimes. Just . . . keep on trying."

"Of course," Aguilar said glumly. "That's what I do every night of the week. Fifty-two years old and I look like an old gentleman of seventy-five. But it's the only consolation I have. That and . . .

365

my ambitions. To the devil with everybody, Adam. Most of all, with that misshapen toad I have to call my son."

He drained his goblet and poured more wine. Studying the map as he sipped, he said, "The Alcaides still causing us trouble. At Cueto, and at Jiguani. You know about that too, I imagine?"

"Oh yes, of course. I have a man in Cueto. He feels the Alcaide there can perhaps be bought, and if the price is not too high I feel we should do that. As for Jiguani . . . I hear there might be a little trouble there soon, a handful of fugitive slaves seem to be planning an assassination. I hear it might be the Alcaide. His chief lieutenant is very much in favor of our aims, it seems. It won't even cost us very much."

"Ah, that's good news indeed, Adam. They've both long been a heavy cross for me to bear. Then, how long to clean up the whole of the Province?"

"You gave me three months, I recall."

"Enough time?"

"I would say so. We'll try."

"And the rest of the island? What do you think, Adam?"

Butrus said slowly, "We have fourteen hundred men under arms now, most of them good and getting better every day. That's more than enough for the Province. By subduing Oriente, we'll more than double that number. The rest of the island? It's only Havana we have to concern ourselves with. And I'll like to see Havana sacked by a twin-pronged assault, a heavy bombardment first from the sea . . ."

"From the *sea*?"

Aguilar was startled and Butrus said firmly,

"Half a dozen small, good ships, with mounted cannon, almost all the cannon we can lay our hands on—there are eleven at Cueto, remember, which will be ours in a few days. We'll drive a few of the ships onto the beaches, lose a few men in a diversionary assault while we bring their main forces out to meet them. Then, the main body will sweep down off the mountain, horsemen first, closely followed by footsoldiers. In two days the town should be firmly in our hands, and once you proclaim yourself Governor-General of the island . . . I'll need no more than a month to wipe out any dissidents."

"Then by the end of the year?"

"Long before then, Excellency."

Aguilar slapped him heartily on the shoulder. "What would I do without you, Adam?" he said.

Butrus answered smoothly, "Without me, Excellency, your future would not be so assured. Did you know that there is a spy among your servants?"

The Governor stared. "Among *my servants*? Good God, man!"

"Yes. There is a merchant in the town named Robert Duval, a Frenchman from Haiti, but a long-time resident of Santiago. It seems that he was hired by the Havana faction more than a year ago to report to them on the shipping in the harbor, quite innocuous stuff really."

"A year ago? But how do you know this?"

"Oh, he told me," Butrus said calmly. "And two days ago, on instructions from Havana, he engaged the services of someone in the palace itself to report on your own activities. Last night, she went to Duval and gave him a very long report . . ."

367

"She?"

"Yes. A serving-girl named Gabriella. She's been sleeping with your friend Manteras for some time, a man whose loyalty is beyond reproach, but whose discretion is sadly lacking."

The Governor said, aghast, "Gabriella? Good God! I knew about Manteras's interest in her, of course, in fact I gave her to him! But she's such a sweet child!"

"No child and not very sweet either. Her report was verbal—she can't read or write—but she's quite intelligent, it seems. In a few minutes she became aware that Duval, who had been told that his life depended upon his cooperation, was unaccountably extremely nervous. She tried to break off the report and take her leave, but . . . my men were in hiding there, and they arrested them both."

"Good God!" Aguilar's mouth was open and he closed it with a snap. "Gabriella! I've had her myself, a dozen times!"

"So she tells me," Butrus said smoothly. "And you have a man named Pedro Velasquez, a pigeon-handler."

"Not him too? I can't believe it!"

"No. Pedro's loyalty is beyond question. I have taken the liberty, since he has been with you so long, and knows everyone on your staff, of having him go through the list of them with a fine-tooth comb, checking them over very carefully. We don't want any more spies in the palace."

"Good, good . . . but Gabriella! I still can't believe it! Where are they now, these two?"

"Duval, unhappily, met with an accident. He fell into the harbor during the night, poor fellow. Gabriella is in my quarters now, under guard. I propose to interrogate her tonight, and have her quietly buried in the morning. Unless Your Excellency has any objections?"

"No, no," he muttered. "Do whatever you have to do, Adam."

"Good. And from now on, when your majordomo engages staff for your residence, if you will allow Pedro Velasquez the final word? I am training him in these matters, and he's learning very fast. A good man."

"Yes, yes, of course."

He said again, muttering, "I'll have a word with Manteras too. He always was a little voluble."

"It would, indeed, be wise. From this day on, please . . . remember that discretion, in military matters particularly, is worth its weight in gold. Even the walls, shall we say, have ears."

"Yes, yes . . ." He hesitated. "But Gabriella," he said at last. "Is it really necessary to have her killed? Perhaps, if you were to . . . to warn her, to frighten her . . . and send her back to her village?"

"I omitted to ask her," Butrus said, "how long she has been in your service."

"A year, I think. Maybe a little more."

"Then she will have a great deal of knowledge stored away in that not-so-childish mind of hers. Knowledge that any competent Havana spy—and they are not all fools—can easily persuade her to part with."

"Yes, I suppose you are right, as always." He was terribly upset about her. "But if you can find it in your heart to . . . to give her a chance? To be charitable?"

"Of course," Adam said smoothly. "I will warn

369

her, and see how she reacts. Perhaps, as you say, I can simply send her back to her village."

One hour after her arrest, when he had already dragged from her every iota of information that could possibly be of interest to him, he had decided what he would do with her.

But he said now, easily, "Let us see what will happen. These things should never be decided ahead of time."

"Of course. How very right you are. And why don't we have some more wine?"

Butrus had caused Gabriella to be stripped and tied down, spreadeagled, onto his bed, ready for him when he might return. He used her three times during the night. In the morning he got up and dressed himself carefully in all his finery, summoned Captain Jake Ollie to his quarters, and said to him, standing in front of the mirror and adjusting the set of his jacket just so, "A present for you, Jake. When you've finished with her, strangle her, take her out and bury her. Behind the north tower, in the sand there. And I want no marks on her grave."

Jake Ollie, a ludicrous figure in his uniform, saluted clumsily, "Aye, aye, sir, Colonel, sir." He could not take his eyes off the slender brown limbs, and when Butrus left to go about his business, he was already fumbling at the drawstring of his breeches.

The midday silence of the forest was absolute. The animals, even the birds, were resting in the heat of the day, and the sonorous pounding of the waterfall seemed somehow muted.

370

Clifford and the green-coated stranger had withdrawn from the terrible dead-man confines of the camp itself, and had found a little clearing a half mile or so away, where fine mahogany trees reared up into the blue sky high above them, their spreading branches providing a pleasing and welcome shade.

Amos Woodchuck was rooting into the saddle-bags of his donkey, pulling out long strips of beef jerky, and Clifford said, "I have been searching, sir, for an English lady who is lost here somewhere. If you have seen any signs, along the trail?"

Amos shook his head. "No, sir, I have seen nothing. And you . . . you know this accursed forest well, I take it?"

"Not well enough, it would seem."

They sat together on moss-covered slabs of rock, chewing on the jerky and drinking from Amos's flagon of wine. A long-beaked bird with blue and green feathers shining in the rays of the sun was perched on a branch nearby, eyeing them as it cocked its head from side to side. In a moment it swooped down and stole a piece of the meat and flew off with it, back to its perch. Amos swore and hurled a stone at it, and it flew off into the forest.

"And you have been here, how long?" he asked. "Shipwrecked some time ago, I think you said. How long is 'some time'?"

"Three months, perhaps."

"Ah. And in that time, have you had the opportunity to acquaint youself with the, eh, the political situation here?"

"No, sir, I have not."

"What a pity."

Clifford was watching him curiously as he ate

371

and feeling inexplicably uncomfortable in his presence; the eyes were too shifty, darting everywhere.

He said slowly, "You told me, Mr. Woodchuck, that you count trees. It seeems a strange occupation in a forest."

"Ah, but not just any trees. Very special trees." He said happily, "I have observed that my donkey can travel for four hours, or approximately for a distance of ten miles, before he starts to wheeze and I have to give him a rest. In that time, I make a little mark in my book for every tree I see of the kind my company is interested in—mahogany, ebony, *ramir*—all the good cabinet woods which can turn a profit. At the end of every day, I can estimate, with reasonable accuracy, just how many of these very valuable trees there might be in any given area. But you, sir?" He was peering at him intently, worrying over a problem. "You were shipwrecked. But you are a long way from the coast now. How came you here, sir?"

"We were taken," Clifford said, "or perhaps captured is the right word . . . by a group of slaves who found us near the beach. My wife is an astrologist, and they thought, it seemed, that she might be useful to them."

"Ah, astrology! An otiose study, if you ask my opinion. Our fate, dear sir, is in our own hands."

"Perhaps. I do not know."

"Not to be decided by the whims of the Heavens."

"Perhaps. They brought us here . . ."

"The slaves?"

"Yes. They held us prisoner for . . . just one day."

"Savages, sir. Savages. Little removed from the apes. But without the apes' undoubted intelligence."

Clifford stifled the angry comment he was about to make. He realized, with a sense of distaste, that those sharp eyes were on him, as though the remark had been made specifically to search out a reaction.

Amos went on smoothly, "And have you, in your wanderings, come across any Spaniards? Or Creoles?"

"Spaniards, only at a distance. And I do not, I fear, know what a Creole is."

"A Creole," Amos said, lecturing now, "is a person born in the Indies, where we unhappily find ourselves now. Do you speak Spanish, sir?"

"No, I do not."

"A pity. Well, Creole is their own interpretation of the Spanish word *creadillo*, which comes from the Latin *creare*, to create. You have no Latin either?"

"No, sir."

"And yet you speak like an educated man. Well, so be it. It takes all kinds to make a world. The Creoles, Mr. Hawkes, are a *created* race, with the worst of the untrustworthy Spanish, the worst of the shiftless Indians, and the worst of the good-for-nothing Negroes bred into them. And, like the Negroes, they are an *excrescence* on the face of the earth."

Clifford could hold himself back no longer. He said stiffly, "Are they not fellow human beings, sir?"

Amos answered him tartly, "Since you have never seen a Creole, you cannot speak with such authority about them. And since you were cap-

373

tured, as you say, by slaves, I cannot credit that you should be on their side either." He wiped at his mouth with the back of his hand. "You are surely not in favor of anarchy?"

"No, sir, I am not."

"Good. That is all I really need to know."

"*Need* to know, sir?" Clifford asked, puzzled. "I do not believe that I understand you, Mr. Woodchuck."

Amos turned and pointed down the trail, and said eagerly, "There is a French settlement some seven or eight days' march from here, called Guantanamo. Now, everyone on this dreadful island is fighting against everyone else, it seems. I wish to know where the sympathies of the people in that settlement, some two hundred of them, really lie. I have to find someone to go there, talk to them, listen to them, find out what they think, and report back to me. Unfortunately, I cannot go there myself without dire risk to my personal safety that I would prefer to avoid. It requires a man of daring, of education, of ability, and there are not many such in the jungle. I have been searching hopefully for such a man for a long time now, as far afield as Santiago de Cuba, knowing all the time that the task was a hopeless one, that I would simply have to give up any idea of finding out what goes on in Guantanamo. But lo! The jungle has produced what I might call an ideal recruit. Would you be prepared to undertake this mission for me, Mr. Hawkes? With your pockets, needless to add, filled with heavy gold?"

"A strange request," Clifford said, "from a man who counts the trees of the forest for a living."

"I am delighted," Amos said happily, "to find out

that you are in fact so perspicacious. I do indeed keep a record of the hardwood trees to account for my presence here should I fall into undesirable company on my wanderings. But . . . you know, sir, that President Polk is still trying to buy this island?"

"I did not know that, sir, no."

"You know that in the United States, the abolition mania, alas, is growing, unchecked, from day to day?"

"I had heard something to that effect, yes."

"Then pay careful attention, young man. There is a very large slave population here, and while the price of almost all agricultural products is rising elsewhere at an alarming rate because of this new mania for paying workers in the field . . . here, sugar, coffee, all the plantations can be worked by cheap labor, which can only add to our national prosperity. An advantage which, I am sure, is as dear to your heart as it is to mine."

"When you say 'cheap labor,' sir, you talk of slaves?"

"I do indeed. We cannot increase that prosperity without a large force of these apes. Exactly what we have here. I have the honor to represent the pro-slave faction in the Unites States. It is my job to find out just who, on this island, might be bribed to join forces with us, and stop the march of Abolition before it can take hold here. Are you prepared to help me in that laudable endeavor? For very substantial reward, cash on the barrel? Your answer, sir?"

Clifford said clearly, "My answer, Mr. Woodchuck, is *no*. I will also say that I find your ideas detestable."

There was a little silence and then Amos said mildly, "I have told you who I am, and what I represent, and I have opened my poor heart to you . . . these are secrets that may not be shared, Mr. Hawkes."

He was drawing the cutlass-pistol from its scabbard, and pointing its hilt at him. Clifford threw himself forward and wrestled him to the ground, fighting for the deadly weapon . . . its handle exploded in a cloud of blue smoke, and its half-inch ball went through the underside of Amos Woodchuck's chin and blew the back of his head off.

Clifford clambered heavily to his feet and stood for a moment looking down at the body of his adversary. He had not wanted to kill him; but he could find no remorse in his heart that this loathsome man was dead.

He went to the donkey and emptied its saddlebags. There was a small pouch of gold coins there, some cheese, bread, and onions tied in a rag. There was a pair of leather breeches, two woolen shirts, one blue and one brown, a spare pair of good boots, two pairs of linen drawers, recently washed and fairly clean, some black powder and balls for the pistol. There was a large bottle of a dark brown liquid with a label on it that read: *Iodine, an extract of kelp, for external medication on wounds, Fletcher & Son, New York, 1839.* There was a cooking-pot, a roll of charred linen for use as touch-paper, contained in a metal box with its attendant steel wheel and flintstones, for making fire. There were two rolled-up blankets, and a bag of grain for the donkey.

He tried the iodine first. He had heard tell of it, though he had never seen it before, and he stripped off the torn shirt he was wearing, poured some of the liquid into the palm of his hand, and slapped it into his wound, gasping and biting his lip at the unexpected sting of it.

He ate an onion and a piece of bread and cheese, while sitting on the trunk of a fallen tree. Then, slowly, thinking that he seemed to be condemned forever to wearing dead men's clothes, he dressed himself in the leather breeches and boots and the brown woollen shirt, all a little tight on him. He wondered for a while about the donkey, but seeing that it was feeding itself from the shrubbery, he took off its halter and turned it loose to fend for itself. He hefted his machete and strode off into the forest.

He did not know where he was going. In his youthful mind there was only one thought: *Find Mercy, wherever she might be.* . . .

He did not even know how to begin his search. He knew only that he would scout the jungle, for a hundred miles around if necessary, till he found some sign that would lead him to her.

It was all that mattered to him now.

CHAPTER EIGHTEEN

For five days, the wagontrain had plowed its slow and laborious way toward the eventual goal, Santiago de Cuba.

They set off every morning at sunup, and by the time the sun set, they covered, perhaps, twenty-five miles if the going was good. When the trail narrowed and squads of fusiliers had to move on ahead, cutting through the heavy brush with their sabers, that distance sometimes shrank to as few as five miles.

They camped every evening, drawing up the wagons in a kind of *lager*, with sentries posted on all four sides. Captain Cordoba would order the officers' tents to be set out, and the men would select their own little pieces of territory under the trees, or sometimes drop back a mile or so to where the

Creoles who followed them set up their own little camp for the night.

There was rum to be drunk, provided they had a few coins in their pockets, and women as well, more than thirty of them, ranging in age from well under fifteen to well over forty, some slim and sensually beautiful, some not so.

There would be music too, and sometimes even dancing in the firelight, with the slapping of iron cans for a counterpoint to the rhythm of the guitars and the flutes. The men, some of them hopelessly drunk, would stagger down the trail, their arms over each other's shoulders, and collapse to the ground in what was their temporary home. Some of them, bedded down with the girls there, would be fetched hurriedly in the morning as soon as the bugle sounded the advance.

And then, the long rigmarole of getting underway would begin. The mules would be hitched to the wagons, at which time the advance guard of scouts would move out along the projected route, to make sure that there were no insuperable obstacles (put there either by nature or man) to cause them any undue problems.

The men would then be paraded and inspected, and divided up into their companies of the day—part of them to precede the wagons, a detachment to follow them behind, with scouts on either flank. Two of the officers, and Cordoba himself, would ride tirelessly up and down the line, sometimes penetrating deep into the forest, searching out security from brigands or rebel slaves, sometimes merely checking on everything in the train, from the harness of the mules to the military bearing of his men.

From time to time, the scouts would report back.

"... a stream to cross, *Señor Capitano*. Too deep for the wagons, we will need a bridge of logs ..."

"... four mounted *bandoleros*, *Capitano*, on the left flank. I have sent three men after them ..."

"... the trail divides one hour ahead, *Señor Capitano*. We should take the left fork ..."

And once, "There is a swamp ahead of us. We will need three hours to find a way around it ..."

And so, the cumbersome wagontrain lumbered on, inexorably but with painful slowness. At the end of every day, when the camp was being made, the cartographer (an earnest, elderly man who thought only in terms of contours) would present himself to his weary Captain and say, "More than a thousand feet to climb tomorrow, *Señor Capitano*. If we can cover seven miles, we will do very well indeed. But once we reach the plateau, we leave the forest behind us, and we can move much faster."

His name was Ernesto Fantera, no more than forty years old but crippled and bowed with arthritis. On this late evening, Cordoba was studying the sketches he had made in crayon. (Those hands were so bent and rigid, that Ernesto had caused his crayons to be tied to his fingers.)

The Captain tapped at the map, worrying about the cover sketched in there; it was never good for the wagontrain to be visible for too many miles. He said. "And here, Ernesto, the mountain is close to our flank?"

"*Si, mi Capitano.*"

"And no trees till we reach ... this place, is that true?"

"True, *Señor Capitano*."

"And this is a trail, leading back into the forest?"

"A trail, sir, a new one. Cut, perhaps, by renegade slaves. Or by *guerrillas*. This mountain is infested with them."

"Do we know the extent of their armament?"

"They have a few guns. One of our scouts was fired on."

Captain Cordoba studied the sketches long and carefully. He said at last, "Then when we reach the plateau, we take this track to the north. See to it."

"*Si, Señor.*"

The cartographer moved off, hobbling painfully, and Cordoba went to his tent and said to the orderly there, "My compliments to Señorita Estrellita, and would she be kind enough to attend on me."

The orderly saluted and hurried off and the Captain poured two glasses of wine from the decanter that had been set out on the campaign table outside his tent. When Estrellita appeared, moving swiftly and with great assurance over the broken sod, he said, "Estrellita . . . how good of you. Come, sit down, we will have a glass of wine together."

Her hands were exploring and she found the edges of the chair he was holding out for her, sat herself down, and touched the edge of the table too, her hands creeping to the wine glass with marvellous delicacy. Finding it, she took it to her lips. "Your good health, Juan," she said. "We covered very few miles this day, I think?"

He sat down heavily and sighed. "Havana must believe that by now I am hammering at the fortifications of Santiago. If they only knew . . . and you, are you well?"

"I am well, Juan. And you?"

"Dispirited, I must confess. Though I do not know the reason why. We are, are as you suggest, moving very, very slowly. I could wish for greater speed."

He picked up his glass and sipped from it. "Tell me about *la Señora* Mercy Hawkes, Estrellita."

"And what is it you wish to know about her, Juan?"

"Is she well too? I wish I had more time to devote to her comfort."

"She is in very good hands . . ."

"Yes, I am sure of it. You do not find her . . . an emcumbrance?"

"An encumbrance?" She laughed. "Far from it, Juan! I delight in her company."

"Good."

"We are already the best of friends."

"Good, good . . ."

"She studies astrology, did you know that? And history too."

"History? Oh, really?"

"Yes. Her knowledge of . . . all kinds of little tidbits . . . her father, it seems, taught history in London, and she was telling me . . ."

Estrellita was laughing at the memory of it already and Cordoba felt a warm glow creeping into his blood as he watched her, delighted that she could be so happy. Estrellita went on. "She was telling me about a race of warrior women, can you believe that? Women who were soldiers? They were called *Amazons*, and I must confess, I never heard of them before."

"A river in Brazil," Cordoba murmured. "Perhaps they came from there. Or perhaps . . . the river was named after them?"

"Oh yes? But I was thinking . . . if they were the fighters, did they carry a wagon in their train filled with handsome young men to serve them? Mercy could not tell me that, she thought that perhaps they did not. But we had such a good laugh about it. Only . . . those warrior women cut off their right breast, so that they could better wield a sword. I don't think I like the idea of that very much. And she says, very seriously, that the stars will be right in a very few days, but not yet, for what she calls 'worthy causes.' Is ours a worthy cause, Juan?"

Cordoba said tartly, "We go to stifle an incipient rebellion against Her Majesty, Queen Isabella of Spain. Yes, I would say that is a worthy cause. And what is she doing now, *la Señora* Hawkes?"

"Dreaming of her lost husband."

"Perhaps we should invite her to join us. What do you think?"

"I think that that is an excellent idea."

Estrellita, very much at her ease here, raised a hand. When she heard the sound of the orderly's feet, stopping close by them, hearing even the light touch of his fingers on his cap as he saluted, she said, "My wagon . . . ask the English lady if she would care to honor us."

"*Señora* . . ."

The orderly hurried off and returned in a few moments with Mercy.

She was wearing a marvellously complex dress of dark burgundy color, the bodice drawn down to a long point, with a wide band of pleated fabric at the neckline, mitred at center-front, and a trailing black scarf. The white sheen of her bosom was shining in the light of the yellow flare and she was gorgeous.

Cordoba was getting to his feet, taking her hand,

bowing over it and kissing it. "*Señora*," he said, "you honor us with your presence. If you would partake of a glass of wine with us?"

"You are most kind, sir." Mercy murmured. She raised the glass he poured her and said, "Your health, Captain. And to the success of your mission."

"To success, for all of us, in all our endeavors, whatever they might be."

They drank together, quite solemnly. The distant sound of music and the voice of a woman, singing, in a strange, melodious language came to them over the still night air from the Creole camp. Estrellita, listening, said quietly, "The song of a lost love, to tear the heartstrings of your soldiers, Juan. There was a man she loved . . . and he left her for a younger woman . . . and he tired of his new love and returned . . . and found her . . . and every time he loved her, he called her by the other woman's name. It is really quite charming, is it not?"

She sipped her wine, leaned back in her chair, and said, "There is a cold, dry scent in the air tonight. The stars are very bright, I think?"

"Yes," the Captain nodded. "They are bright tonight."

"And Mercy tells me that for a short while there are perhaps hard times ahead of us because of them,"

"Because of the stars?"

He looked at Mercy quizzically and she said, nodding, "For just the next two or three days . . . yes, there will be difficult times ahead of all of us. What is your birthdate, Captain?"

He said, startled, "My birthdate? I was born, *Señora*, on February the tenth, in the year 1798 . . ."

"Ah, Aquarius, I should have known it!"

"Aquarius? I don't think I understand what you are saying, *Señora*."

"The eleventh sign," Mercy said patiently; his eyes were on her, not understanding at all. "Ruled by Saturn and Uranus, a sign of brotherhood, of humanitarian ideals. But . . . you are very set in your ways, I think."

He nodded. "Of course. I am a soldier."

"With a high sense of duty? Even of . . . logic?"

"I would wish to think so."

"Yes, yes, of course . . . and the relationships you have with your friends are of the utmost importance to you, no doubt?"

"They are indeed. In some cases, of the greatest possible importance."

His eyes had moved to Estrellita, studying the outline of her delicate, sensuous features, edged now by the light of the flares. She said, almost mocking him, "Are you looking at me, Juan? I believe you are . . ."

He was overwhelmed by confusion. "Estrellita," he said, "you confound me."

He was suddenly very grave. "And most unhappily, I am wondering whether or not I should send you back to Havana. With, of course, all your young ladies, and *Señora* Hawkes.

Mercy heard the quick intake of breath from the blind woman. "Send us back, Juan?" she echoed. "But why? Will you tell me why?"

Mercy too was staring at him. He got to his feet and began striding up and down, in and out of the yellow pools of light.

386

He said slowly, "This afternoon, a runner, near dead from exhaustion, came in from Santiago with a message from one of our spies there. It seems that Governor Aguilar knows that I have been sent to arrest him. It seems that he knew just a few days after my wagontrain had left the capital, though how he got the intelligence so speedily I cannot imagine. Perhaps a relay of very fast horses, though there is talk there, it seems, of birds that bring him messages. Pigeons, I believe. I find this very hard to believe, but . . . somewhere in the recesses of my mind, I seem to have heard of . . . is the word *homing* pigeons? Birds that once taken from their home will fly back there at great speed? With messages attached to their legs? It all seems very unlikely."

"The pigeon post," Mercy said, "is six or seven hundred years old. In England, pigeon racing—the birds carrying numbers fastened to their legs and flying from one predetermined point to another—is one of our favorite sports."

Cordoba was watching her, a very considerable respect in his eyes. "Then perhaps," he said, "it is not so unlikely after all. Be that as it may, he knows all about us."

"But when we reach Santiago," Estrellita said, protesting, "we will have no part of the battle! Surely, we will be camped somewhere away from the fighting, as always? It should not be necessary for us to leave you now, so far away from our goal."

"If he were to meet us *there*, perhaps you are right," Cordoba said. "Aguilar is no soldier, but he has a large and well-armed force of mercenaries of his own—renegade Spaniards, Frenchmen, Englanders, a few Germans, even Creoles . . . who commands them, I do not yet know. But perhaps it is a man named Manteras, a colonel of more than adequate expertise in the field. If it is indeed Manteras, or anyone else of military competence, he will not wait for us to place our cannon outside his fort and blow him to perdition."

He stared out for a moment at a work-party who were grooming the mules, and he went on.

"He will meet us in the mountains. My troops are the best on the island, but . . . if Aguilar sends more than five or six hundred men against us? I have a hundred and seventy fusiliers, twenty-two of them at this moment suffering from fever, carried in the wagons, and unable to fight. He will lay an ambush for me somewhere near Sagua de Palmirito, and we will be at a very considerable disadvantage. I have asked myself, therefore, whether I should not sent you back, Estrellita, with your young ladies, and with *Señora* Hawkes, to the safety that only Havana can offer you."

Mercy had reached out to put a hand on Estrellita's, and the blind woman said quietly, "If the worst should happen, Juan, and for myself I doubt it, then some of my girls would change sides happily, some of them with the greatest reluctance. But even mercenaries do not harm whores. They need their services too."

"And you, Estrellita?"

"Need you ask?"

"I think not. I want to hear it from you."

"I myself," Estrellita said clearly, "would rather die in your company than give up my allegiance to Spain. I have good friends among the girls. They have, for the most part, little in their favor except

388

their bodies, but yet . . . I have grown close to them and the parting would grieve me deeply. Nonetheless, I would never serve Aguilar in any capacity whatsoever. You must know that, Juan."

"And *Señora* Hawkes?"

"Mercy is in my charge," Estrellita said, "and I promise you that no harm will come to her. Though that decision must, of course, be hers. I have only one thing to say. If Manteras, or even Aguilar himself comes out to meet you . . : you will win that battle, Juan. Just as you have always won all your others."

"I am gratified by your confidence," he said dryly.

He turned to Mercy. "There may be dire trouble ahead of us, *Señora*," he said.

She interrupted him calmly, "Yes, I know it. I already told you of them . . ."

"And be that as it may . . . what say you? Would you not feel safer on your way back to Havana?"

She shook her head. "If Estrellita prefers to stay with you, Captain," she said firmly, "then I will stay too. My friends . . . are in this camp. I will stay with my friends."

She was barely conscious that Estrellitas' hand, in the darkness, had found hers.

Adam Butrus, driving his pony almost to its death, had ridden hard for three days and three nights. Jake Ollie rode beside him, a squat uncomfortable figure perched atop a horse that was far too heavy for him, his short legs reaching barely down its heaving, foam-specked flanks.

Ollie was not a good horseman.

389

He said, as they galloped hard along the tightly packed sand of the beach, "Adam . . . if I'm to ride another mile . . . in God's name, let's stop for a drink of rum."

Butrus was riding easily, his body straight and muscular, part of his mount. He called back, "Another few miles, Jake, and we turn into the forest. Then, the village is only an hour's ride away. If we can believe this damned map."

"And if we can't?" He was panting heavily from the exertion, the sweat soaking his woollen shirt.

"Then we ride on till we find it."

The sound of pounding hooves was a counterpoint to the susurration of the surf beside them. They passed the headland which was their marker and in a little while they found the old muletrack that turned north and cut its way into the jungle, already overgrown with long, probing lianas. They slowed to a canter and then to a walk, then Butrus jumped down and led the horse by its halter, using his saber to cut a way through, his fierce energy inexhaustible. Ollie eased himself in the unaccustomed saddle and swore volubly. It was not until more than two hours had passed that they came to the clearing in the forest and the little hamlet that was called Sagua de Palmirito. ,

They rode their horses easily down its single, mud-packed road, the women, the old men, and children coming out of their ranshackle houses to stare at them, knowing that a fine Spanish *Hidalgo* had ridden into town with his servant, and that it could only mean trouble for them. The sun was sinking, casting oblique beams of light that cut through the foliage of the trees and gilding the dust the horses' hooves were making.

They rode to the tavern together, and dismounted, dropping their horses' reins over the horizontal pole set there. The tavernkeeper was at the door, bowing to them obsequiously, his straw hat in his hand. Smelling their money, he said, "Gentlemen . . . welcome to my miserable tavern, where the best food in the whole of Oriente is served . . . and how may I serve your Excellencies?"

He bowed them into the warm and smoky room. Butrus looked over the four men there with hard, uncompromising eyes. He turned back to the fawning man and said, "First, your name, Innkeeper." There was an old woman crouched by the fire in the corner, looking at him with hatred in her eyes. But the landlord was bowing, bobbing up and down, knowing his safety depended upon his humility.

"Sistera, Excellency," he said. "Sistera Manuelo, at your service."

"And these fellows here? Each one of them, Sistera."

The tavernkeeper said, indicating, "Aruba, a farmer, and Fedora, another farmer, but they have no cattle left. They were honored to supply one of your patrols with their last few beasts. And Sinara, who cuts wood in the forest, and Escobar, who does not work at all because he is lazy and says that he is too old to work. All loyal subjects of Spain, Excellency, and devoted to His Glorious Majesty King . . . ah, King . . . no, *Her* Glorious Majesty, our Queen. And what will you take, good sirs? My beer is truly excellent, much praised in the neighborhood, and I have a powerful rum which is made for me, to my express order, you understand, in Santiago itself."

"Then give these fellows enough of your filthy beer to fill their miserable bellies and bring us a jug of rum. And food? What have you for food?"

"A roast suckling pig, Excellency?"

"Good. See to it, Sistera."

They sat down at a table and Jake Ollie lowered his head into his hands, saying, "Holy Mother of Christ, if I'd had to ride another mile . . . the horse is not a fit creature to carry a man on his back, Adam. He's shaped all wrong."

Butrus took off his *shako* and laid it down, ran his fingers through his long, dark-brown hair, and said, "An hour or two to rest and eat and drink, Jake, and then we move on. There's a gorge ahead of us, a hard night's ride to the west. I want to look at it."

"Mother of God," Ollie said. "Cordoba will never leave the beach. So for the love of Christ, what the devil are we doing in these damned mountains?"

"If he's on the beach, which I doubt very much, he'll have to leave it. And he'll have to pass through that gorge if he hopes to reach Santiago before he dies of old age."

He slapped his hand on the table and roared, "Landlord! Where in hell is that rum?"

"Coming, Excellency, coming . . ." Sistera was bustling out of another room, a large jug of crude, discolored pewter on a wooden tray with two tin mugs. He set them down and said, "The food, Excellency, in half an hour?"

The old crone was on her knees at the fire, blowing onto the embers to make them glow. As they began to drink, Ollie's eyes went to the door, bulging, and he said, whispering, "Mother of Christ . . . look, Adam."

The twins were there, carrying between them an already cooked young pig on a stake, taking it to the fire and placing it in the notches of the iron holders at its sides. As they bent over it and eased it into position over the hot coals, Butrus studied them both, admiring their rounded haunches. Ollie whispered excitedly, "We're in luck, Adam. Two of us, two of them."

Butrus said mildly to the tavernkeeper, "I am surprised, Sistera, that you keep such jewels in such a pig pen. Bring them here."

"Con mucho gusto, excelencia . . . they are my daughters. Their poor mother died and they are all I have left in a cruel, cruel world, to comfort me in my old age."

"Call them over, Sistera."

"Of course, Excellency, at once." He raised his voice, authoritatively. "Over here, both of you, come, come . . ."

The pig was set in its bracket and the old woman used a stick to turn it heavily on its axis. She crouched there in front of the fire with her long black dress a shroud around her. The girls came over and stood close by the table, looking at the handsome and elegant *Caballero* and trying to avoid the leering eyes of the gross fellow with him, his servant, no doubt, even though he was drinking with his master.

Butrus said to Sistera, "And they speak Spanish too?"

He was rubbing his hands together, pleased that something here, at least, had found the approval of this very rich-looking gentleman. "Of course, Excellency. We are all loyal subjects here. We all speak His Majesty's language, even among ourselves. Except for Escobar, he speaks only Creole, an old man, only Creole . . ."

Butrus, smiling gently, was looking the two girls over, from head to foot. They wore long skirts of coarse cotton, not padded out, it seemed, with many petticoats, and identical blouses of heavy, off-white calico that had been made from floursacks but were decorated at the deep necklines with intertwined pieces of blue ribbon. The blouses were very loose, quite high on the shoulders but gaping wide, so that the upper part of the bosom, and rather more than that, was exposed.

He said, still smiling, "You are twins, no doubt, identical twins at that . . . And your names?"

"Almira, Alvira," they answered, almost in unison.

He laughed. "And how shall I tell one of you from the other, can you tell me that?"

"One of us," Almira said slyly, "has a tiny mole on her thigh, just above the knee."

"Ah . . . And which one of you is that?"

"In truth, sir," Alvira said, "we are never quite sure ourselves."

He was thinking: Ha! It augurs well!

He said, "And your father? Can *he* tell you apart?"

One of them answered innocently, "No, Excellency, never. He says: 'Almira, come and light the fire,' and I light the fire, and I am Alvira. Or he says: 'Alvira, put more bread in the beer barrels,' and I say yes, Father, and do it, and I am Almira . . ."

He sighed. "And I think you are playing a game with me now."

"Of course, Excellency. It is always good to play

394

games. After all, we are both . . . children. Your servants, but children."

There was a light of pure mischief in their eyes, and one of them said, "Will you stay here tonight, Excellency? We have beds here, good clean beds, if you would like to sleep?"

Butrus shook his head. "Unhappily, *Senoritas*, I am on a mission of importance."

Ollie said hoarsely, "Adam . . . Adam, I can't ride another mile tonight . . ."

Butrus went on, "I could wish that it were not so important."

"Our mattresses are made of good kapok," one of them said, "not straw. The beds are very comfortable." The other chimed in, "And very warm, Excellency. It is certain that you would be comfortable, an honored guest."

"And you have a stable? And a stableboy?"

"Yes, Excellency."

Butrus considered for a moment; the game, he thought, was a pleasant one, even though he had not initiated it himself. He made a mental note to keep his knife close by his side during the night, and raised his voice to call "Innkeeper!"

Sistera came running, chased the girls away, and waited, fawning. Butrus said, "I see that my companion is very tired, so perhaps, if you have lodgings, we should spend the night here and leave in the morning. We have both ridden very hard this day, and a good night's sleep . . ."

"Of course, Excellency, we have splendid rooms, three of them . . ."

"Two will be sufficient."

"Of course, of course . . ."

395

"And if you will have someone feed and water the horses, rub them down well, stable them?"

"At once, Excellency."

He hurried off outside.

Butrus stared absently at the fire, another problem pressing into the recesses of his mind, the girls forgotten now in a sudden and unexpected onslaught of awareness. . . .

He had cast his mind back to the days of the *Capricorn*, and he was sure it could not be possible, and yet? He said to himself. "But why not? It's entirely possible. And if so?"

The men were gathering about him, aware, perhaps, of a sudden distraction and hoping that his evident worries did not concern them. He looked up sharply and saw the four of them advancing on him, their tin cups of beer extended. One of them cleared his throat and said slowly, in execrable Spanish, "Her health, Excellency, the health of your Queen . . . no, of *our* Queen, the Lady, the Lady . . . Maria?"

"Isabella," Butrus said, and the man nodded eagerly.

"To the health of the Lady Isabella, Excellency, and to your own."

He raised his own mug and said automatically, "The health of the Queen."

Someone murmured, "*A todos los Peninsulares*, to all the Spaniards."

They hated them with an undying and virulent passion; but they kept it well concealed.

The movement toward independence was very strong, but it was dangerous because the arms of the Spanish overlords were stronger. If a man dared raise his voice (or even, on occasion, not smile

when he should have smiled) he faced the danger
of the hangman's noose, or—worse, far worse—the
terrible *garrotte*, an instrument of execution that
terrified them. They had seen too many of their
fellows seated in the dreadful chair with the collar
around the neck, the wooden screw, sometimes, not
quite driven home to break the spinal column as it
was meant to do, but merely cutting off all air so
that the hapless victim strangled to death, very
slowly. Sometimes people were garroted for so trifling an offense as hiding the food that was needed
for the support of their own families.

But where one Spaniard went, or two or three, it
always meant others close by, in force. And there
was nothing they could do but conceal their loathing and doff their peasant hats, hoping they would
be regarded as loyal subjects of the Crown, or even
as friends.

So, they drank their cloudy beer in a toast, and
were grateful when Sistera came back to fill up
their mugs once more, and again and again as the
evening wore on and the night came in its wake.

The twins had sliced off great quantities of pork,
setting it on the table on two tin plates. Butrus took
Ollie's shoulder and shook it to wake him up, saying, "Ollie, wake up, the devil take you! Food! Eat,
man, eat!"

Ollie grunted and rubbed a hand over his bleary
eyes, trying to focus them. He began tearing at the
succulent flesh with his hands, wiping the grease
from his mouth with the sleeve of his coat.

Butrus said, almost casually, "Jake, take a good
look at that hairshirt that abominable fellow is
wearing. The innkeeper. Did you ever see it before?"

397

Jake Ollie was well into his cups. He tried to steady the swaying of the room and stared. He said, "A hairshirt, the kind the whalers wear. Nothing . . . nothing special about a hairshirt, Adam."

"A whaler's shirt? In the middle of the Cuban jungle?"

"Well, maybe they've got whales in these waters too, who knows?"

Butrus was sure, but he could not believe it. He said urgently, "The brown binding at the neck and the cuffs, Jake! The pocket that someone sewed onto the sleeve to hold a splicing-knife! There can only be one hairshirt just like that in the whole of the whaling-fleet."

Ollie grunted. He banged his mug on the table and roared, "Landlord! More rum! Damn your eyes, more rum!" There was a piece of pork gristle hanging from the corner of his mouth.

"Coming, sir, immediately, sir . . ."

Sistera waddled quickly to them, took the jug away and refilled it before setting it down for them again. Butrus said mildly, "A fine shirt you wear, Innkeeper. Not from these parts, I think?"

Sistera was taken aback, a moment of alarm showing in his wary eyes. "But . . . honestly come by, Excellency. I assure you."

"I'm sure of it."

Butrus's eyes were like flint. "You bought it, no doubt, from someone who passed through here?"

"No, sir, Excellency, in truth . . ."

He was stammering, sure that somehow, somewhere, he had done some sort of wrong. "It was found, Excellency, in the forest, by my daughters. On a dead man, and what would a dead man do with a good shirt? It would only be wasted, torn to shreds by the birds to make their nests with."

"A dead man? You are sure that he was dead?"

"So they told me, Excellency. If you wish, I will call them over . . ."

"No. I will talk to them later. I am interested in the man who was wearing that shirt. The dead man."

Sistera could only blink his eyes, wondering what sort of trouble he might have stumbled into. A man could never tell with the Spaniards; they seemed to look for trouble wherever they went. And if they could not find it, they made it.

The twins were sweeping out the room that the fine *Hidalgo* was going to use, sweeping out weeks of dirt and the droppings of the rats that made their home in the rafters. They were deciding between themselves just what they should do about him, with a fine Creole nonchalance.

Almira, who was a little more reckless than her twin, said dispassionately, "I think we have a good chance to kill him. To kill both of them."

"And in the morning," Alvira said casually, "there will be a patrol of troops passing by, and they will say: Where is the Spanish *Hidalgo* who came here last night? Where is his fat and bloated servant?"

"No. They came alone, I'm sure of it."

"But he's an officer! What is it, a captain?"

"No, a colonel, I think. I'm not sure about that."

"Well, then . . ."

"We could get a fine price for their horses, and for the captain's uniform . . . and he must have a lot of money, too."

399

"Not a captain, a colonel."

"So much the better. The whole village would welcome it."

"The whole village just might be strung up on the trees. Or garroted."

"It seems such a good opportunity. A pity to waste it. We don't even have to do it ourselves. We could get one of the men . . . we could even suggest it to Father, he'd think it a wonderful idea too. If he hasn't thought of it already."

"Father!" Alvira said scornfully. "Father would tremble at the mere thought of it. And he'd beat us for thinking about it."

"Yes, that's true enough. But if we can find out where his troops are, and send word to what's-his-name up in the Sierra? What's his name?"

"I can never remember it. We'd have to know how many of them, too."

"The way he's drinking, he'll be dead drunk by the time we bed him."

"He may not talk about his troops quite so easily, even so . . ."

"Why not? He's man, isn't he?"

She was giggling. "Very much a man . . ."

"So he's a fool! He'll tell us everything we want to know. And what's-his-name will pay us handsomely."

"Handsomely! He's handsome too! We can make much better use of him."

They were both laughing suddenly, and Almira said, "But his skin is so white! It looks like lard."

"I know, it's really disgusting. But did you notice the bulge in his breeches?"

"Of course I noticed it, silly! It looked enormous. I'd *love* to feel that inside me. Like the trunk of a coconut palm."

"Only warmer . . ."

"I know, can you imagine it? I wonder if he's very hairy? I don't really like too much hair on a man."

"Oh, I don't mind it. As long as he knows what he has to *do*."

"I'm sure that one does. Why don't we both have him?"

"Well, of course it's not going to be just *you* . . ."

"Me first, and you can watch. And then you."

"No, we'll play with him, you on one side and me on the other, and see what he does."

"What he *does*?" She was laughing hysterically. "We *know* what he's going to do!"

Almira sat on the edge of the bed and held her hands between her thighs, pressing her knees together. "And I'm getting all hot and sticky."

"Me too . . . we'll have to ask him for money. We can't just *take* it from him."

"I don't see why not."

"Unless we really do kill him. And it would be terribly dangerous, Mira."

"Well, let's have him first, and then . . . just see what happens. *Mi Dios*, it really is like a coconut palm, you know . . ."

"But they're really quite small, the Spaniards, I mean, if you compare them to our own men."

"Not that one. I saw! I can hardly wait."

"Wait, Mira. Don't waste it all, keep it in, I'm going to."

"Yes, I suppose so . . ."

She got up off the bed and looked up into the rafters. In the light of the two hanging tins of tallow, a rat was scuttling from one side of the little room to the other. She said, not very enthusiastically, "Should we make smoke and drive them out for a while?"

"What, the rats?" Vira shrugged. "It's not worth all that trouble, he won't mind. I hope his attention is not going to be on rats."

She looked around the room and said happily, "Well, that's clean enough. Why don't we go and tell him: 'Your Excellency, your room is ready, and if you are, we will be happy to show you where it is'?"

Almira spat onto the floor. She said savagely, "Excellency! A Spanish bastard, nothing more!"

"But bearing a tree trunk between his legs. Let's enjoy it. And remember to be servile, all the time. *Yes, Excellency, no Excellency, what would you like to do now, Excellency? Shall I turn over, Excellency?* And all the time too: *Where are your troops, Excellency? How many guns do they have, Excellency?*"

Alvira was not laughing anymore. She also spat, and she said, "I spit on their graves! And I still think we should kill him. Both of them. It would be so *easy* . . ."

They went out to fetch Adam Butrus, to tell him that everything was ready for him.

He lay back, naked, on the kapok-stuffed canvas bag that was his mattress, thinking: *The Creoles, all a man has to do is snap his fingers . . .*

He watched in deep appreciation as the twins stripped off their clothing in the faint yellow light, a light in which the soft glow of their skins seemed to take on a luminescence of its own that was almost amber.

They were slender and willowy with a marvellous articulation to their movements. Their breasts were very high and firm and swelling, with tiny, very dark nipples. Their long black hair fell untended about their shoulders. As they moved to clamber onto the bed with him, one on each side just as they had planned, he ordered, "No. Stay there for a moment, I want to look at you."

As though driven by the same thought, they were both shaking their heads. One of them said softly, "No, Excellency, *we* want to look at *you*. Such beautiful white skin, there is nothing more beautiful than truly white skin . . ."

The other twin was stroking his body delicately, and his hand was at her thigh, finding the little mole and touching it lightly with his fingertips. "Almira?" he asked.

"No, Excellency," Almira said. "I am Alvira." There was a little frown on her lovely face, and he said, "Something disturbs you, Alvira?"

She shook her head and brushed her lips against his. "Only . . . only that it worries me that you come here alone. In Sagua, you are safe. Of course you are safe, this is a loyal village. But the hills are full of *bandidos*, and if they know you and your companion are here, alone . . . you are alone, are you not?"

"Not alone, Alvira."

"Almira, Excellency."

"Ah, yes, Almira is the one with the mole." He leaned over and kissed it. "I am not alone, Almira."

"Alvira."

"Yes, of course. Alone? No. My men are camped at the river's edge, less than a mile away."

"Good. I am so happy for you. Fifty, a hundred men there . . . the *bandoleros* will know, they have their spies everywhere, and this means that we are safe from them."

"Not fifty or a hundred, Alvira. More than three hundred of Spain's best soldiers."

"Three hundred? *Madre de Dios!* Then we are indeed safe, and I am happy for us all. At the river?"

"At the river," he said gravely, "where the mango trees are."

It was a lie.

One hundred and forty horsemen would indeed have crossed the river by now and taken up their allocated position on the lower slopes of the Sierra. Two hundred and eighty fusiliers were enduring a terrible forced march at breakneck pace and were only half a day's march away. A third contingent of one hundred and ten, having left twenty-four hours earlier and marched through the forest itself, moving only by night and hiding during the day, was already concealed in the valley that ran down to the cliffs at the edge of the beach and awaited the runners who would bring them their orders. And eight cannon, broken down and carried on mules, were on a high peak overlooking the village.

Almira stretched her mellow, pliant body close to his and fingered him, brushing her sister's hand away. He put an arm carefully about each of their necks and reached down to cup a golden breast in each hand. He said casually, "Tell me about your dead man, the dead man you found in the forest."

They were both startled. The probing hands stopped their motion. "The dead man?"

"Your father told me. You found a dead man in the forest. Tell me about him."

"But . . . what is there to tell? He was dead, and we took his clothes, and his pouch, a good knife in it, the kind that folds up, and some pieces of rope . . ." She was alarmed now. "He was not a Spanish soldier, Excellency, but . . . a *Norteamericano*, I think."

He turned to the other twin. "And you, Almira-Alvira? You too think he was a *Norteamericano*? No, don't stop your caresses, they please me."

"Of course, Excellency, whatever pleases Your Excellency." She continued her manipulations, and said, "Yes, he was a *Norteamericano*, I think."

"And he was dead?"

"Yes. At first, he was dead."

She felt the body stiffen under her touch. "At *first*?"

"We did not see it, but . . . he got up and walked away. With no boots, no clothes . . . into the jungle." They were giggling again at the memory of it.

For a long time, Adam Butrus said nothing. He murmured at last, "And there was a woman with him?"

"A woman? No, Excellency, there was no one with him. We found the tracks in the mud where he had gone off into the forest."

"And had there been someone with him? You would have known?"

"But of course, Excellency. His tracks in the mud, no one else's."

"And this was when, precisely?"

"Three days ago, Excellency."

"Three days ago . . . well, let us forget your dead man who mysteriously comes to life again, and walks off into the forest without the help of a young woman who was undoubtedly with him. It is really of no importance at all."

For one terrible moment, the twins thought that his interest in them had quite gone. But his erect manhood had not lost its strength, and they played with him for a while as he thought, unknown to them, of another woman.

He said to himself? *If he is in Cuba, then she is here too, and I will find her, and I will enjoy that tender, unspoiled body of hers. Again and again and again . . .*

The thought of Mercy aroused him. He rolled over on top of Almira and and drove himself furiously, without any preliminaries at all, deeply into her. When he was fully contained, and his loins were moving of their own volition, he thought: *This sweet young child wants to know where all my troops are . . .*

He heard the other twin's gentle voice, "And what would you like *me* to do now, Excellency?"

He reached out for her hungrily, and pulled her down close beside him, and buried his face between her soft, full breasts.

In a little while he eased himself from Almira, and poised himself for a moment between Alvira's welcoming thighs. Plunging fully into her, he satiated himself completely, not caring which of them was which now, knowing only that they were supple-bodied young women and that they were his to enjoy as he wished, not only because he was—at least in this moment of his career—a Spani-

406

ard; but also because he was a man. They were merely chattels to be enjoyed in any matter that pleased him. The thought gave him great, masculine satisfaction.

He slept for a while, conscious always of their ripe and beautiful bodies enfolding his, and he took both of them again, then, at last, fell into the final sleep of exhaustion.

And he was thinking, when the oblivion came over him: *Where are you, Mercy Carrol?*

CHAPTER NINETEEN

The wagon-train had indeed left the beach.

The red cliffs were towering high, right down to the water's edge, gilded now in the evening sun, blocking any further progress along the sand. They halted for a while, waiting for one of the advance scouts to report back. When at last he had come galloping in, his pony quivering and drenched with sweat, he had reined in sharply. The pretty little mare pranced on her hind legs, and he had called out, pointing back into the forest, "An abandoned *hacienda, Señor Capitano*, a good place to camp, one hour away from the train."

Cordoba took from his pocket the beautiful silver timepiece that had been in his family for two hundred years. Its ornate case was deeply engraved, and its movement bore the minute signature: *Jean Houbert, Rouen, France, 1646.* It had first been worn by the French general who commanded the troops sent by Cardinal Richelieu into the then-French province of Catalonia, back in the 1640s, and had been taken from him by Juan Cordoba's great-great-great-great-grandfather, the famous General Alonzo Montero-Cordoba. Ever since, it had been carried into battle, a reminder of a proud heritage, by seven generations of Spanish officers.

It was a little after five. He lifted the watchglass, wound it carefully with the little key that was attached to the fob, and mechanically, a matter of habit, pushed over the lever that rang the last hour to have passed, a pleasing, tinkling sound.

"A *hacienda?*" he asked. "Protected, trooper?"

"An adobe wall around it, Captain. A good house, four other buildings."

"Abandoned?"

"No sign of life there at all."

"And beyond it?"

"A good trail to the east, Captain, the scouts are checking it now."

"Very well, we will make camp there. Tell the officer of the day."

"At once, *Señor Capitano.*" He spurred his horse and galloped off.

The wagontrain wheeled its cumbersome way around and entered the forest vastness. One hour and fifteen minutes later, when the last light of the evening was in the sky, they came to the wide clearing where the old *hacienda* stood.

The gates in the adobe wall were open, and guarded by two of the scouts. One of them, a sergeant, eased his mount over to Cordoba and saluted, grinning. "A fine camp, *Señor Capitano.* A good house, fully furnished, food in the pantry not

410

yet rotting, a stable of eight horses that are hungry, but . . . they must have been fed just a few days ago. They're dried out and being watered now . . . we've set up your quarters, sir, on the second floor, some fine bedrooms there."

"And no people here at all?"

"None, sir. We broke down one of the doors to gain entry. The place looks as if it was left in a hurry just a day or two ago."

"Is there any indication, Sergeant, for their haste? Our approach, perhaps? Or might it mean that there is some other army nearby? Creoles? Or slaves seeking their freedom? . . ."

He was an elderly man and a little philosophical. He shook his head. "For myself, Captain," he said, "I've always found it easy to accept the inexplicable. Seems to me that life is made up of mysteries, and if we tried to find an explanation for all of them . . . We'll leave at sunup, sir?"

Cordoba was lost in thought. He said at last, "I don't know yet, Sergeant. Have we good accommodations for the men here?"

"Excellent, sir."

"Then have the bugler sound officers' call in . . . fifteen minutes. I want evey building in the compound searched from top to bottom. Report to me yourself when it's been done."

"Very good, sir."

He rode off and Cordoba walked his horse slowly around the perimeter of the wall, wondering what had become of the residents here, and just who they might have been. He thought about the sergeant's comment, adding to it: *And in Cuba, the inexplicable is constant . . .*

The wall was a little less than the height of an

411

average man, with recessed embrasures down its sides and twenty-foot-high towers at each corner, also of adobe. He was pleased to see that each of them was already occupied by a sentry.

He gave his horse to his orderly and went on into the main house.

It was very large and comfortable, with a timbered hall and a mahogany staircase, good carpets everywhere and tapestries on the walls, and a great deal of very fine French furniture. The home, then, of one of the French planters.

An orderly was carrying a taper around, lighting all the fine oil lamps. He heard the bugle call out there in the grounds, and another orderly was lighting lamps and waiting to show him his quarters.

It was a large, airy room furnished with: a long and highly polished table, a number of bookshelves filled with books in French, a lot of portraits of what he presumed were family members on the walls, a huge Oriental carpet on the floor. Whoever had lived here—or still lived here—was apparently a man of great wealth. There were heavy cabinets everywhere, and he opend them one by one and looked at all the secrets of an unknown stranger's life—pieces of fine china, excellent glassware, a dozen or so bottles of French wine, objets d'art in ceramic or porcelain, a few leatherbound ledgers. He felt oddly ill at ease and he was glad when his lieutenants entered in answer to the sounded summons.

They stood there respectfully, waiting for him to speak, and he said, "The officer of the day is?"

One of them clicked his heels and inclined his head. "Lieutenant Barbastro, Captain."

"Ah yes . . . well, Barbastro, you will find in the cupboard there some excellent French claret and a fine array of Bohemian crystal glasses . . . if you would be kind enough?"

"Sir." He was very young, Barbastro, barely out of his teens, clean-shaven with very long curly hair and dark eyed filled with innocent wonderment. He set out the glasses on the table and opened two of the bottles and poured.

Cordoba, sunk in thought, began pacing, a heavy load on his shoulders.

He said at last, "Gentlemen . . . there is something very wrong going on, and I confess that I do not know what it might be. For five days now I have received no word, no word of any sort, from the man in Santiago whose duty it is to keep me informed of what is happening there. His name is Fernand Duval, A Frenchman who lives by the harbor, and he has long served us well. But for five days . . . nothing from him, and it troubles me."

They were all waiting for him to drink first. He picked up his glass and said, "To Her Majesty, Queen Isabella. Long may she reign."

"To the Queen . . ."

He went on, stabbing at the air with his hand, "We know, unhappily, that Governor Aguilar is at least aware of our presence somewhere between Havana and Santiago. We are on the somewhat ill-defined border of Oriente Province, which means that in the next few days we should prepare ourselves for a possible attack. I cannot really believe that Aguilar will make such an overt move against us, but we cannot be sure of that. Only Duval can

413

tell me whether such an eventuality is, in truth, likely or not, and Duval is strangely silent."

He was trying to hide the worry that was gnawing at his mind: How long was it that the devious Frenchman had been sending off his reports? He could not remember.

He went on, "I will be frank with you, gentlemen, my superiors in Havana believe, quite strongly, that all we have to do is to march into Santiago and arrest its governor. I do not share that view. It is known that his army has grown far beyond the bounds dictated by provincial security; it is known that he had ambitions concerning the whole of the island; it is known that his loyalty, so often and so volubly protested, is in very considerable doubt. In short, gentlemen, I think the possibility is very strong that Aguilar will meet our arms, when we reach the city, not with a meek surrender that he knows must lead him to Madrid and a trial for treason . . . but with his own arms. We do not know the strength of his army in definite terms, but we do know that—quite illegally—it is composed largely of mercenaries. Which means that their devotion is to him, and not to the Crown. I have, therefore, made certain decisions."

He looked over his officers, knowing that they were good men, all of them. Yet he was unable to drive away the terrible sense of loneliness that had come over him, nor even to account for it.

He went on, "A fast horse can reach Santiago in about forty-eight hours. The home of Fernand Duval is easy to find, a shop in the harbor with his name on it. I want one of you to leave this place tonight, accompanied by one sergeant, both of you out of uniform, and to ride hard to Santiago, to

414

find Duval, to learn from him what Aguilar's probable intentions are, and report back to me here."

He looked at one of the older lieutenants, a dark and swarthy man in his forties named Valverde, who came from Cadiz. "I thought you might undertake this task for me, Valverde," he said.

The lieutenant sprang to attention and said, "At your command, Captain. I will take Sergeant Tivisa, with your permission?"

"Of course. When you meet with Duval . . . I leave everything to your discretion. You know what is required of him."

"And . . . he is to be trusted, Captain?"

Cordoba gestured wryly. "A Frenchman," he said. "But within limits imposed on all Frenchmen by their devious intellectuality . . . yes, he is to be trusted. If only because he knows that the Crown, in the end, will triumph. As always. I have driven all of you hard, the men too. And the time has come for rest before we undertake the last leg of our journey. We will spend the next few days here awaiting your return. It would be best if you were to leave at once."

Valverde saluted, clicked his heels, and hurried out. Cordoba continued, "Four days, gentlemen, we will stay here. We will regard it as a fortified compound, and we will take the usual precautions for its defense. Barbastro?"

"Sir?"

"My compliments to the cartographer and tell him I want a detailed map of this compound before he goes to bed tonight. It will not be easy for him in the darkness, he can amend it at first light. I want scouts out to examine the approaches. Tell them to find whatever Creole villages there may be

415

here and question the inhabitants closely for news of the passing of any troops. Closely, I say . . . but they are to be treated as friends of Spain, and with respect, is that clear?"

"*Si, Señor Capitano.*"

"I want a constant patrol around the perimeter, I want another to circle the clearing, and I want yet a third about two hours' ride out. They will all keep in constant touch with the Officer of the Day. The camp followers may camp within the walls. The troopers, except those on patrol, will not leave the confines of the compound at any time, or for any reason. A state of stand-by-arms will be posted immediately. Now . . . if there are any questions?"

One of them, an elderly and sickly looking man who had distinguished himself in combat so many times that the name *Lieutenant Carpio* had become a legend to marvel at, said mildly, "It is apparent, Captain, that you expect an attack *here*? A week's march for a body of troops from Santiago?"

"No, Carpio," Cordoba said. "I do not *expect* it. I will, however, *anticipate* it."

"There are three places where the wall needs strengthening. The decay of old age. Which all of us suffer from . . ."

Cordoba smiled thinly. "So I observed. I assume it will be attended to. Barbastro?"

"I will put some men on it at once, Captain."

"Good. And the sick roll today?"

"Thirty-seven men, sir, "Barbastro said uncomfortably. "And three sergeants."

Cordoba felt himself paling. "Forty men on sick roll?"

"Yes, sir. Almost all of them with the fever. I fear that we will lose perhaps three of them."

416

"Forty men out of a hundred and seventy," Cordoba said angrily, "is not an acceptable figure! Do we still have quinine?"

"The medical orderlies are worried that the supply is running very low, Captain. But if we are staying here for a little while . . ."

"Yes, yes," Cordoba said, interrupting. "There are cinchona trees and shrubs growing here everywhere. Send out half a dozen men in the morning to strip the bark off every tree they find, let us profit by the delay and build up our supplies of medication."

"We passed a fine stand of it just before we entered the compound, *Señor Capitano*. I will see to it."

Cordoba, aware that Carpio was lost in thought, said quietly, "What is it that troubles you, Lieutenant Carpio?"

The old man answered, slowly, "As we entered the compound, Captain, I observed a bluff to the north of the *Hacienda*, thickly wooded . . ."

"I saw it."

"No more than five hundred paces away, and high enough to . . . to *threaten* us here. I would like your permission, Captain, to take a patrol up there. Just two or three good men. Or alone, if necessary."

"Please do so. And if there are no more questions . . ."

There were a few polite murmurs, and they left him alone again—terribly alone. He went through the open door into the adjoining bedroom and stared at the big brass bed there, already made up for him with the covers turned down in military precision, his night-robe laid out ready for him. He knew he would not sleep at all this night unless, somehow, he could shake off the feeling of apprehension.

He went back into the other room and saw the orderly setting out the solitary service for his dinner, his unknown host's excellent pewter, no less! He said, shaking off the malaise, "What are we eating tonight, trooper?"

The man stood rigidly to attention. "Goat, sir. There was a fine young goat careless enough to walk right past the kitchen quarters just when the cook was wondering what to feed you this night."

"Splendid! Then set two more places. Find *Señora* Estrellita for me, give her my compliments, and ask her if she and the English lady would honor me with their presence for dinner."

He went to the big intricately carved cupboard, selected a particularly fine claret, and uncorked it, laying the cork across the top of the bottle while it breathed, just as his illustrious father—an officer in the army of King Ferdinand VII, who had been killed during the Cadiz mutiny of 1820—had taught him to do. He took out the little watch that he had been given by the old man as he lay on his death bed, and touched the lever for the pleasure of hearing the tiny bell inside it.

And when they came to him, dressed in splendid gowns of tulle and silk, one a dark, tempestuous Spanish beauty and the other a milk-white-skinned English beauty who somehow contrived, in spite of her heritage, to appear equally desirable, he could only catch his breath at the sight of them.

They stood for a moment in the doorway, Estrellita a little ahead of Mercy, as though showing her the way; as though she knew every inch of this unaccustomed territory.

418

The Captain moved a little to one side, so that the inlaid table that stood between them should no longer be in that straight line between his voice and her ears. The moment he spoke, Estrellita was moving to him, knowing that there would be no obstruction there. Mercy followed her, marvelling, and Cordoba took both their hands in his and said, smiling happily, "I am entranced. Never have I seen such visions of pure beauty, it is almost more than I can bear."

He escorted them to the table and held out their chairs. As the orderly brought them their plates of food, Mercy said, "I take it, sir, that there is still no news of my husband?"

He shook his head. "Unhappily no, *Señora*. My scouts are still searching hopefully. In every Creole village they come upon they ask the necessary questions. But it is my belief . . ."

He hesitated, then went on, "If I were in his position, that is to say, searching an empty jungle for someone I loved, as no doubt he is, while we search with equal patience for him . . . I would find my way, sooner or later, to whatever town might be relatively close by. There is only one town of any consequence within a hundred miles of here and that is Santiago de Cuba. I believe that in the course of time, one way or another, he will discover this important fact and will find his way there. A town, so to speak, is a magnet. I believe that it will draw you both there and in Santiago, when we reach it, you will find him."

"But you believe that I *will*?"

"In the course of time, yes. And meanwhile, you must be patient. Tell me, how you are managing to survive the rigors of a wagontrain?"

419

"Rigors?" Mercy could not help laughing, a little trill of a laugh that escaped her involuntarily. "I sleep in a comfortable bed with the softest feather mattress. I eat royally, far more than is good for me. I have found a dear, dear friend . . ." Her hand reached out and touched Estrellita's. "And you talk of *rigors*? I have seldom been so well cared-for in my whole life."

"I am glad. We will be staying in this pleasant *hacienda* for a few days, perhaps they told you already?"

"Yes, they told us."

"And have they found rooms for you? If not, I will arrange it. If only as a relief from the confines of that very small wagon."

"They found us a room already, a beautiful room," Estrellita said. "There is a very large window and a veranda with honeysuckle growing over it, the most sweetly scented room I have ever known. And if you listen at the window, there are the songs of a thousand birds out there in the forest. The bed is big enough for ten people, and very comfortable. Why are you so depressed this evening, Juan?"

He was startled, and for a moment he did not answer her. He said at last, "Depressed? How could I be, in such excellent company?"

"You cannot fool me, Juan," Estrellita said. "You never could, you know that."

"Yes, you are right . . . well, I was, I must confess, unaccountably sad this evening. But now, all is well again."

"Is it, Juan?" she asked. "In truth, is it?"

"In truth, everything is all right now," he answered.

420

She could hear the sigh in his voice and it pained her acutely.

When they had finished their meal and had taken a small glass of good French cognac each, they went to the room that had been prepared for them and left him once more to his worried solitude.

Estrellita went unerringly to the window where the honeysuckle was and stood on the little balcony there, gripping the wooden balustrade with both hands. Mercy could have sworn she was actually looking down into the yard below them. There were half a dozen men moving around below, going about their business. In a moment Estrellita said, "There is a man patrolling to our left. He is a sergeant, I think. Three red stripes on his arm?"

Mercy gasped. "Yes, but . . . in Heaven's name, Estrellita! Can you tell a soldier's rank by the sound of his feet?"

She was laughing softly. "This one, yes. It is either Arenas, who is a fusilier, or Azuaga, who is a sergeant. They both walk exactly alike, I find it very frustrating . . ."

She called down softly, "Azuaga? You are on patrol?"

"Si, Señorita. Making sure you can sleep well this night."

"Then will you do me a favor?"

"Anything, Señorita."

"Send one of your men to find Carmen for me. Or if not Carmen, then Tina. Or Miranda . . . I do not know where anyone is in this . . . this unaccustomed place. Any of the girls, Azuaga, but preferably Carmen. Will you do that for me?"

He was nodding eagerly, a friendly, happy young man who was delighted that this lovely blind woman knew him even by his footsteps. "I will do so at once, *Señorita*," he said.

Mercy, marvelling at the exchange, watched him hurry off. She put an arm around Estrellita and murmured, "You have them all eating out of your hand, don't you?"

Estrellita was smiling, delighted. "No, not really. It is a great deal simpler than that. They all love me, Mercy. From a distance, perhaps . . . but they love me. And I am grateful for it. Now, come before we go to bed, you have to help me just a little. I know where the bed is, and the commode, and three of the chairs, and one table. But there is another chair, to the left of the window somewhere, and another table that I have quite lost. So come, take my arm and lead me. First, around the room . . ."

As they moved off together, she paused and said, one hand reaching out and touching Mercy's cheek, "I have never before asked anyone to help me like this. Am I becoming dependent upon you, dear Mercy? Perhaps I am."

"Does that disturb you, Strellita dear?"

"No, it does not. Ah, that damned table, there it is!" Her hand was on it, shaking it infinitesimally, almost imperceptibly. "A piece of china on it. What is it, a vase?"

"No. I don't quite know what you'd call it. A china angel with no clothes on, carrying a harp, and a sweet little cherub lying at her feet . . ."

"And something else, I think, of glass?" The hand was probing. "Ah, yes, a *bonbonniere*."

They continued their exploration of the room, and Estrellita murmured, "How good it is to have someone to guide me! Perhaps I have been too independent . . . for too long."

There was a timid knock at the door and she said, "Come!", looking toward the door as if she were able to see who it was. It opened, and a young girl was standing there, waiting. Estrellita said patiently, "Well, come in, child." The moment the footsteps sounded, she said, "Ah, Carmen."

She was a gawky-looking young woman in her early twenties with a wide, high forehead and dark, intense eyes, she had very full, dark red lips and her long hair was piled high on her head and tied with green ribbons. She wore an elaborate dress of pale-gray muslin with three large flounces, cut very low at the fine, upstanding, coffee-colored bust, with a border of lace running along it. There was a little collar of black velvet around her throat, fastened with a pearl brooch.

"*Si, Señorita*," she said, "Carmen . . ."

The black eyes flashed once to Mercy, then found the floor and stared at it, as though a little uncomfortable in her presence.

Estrellita said gently, "Our Captain is not happy tonight, Carmen. Go to him. Be very gentle with him."

"I am always gentle, *Señorita*, you know that."

"Yes, I know, But tonight, more than ever. There is a very heavy cloud hanging over him tonight. Chase it away for him."

"I will."

She hesitated, before saying, "And if, in his sleep, he calls you Estrellita . . . do not correct him. Do not say: 'But my name is Carmen, *Señor Capitano*.' You understand me?"

"I understand, *Señorita*."

"Go then. Comfort him. Drive those clouds away as only you know how to."

"I will do so, *Señorita*." Those huge black eyes went to Mercy's for a moment and held them, then dropped again. She turned and went out, leaving them by themselves.

Mercy turned the wicks of the three lamps down low, went over and closed the windows, and drew the heavy velour drapes. Estrellita reached back to unhook the tight confinement of her silk dress and said, "Ah . . ."

She laid the dress over the chair that had given her so much trouble, stepped out of her pantalettes and shoes, and ran her hands over the svelte body for a moment. She said, frowning, "A lovely room . . . but I do not know where anything is."

"If you will tell me what it is you need?" Mercy asked.

"My bottle of oil. I am sure that they must have put it here somewhere."

"I see it." It was on the table by the side of the bed and Mercy took out the glass stopper and smelled it. It was lavender-scented, the delicate perfume of an English herb garden. "In London," she said dreamily, "I used to make *cachets* of lavender and put them in the drawer where I kept my unmentionables. It makes them smell so fresh and clean."

"Oh, really? I never heard of that."

"Yes, you just pick the flowers and dry them, and put them into a little bag that lasts for years."

"It sounds like a very good idea."

Estrellita had stretched out her supple, voluptuous body on top of the bed, quite naked, a forearm

424

across the upper half of her torso. "Will you do it for me, Mercy?"

"All right."

"Just a few drops in the palms of your hands. My shoulders, my breasts, my legs . . . I do not like to sleep smelling of the day's exertions. And the oil is good for the skin, it keeps it soft and smooth."

She reached out and found Mercy's hip, resting on the crisp tulle. "But . . . will you take off your dress first? It gives me such pleasure to know that you are naked beside me."

It was a whisper now. "All right, Strellita, if you want me to."

Mercy took off her clothes, conscious now of that uncontrollable shaking. She laid them slowly and with meticulous precision on the chair. When she was completely disrobed, she climbed onto the bed beside her dear blind friend, and studied the smooth curves of that demanding body with something akin, at first, to detachment, as though she herself could remain unmoved and yet know that to Estrellita their close touch was of overwhelming importance, the whole substance, now, of her desires.

She poured a little of the lavender oil into her hand, holding it there for a moment and watching it spread over her palm, an offering to the Gods. She put the bottle aside and began a leisurely caress of those soft arms and shoulders.

"My father grew it," she said. "The lavender, I mean. In the spring he would wheel himself out into the tiny garden, and he would pluck the stalks and bring them to me, saying 'Mercy, child, hang these in the kitchen over the stove for a few days, and then you can make them into your *cachets* . . .' "

425

There was a long, trembling silence and Mercy studied the inviting body under her touch almost as an artist might. Her hands found the firm, resilient breasts, cupping them and moulding them gently. She still tried to force the detachment on herself, and knew that she could do so no longer.

"There was always an old petticoat," she whispered, "that could be cut up into little squares of calico . . . to make the bags for the lavender florets. And I would stitch a whole lot of them all at once . . ."

Her fingers were caressing the tiny nipples, lingering delicately, and her own emotion was rising fast now. "I used to give some of them," she said, "to a friend we had, her name was Genevieve, Genevieve Doren. So long ago!"

She moved a hand infinitely gently down over the smooth stomach, quite deliberately now, and knowing the course that she had chosen, and exactly what its inevitable conclusion would be, knowing that she would let her own sensuality run its full course, and relishing the tremors that were shuddering through her body.

She found the soft, expectant thighs that opened to her touch, parting slowly and awaiting the rapture. Estrellita's eyes were closed, that fine hair lying over her shoulder, and her body was undulating, the tiniest of movements.

"Tell me, dear Mercy," she murmured, her voice almost inaudible in the silence, "about your friend Genevieve? Was she . . . a very close friend?"

"No, she was not . . . not a friend in the way that you and I are friends, though she was almost as beautiful. Sometimes, as she sat by our fireplace, so graceful and composed and so sure of herself . . .

yes, sometimes I wondered, I will confess it, what she would be like without her extravagant French gown."

"And did you ever discover the answer to that question, my love?"

"No."

"Then this love, of woman to woman, is new to you?"

"Yes."

"I was convinced of it. Does it disturb you?"

"No."

"Are you sure of that?"

"Yes, quite sure."

"I am glad . . ."

The movement of her loins was stronger now, as she thrust herself to meet the probing. In a little while she reached up and twined her fingers in Mercy's hair, and pulled her down and kissed her on the lips. Mercy lay close beside her, one long thigh finding its counterpart, and Estrellita whispered, "Love me now, Mercy. Love me?"

She felt the light weight of that slender body easing itself onto hers, and their arms and legs were intertwining now.

They could feel the zephyr of a breeze whispering over them from the open window, bringing the scent of the honeysuckle there that searched out with its tendrils for the warmth of that mysterious, life-giving force on which it nourished itself.

There was the rhythmic cadence of their limbs together for a long, drawn-out time, a time that stood still for them both, the lover and the loved, as though the harsh realities of the world outside this room did not exist any more.

Soon there was the seething and the foment, and

when the excitation took them completely, there was the perfection of a mutual delirium in which that other world could be forgotten.

They fell asleep at last, tightly clasped in each other's arms, to dream of all that was beautiful.

CHAPTER TWENTY

Valverde and his sergeant, Tivisa, had ridden in the darkness for scarcely more than three miles.

They had left the main trail that led down to the beach and were following one that, the cartographer had assured them, would bypass the cliffs that had been such a stern barrier to the wagontrain, and would lead them eventually out of the forest and into good riding country.

They had come to a point where the track narrowed to little more than ten feet across, inclining very steeply upward, and winding this way and that over ground that was getting more and more treacherous every inch of the way.

They dismounted and led their horses in the silent darkness. Tivisa was a bright young man in his early twenties who was probably the best horseman in the expedition and Valverde was much older and wiser, and somehow, quite unaccountably, worried about his foray. Tivisa said, some of that worry brushing off onto him: "Two days the Captain gave us to get to Santiago. It might be more, Lieutenant."

Valverde shook his head. "We climb this damned mountain, Sergeant," he said, "and on the other side, if Ernesto is to be believed, there's easy going all the way to the river. With luck, we'll cover forty miles or more this night, and tomorrow, in the easy light of day, sixty more. We'll rest up when we're half a day's ride from the town itself. I don't want to meet that damned Frenchman with the weight of exhaustion on my shoulders."

"You know him, Lieutenant?"

"No. But he's a Frenchman, and so . . . I distrust him instinctively."

They were dressed now in simple farmers' clothes that were very much out of place with their military bearing, their pistols hidden in their saddlebags, their rifles slung over their shoulders. They were hoping that should they be seen they would be taken for hunters out after wild boar.

They were good friends, these two, in spite of the difference in their ranks. Valverde had studied at the Military Academy of Horsemanship in Madrid, passing all his tests with flying colors, winning the coveted *Medallon de Oro de Santa Teresa de Cepada*. He had come to Cuba to discover that a young untrained sergeant was a better horseman than he was. It had brought them together, the middle-aged officer on the one hand and the boyish young sergeant on the other.

They plowed steadily and laboriously upward along the winding, slippery trail, covered now with protruding slabs of shining gray rock over which their horses stumbled, even though their hooves had been wrapped in rags as a precaution against undue noise. A large tree rat, a *hutia*, dropped from an overhanging branch onto one of the saddles and the horse reared up, protesting in a loud and frightened whinny.

The character of the trees was changing as they climbed doggedly up and a light and gentle rain began to fall, the rain drops making a strange, insistent chatter on the foliage above them, like the tapping of a thousand light fingers. The clouds were dark above them, broken here and there with patches of lighter sky through which the moonbeams cast their pale, slanting rays down through the trees.

The track narrowed and divided itself into two paths, both overhung with vines. Tivisa said, "The right, I think?"

"Yes. We should keep as close to the sea as possible. Perhaps this way will lead us to the top of the cliffs."

They were whispering in the great arched cathedral of the forest. In a little while Valverde stopped and peered at the white, cut end of a branch and touched it with his fingers, feeling the sticky sap there. He said, his voice very low, "I think this trail has been cut but recently . . ."

Tivisa had found a blaze cut into the trunk of a tree and it too was still sticky. "We are not alone on this mountain," he whispered.

They unslung their rifles and moved on cautiously in near silence, leading their horses in single file now. Valverde, in the lead, stopped and held up

431

his hand in a gesture and they listened, straining their ears in the darkness.

There had been a tiny sound ahead of them, a stirring in the bushes. An animal, perhaps? There were very few animals on this island. A night hawk fluttering it wings? It was impossible to guess; the sound had stopped.

As they peered out into the dense shrubbery, blacker now than the night itself, six, eight, a dozen men rose up silently out of the bushes. No more than shadows, their uniforms were covered with draped sackcloth and only their weapons showed.

Valverde fired the charge from his rifle and heard the answering volley, more than a dozen shots fired in rapid succession. He was aware of the incisive, clipping sound the lead balls made as they cut their way through the leaves and of the smell of powder, and he could not understand why he was lying in the mud with his legs thrashing. The pain in his chest seemed a very trifling thing. Nor could he understand why young Sergeant Tivisa was lying close beside him, so very still, with his eyes wide and staring. He saw, but only dimly, that one of the ghouls was poised above him, a fiercely bearded man with his ringlock bayonet held high. He saw, in the moonlight, the glimmer of the sharp steel coming down on him; and then, everything was darkness and death.

They knew nothing of this in the *hacienda*, though it was only three miles away. There, the sentries were alert at their posts, the patrols wide awake and prowling and there was the cheerful sound of music coming from the Creoles' camp in one corner of the grounds. Everything was as normal as it could be.

The sentry at the gates, closed now, was sitting atop the adobe wall and listening to the strains of the guitar coming to him from the firelight, thinking about a girl there he had slept with a few nights ago, wondering if he should visit her again when his four hours were up and he would be relieved.

The pounding of galloping hooves brought him sharply back to reality, and he leaped off the wall and held his rifle ready. As the horse reared up in front of him, he looked up at Lieutenant Carpio and said automatically, "Who goes there? Identify yourself."

Carpio roared, "Open the gates, idiot!" The sentry swung the heavy timbers open and watched the officer ride furiously to the house and dismount.

The sentry at the door snapped to attention, and Carpio snapped, "Get the Officer of the Day and send him to the Captain's quarters." He hurried inside as the man ran off and went up the stairs two at a time. He knocked thunderously on the door to the Captain's apartment.

It was Carmen who woke him, saying in sudden alarm, "*Capitano*, wake up, wake up!"

He was instantly awake, He leaned over and turned up the lamp on the table, looking at the little silver watch he had placed there and pressing its chime lever to assure himself that it was indeed after four in the morning. He called out, "*Vengo, vengo*, I am coming!"

He slipped into his robe, went into the other room and opened the door. One look at Carpio's face told him that something terrible had happened. But he said quite calmly. "What is it, Lieutenant?"

There was a strange excited look in the old man's

433

eyes and Cordoba thought, mechanically: *Fifty years old and still a Lieutenant, one of my very best men, and how can I effect his promotion?* He shook his head to clear the sleep from it and said, "Come inside, Carpio."

He moved from one table to another, turning up the lamps as Carpio strode into the room and wiped at the sweat on his forehead. He said softly, almost delighting in it, "A thousand pardons, *Señor Capitano*, not a fitting hour to disturb you. But we have trouble on our hands. Quite considerable trouble, I fear."

"Oh?"

He could not fathom that maniacal look and thought it might be the prebattle excitement of the seasoned soldier.

The lieutenant went on, "I have recconnoitered the bluff we spoke of, Captain, together with Corporal Adamuz. There are a great number of men up there."

Cordoba said sharply, "A great number? How many is a great number, Lieutenant?"

Carpio felt quite secure in his age. "We could scarcely make a head count," he said smoothly, "but I would estimate sixty or seventy."

Cordoba accepted the rebuke. "Soldiers? Or *bandoleros*?"

"I think perhaps soldiers," Carpio said slowly, "though unhappily I cannot be sure of the answer to this very important question. There is a great deal of heavy cloud tonight, and the men we saw ... we saw with very little clarity. They were wearing, I think, *ponchos* of a very dark color which hid them quite effectively. But I had the impression that under those *ponchos* they were wearing uni-

434

forms, the uniforms of Spanish soldiers. I caught a glimpse, I think—and I cannot be certain—of crossed white leather."

"Soldiers?" the Captain said sharply. "Hiding their uniforms? It suggests that they have very little pride."

"And also that their leaders may have fought in Haiti. The French there discovered—and not really a very surprising discovery, is it?—that they could more easily approach an enemy in the forest, if they covered the bright colors a soldier wears. They even had a name for it, *camouflet*, a puff of smoke in the face to hide behind."

"Their weapons?"

"As far as I could see, all the arms were identical, the rifles of the Royal Spanish Fusiliers. Above all, they seemed to be . . . well-disciplined. No one was smoking, no one was talking, not even whispers. They were well hidden among the trees like *guerrillas*, but yes, I am convinced that they are soldiers. My experience of *bandoleros* is that they swagger around and talk loudly, and sometimes even fire off their guns to show the world how brave they are. But among these men, there was only *silence*. They were *waiting*, well-disciplined and ready for . . . for *something*. For what, I cannot guess. They were all well within earshot of our camp. I could hear the music the Croeles were playing. I heard someone, Sergeant Azuaga, I think, dressing down a sentry because he had not heard his approach. The edge of the bluff is scarcely five hundred paces from our perimeter, Captain. At that elevation, well within rifleshot."

There was a sharp knock on the door and Cordoba said, "Come!"

435

Barbastro entered and saluted and Cordoba told him what Carpio had reported. He said, "All fires to be doused at once. One half of the men to be posted to duty on the walls, the others to continue their sleep and take over at seven o'clock, with stand-by-arms until further notice." He thought for a moment and said, "No, let the fires *not* be doused. Whatever nighttime activity there may be in the camp, let it continue. We can be seen from up there. Let them not suspect that we know of their presence. But warn the men that they are under observation. The other patrols, are we in touch with them?"

"A runner every hour, sir," Barbastro said.

Carpio interrupted him, "By your leave, Captain. On my way back to the *hacienda*, I came across Sergeant Cabra on patrol. I alerted him to the situation. He is sending a runner up there to join Trooper Adamuz, to report to us if and when necessary. Adamuz is still there, watching. If those men make any offensive move . . . we will know it within fifteen minutes."

"Good. And we have a question of tactics here, I think. Do we not, Carpio?"

The old man was nodding, his eyes gleaming bright. "We have indeed, Captain. To the west of us, there is an easy way out of whatever trap they may have set for us. A good, wide trail that leads to open country where we can deploy our troops to best advantage. If there are more of them . . . and how can we know about this? Certainly, if the enemy's main force is up on the bluff, we can easily fight our way out to the west. But if I were in that enemy's shoes, whoever he might be, I would block that escape route. With my main force."

436

Cordoba was pacing, wrapped in deep thought. He said at last, "An opinion, Carpio. An estimation, if you like. Are they Aguilar's men out there?"

"I think so," Carpio said carefully. "I cannot be sure. But if I must guess . . . yes, Aguilar's men."

"He can throw two hundred, perhaps three hundred men against us. We have a good defensive position, my men are better trained than his. We shall win this battle, Carpio."

"I am sure of it."

"*If* he chooses to attack us here, it would be a mistake. But Aguilar's history is drawn in the heavy lines of mistakes. He may, of course, be merely watching us and waiting for a more favorable opportunity. An opportunity which we will be at pains not to give him."

He turned to Barbastro. "I want this *hacienda* made secure *now*," he said. "If it comes to a battle, the first line of defense will be the wall. Has it been repaired?"

"Not yet, sir," Barbatro said. "They are working on it now. The adobe takes a little time to harden, but by midday tomorrow it should be strong enough to stop a rifle ball."

"I wonder if they have cannon? Perhaps not. The second line of defense will be the buildings here. The third, this house. Let us hope that it will not come to that, but let us also be ready for it. We will be outnumbered by two to one, perhaps, though we cannot be sure of this. It is possible that his force may be smaller than ours. And, Carpio? I want to know about that."

"We will know very shortly," the old lieutenant said.

"Odds of two to one, even three to one, which is

unlikely . . . the odds do not disturb me unduly. But I want to know what they are, Lieutenant."

"We will know soon," Carpio said, and his eyes were gleaming. Cordoba thought: *This old man is spoiling for a fight; well, maybe he will get his wish.*

Barbastro said, the fever of battle on him too, "If I may be excused, Captain?"

Cordoba nodded. "Go about your duties, Lieutenant. I want to be assured that the *hacienda* is secure, from this moment on. And you, Carpio, look to the west and the south. Let us know if they have any more soldiers there dressed in *ponchos.* I need a perimeter we can hold and a route by which we can escape if necessary. See to it. Keep me informed, constantly."

They saluted and left him.

He paced the room for a moment, lost in his own solitude. He thought: *With less than three hundred men, they will not dare to attack me here. If they have more than that, which I doubt, we can still win easily. And Aguilar's ambitions will be stifled forever. Long live the Queen!*

He could guess how great the odds against him really were. Havana had told him, "*Yes, Aguilar has a rabble of untrained mercenaries, but they can offer little resistance to you, Cordoba.*" Had he noticed a certain . . . malevolence in their instructions?

He went, worried, back into the bedroom and looked down at Carmen's lovely face, framed in the black hair that cascaded down over the white satin pillow, the sheet pulled up to her chin. He was thinking: This sweet child knows nothing of the problems which beset me, and if they break in here tomorrow she will say, "*I am at your service, Cap-*

tain." Only it will be a different Captain, a traitor to the Crown.

He mused on this point for a moment, then decided: *Well, that is as it should be. What part should these lovely child-women have of our eternal and quite senseless bickerings? They are right; there is more to life than death, and their thighs are more important than all the swords in Spain.*

He leaned forward and took the sheet in his hand, pulling it gently down from that slender ivory body.

She was fast asleep, the sleep of innocence, and he dropped his robe to the floor and stood looking down at her and admiring her. Then he knelt on the bed beside her and gently touched a breast, a thigh. She half awoke and murmured an endearment as his hands explored her. "You are such a very beautiful child, Carmen," he whispered.

"Not a child, my Captain. A woman."

"Yes, I know it . A very lovely woman."

Her fingertips were on his erect manhood, driving him to distraction. "And you are so strong this night . . ."

"Because of your loveliness, Carmen. Your breasts are like . . . like Solomon's two young roes that are twins, which feed among the lilies."

"Solomon? Who is Solomon? I do not know him."

"He was a great King once. He too loved beautiful women. He wrote a famous poem to one of them."

"Ah, that is nice . . . did he truly love her?"

"Very much."

"And what was her name?"

"He called her the *Shulamit*. And she said, "*My*

439

beloved put his hand by the hole of the door, and
my bowels were moved for him."

"What a strange thing to say . . ."

"And do I move you now, Carmen?"

"Yes, oh, yes . . ."

His fingers were probing, exploring, his lips brushing her breast, the tip of his tongue finding a ripe and hardening nipple and teasing it. She opened her thighs as he moved atop her, her long legs entwining him. Crossing her ankles behind his back she demanded more and yet more of him. He took her wrists in his hand and pressed them into the pillow at her head, and he held his body up so that he could watch his entry as he inserted himself into her, looking at the fusing of their bodies as they became one together.

When he was completely engulfed, enfolded by her, he lowered his chest onto her breast and found her lips with his. She thought: My beloved Captain is filled with pain this night, and only I can ease it for him . . .

She thrust her hips up at him, a gentle and rhythmic movement to match his own, growing in measured intensity until the long, shuddering climax came for both of them, almost instantaneously.

He lay quite still for a long time, savoring the warmth of her while she held him tightly within her, knowing that this kind of gentle man was part of her, still deep inside her, still throbbing there with an infinitesimal pulsation that was bringing her again to the borders of ecstasy. She prayed that he would not pull himself away from her, and he did not. She wound her arms and her legs about him, and he cupped a breast in his hand and laid his head on her shoulder. She contained him there

440

while he slept and she traced the outlines of his handsome face with her fingers, knowing that for the time being at least, he was hers to enjoy whenever the desire would come over her again.

Once, in his sleep, he half moved away from her, but she clutched him tightly, enfolding her legs around him. She murmured, "No, *mi Capitano*, do not move . . ."

The throbbing was still there, and she let the rapture overtake her again.

It was a day of intense activity. And it was alarming in the extreme.

Lieutenant Carpio returned with Barbastro at ten o'clock. There was still that strange look in his eyes, almost demented now—though the youngster, he saw, looked pale and anxious—and he said, "The light of day is disclosing many secrets, Captain. There are not sixty or seventy men up there on the bluff, but more than two hundred. I have relieved Corporal Adamuz, who is too good a man to waste on a watching brief, and sent him on a search to the other side, with runners who are coming in now. First of all, I have to report with great sadness that Lieutenant Valverde and Sergeant Tivisa are dead. Their bodies were found only three miles away, four balls though each of them, Valverde bayoneted too. It seems he did not die quickly enough . . . So, two hundred men, at least, to the north of us. On the east, Sergeant Crespos reports another force that may be a hundred and fifty strong. To the south, another two hundred and fifty spread across the trail by which we reached this deathtrap. And to the west . . ." He sighed. "To the west, Captain, our only possible escape route . . . to the west, there are no less than four hundred men waiting, half of them mounted." He sighed and said gently, "It seems that we are surrounded, *Señor Capitano*, by more than a thousand troops of . . . of *somebody's* army."

Cordoba looked at Barbastro. "And our effectives this day, Lieutenant?"

"One hundred and twenty-eight active men, sir," Barbastro replied. "Twelve of the sick are ambulatory and capable of bearing arms. They are already on the wall."

"One hundred and forty all told?"

"Yes, sir."

"How many of the Creoles among the camp-followers can we trust to load rifles for us?"

"None, sir. I fear there is not a single Creole left in the compound. The men, women, girls . . . they've all gone, every one of them. It seems that . . . they *know*."

"Yes, they always do, don't they? So . . . we are outnumbered seven or eight to one. Those are not insuperable odds, gentlemen. And what do we know of the enemy's efficiency? I could wish I knew who commands them. Carpio?"

"Whoever their commander might be," Carpio said carefully, "he is no fool. He has his men adequately trained, I would say. I watched one of them for more than half an hour this morning. I observed that when the sun moved around and cast its rays across his body, he just naturally moved back a foot or so into the shadows. And in all that time, from two hundred men, there was not a sound of any sort. These are well-disciplined troops we have to face, Captain."

"And ours are too, let us not forget that," Cordoba said sharply. "And we are stronger if we remain here, than if we attempt to break out. I take it that the consensus of the officers' opinions would agree with me there?"

"They would indeed, sir. The wall is of a good height . . . yes, we should be able to hold it. And they will probably strike . . . when, I wonder?"

"They are soldiers," Carpio said, making a point of it, "but trained as *guerrillas*. Their uniforms covered, and hiding themselves expertly in the forest."

"In that case, they will undoubtedly choose to attack by night."

"I would say so, yes."

"And they can sit out there for a week, ten days, a month even, waiting for us to collapse from lack of sleep. We are a long, long way from Havana. They must know that there is no one who can come to our assistance. So . . . tonight perhaps. Or tomorrow night, when we will all be a little more tired. Or the night after, or the night after that. Or ten nights from now, when there will be scarcely a man among us capable of standing on his own two feet, through the sheer exhaustion of keeping watch and waiting."

"Since they are so strong," Carpio said gently, "they may not think it necessary to wait so long."

Cordoba took the little watch from his chamois pouch and pushed the lever. He said, listening to the gentle sound of the bell, "Eleven o'clock in the morning. Barbastro . . . your turn of duty is finished, I think?"

"No, sir. In view of the emergency . . ."

"Very well. I want you to withdraw all of our effectives at once, except for the patrols and . . . six men at each wall. The others are to *sleep*. Explain

443

to them that from this moment on, sleep is their most important commodity. They are to sleep with loaded rifles at their sides, their pouches filled with balls, their powder-flasks ready. Two buglers are to be ready to sound the alarm at all times. At sundown, man the walls with half of our effectives in shifts of four hours each, those off duty to *sleep*. The officers will sleep for three hours in every twelve from now on. See to it, Barbastro."

"Yes, sir."

Barbastro saluted, and when both turned to leave him, Cordoba said, "A moment of your time, Carpio . . ."

The old man turned and when the door had closed behind the young lieutenant, the Captain said, "Well, Carpio . . . you must know that I have always had the highest possible regard for your sagacity. What think you?"

"I think," Carpio said carefully, "that within forty-eight hours or so, every living man in this *hacienda*, Captain, will be a dead man."

There was that strange, maniacal gleam in his eyes again.

Throughout the day, the scouts reported in at regular intervals, all but two of which, it would appear, had been discovered and promptly killed. The enemy was still poised there, waiting in silence, his own patrols constantly on the move. They could not know it in the *hacienda*, but Butrus was awaiting the arrival of his cannon.

Jake Ollie said, "We don't really have to wait like this, Adam." Butrus's eyes on him were cold, but Ollie was learning now, learning the value of the Colonel's own self-assurance. "A diversion," he

444

said, "send in a hundred men from the other side and have them withdraw after a dozen volleys or so! Then we can be over those walls in a couple of hours, maybe even less."

"Yes, you are right," Colonel Adam said. "And it would cost us, perhaps, half a hundred men, no more. But we will reduce that place to rubble, pound it into the ground before we even move out from under cover. And we will lose scarcely a single trooper."

"Yes, sir."

"We wait for the wagons."

They were little more than half a day away, the muleteers swearing and sweating as they belabored their animals, dragging the heavy loads of cannon-balls and barrels of black powder, onward and upward through the forest. The mules strained their stubborn muscles between the shafts, the wooden wheels slipping in ruts that the others had made.

It seemed an impossible journey for them; but slowly, they were reaching their objective.

CHAPTER TWENTY-ONE

Throughout the long, expectant day, Captain Cordoba sat at the long table in his quarters, poring over the map of the compound that Ernesto had prepared for him, checking over the number of men on each of the four walls, the men in the watch-towers, the men on patrol, and trying to guess at what hour the enemy might strike.

At around four o'clock in the morning, he thought, the time which a man who has been denied his sleep is at his least alert; but which morning? The next? Or a week or more from now, when our food has gone and we can no longer forage? He was glad to see that Barbastro had marked on the map, with little pencilled arrows: "*At three o'clock in the morning, eight more men here, six more here, twelve more here . . .*"

The young duty officer, still wide awake and

alert after a night of no sleep, was bringing him reports every hour. There was still no movement from the hills and at four o'clock he sent for Estrellita.

She came unerringly into the room and sat in the chair he silently placed for her. She said, whispering, "I have heard, Juan . . . is it as bad as they say it is?"

He would not lie to her, nor could he. "Yes," he said simply. "As bad, and perhaps a great deal worse. I want you to listen very carefully to what I have to say to you."

"Very well."

She sat in the heavily brocaded chair, her hands in her lap, her huge, dark, unseeing eyes cast down, as though not wanting to meet his.

He pulled his chair close to hers, and laid a hand on her knee, saying slowly, "I am, as you know, a man of supreme confidence. I have been engaged in, and have won, so many battles, sometimes against odds that seemed insuperable. This time, I will confess to you, I know that only a miracle can save us. Unhappily, I see no sign of a miracle on the horizon."

"But Juan . . ."

"No. Listen to me, Estrellita."

She fell silent, waiting, and he went on, "Perhaps we will be lucky. Perhaps some of us will survive, but I think it unlikely. Now, I have a plain duty to my men, but they are in Her Majesty's service, as I myself am. And a soldier . . . he learns very early in his professional life that he must expect . . . not always to win. He accepts that. He has been trained

448

to expect it. I also have a duty to you, to your young ladies, and to *Señora* Hawkes . . ."

"Juan . . ."

"Listen, Estrellita. We know that if this battle goes against us, you and your ladies will be in no great danger. You are—forgive the blunt word—camp followers. And historically, the young ladies serving an army are never harmed, provided that they can accept, with whatever good grace they can summon up, the undeniable fact that their masters have changed, but not the duties expected of them. In other words, though your girls will weep for us at first, they will soon recover, and then, accepting the inevitable and at no cost to themselves, go about their work once more in the capacity they have always filled so well. No opprobrium attaches to them for this. To the victor, the spoils. We accept that. You agree with me there?"

"Juan, I will never even begin to think . . ."

"In principle," he insisted. "The principle is correct, is it not?"

"Yes, it is correct, but you must listen to me too!"

She made a sudden motion under the long blue dress, and there was a thin stiletto in her hand. She said, gesturing with it fiercely, "I will drive this into my bosom before I let them lay a hand on me!"

Cordoba laid a hand on her wrist. "Put your dagger away, Estrellita," he said. "And tell me about the ladies in your charge. What will they do?"

Estrellita sighed and placed the knife carefully back in its sheath at her thigh. "You said it yourself," she answered. "My girls know nothing of

loyalties, of causes, of the Crown or of treason to
it. They will continue their work, and after a few
days of sadness, perhaps . . . they will forget that the
weather vane has moved around. I too have given
some thought to the problem that concerns you so
deeply now. The future of the girls is acceptable to
them, though it would not be to me. But Mercy . . .
she, I believe, is the cause of your worry, is she
not?"

"Yes. I must admit it. She is in my charge, and if
those men out there are indeed Aguilar's mercenaries, as I believe them to be . . . then the prospects
that await *Señora* Hawkes appall me."

"I told you, Juan," Estrellita said gently, "that
you must listen to me. It is quite true. If Mercy is
found living with a wagontrain of whores, inevitably she will only be accepted as a whore herself.
Her protests will mean nothing to men like these.
And I will not allow it."

"And so?"

He had come to regard this lovely blind woman
not only with great affection, but with confidence
and respect too. There was a glimmer of hope for
him in what she might have to say.

She went on, very calmly, "My death, at my
own hands, will mean nothing to me. But it will
serve nothing, too, for, without my help, Mercy is
lost, I am sure of it. She is a bright and intelligent
young woman . . . but she is not as hardened as we
are. And if the mercenaries capture her . . . I too am
appalled by the thought, Juan."

"And you have found a solution?"

"Yes. I have."

"Tell me."

450

"First of all," Estrellita said clearly, "I believe you will hold off these ruffians. I believe that eventually you will destroy them."

"I find great satisfaction in your confidence," he said dryly, reaching out again to touch her.

She laid her hand on his, "But if the worst . . ." There was a tiny break in her voice. ". . . if the worst should happen, then I will see to it that Mercy is not captured. If they should break into the *hacienda* . . . then we will find a secure hiding place, a cellar, perhaps, or an attic. And we will wait there . . . as long as we have to." She was conscious of the tears welling into her eyes, and she touched them with a lawn handkerchief. "I hate weakness more than anything," she said. "Even though, yes, I have weaknesses of my own. But tears? Seldom before. I forgot, many years ago, how to weep."

"Then you will hide," Cordoba said steadily, "and you will both *wait*. It may be for quite a long time. But you will wait until the silence tells you that it is all over. And you will still wait, for a full day, before you stir, by which time we can be sure that they will have gone. A full twenty-four hours, Estrellita, a day and a night. Promise me that you will not stir till then."

"I promise, Juan."

"And Mercy . . . *Señora* Hawkes, she knows of all this?"

"I told her, yes. It confuses her a little, I think. She is aware that if it were not for the need to help her, I would kill myself. So, while I save her life . . . she is saving mine too. She wants to talk with you, Juan."

451

"Yes, of course. I will see her later. And meanwhile . . ." He reached into his pocket and took out the little silver watch. "I wish you to accept a present from me, Estrellita." He touched a lever and she heard the tinkle of its chime. The tears were in her eyes again and she could not contain her emotion. "Your watch? No, Juan, I will not accept such a gesture of . . . of finality."

"I insist that you do, Estrellita. Here, give me your hand."

She did not move. "You told me once that it had been carried by seven generations of your family. And you give it to a whore?"

"Not to a whore. To a fine and gracious lady who has long commanded my deepest respect. Even . . . my love."

He took her hand and placed the watch in it carefully. She took a long, deep breath, almost a shudder, and said quietly, "I will hold it for you, Juan, until the battle is over."

"Yes. Do that, then."

She heard the slight movement as he rose and she laid the watch down on the table holding out both her arms to him.

"This might be goodbye, Estrellita," he whispered. "And yet, it's all rather foolish. If they don't come tonight, then I will be saying goodbye to you again tomorrow. And the day after, perhaps, and the day after that . . . for who knows how long?"

"Not foolish." She held him tightly for a moment, then broke away, her hand on his shoulders. He could have sworn that she was looking straight into his eyes, even reading his thoughts there. A

452

hand went to his face, touching his eyebrows, following the line of them.

"In all the time we have known each other," she said softly, "I have never read your features, your body. In my mind, there is a picture of you, yes. I never quite know how true it is. Your eyes, of course, are dark, like any good Spaniard's. And very gentle, I am sure of that too."

"No," he said, mocking. "they are hard and cold, the eyes of a soldier . . ."

"No. Your voice told me otherwise, a long time ago. But I never knew how finely arched your eyebrows were. The hair, they tell me, is gray?"

"More white than gray now, I fear. Once it was jet black."

"When we first met, three years ago?"

"Yes, it was black then, beginning to turn gray."

"I was never conscious of its changing. They say the lines on your face are deep, and yes, they are indeed." The fingers were touching his cheeks lightly. "And the moustache . . . larger than I had imagined."

"Ever since we left Havana, I have not had the attentions of a barber."

"And the shoulders . . . strong, very strong. I always knew that too." Her hands were at his waist now. "But I did not realize how slim you were. And straight, very straight."

"Because I spend too much time astride a horse."

"And the hips . . . very narrow. Yes, I might have expected that."

Her gown, of pale blue tulle, was trimmed with silk roses, and there was a row of them across the lines of the very deep decolleté. He could not remove his eyes from the smooth mounds of her breasts; just the edges of the areolae were visible, and it was not easy to resist the temptation to touch, to plant a kiss there, even. He was thinking: *Last night, I was with Carmen, and her breasts are as small, and as smooth, and as pointed.* But with this lovely blind woman, there was more than physical perfection, there was also an intellectual relationship, a deep understanding that could never be achieved with the girl who went, the next morning, to the paymaster and said, "Last night with Captain Cordoba, and may I have my five *reales*, please?"

Those infinitely tender hands were on his taut, hard stomach, moving lower and feeling the swelling hardness there. She whispered softly: "I think you want me, Juan . . ."

"Yes, Estrellita, I want you. I will not take you."

That seductive hand did not stop its caress. "You will not take me?"

"You told me a long time ago that you would never again give your body to any man . . ."

"And all these long years, you have respected that?"

"Of course."

"We could have been so happy together! I send Carmen to you, or Inez, or Dolores, or Linda, or Clarina, or even Francesca. And in the morning, the first question I ask, always it: Did you truly make my Captain happy? But now, Juan? There is a bedroom behind us. Will you let me lead you there?"

He ground his hips into hers for a moment and laid a hand on that splendid breast, whispering,

"Oh, yes, Strellita! I do need you, so badly now . . ."

"Then come."

She took his hand and led him, with no blind hesitation, to the bedroom. She said (it seemed to him that her voice had a shy and almost virginal aspect to it now), "If you would like to undress me, Juan?"

His unaccustomed hands were fumbling and she whispered: "At the back . . . there are hooks there."

"Ah yes, of course."

He unfastened them and slid the tulle down over her smooth shoulders, untied the bodice and let her magnificent breasts stand free, and bent and kissed them. He knelt before her to pull down the pantalettes and remove her shoes. He pressed his cheek against her stomach, his hands at her back, held her tight and whispered, "Oh, Estrellita . . ."

He picked her up bodily and laid her gently down on the bed, quickly stripped off his own clothes and lay beside her.

He had dreamed of her for so long! His hands explored her long, slender, unblemished body, so smooth and soft to his touch, like the fragrant petals of a magnolia. But the fragrance was of lavender where she had oiled herself carefully for just this experience. She thrust a thigh over his, moving herself against his hip bone slowly till the excitation was almost more than she could bear. Then she straddled him and took his pulsating manhood in her hand and gently guided it into her, lowered herself on him, knowing that this great love, so lately flowering, would soon be over, shattered by an enemy bullet. . . .

He filled her completely, undulating his body up and down again, his hand reaching up to clasp

455

those magnificent breasts, carefully placing his hands so that the hard nipples were in the clefts of his fingers, at the sensitive base of them. She collapsed on him as the spasm took hold of her, her breath escaping in short, anguished gasps. Still, he was plunging in and out of her, demanding more and more of her, and she accepted all of it with a sensation of perfect rapture.

As the orgasm mounted in her again and flooded over her, she cried, "No more, no more . . ." But she still demanded more, and held him tightly imprisoned in her, clutching at him with every muscle in her loins. His own explosion came, flooding into her, and she whispered, "My love, my love, oh, Juan . . . I love you so dearly . . . and I have loved you for so long, so very long . . ."

"Shhh . . . sleep, my love. I want to dream that . . . in these last few hours, you are part of me. I want to know that I am . . . deep inside you, that your body is part of mine, that we are in each other's arms . . . and part of each other."

Her fingers were twining themselves in his hair, where it curled up over the nape of his neck and she was brushing his eyes with very tender little kisses. "Sleep?" she echoed. "No, Juan, I will not waste this precious time in sleep."

"But I must, my love, for just a little while."

"And I am heavy on you, I think?"

"A fragile weight that I can bear. Lie still, my darling."

"But soon I will move again."

"I wait for you to move."

Her lips found his, then she nestled her head into his shoulder as he slept, and soon, no more than half-awake, he was stirring in her again, very

456

slowly and with great gentleness. His hand was travelling down her spine, the fingers finding the bones there and pressing them, moving on to her hips and clutching at them. She could hear his frenzied breathing as he pressed their naked bodies together. The turbulence was there again, rising in intensity, the convulsions multiplied a hundred-fold now, stimulating her beyond the borders of passion, and she felt the caress of the flooding inside her, then let her own delirium come again.

She still did not move. She lay atop him and slept.

The harsh awakening was the sound of a single cannonshot, followed by a silence that was broken only by the restrained shouting in the compound below and the strident call of the bugle.

He was still between her thighs and he lay there for a brief moment, knowing that the long, slow process of the cannonade would begin very soon now. He eased himself from her, wishing that he could take his mind from her as easily as his body. He said very calmly, "I must leave you, my love . . . The moment that we both knew would come . . . has come."

She lay there, desirable still but terribly vulnerable; and as he struggled into his breeches and his boots, she found her clothes unerringly and dressed herself in silence. Now there was a thunderous knocking at the door and he said, "Come!"

It was Barbastro, a look of extreme excitement on his boyish face. He threw a look at Estrellita, calmly fastening the cords of her bodice, and he said, stammering, "An attack, *Señor Capitano*, on the west wall of the *hacienda*."

Cordoba said quietly, pulling on his shirt, "A single round, Lieutenant, it means they are searching out the range. In a few moments there will be others, a dozen perhaps until they find it. Where did the ball hit?"

"Fifty yards beyond the wall, sir. We recovered it, of course. It is about thirty pounds in weight."

"Ah, the Rodman cannon, no doubt. You know what has to be done now, Barbastro?"

"Yes, sir. It has been done already."

"How many men on the walls?"

"Ninety-seven, sir."

"And they will hold their fire, until? . . ."

"Until they find targets of opportunity, Captain. The senior lieutenant has ordered . . . no firing until there might be a charge."

"And that is Lieutenant Carpio?"

"Yes, sir."

He felt in the pocket of his jacket for his watch, then he remembered and was glad of it. He asked, "What time is it now?"

"A quarter before six in the morning, Captain."

"Ah! Then they are well supplied with ammunition, or they would not have begun so early. I do not believe they will leave their cover in daylight. For the next ten or twelve hours, expect them to break down the walls. Send half of the men back to sleep."

"Sleep, sir?" Barbastro sounded incredulous and Cordoba nodded.

"When night comes," he said, "they will need to be wide awake and refreshed. Even so, it may help us not at all. We must be ready for a charge of infantry, followed by cavalry, some time after sundown. As they breach the walls, have the breaches filled with whatever is available. And when they come . . . let us give a good account of ourselves, whatever the outcome."

"Yes, sir."

"That is all, Barbastro."

"Yes, sir." The young lieutenant hurried out, marvelling that his Captain could be so calm in the face of what he already knew was certain death. And with the Senorita Estrellita indeed, a woman whose chastity, in spite of her profession, was known to be immaculate. With the understanding of extreme youth, he wondered if it might be a portent . . .

Cordoba was fully dressed now. He took Estrellita in his arms and said, smiling, "Our last farewell again, and perhaps it will be one of many, who knows? But now, there are duties that await me, though I must confess . . ." He grimaced. "I could go back to sleep in the sure knowledge that everything that has to be done down there will be done. Your hiding place. Have you decided upon it yet?"

"No . . . I could not bring myself to think of it. I will do so now."

"Take Ernesto as your guide. He has mapped every inch of this place for me. And let me know where it is, Estrellita."

"Yes, of course. You must know where to find us, should we be too frightened to disclose ourselves."

"Not in the cellars. There are wines there, and this is the first place they will search. But, if possible, somewhere in this great house. When you have decided on a secure retreat, find me again, and if you would bring Mercy with you?"

"Yes . . . She is very anxious to talk with you."

459

"And I with her. And since this may be the last time we can be alone together . . . goodbye, Estrellita my love . . ."

His arms were tight about her, their bodies pressed tenderly together. "*Hasta mañana*, Juan," she whispered. "Until tomorrow."

"Until tomorrow, and the next day, and the day after that. You have given me courage."

He was aware of her trembling now, and he knew that the parting was as grievous for her as it was for him.

As she turned to leave, their hands lingering, their fingers touching as though reluctant to break their hold, her eyes were very moist. But she held herself straight and proud, and she paused for the slightest moment at the door before closing it softly behind her.

He heard the sound of the cannon again—more of them now as they searched out the range—the deep, throaty roar of four, perhaps six pieces of ordnance on the west and on the south. He took his sword, and went downstairs to inspect his defenses. There was calm, controlled excitement in him now, as there always was at these times; but at the back of his mind, the question of Estrellita and of Mercy Hawkes was tearing him apart.

Carpio galloped across the grounds the moment he stepped outside, flung himself off his horse and saluted. "Five cannon to the left of us, Captain," he said, "and four more over on the south. The ones up on the bluff there, they're doing more damage to the walls."

"And your assessment, Carpio?"

The old man's eyes were on fire, giving the lie to his sickly complexion. He said mildly, "The walls

460

are only adobe, Captain. They'll stop a man or a horse, but they won't stop a cannonball. My assessment, then, is that they will take their time and demolish the walls at their leisure. Then, in the dark, I suspect, they will charge us. With your permission, Captain . . ."

Cordoba knew what was in his mind. "A sortie?" he asked, and Carpio nodded eagerly. "I need ten fusiliers, no more. Perhaps, just possibly . . . we can silence the cannon on the bluff. And if we can do that . . ." he grimaced. "Then we can stave off the inevitable for a few hours longer."

"Very well," Cordoba said. "Ten men, no more. And every ball they fire will have to count."

"Of that, I can assure you, *Señor Capitano*."

"See to it then, Carpio. And bring back as many of those ten as you can. We shall need them, come darkness."

He reached for his pocket timepiece instinctively, and thought of Estrellita, knowing that she would be weeping for him now, those sightless eyes filled with tears that she had never learned how to spend.

He watched Carpio ride off in a fine flurry of dust, and saw the medics running with a stretcher to where a trooper had been hit by a cannonball. He saw a file of half a dozen of the sick, wrapped in their blankets, wandering slowly, as though in a daze, to their allocated positions along the walls. Their aim, he knew, would not be steady enough. They would load their comrades' rifles for them.

He was surprised to find Barbastro beside him, strangely subdued, his youthful face very pale now; he had not heard his approach. He said

461

calmly, "Barbastro? There is a difficult time ahead for all of us now."

"Yes, sir, so I believe."

"The men know, by now, the strength of the enemy, no doubt?"

"Yes, Captain. We all know it. Do we . . . do we have any chance at all, sir?"

He was about to say quite coldly, "None, whatsoever, Lieutenant," and follow the comment with a few well-chosen words about a soldier's duty, about dying for the glory of Spain. . . . But he thought: *Twenty-two years old, and flowering into a fine young man, perhaps never having even known the love of a fine woman* . . . and he said instead, very gently, "Yes, Barbastro, we have a chance, a good one. We have the finest soldiers in the Imperial Spanish Army. And if we foster the bravery of our men by a show of our own . . . Yes, Lieutenant, we have a good chance."

"If I may say, sir . . ."

He was stammering and trying desperately to control the anguish inside him. "If I may say . . . how honored I have been to have served under you?"

He produced a large whitish handkerchief and blew his nose loudly, saluted, and hurried off.

All through the long day, the cannonballs, sometimes one by one and sometimes in volleys of ten or more, smashed into the fragile walls on all sides. The guns were being moved out there in the jungle, speedily and effectively, from cover to cover as the sweating mercenaries struggled with their wheels. Only once was it interrupted: a little after ten in the morning, a fierce firefight broke out on the bluff, the sound of rifleshots taking over as Carpio's men mounted their attack at very close range.

But an hour later, the cannons began to sound again. Not Carpio, nor a single one of his men returned to the *hacienda*.

By three o'clock that afternoon, there were eighteen fearsome breaches in the adobe walls. They had been filled with wood, the dead trunks of coconut palms, overturned wagons, anything that could be utilized as a barrier. There was even one place where a huge iron kitchen range had been manhandled into the gaping aperture. And still the defenders, conserving their ammunition for when they would most need it, and seeing almost no targets of opportunity, had fired scarcely more than a score of bullets.

The time for the disciplined, yet desperate volleys would come; it was not yet.

All they could do now was wait and wonder how many hours of life were left to them.

CHAPTER TWENTY-TWO

It was an endless spread of jungle, forest, and mountain, even though it was, in reality, scarcely seventy or eighty miles from coast to coast.

The towering *sierras*, the deep, lush valleys, and the myriad rivers that found their insistent way among them, seemed to give it a wildness without definable limits, as though the distance could not be counted in miles, but only in the hours it took a man to carve his wearisome way through all the vegetation with his machete.

. Though there were birds here without number, there were very few animals, perhaps fewer than on any other tropical island in the world. Except for a scattering of wild boar, none of the host of indigenous species of nearby Central America, nor of Florida to the north was to be found here. There were rodents and caymans and *cocodrillos* in the marshes, and seacows at the mouths of the rivers; freshwater turtles and a profusion of lizards; and a few snakes (none of them poisonous), but not much else.

The Spaniards had introduced horses, sheep, goats, asses, pigs and cattle; they thrived here, together with the dogs and cats they had brought with them. But these were on the small and sparsely dotted plantations; in the jungle, there was almost *nothing*.

The forest, however, which gave its shelter to little else, did provide homes for the Creoles, a people who had been created (as Amos Woodchuck had said) from other races. For three hundred years they had made their home on this "Paradise of the Sea."

They were a people of wondrous beauty, with coffee-colored skins and straight, dark hair. If the hair was crinkly, the admixture of Negro blood was considered too strong, and the subtly different word *mulatto* was used.

They were of medium height, and usually very strong physically, with an aspect of laziness combined with a remarkable endurance. They never liked to work too hard, but once committed to a project they would pursue it far beyond the bounds of normal human endeavor. They were sensual in the extreme, with bright, alert, discerning minds and a peculiarly Latin volatility. And the homegrown Spaniards, the "Peninsulars" had quickly learned to be wary of them. They suffered the indignities that an exarchy imposed upon them with an apparently resigned acceptance, but that acceptance was not without its limits.

They were terribly treated. They had no say at

all in the island's affairs. They were looked down upon, sometimes with contempt, but sometimes with fear, as *mestizos*, people of mixed blood; as though purity of bloodline had—ever—been of importance in the advance of *any* culture.

For some of them, the position was intolerable.

And for these, who did not dare raise their voices for fear of the *garrote*, there was only one solution. And that—a bad answer at best—was to hide out in the jungle where they would not be found, in hidden forest hamlets where they could perhaps hope that they would be allowed to continue, unrestricted by a foreign and burgeoning bureaucracy, the indolent kind of life they preferred.

Sometimes, among them, a leader would come forth who preached rebellion. He would exhort his handful of followers to violent protest; and the result would always be the same—more suppression.

One of these new messiahs was a Creole named Narcisio Dacis. He was the bastard brother, he claimed, of the great Miguel Dacis, though there were some who did not believe his claim. There was too considerable a difference in their ages.

Miguel was younger, a shrewd and wily man who many thought was far too friendly with the Peninsulars. He firmly believed in the value of arbitration, of talk and requests and "Special Laws," and for some years the Creoles all over the island followed him almost slavishly, listening to his placatory speeches, and believing him when he told them, "Our exit from oppression will be through entrance into their politics."

And indeed, for a while it seemed that those Special Laws for the Creoles, so reluctantly passed by the Spanish *cortes*, might effect an improvement in their condition. Even though, in effect, they granted little more than freedom to mix their own varied religions with the more rigid discipline of the accepted Church.

But though the *cortes* in Spain, wearied by the constant agitation, were amenable to a loosening of restrictions, the local governors—Peninsulars who had deeply entrenched themselves in privilege—had no interest whatsoever in changing the *status quo*, and continued their selfish exploitation to their hearts' content. Their constant show of force, their equally constant show of the most prodigal wastefulness and luxury, was slowly driving the great mass of the Creoles from their adherence to Miguel —and into the waiting ranks of his rambunctious bastard brother. A man who promised them not talk, but action; not the laborious processes of arbitration, but accession to their demands by the force of arms.

And so it came about that the mutually hostile Spanish governors, warring among themselves, and the rebel slave-groups who were also at each other's throats, and the brigands and guerrilla chieftains to whom conspiracy had become a way of life . . . all these factions found in their midst a new and startling danger—the rise of scattered armies of local inhabitants who knew every mountain, every river, every valley of the island and were prepared to fight for them.

The name Dacis had come to mean now, not the young politician Miguel; but the old soldier Narcisio.

He was a cypher, and a man of immense character. He was reputed to be in his sixties, though he had the boundless energy of a man half that age.

He had travelled widely in Louisiana and the Florida parishes, and he spoke English, French and Spanish as fluently as his native Creole. He was very thin, wiry, and he moved like a cat, preferring the darkness to the light of day.

He was never where he was thought to be, moving his hideouts speedily through the forest, sometimes alone, sometimes with a strong band of his followers. And when, as so frequently happened, one of the Spanish punitive patrols simply disappeared from the face of the earth, Havana would send out stronger forces, knowing that once again they were looking for Narcisio Dacis and that they would never find him. He was rumored to control more than four thousand armed men throughout the length and breadth of the country, and to have his spies everywhere.

He was known to be a patient, thoughtful man, and very, very dangerous.

Clifford had fought the jungle for three days and nights, searching, searching, searching with a kind of helpless desperation, for any sign that might lead him to his beloved Mercy.

There was only one thought driving him on, indefatigably, and that thought was: *However large this island might be, she is on it, somewhere, and I will find her.* He was sure that somehow, in the course of obstinate time, he would learn, from someone, somewhere, some news of her.

There would be plantations here, and little villages perhaps, and settlements . . . and if it were to take him a hundred years, he knew that he would never give up.

He was beating a pattern, an ever-widening

circle around the camp where the slaves had been massacred, following every path and trail he came upon, cutting his way through the heavy tangle of undergrowth and, at last, deep in a hidden valley, he had found a village. . . .

He lay on his belly, cautiously, under the cover of a mass of twining creeper, and watched it for a long, long time.

The trail he was on led steeply down into a hidden valley of great charm and beauty, a thousand different shades of greenery interspersed with brilliant pinpoints of red, yellow, blue, and purple, where wild flowers grew and brilliant birds fluttered their glorious plumage. There was a shallow stream there, meandering past a dozen or more houses of adobe or palm-frond—quite a large village—and at the stream there were dark-skinned women in colorful dresses with bright *bandanas* around their hair, washing clothes.

It occurred to him that there were no men in sight, only women and children, and he tried to puzzle out what that might mean. He counted the huts carefully, fourteen of them, with one long building in the center that might, perhaps, be a communal hall of some sort. There was a huge tree spreading over it, the lacy branches reaching out over its palm-frond roof.

He needed help; and he thought perhaps he could find it here. He got to his feet and walked on down the steep slope into the hamlet.

He was conscious that they all stopped work at his approach, eyeing him warily. He saw a woman at the water's edge bend down and whisper to a child at her side, saw the child run off to the long building under the huge tree, his feet and arms pumping rhythmically. He could not help smiling at the earnest determination of his efforts.

He reached the center of the tiny street and stopped, standing there and waiting patiently, knowing that someone would come now to find out about his business here. There would be, he knew, the difficulty of language, and he was already rehearsing the gestures he might make to explain his purpose.

Then, quite slowly, men began filing out of the long palm-roofed building to gather around him. Many of them carried guns, and they were menacing him in silence. There was one man among them for whom the others seemed to be parting their ranks, giving him access, an unbelievably thin and bony man with parchment skin tightly stretched over hollow, sunken cheeks, with white, wispy hair, and extraordinary eyes that belied the evident great age. They were very dark, almost black, the eyes of a much younger man, with a sharply inquisitive look in them.

There were subdued murmurings now, comments he could not understand, and the white-haired old man raised a hand for silence. He said, very mildly but with a latent menace, "*Se ha equiv-ocado de lugar, Señor.*"

Clifford said, holding his arms wide, conscious of the guns and wanting to show that he had no intention of drawing his machete from its scabbard, "Forgive me, *Señor*. I have no facility in Spanish, I fear. If someone here speaks the Queen's English?"

Those alert, all-understanding eyes seemed to narrow, and the old man said in good English, "The *Queen's* English? Would that indicate, sir,

471

that you are neither Spaniard nor yet American? I do believe it does."

Clifford was astonished at the fluency, the ease with the language; he could have been talking to one of his officers on board the *Northern Wind*. "But . . . you are English too, sir?"

There was the slightest smile in those eyes—though they were still very wary, he thought. "No, sir. I am proud to be Creole. But some of us have been fortunate enough—dare I say *un*fortunate enough?—to have spent all our lives in the company of those who seek to rule us. Spaniards, Americans, Portuguese, Colombians, French, Dutch. So many foreigners are seeking to control our destinies! And if you will tell me who you are and where you come from . . . then I can more easily decide whether or not you should be killed."

"Killed?" Clifford echoed calmly. "But why should you want to kill me? I came here seeking help, sir."

"Your name, then? What do you do here?"

"My name," Clifford said clearly, "is Clifford Hawkes. I am a seaman from a ship named *Capricorn*, and I will not bother you with the history of my arrival on this island. Suffice it to say that I was cast up on your shores with . . . with my wife. I have lost her in this jungle. I am searching for her. And I seek any information which may lead to my finding her. News of . . . of any sort. A footprint in the mud, a piece of tavern gossip, a rumor, anything at all which might lead me to her."

The old man's eyes did not leave his—but was there a kind of sympathy in them now? He was talking quietly in his own language, explaining

472

what was happening to the others there; but they were still wary, and no weapons were lowered.

Clifford said, begging now, the desperation apparent in his voice. "If you, or your people, sir, have any news of this kind? A young English woman, alone and helpless, wandering in this terrible forest?

There were tears in his eyes as he thought of her. "This is all I seek here," he said, ashamed of his momentary weakness.

There was a long consultation again, and still those extraordinary eyes were on his. The old man said at last, "I am Narcisio Dacis, Mister Hawkes. I and my men . . . we have other, perhaps more pressing business on our hands at this moment. But the forest, indeed, is full of my men, and maybe . . ." He sighed. "In the press of that business, I find it . . . refreshing—is that the word?—that we can interest ourselves in so prosaic a matter as a woman lost in the jungle. Ah . . . if all our problems were open to so simple a solution! But . . . you are English, I am convinced, so tell me, if you will . . . where do the English stand on the matter of the Creole's freedom? Will you tell me, sir, quite honestly?"

"Quite honestly," Clifford said, "until a few days ago, I had never heard the word Creole. Nor did I know who your people were."

There was that long, weary sigh again. "An honest answer indeed . . . Then tell me, are you on the side of the Spaniards?"

"I have met the Spaniards but once, *Señor* Dacis. I must confess that I was not mightily impressed with . . . with their sense of humanity."

It seemed that the old man was making up his

473

mind. The conference in Creole went on for a little while, and then he said, with a broad gesture of hospitality, "Let us sit down and talk, Mr. Hawkes. Are you hungry? Thirsty?"

He led the way back into the longhouse they had come from, and there were tables there with benches set beside them. Only half a dozen of the men had entered with them. They sat together and Dacis said quietly, "Tell me about the lady you are searching for, Mr. Hawkes. Perhaps we can be of assistance."

Clifford told him at great length of the home they had made for themselves down there by the waterfall; of the advent of Theophilus; of the attack on the camp by the Spaniards; and of his own fortunes and misfortunes since then.

Dacis listened in quiet, understanding patience, and he said at last, very hesitantly, "It seems to me, Mr. Hawkes, that your determination to find your wife is much to be commended. As a Creole, I find in my heart a great deal of sympathy for you. Certainly, my people are at home in this jungle and perhaps . . ." He thought about it for a while, and said, "There are more in the mountains here, and for purposes of my own I am in touch with all of them. I can, and I will, ask for news of the lady, though the question of survival, for someone who does not know what trails to follow, what berries to eat . . ."

He broke off. A lank and agitated man was striding into the room, dressed in little more than rags but with a strange authority on him. He threw an angry, suspicious look at Clifford, and spoke sharply to Dacis, gesticulating wildly. Clifford was very conscious that whatever news he was bringing was bad.

There was a deep frown on the old man's face as he listened, interjecting a question here and there, and he made a little gesture to the new arrival at last, a gesture that seemed to say: Wait . . .

He turned to Clifford; his voice was heavy with anxiety. "This meeting has given me great pleasure, Mr. Hawkes, and I fear I have been neglectful of my duties as a host. If you will forgive me, there are matters I must discuss with one of my lieutenants. He has ridden hard and fast for a day and a night from a *hacienda* where, it seems, a battle is under way between Spaniards of opposing philosophies. I must know who they are, how strong they are . . . You understand, and forgive me?"

Clifford rose to go, but Dacis restrained him. "No, please, do not let us drive you away without at least a small sign of our hospitality. I will have someone bring you food."

He gave an order to one of the women there, and as she hurried out, Clifford said, hesitant yet patient, "I have one favor to ask, *Señor* Dacis. If your lieutenant has been riding through the forest?"

There was a long and earnest consultation in Creole, then, suddenly, Dacis was frowning again and looking at Clifford. Clifford said urgently, "Sir, if there is news, any kind of news?"

That expressive hand was slowing him down again, and the conference went on and on and on. Dacis stared out into space as he listened and rubbed his cheek, thought deeply in silence for a while, then at last he said, "It may be, Mr. Hawkes, that some kind of perverted destiny, in which all

475

Creoles believe, is drawing us together, you and I. Your search and mine . . . perhaps their paths are crossing. But let me pursue this further . . ."

There was a long talk in dialect again, with gestures and gesticulations on both sides, and Clifford could scarcely restrain himself. After what seemed an eternity, Dacis turned to him and said, "I am forgetting my manners again. This is Lieutenant Linares, one of my confidantes, who has been with a trifling force of Spaniards under a Captain named Cordoba . . . who is, I say reluctantly, a good man, though a Peninsular. He has been for a long time now on his way from Havana to Santiago to arrest Governor Aguilar on charges of treason . . . and Aguilar, you must understand, is our prime enemy, a vicious, depraved man."

"But sir," Clifford said desperately.

Dacis made that little Creole gesture again. "Patience, my son, we must all have patience now. Tell me, if you will, the name of your lady?"

"Mercy," Clifford said quickly. "Mercy Hawkes."

That long and frustrating talk again!

Clifford heard him say, repeating it, "Mercy, Mercy! *Clemencia, Misericordia, Gracia* . . ." And the answer: "*Gracia.*"

The woman was returning, as they talked, and she set a plate of roast meat down before Clifford. He threw up his hands and said, "For God's sake, Señor Dacis! Tell me!"

Dacis was so calm and unhurried! But he nodded gently, wisely, and though the ancient lips seemed to be smiling, there was anxiety in his eyes. "Eat your food, Mr. Hawkes," he said, an elder addressing a child. "This is not a time for impatience, or for hasty decisions. And yes, I will tell. It may be that we know where your lady is."

Clifford tried hard to control the terrible impatience, and Dacis said, explaining and taking his time over it, "There is a *hacienda* on the way to Santiago de Cuba. It seems that Captain Cordoba is camped there. Linares tells me that among the . . . the camp women, there is an English lady who is being treated, please be assured, with the greatest respect. She is known among the troops as *La Señora Gracia*, which could be translated as "The Lady Mercy" . . ."

"Then I must go there at once!" Clifford said eagerly, and Dacis gestured again. "Patience, patience," he said. "I am told that Cordoba, with one hundred and seventy troops, is at this moment under attack by a very large force of Governor Aguilar's mercenaries. In Linares's opinion, which I value, they cannot last more than twenty-four hours."

Clifford could feel the blood draining from his face, and his urgency was overpowering. "If you would just tell me where this *hacienda* is! Where, *Señor?* I must know! And at once!"

"Wait, wait," the old man insisted. "There is a question here to be examined very carefully. You must go to the *hacienda*, without a doubt. And so must I. And I must ride on to Santiago and join my men, with the few troops I have here following as fast as they can. We are almost ready for an assault on Santiago, and what has held me back is that huge mercenary army of Aguilar's. But if we can reach his citadel before his army can return . . . come, sir, we will ride at once to the *hacienda*, you about your business, and I about mine. Our destinies

477

do indeed seem to be converging on each other, at least for the moment. But give me a few moments first with my lieutenants."

He strode out and Clifford pushed the plate of food away from him, jumping to his feet to pace up and down intolerably as he waited. Linares gesticulated at the meal, a question, and when Clifford shook his head, he took it and wolfed down the meat hungrily.

It was ten minutes before Dacis returned and he carried a rifle slung across his shoulder, a brace of good pistols in his belt. There were six other men with him, similarly armed. One of them carried a spare rifle, and he handed it to Clifford. The old man said, "You know how to use a rifle, sir?"

Clifford grimaced. "I have fired a harpoon gun in my time, *Señor* Dacis, nothing more."

"Then we will take a few moments more in your instruction."

He pulled the ramrod from its casing, set down both the main-charge powder and the fulminating powder on the table, and began showing him carefully how to load the weapon.

"The Shaw rifle," he said, "fired by a square-headed hammer onto the percussion powder, so igniting the charge . . ."

Clifford interrupted him anxiously. "Sir, we are wasting time."

Dacis shook his head, his old eyes gleaming. "No, Mr. Hawkes, we are not. If you are to be killed before we reach the *hacienda* because of your inability to defend yourself . . . instruction is never a waste of time, and I will have no one with me who cannot use a rifle. Now, watch carefully what I do, and *learn*."

Clifford controlled his restlessness and watched the slow and laborious loading process. When the rifle was charged there were still other lessons, it seemed. Dacis took him outside into the gathering dusk, and aimed the rifle.

He said, "You look carefully along the barrel at your target, and you press the trigger with your first finger. These are very accurate guns, new guns from the United States, so accurate that if you are to aim at a group of charging men, three or four of them shall we say, at fifty paces, you are almost certain to score a hit on one of them. Now . . ."

He handed him the gun and said, "Put the stock tightly into your shoulder or the recoil will knock you off your feet." He pointed and said, "That stump there, show me that you can hit it."

Clifford fired and missed, but saw the lead bullet hit the ground close by, and Dacis nodded his appreciation. "Yes, had that been a man, perhaps you would have hit him. Now, please load the rifle again, in the way I showed you."

He was fast losing all patience, but he went carefully through the business with the two powders, and the ball, and the pressed wadding, and the ramrod. He could not credit that it took such an unconscionable time. He wanted to throw the gun down angrily and rush off on his own, and to the devil with their patience! But how would he find the *hacienda* alone? He said instead, growling, "A man could be killed a dozen times over while he loads one of these infernal things! And while we stand here talking . . ."

"Time spent in preparation," Dacis said placidly, the teacher again, "is soon recovered. And I hope

479

that in the course of time you will learn to do that very much faster."

Linares was riding up with a string of ponies, and Clifford was faced with another problem. He watched Dacis leap onto the saddle with an agility he found remarkable, and when he tried to emulate him he failed miserably. He was conscious of their eyes on him and he straddled the mount awkwardly while someone lengthened the stirrups for him. He saw that the old man was smiling gently now. "You will learn, sir," he said. "I am sure that you are the kind of man who learns fast."

Linares took the lead as the little party set off, and Dacis said, "Be prepared to ride hard, my friend. We have a long, long way to go."

The forest was closing in on them, the shadows lengthening as the hooves drummed their muted thunder into the red-brown, leaf-strewn trail. Clifford said, easing himself in the unaccustomed saddle, "There is one thing I do not understand, *Señor* Dacis."

"Only one thing? Then you are a very lucky young man."

Clifford felt his face reddening. "I mean, of course," he said, "in the matter of this business we are undertaking."

"And if I can help you to understand, I will."

"You spoke of a Captain Cordoba, presumably a Spaniard, under attack by . . . other Spaniards I think? It seems strange."

"In Cuba these days," the old man said sadly, "there is so much that is strange! But this . . . no, it is not. It is a very simple matter, Mr. Hawkes. The Spanish Empire is breaking up. Should Spain lose Cuba, as one day it surely will, the local governors will not want to return to the peninsula they came from. They will want to continue their exploitation of my country, no longer for Spain, but for themselves. One of these men, perhaps the worst and most dangerous of them, is Governor Aguilar. Even Havana—and the Spaniards there are just as venal, just as preoccupied with their own futures—has had more than enough of his excesses. And so, they are making war on him. Not in the name of justice . . . but in the name of venality."

They rode on in silence for a little while, stooping low to pass through the overhanging foliage, and Linares, a little ahead of them, was slicing at branches and tangled vines with his machete.

"And yet you told me," Clifford said, the thought troubling him deeply, "that my wife is being treated . . . I think your words were *'with the greatest respect.'* If she is with these . . . the evil Spaniards you speak of, is it of her own free will? Or as a prisoner?"

"Of her own free will it seems," Dacis said carefully. "And now, for a moment at least, I must thrust aside my hatred of all Spaniards and tell you that Captain Juan Cordoba . . ." He sighed. "If there were such a thing as a good Spaniard, it would be Cordoba. He is a simple, straightforward soldier, and I will admit that he is a very good one. We are coming to a marsh now, grip your mount very firmly with your legs, Mr. Hawkes. You are not, I think, a practiced horseman?"

"No, sir. You were telling me about Captain Cordoba."

"And about your wife, yes. Well . . . there is hardly a man among the Spaniards whose hands have not been stained with Creole or Negro blood,

481

whose pockets have not been lined by a corruption so blatant that it has become a festering sore on the island. Any man who dares to raise his voice in protest . . . they do not listen to him, Mr. Hawkes, they execute him. In my own village . . ."

He broke off, staring straight ahead into the darkness, his eyes glazed with the memory of it. He went on, speaking very quietly, "A patrol of a hundred men, just like Cordoba's patrol, went there one day, carrying with them the chair and the *garrote* for a public execution. Narcisio Dacis to be strangled ceremonially before all the assembled villagers. I was not there, merely because I had gone into the forest to gather food for my family. When I returned, the soldiers had gone, and they had left behind them a burning village, only a handful of survivors among the forty souls who lived there. There were twelve men hanging from trees, there were eight women who had been raped and murdered, there were six very small children who had been thrown into the flaming huts. And the reason? It was my village, Mr. Hawkes, and the fact that I was not to be found there, and executed, was reason enough for them. Unhappily this is by no means an isolated example of the oppression we suffer from. It is the pattern of it."

Cifford said tightly, "And my wife is in the hands of these . . . these savages?"

"No, sir. I am happy to say that she is not. Cordoba, without a doubt, knows of these terrible crimes. How can he not know, they are all around him? It is even said that he has, on occasion, protested them vigorously, and that this is why, a man in his fifties and one of the best soldiers ever to be sent here, he has not risen beyond the rank of captain. For Havana, a colonel, even a *commandante*, must be a monster, and Cordoba is not. My people in Havana tell me that this is why he was sent against Aguilar with such an insignificant force. Havana *knows* he is going to his death, they *know* that Aguilar will annihilate him. It will give them further, more positive grounds for splendid rhetoric at Aguilar's eventual trial . . . and it will rid them of a man they detest because he is not evil. And I am sure he does not even suspect their duplicity."

"Your lieutenant said he can hold out for twenty-four hours, and you spoke of your confidence in his opinion." He was instinctively trying to urge his horse faster through the deep mud of the marsh. "You also spoke of the camp women she was with . . ."

"Pray God," Dacis said, "that they will escape."

Clifford said steadily, "And if they can not?"

Dacis would not answer him.

They rode on in silence, plodding their way heavily through the swamp, and when they reached the open country on its further bank, they broke into a trot, a canter and then a very fast gallop.

Clifford could not contain himself. He shouted desperately, "How long? How long before we reach them?"

Dacis answered him, "Ride, Mr. Hawkes! Ride hard . . . and pray."

CHAPTER TWENTY-THREE

Mercy had never been so terrified in her life.

The awesome fear that had been upon her during those hard days and nights on the open ocean, when sometimes she had felt sure that there was only loneliness and death ahead for both of them, was nothing compared with this.

Then, Clifford had been with her to comfort her and sustain her courage, and the dangers were the casual dangers of Nature. But now he was no longer by her side, and the relentless hail of bullets that poured steadily into the grounds was somehow more frightening because it was deliberate, methodical, and utterly ruthless. There had still been no visible sign of the enemy, just the smoke of his black powder and the incessant roar of volley after volley after volley from massed rifles.

Cordoba was running from wall to wall, placing

men here, withdrawing them from there, checking on the wounded, shouting encouragement to his troopers everywhere, hoping his own fortitude would somehow be contagious.

All of the girls, save Estrellita, were working now as *vivandieras*, carrying water and food to the men on the walls, crudely bandaging those who had been hurt, collecting the rifles from those who had been killed—and there were many of them—and bringing them to the living.

The wall was a shambles and the cannonballs were still coming; and yet very few of the defenders' guns had fired. The men, well disciplined, were conserving their ammunition against the time when, they knew, the enemy would be forced to leave the dense cover of the undergrowth and show himself in the final charge.

Estrellita, knowing herself to be useless now in her affliction, had refused to take cover while her girls were still out there, and she sat alone and very calm on the steps that led up into the house. She listened to the sound of the gunfire, to the screams of the wounded, and to the sound of lightly running feet that told her just where all the women were. The warmth of the sun had left her face and she knew that there would be now that strange gray light over the landscape that once she had loved so much. She knew that the end would not be long now. And in a little while, Captain Cordoba came to her and she could hear that he was limping, hear the pain in his voice.

He said heavily, "I am sending the girls into the house, Estrellita. All of them save . . . Inez. I'm afraid Inez has been killed."

She could no longer feel any pain. "And your men, Juan? Your officers?"

"Barbastro, my youngest lieutenant, is dead. So, I must assume, is Carpio, my oldest. Malagos, Perez, and Barrato, all wounded but still waiting and ready to fight. We have lost, at the last count, seventy-two men. That was an hour ago. I no longer have an Officer of the Day to make the tallies."

"And you, Juan? You are wounded . . ."

"A bullet in my thigh. It is no longer of importance. I am worried about Mercy Hawkes. I last saw her loading a rifle for a trooper who had lost his left hand. Inexpertly, I am afraid . . ."

"She is in the house, Juan. Sergeant Azuaga is gravely wounded, and she is tending him."

"Then we will go to her now. Come."

"We will wait for the girls to be sent to their quarters, Juan."

"I have already given the order. Do you want to . . . to talk to them first?"

"No. There is enough pain for all of us without fare-thee-wells. Yours and mine, Juan . . ." She caught her breath, biting her tongue and stifling the flow of tears. "More than I can bear," she whispered.

"Come."

He held out an arm for her, and she reached out and took it as though she could see it, unerringly, and they went into the Great Hall where the wounded had been laid out on the floor. Mercy was there, crouched dry-eyed over the dead body of Sergeant Azuaga. Her voice was hollow and filled with anguish. "I will not hide, Estrellita," she said, "while so many good men are dying . . ."

Estrellita reached out and touched her arm. "We will hide," she said quietly, "just as we planned."

"No, I will not!"

"It is not death we are hiding from," Estrellita said softly.

Cordoba took Mercy's hand and said stiffly, "I cannot express my regrets, *Señora*. Please . . . hide my Estrellita for me, hide her as you have planned. She is helpless now and I can be sure of her survival only if I know she is in your hands." He knew they were both ready to die, lost in that awesome limbo of despair, and he said stiffly, urging them, "Please . . . if only for my sake, I beg of you."

Mercy's arms were around him suddenly, clutching him tightly, a man about to die and facing it calmly, with thoughts only for the woman he loved. She said very quietly, "I will take care of her, Captain Cordoba. Trust me. She will not be captured."

"I trust you, *Señora* Hawkes. But you must go quickly now. Take her for me to your hiding place . . . the attic, I believe?"

"Yes, the attic. There is a place there that . . ." She looked down at Azuaga's still body, and whispered, "A place that Sergeant Azuaga found for us."

He kissed her almost ceremonially on both cheeks and said abruptly, "I will not say goodbye. As Estrelitta says, we have pain enough."

Mercy turned away, a load on her heart more heavy than she could tolerate, as Cordoba took the blind woman in his arms. She heard him say, "I must return to my men now. In Heaven, Estrellita, there are no blind angels. And when we meet there . . ."

He held her trembling body tightly for a brief moment, kissing her passionately, then turned sharply away as though he felt she could see his face, and hobbled out.

Estrellita heard the door close behind him, heard Mercy's terrible silence, and took her hand. "Come," she said. "I will take you to the attic, and then . . . you will take me to this loathesome cave we are to hide in, like frightened children, while so many good men we have known . . . come."

Arm in arm, they went up the wide staircase to the upper floor, and found the ladder that went up from it to the garret. There was almost no light there at all, and Mercy said hesitantly, "I will show you the way now . . ."

"You will need a tallow," Estrellita said. "There is one burning somewhere nearby."

"Yes . . . yes, of course." She found the candle, a wick in a little ceramic bowl of oil, and carried it carefully as she climbed the ladder to the top. She set it down and whispered to Estrellita, "All right, can you manage?"

She climbed the ladder easily, and crouched on the upper sides of the rafters, very sure of herself now, and said, "All right, the cockloft is above us, I believe."

"Yes. Take my hand."

There was another ladder there; in the pale glow of the rushlight Mercy stared up at it. It looked very fragile, not much used, and it had been laid loosely against the entrance to the upper chamber. She said, her voice hushed, "We can drag it up there after us, and no one will know that the loft is even there." She took Estrellita's hand, laid it on a rung, and said, "I will go first."

"No, let me. We have already explored this place, you and I. I know it better than you do."

Mercy followed her carefully into the tiny chamber. It was not more than eight feet by five, very low-ceilinged, with a single miniscule aperture in one wall that served as a window. The flooring was of rough planking and one side was covered with richly smelling little bamboo cages that once had held pigeons.

The sound of the gunfire was coming to them from far down below there, but it was quite dark outside now, and the flashes of the cannon were bright against the night sky.

Mercy set the tallow down and saw that Estrellita's hands, the only eyes she had, were exploring, reaching up to find the height of the low rafters over their heads, groping along the floor to find the overlying beams. In a moment or two, the blind woman lay down on the timbers, her sightless eyes staring, the tears running from them unchecked. She whispered, "The ladder. We must not forget the ladder."

"Yes, of course . . ." She pulled it up carefully and pushed it along the wall out of their way, closing the wooden hatch that was part of the ceiling below.

"And the candle . . . it must be extinguished."

Mercy pinched the flame with her fingers, and in the darkness she whispered, "Do you feel as I do, Strellita?"

"Yes. I am sure of it. We are waiting for all the good men we have known to be killed."

"Oh dear God . . ."

490

"Juan Cordoba . . . he was such a good man."

"Yes. I know it."

"I have known him for so long! And yet, it was only a few hours ago that he became my lover. And even then, if I had not deliberately aroused . . . yes, I seduced him, I will confess it. He wanted to love me so very much. I think now that this was what he had always wanted. We dined together very often, and he would talk to me about his home, his childhood, and all the foolish things a man will talk about to a woman when he fears to ask for the love that he really needs so intensely. And he would never lay a hand on me, because of a foolish promise I made so many years ago, denying myself all that is good in life. There was always, between us, a kind of—how shall I call it?—a kind of intellectual passion. I admired him as a man, and he admired me as a woman. And yet, there was never that intimate touch of affection . . . he would kiss my hand. He never laid a hand on my breast, nor my thighs, until in those last hours, when he knew he was dying. I read his body then, for the first time . . . his hair, his eyebrows, his lips and his strong chin. His shoulders, his chest, that tight muscular stomach. I touched, for the first time, his manhood, and found it erect and powerful, and I knew that he wanted me as desperately as I had always wanted him. And even then, it was I who led him into the bedroom . . ."

The tears were streaming down her cheeks now, and there was a terrible tightness in her voice. "He loved me, Mercy," she said, "so long and passionately. He would not leave me, as though the embrace of my flesh were a kind of ecstasy for him that had been denied him too long. His hands, his

491

lips were all over me, exploring, caressing, tasting
. . . I could not believe that I could lose myself so
completely in . . . in such delirium. And now . . .
there will never be another man like my beloved
Juan."

Mercy, sitting beside her on the hard planking,
touched her cheeks and knew of the tears there.
She was thinking: *in the darkness, she is more
aware than I am* . . . she leaned down and kissed
those wet eyes and said softly, trying to stifle her
own emotions, "You must not talk of him as
though he is dead, dear Strellita. He is not. There is
still hope."

"He is dead," Estrellita whispered. "I know it.
There is no hope at all."

While the light had lasted, the men up on the
near bluff, and the others on the south, had been
firing their orderly volleys into the grounds of the
hacienda. The range, on both sides, was from less
than five hundred paces; and every ball in ten—perhaps more—found a mark. Such calculated slaughter could not last for long and Adam Butrus was
almost bored with the ease of it.

They were exposed down there, with no visible
foe to answer with their guns, wasting their bullets
once in a while by firing blindly at where they
hoped that foe might be as their self-restraint broke
down at the sight of so many dead or dying comrades. The walls now were reduced to a useless
rubble by the cannonade which had gone on hour
after hour with such prodigious profligacy.

It was not a waste of the cannons' ammunition;
in the morning, almost every heavy ball they had
fired into the compound would be recovered and

loaded once more onto the ammunition wagons. And there would be nearly two hundred good rifles to add to their stores, and Havana would learn—in the course of a long, long time—that Captain Cordoba's miserable little force had been wiped out by some other provincial governor's forces, or by those abominable Creoles whom Narcisio Dacis commanded, or even by a well-armed party of rebel slaves. It was all so impossibly easy, and Butrus was thinking: When I report to that peacock Aguilar, there will be more gold coins for my chest, no doubt . . . and more, and more, when we have conquered the whole of Cuba.

Like his soldiers, he was wearing a *poncho* over his brilliantly colored uniform, and he looked at the last streaks of gold in the western sky, saying to Jake Ollie, "All right, Captain. I need a count of cannonballs, and of ammunition for the rifles."

Jake Ollie saluted. He had grown considerably in stature under Colonel Adam's indomitable command, learning fast from him, his natural niche in life found at last. He saluted and said, "At the last count, we've fired over six hundred balls down there, Colonel. We've broached our seventh barrel of powder. And by God, there's still plenty left. Its' a good way to fight."

"The *only* way to fight, Ollie," Adam Butrus said. "Get me an exact count."

"Yes, sir."

He hurried off and Butrus took a long drink from his bottle of rum. He began to wonder if Jake Ollie were ready now for the honors he was about to bestow on him.

The shooting had stopped and there was nothing now but an ominous silence over the forest. In ac-

493

cord with his orders, the men were gathering together under their sergeants, lining up and awaiting their orders patiently.

He decided that he would favor them with a little speech, and he said, "There were a hundred and fifty men down there. If your marksmanship is in accord with the training I've given you . . . there are probably not more than thirty or forty of them left alive. I am taking three hundred men down there, and our objective is simply to ensure that there are no survivors left. This is the time to use your bayonettes as I've drilled you to use them. Every man, woman, or child still within the grounds of that *hacienda* is to be killed. When it's all over, we will march back to Santiago, where a grateful Governor will be anxiously awaiting the news of our great success."

He called a sergeant to him and said, "Go down to the southern assault force. Tell Lieutenant Tacon that we move in on the sound of a single rifleshot, which I will fire shortly. Tell him what I have told you . . . that I want no survivors. Not man, not woman, not child. Go now."

The sergeant saluted and scurried off, and Butrus paced back and forth. When Ollie returned, panting and out of breath, he asked, "Well? Your report, Captain?"

Ollie said, grinning, "Seven hundred and eighty cannonballs fired, Colonel."

"I want them all recovered, Ollie."

"I'll see to it, sir. And two thousand six hundred rounds of lead shot fired. The men on the south have fired off almost all their balls, the men up here still have plenty left."

"They won't need them. We use the bayonettes now."

"Aye, aye, sir."

"And you do know, don't you?" he asked, "what we have achieved this day?'

"Yes, sir. We wiped them out without giving them a target to fire at."

"More than that, Jake. Like disciplined troops, they held their fire till they could see something to shoot at, and we never gave them that satisfaction. So we not only get their rifles, we get their powder too."

"Yes, sir."

"Powder is vauable, Jake. It has to come all the way from Spain, or from America. We have used up a great deal of it. It will be replaced because we gave them nothing to use it on."

"Yes, sir."

"Remember that. We wait for one hour now."

And precisely one hour later, the mercenaries moved in, like shadows out of the darkness of the forest. The defensive walls were no more than piles of dried mud, and the pathetic resistance of the forty or fifty men who had survived the bombardment was nothing more than a desperate gesture.

The main body of the attacking force held their positions, while the chosen three hundred of their fellows went through the camp methodically, using their steel in the moonlight.

Cordoba, mercifully, was already dead, with four bullet-wounds in his poor body. The girls, lining up in the cellar that had been chosen for their refuge, with forced, expectant smiles on their hopeful faces, were raped repeatedly, the men lining up for their acquiescent, yet still apprehensive bodies.

Then, on the personal order of Colonel Adam, who wanted no testimony left to haunt him, they were all killed.

Adam Butrus explored the grounds and found nothing but death there. He ordered the collection of all the cannonballs, the enemy rifles, the mules, the wagons, and all of the other supplies.

He said to Ollie, "There's a fine selection of wine in the cellars, Captain. Find room for it on one of the captured wagons."

"Aye, aye, sir. And we camp here tonight?"

"No." He hated this uncouth, idiot man, and yet . . . he had need of him. He said, "We camp on the bluff, where the rest of the men are. Meanwhile, put the torch to this place. Burn down every building there is here, the way the Creoles do after their attacks. See to it, Ollie."

Estrellita was the first to smell the smoke.

There had been long and terrible hours of fear as they heard the sounds of sporadic, nearby shooting and knew what it meant.

There was an intolerable state of exhaustion upon both of them, not the exhaustion of effort, but that far worse fatigue that is the result of inactivity in the face of great endeavor.

They lay close to each other in their hidden chamber high up in the roof, and that state of mind had set in which is beyond all rational comprehension. The *hacienda*, so recently a place of ebullient life, with the guitars of the campfollowers strumming, the little campfires burning everywhere, the troopers quietly, contentedly, polishing the jacked leather of their boots . . . all was silent now. And the silence could only mean the end of an era.

496

Mercy said quietly, "What now, Strellita? A part of our lives has been cut off so . . . so brutally! What now?" She was grateful that she could not see, in the darkness, the pain that she knew was there on that lovely face.

"What now?" Estrellita echoed. Their voices were subdued, no more than zephyrs in the night. "I do not know, Mercy. In a little while, when I have had time to think, to overcome this . . . this terrible sadness . . . then perhaps I will know what we must do. For the moment, we must do as dear Juan said. We wait."

"For what?"

"I do not know, dear Mercy. For . . . for silence, For a day and a night, he said, or a night and a day . . . and then, perhaps, we should try and find our way . . . where? I do not know. Santiago? An evil place. Havana? It was my home once, but I must confess that Havana too is a place of even greater evil. Wherever we go, how shall we live? There will never be another Juan Cordoba."

"And Clifford, dear Clifford . . ."

"Yes. Your Clifford. Perhaps you should forget him."

"No! I will not! Never!"

"Then think of him always."

"I will."

Estrellita whispered, "All there is to do now, dear Mercy, is wait . . . and try to forget . . . what has happened down there. In God's name, it is not easy."

And then, there was the first whisp of smoke finding its way up there, and Estrellita was brought sharply back to earth by the danger of the moment.

She said urgently, "*Madre de Dios* . . . they have fired the house!"

Mercy's eyes were wide with alarm. She moved to the tiny aperture and peered out, then hurried back to the hatchcover that separated them from the rooms below, lifed it, and let it drop back into place as the smoke billowed up into their tiny sanctuary. She went to Estrellita and took her arms, saying, "We have to climb down over the roof. It will be very dangerous, but you will hold my hand all the way. Do not be afraid, Strellita, I am with you."

Together they went to the little opening in the wall. There was hardly room for them to move through it, but Mercy eased her body over the sill and held out a hand for her blind friend. She led her carefully over the steeply sloping palm-frond roof that crackled under their touch, tinder dry.

She said urgently, "Keep hold of my hand, Strellita, it is very steep, but there is a way down, rooftop to rooftop."

They slithered cautiously over the thatching and dropped down from one level to another until they finally reached the ground. Now the flames were crackling, beginning to roar with the powerful updrafts generated by their own heat. They began to run, Mercy holding tightly to Estrellita's hand, as they sought to escape the fierce heat of the fire, engulfing the whole building, a torch of long-dried wood and thatch.

Mercy pulled up short, gasping. Three men were barring their path. One of them, in a *poncho*-covered sergeant's uniform, she had never seen before. But the other two . . .

She could not believe the evidence of her own

eyes. One of them was First Mate Adam Butrus, and the other was that equally loathsome man, Bo'sun Jake Ollie, both of the sailing ship *Capricorn*.

Butrus was staring at her, unbelieving. He said at last, drawling, "Well, Mistress Mercy Carrol . . . God's blood, it is a surprise, I must admit! And yet . . . I know that Seaman Hawkes is on this island, and if he is here, then it follows that you must be too, does it not? Nonetheless, I admit to a considerable pleasure that the Fates have been so kind to me."

She could find no words at all. Her hand was tight on Estrellita's and she could sense the alarm there.

Butrus said to his captain, "Ollie, be a good fellow and escort these two ladies—unharmed, you understand?—up to my tent. I would have words with them both."

He was looking, a little bewildered, at Estrellita's fine eyes that seemed to be focused just over his left shoulder.

He said to Ollie, "*Now* . . ." and turned on his heels and walked away. His heart was pounding furiously as he thought of that cabin on board his ship; thought too of her lovely companion with the huge and lustrous eyes that had stared at him so strangely. He could scarcely control his excitement.

His tent had been set up in a little clearing among the tall trees of the bluff.

Outside it, there was a campaign table with a map spread out on it, a single chair, and a flare on a long pole that was stuck into the ground. A dozen men were ringed about it, his personal

499

guards, men whom Butrus had trained in their first and only duty—the safety and well-being of their colonel.

He sat back in his chair with his booted feet up on the table, a wooden goblet of rum in his hand, as Ollie and the sergeant with the two women approached. There was a tremendous excitement quickening his pulse as he looked at them. He sipped his drink, taking his time, relishing their discomfort, and he said at last, smiling wryly, "Yes, the Fates are indeed kind to me this day. And where is your lover Seaman Hawkes, Mistress Mercy?"

"I do not know where he is, Mr. Butrus," she said coldly. "And if you would kindly tell me why you have brought us here?"

"Ha! You will find out, dear lady, in the course of time! But why do you not introduce me to your beautiful companion? A Spanish lady, I perceive, from her dress and her demeanor?"

"I will not present so hateful a man to any friend of mine," Mercy said coldly. "She is a friend, let that suffice."

He ignored the contempt in her voice; it was a quality he had long become accustomed to in his dealings with decent people. His eyes were on Estrellita, peering at her, puzzled. He said: "And you will not meet my eyes, *Señorita?* Am I so unpleasant to look at? I think not."

Estrellita said very quietly, "I am blind, *Señor*. Quite blind."

He stared at her, incredulous. He got to his feet and stood in front of her, passing a hand back and forth in front of her eyes. "Quite blind?"

"For some years now. And I too must ask . . . why are we here?"

His eyes were on the low neckline of her tulle dress, and his hand dropped to within an inch of her breasts, cupping them but not yet touching, moving across her body from one to the other. "You see nothing, *Señorita*?"

"Nothing at all, *Señor*."

"A blind woman . . . in all my very successful years, I have never enjoyed a blind woman. Is it different, I wonder? The breasts, the thighs, they will be the same. But that vague and distant look in unseeing eyes . . . it merits some consideration, I would say."

He raised his other hand, both of them now, cupping but not quite touching her. "And you do not see where my hands are?"

"No sir, I can see nothing, as I told you."

"Charming. Quite charming."

He turned to Mercy, smiling. "You will forgive me, will you not," he asked in mock piety, "if I satisfy my curiosity first on this blind companion of yours? But please do not be alarmed. Your ardent desires will soon be satisfied too."

There was a strangely calm pleasantry to his voice, but Mercy saw that his eyes were feverishly bright and that he was almost trembling with a savage anticipation.

She looked to Estrellita; she was holding herself in firmly, her beautiful face deathly pale now. They reached out and touched hands.

Butrus saw the gesture and laughed. With a sudden, violent movement, he gripped the top of Estrellita's dress and ripped it wide open, and stepped back, still laughing, as she slashed at him with her

501

fingernails, seeking to rake them across his face. Mercy threw herself at him with a scream of fury and he seized her arms and swung her round. He raised his voice and called out, "Ollie! Hold her for me! I want her to watch this."

Ollie was there instantly, grinning like a maniac as he took Mercy's elbows in his powerful hand and pulled them tight together behind her back. She struggled, quite in pain, and he held her there, a helpless woman in the grasp of a violent man who felt the need to assert his masculinity.

And now, Estrelitta was the target of a cruel and spiteful game.

Butrus moved to one side of her and she swung round instantly to face him. He moved again, in utter silence now, testing her; and still she followed his movements. Then again, quieter still, even holding his breath. She had drawn together the torn pieces of her dress and bodice, partly covering herself, and he was moving his feet very carefully, watching for her instant reaction. Her head was cocked a little to one side as she strained her ears for the sound of his heartbeat. She said, whispering, "Mercy? Are you all right?"

Mercy choked and could not answer, then Butrus reached out again and tore those covering hands away. He held her there in front of him, her wrists cruelly held far apart as he feasted his eyes on her. He shouted, a maniac now, "Are you watching, Mistress Mercy? Do you see what a savage animal a man can be when he is aroused?"

Ollie had changed his grip on her, a strong arm tucked under one of hers, his free hand mauling her breast as he bit into her neck. She could not stop her screaming or her livid fury. Then, she saw

502

that Estrellita had freed one hand and was groping under her skirt with it. The little stiletto came up as fast as lightning, ripping open Butrus's beautiful silk shirt and drawing blood from his chin with the end of the movement. He staggered back and swore horribly, and stood there for a moment, an animal poised, as she slashed out desperately again, knowing that he was there but just beyond her reach.

He made a swift movement and caught her hand, and twisted the dagger round as he forced her to the ground. He lay atop of her a moment and twisted the blade in her chest. She screamed once, and there was a terrible, shocking rattle in the last notes of the scream. Then, Estrellita lay still, her sightless eyes sightless now in death as they had been for so long in life.

Butrus staggered to his feet and touched his face, the blood streaming down there. He shrieked, "*Madre de Dios*! She cut me, she cut . . ."

He ripped off a piece of tulle from her dress and began dabbing at the wound as though it was all that mattered now, kicking out savagely at the dead body at his feet.

In a paroxysm of fury, Mercy tore herself loose from Ollie's strong grip and threw herself down on her dead friend's body. She took the lifeless head in her hands and rocked back and forth, moaning softly to herself. She heard Butrus swear again and shout, "She cut my face, my *face*!"

She could not believe what had happened. She drew the torn pieces of cloth together to cover those splendid breasts, and rocked her gently to and fro, saying all the time, "Strellita, Strellita, Strellita . . . speak to me, Strellita . . ."

503

She was conscious that Butrus and Ollie, hard by the lifeboat on the deck of the *Capricorn*, were standing over her and looking down at her as she rocked back and forth, and she said, over and over again, "Your hand, Strellita, give me your hand . . . give me your hand, I must hold it now . . . why are you so silent, Strellita?"

She was conscious that someone—who could it be?—was staring at her, and she looked up and saw a handsome, bearded face. There was blood pouring down from his chin, and where could it come from?

She heard a voice out of the void, coming to her from a long way off. "She is crazed, the woman's dead, blast her soul to hell, she cut my face . . ."

He was still dabbing at the wound, and looking down in anger at the bloodstains on his fine shirt, and still Mercy rocked Estrellita in her arms, whispering softly, ". . . but only till Clifford comes, dear Strellita, and then . . . then I will have to leave you, and why do you not take my hand? I want you so much to hold my hand . . . he is below decks somewhere, but soon he will come, and you will see what a fine and splendid man he is, and he loves me. Strellita, why don't you take my hand?"

She felt a firm grip on her arm, and let herself be dragged to her feet. Clifford was looking down at her and saying—why was he suddenly so uncouth?—"You come with me now, Mistress Mercy."

"Why do you call me *Mistress*?" she asked innocently. "I am your wife, you told me I was your wife now."

She was conscious of a little hesitation, and the

504

voice did not seem like his at all, but after all that he had been through, they had been through together . . . She put her hands on his broad shoulders and said, whispering, "Yes, I will go with you. Wherever you want me, Clifford, my love, my husband."

She could not understand that long, long silence. She heard a distant voice saying: "Get rid of that damned body, Ollie. And then . . . leave us alone." Ollie? Who was Ollie? The name was familiar to her, but she could not place it.

She said suddenly, very clearly, "We must be careful, Clifford. Adam Butrus might come, any minute now. And if he finds us together . . ."

The long silence again. Then Adam Butrus said softly, "Adam Butrus is a long, long way from here, Mercy my love."

"Yes . . . I know it. Take me again, Clifford? I need you so badly . . . I want to feel your hands on my body, I want the touch of your body on mine."

He knew what had happened; and again, it was a new experience to him.

He led her into the privacy of his tent and watched in a kind of astonishment as she slowly and casually stripped off her clothes, watched her as she lay down on the mattress, her limbs gleaming in the half-light. She reached out her arms to him and said urgently, "Clifford, my love, my love, my dear husband . . ."

"Yes, your husband . . ."

He took off his shirt, and stood for a moment above her, his muscles rippling in the yellow light of the candle. He sensed the impatience on her and took off the rest of his clothes. When he was as

505

naked as she was, he lay down beside her, a hand on her breast, a thigh thrown across hers, his fever mounting. He whispered, "Your body is so soft and ... and inviting, Mistress Mercy."

"Not Mistress Mercy. Your wife now."

"Yes. My wife." There was a great excitement for him in the masquerade, an excitement that mounted with every feverish word she spoke.

"There is something ... sacred," she whispered, "in the love we have for each other. My husband now ..."

"Yes, I know it. So show me what a wife can do."

"I will do that ..."

Her lips were on his and her hands were exploring his body. He leaned over and found her breast with his lips, his own hands lightly touching with an unaccustomed tenderness, lingering softly on her thighs, and the soft petals there as they parted to receive his probing fingers.

Her breath was labored now and she whispered hoarsely, "Yes, yes, Clifford my love ..."

She moved to straddle him then, her long thighs wide spread over his loins, and her hands found his face and traced its outline. She whispered, "But your beard, Clifford? What have you done with your beard?"

"I changed it, Mercy," he said swiftly. "It means nothing. Hold me tight, my love. Take me now ..."

The hands slid down to his manhood and inserted it as she lowered herself on him. She reached back and found his thighs with her hands and leaned there and closed her eyes and let the rapture overtake her completely. He reached up and held her breasts and fondled them; and he found it hard to control the fierce exultation which almost, but not quite, dissolved into a terrible, sardonic laughter.

He pulled himself from her at last and laid her down beside him, saying, "Now we will sleep. Lie still, I will need you again later."

His arms were around her, clutching, a leg imprisoning hers, and she said softly, "I am here, Clifford, whenever you need me."

She fell asleep, wondering where Estrellita had gone and why she had not returned. She was barely conscious of those probing fingers when, a little while later, they began their insidious search again.

It was more than three hours later that Adam Butrus left her sleeping, naked body, staring at those long and desirable limbs and wishing he were twenty years younger and could take her again and again and again . . . but he had other plans for her now.

He went outside and found Ollie. He was thinking: I wonder if this gross, obese fellow is capable of taking over command of my army?

His chief lieutenant was supervising the refilling of the ammunition wagons with the cannonballs that were being brought up from the compound below, taking a meticulous count of them, licking his stub of pencil as the men labored up the hill with them. He said cheerfully, "Seven hundred and twelve balls recovered, Adam. We've used up a lot of black powder, but we've still fourteen barrels left. More than enough for what remains to be done."

"And you know what that is, Ollie?"

"Aye, sir. The scouts have all returned. There's an armed party of Creoles gathering not a day's march from here, reported as eighty-five men awaiting word from their leader, a guerrilla chief named Dacis. There's a provincial town forty miles to the west of us, named Riamjara, where the Governor has decided to throw in his lot with Havana. He has less than a score of troops, so that won't take us very long. In a few days we can be back home in Santiago."

"Good. I will leave all that to you, Jake."

Ollie stared at him, not understanding. "Sir?" he asked.

"I myself," Butrus said, "intend to ride directly to Santiago. I have urgent and profitable business there. You've worked well for me, Jake, and I am beginning to believe that some of my own expertise has devolved on you, and so . . . I'm putting you in command of the army, the most highly trained army on the island. You will report to me as soon as may be in Santiago . . . and I promise you a hero's welcome."

Ollie's eyes were wide and goggling. "Command . . . command of the army?" he said, stammering, and Butrus nodded.

"You've earned it," he said. "Don't destroy my trust in you, Jake. Or I'll destroy you, count on it."

"Yes, sir, no sir."

"And I'm making you a major. You're no gentleman, Ollie, and you'll never reach the exalted rank of colonel . . . but *commandante*, yes, and it will be *Commandante* Jake Ollie from now on. Find someone to stitch the braid to your epaulettes, and break out a bottle of rum. We'll celebrate your promotion before I leave."

"Good. There's nothing better than a long drink of rum before a good day's work."

"What happened to the blind woman. What was her name?"

"I don't know what her name was, who the hell cares?"

"Did somebody bury her?"

"There's a river back there, full of crocodiles. God's blood, you never saw so many crocodiles. We tossed her in there. You'd think they hadn't eaten for a hundred years."

He had burned the deep wound with black powder and it was still paining him. Suddenly angry again, he said savagely, touching the scar, "I hope she rots in hell."

There was no thought anymore of Mercy, still lying there in the tent, her mind quite deranged and dreaming only of her husband, wondering why he had left her so soon after he had loved her.

Jake Ollie opened the rum bottle and passed it respectfully over to his colonel.

CHAPTER TWENTY-FOUR

Clifford, Dacis, and the Creoles who followed, had driven their horses like men possessed.

They stopped once to rest their mounts, letting them champ for a while at the grasses in the meadow they had found, and drink thirstily from the stream there. Dacis and Linares and the others, as though from uniform practice, stretched themselves out on the ground, their arms and legs flung wide, and Clifford paced up and down, half out of his mind.

He said, gesticulating furiously, "Why do we *stop, Señor* Dacis? We have no time to rest!"

"If we do not," Dacis said, suffering the impetuousity of this angry young man with commendable patience, "our horses will drop dead beneath us. Bodily strength, Mr. Hawkes, both in men and animals, must be conserved if it is to be put to its best use."

"But in God's name . . . they show no signs of weariness at all!"

"What, you are already an expert horseman?"

Clifford bit his lip. "No, sir, perhaps not. I ask your forgiveness for my . . . my natural anxiety."

"Natural indeed, and not to be condemned, young man. But stop your pacing. Lie down, stretch out your legs, give them the rest they are sorely in need of, whether you like it or not. If we have to fight when we arrive, do you want your legs to collapse under you as though they were made of grass? Rest them, Mr. Hawkes, and they will serve you better when you need them."

Clifford sighed and lay down, knowing that the old campaigner was right, and still hating the inactivity. He watched one of the horses lying down and rolling over onto its back, kicking its feet into the air. He said, muttering, "We are so close, after so long a time . . ."

"I understand your impatience," Dacis said calmly. "Anent which . . . if we find your lady, where will you go with her?"

He shook his head. "I know not, sir."

"Would you, perhaps, be prepared to join us in our struggle against the oppressor? We could use a man of your merit and . . . energy. I should add that I can offer no recompense. All that we have is . . . hope. Not a very valuable commodity, perhaps."

"It is all that both of us have," Clifford said quietly. "But until I find my wife, I will give thought to nothing else."

In a short while they rode on again, up the steep

slopes of the mountains, down into the valleys and across the streams that ran there, and up again on the other side, until they reached the top of the mountain that towered over the bluff that looked down on the *hacienda*.

They slowed down now and rode more cautiously over hard granite rocks. When the trees around them parted at last and the whole of the pretty little valley was laid out before them, Dacis called a halt.

Clifford was in a frenzy. He said angrily, "No, we must go there now!"

Dacis answered him, with that placatory gesture again, "You are a very headstrong young man, my son. Until we know that it is safe to go there, we will *not* go there. We will wait, and watch . . ."

"No, sir."

He was trying to contain his anger. "The horse is yours, and I thank you for the use of it, as I thank you for your guidance. I will leave you now."

He began to dismount, the muscles of his legs so tightly constricted that he could hardly move, and Dacis said quickly, "Then take the horse, Mr. Hawkes. I will be sorry to lose him, and you too. But if you run into danger . . . dig your heels in hard, lie down flat over the horse's neck, and give him his head. We will follow you, but only when we know that it is safe to do so."

Clifford rode off at a fast gallop down the steep slope, holding on desperately to the pommel of the saddle and gripping hard with his tortured thighs. Five minutes later he was riding through the open gate of the compound, more cautiously now, knowing that he had indeed been headstrong. He had not even bothered to unsling his rifle.

There were a hundred, more than a hundred dead men lying there, and many of them were quite naked. There were ten or fifteen Creoles, men and women, going from one body to another, stripping off their boots and the rest of the uniforms, collecting canteens, leatherwork, good shirts of army duck. Some of them were even wearing *shakos* clumsily jammed on their heads. After a few brief and suspicious glances, almost no one paid him any attention at all.

He raised his voice and called out in anguish, "Mercy! Mercy! Mercy!"

They still scarcely deigned to look at him as they went on with their looting.

He dismounted, almost falling to the ground as his legs seemed momentarily to be made of painful rubber. There was nothing there but the still smouldering ruins of what had once been a very large house, and the charred remnants of a half-dozen smaller buildings. Nothing else but dead bodies were lying there, and a few of the living stripping them of anything that might be valuable.

He found a young Creole close by him, sniffing with suspicion at a canteen and tasting its contents. He grabbed him by the collar of his woollen shirt and dragged him to his feet, shouting at him, "A lady! An English lady, have you seen her?"

He was quite beside himself with anguish for her, with the knowledge that he had arrived too late.

The boy looked at him with fear in his eyes and shook his head blankly, answering with something Clifford could not understand. Clifford shouted again, "A lady, *Señora, Inglesa, Inglesa* . . .", trying to make himself understood. He felt a hand on

514

his arm and there was a woman there, short and plump, dressed in a long and loose print cotton smock with a red bandana over her jet-black hair. She was staring up at him, and there was a look in her prematurely old eyes that he thought might be of sympathy.

She said hesitantly, *"Esta buscando una mujer? Las mujeres estan alli . . . Una . . . Señorita?"*

He was sure that he understood her and he said urgently, "Yes, *si, una Señora . . ."*

She still held onto his arm, and she pointed and said, *"Las mujeres estan nel sotano, alli . . . Las vivandieras . . ."*

He shook his head, not understanding at all. She pulled him with her and led him to the ruins of the house, and through a rubble of adobe that had once been the entrance to the cellars, where the ceiling—the floor of the main room—had caved in, the beams lying there and still smoking.

He wanted to vomit. There were eight young women there, all in varying stages of undress, their bodies obscenely exposed even in the solace of death. There were two pairs of them who were twined in each other's arms, as though seeking some kind of comfort, in those last moments of oblivion, in the touch of their closest friends. Their silk, tulle, or muslin dresses, their pantalettes too, were torn and half-stripped off their pathetic young bodies. There were bayonette wounds in their chests and blood everywhere.

There were three of them whose faces he could not see and he forced himself, a terrible fear mounting in him, to turn them over and look into those long-dead faces. The bodies were stiff, like plaster

515

statues, and he stumbled to a corner and was sick. He lay down on the ground and let the tears flow.

She was crouching over him, the unnamed woman, and she said softly, "*Vuestra mujer*?"

He did not understand, shook his head, and he looked up into the face of Narcisio Dacis.

The old man said gently, "You see now, Mr. Hawkes, what I mean when I talk of the savagery that is directed against us."

He climbed unsteadily to his feet, feeling vaguely ashamed. He looked at Dacis and said, "Cordoba's work?"

"No, sir. Cordoba's enemies, without a doubt. And I know the reason. They must have no witnesses, so that Aguilar can say, "No, we did not do this, we are loyal servants of Havana and of the Crown." No witnesses, Mr. Hawkes, so these savages can say, "This was the work of Dacis." Come, my young friend, this is no place for a man to whom death is a stranger. Your lady, I take it, is not here?"

He could not find the words and he shook his head and allowed Dacis to lead him up the stairs and out into the cold light of the evening. Dacis said bitterly, looking over the compound, "You see the people with whom I hope to win our freedom? They are looting dead bodies for pieces of rags . . . a strip of leather, a pair of boots. And these are the men and women who call on me to lead them into . . . into an understanding of what the word *responsibility* means. And you, sir? What will you do now?"

They were pacing together in the twilight. Clifford rubbed a hand over his eyes and said wearily, "I do not know, *Señor* Dacis. For a short moment a

516

while ago, there was hope that I might find her. I still have that hope; without it, I would die. I have been searching, not even knowing what paths I was following or where they might lead me. And now, once again, that is what I must do."

His voice was breaking. "If you can help me, sir, in any way, my undying gratitude is yours."

"Our mutual problems," Dacis said carefully, "must be examined, analyzed, and very carefully pondered. Mine is simple. My troops are perhaps a day behind me." He said sourly, "At least, that is where I hope they are, but I cannot be sure. And now that Colonel Adam and his army are so far from Santiago, this would be a very good time for an attack on the citadel. For you . . . I do not know. There are two possibilities to be examined. The first is that your lady escaped before the slaughter began, or during it. In which case . . ." He shrugged. "My Creoles might, in the course of time, find her; I will instruct them accordingly. The second possibility . . . I do not know, sir. Perhaps she has been captured, though it does not seem likely to me."

"*Likely*, sir?"

"Most unlikely."

"And the alternative?"

"The alternative," Dacis said brutally, "is that she is dead. Or perhaps still wandering in the jungle. How can I even guess?"

"And if these mercenaries of Aguilar's have indeed taken her? Where would they go, *Señor* Dacis?"

"To Santiago, without a doubt," Dacis said promptly. "If only for no other reason than that

Colonel Adam cannot afford to leave the provincial capital undefended for too long."

"Colonel Adam?"

"A guerrilla," Dacis said, "of very considerable repute. He has fought in Haiti, in Colombia, in Florida. He is perhaps English, or American, or Spanish, or even French. No one seems to know his origins. But he is a very dangerous and vicious man indeed. I am told that his real name, and even of this we cannot be certain, is Adam Butrus. Be that as it may . . ."

He broke off; Clifford was staring at him, his eyes wide. "Adam *Butrus*?" he asked incredulously. "*Adam Butrus*, you say?"

Dacis could not know the reason for the astonishment. "Adam Butrus," he said, "is his reputed name, yes. You have heard it spoken?"

"Adam Butrus!" he whispered. "It makes no sense at all. And yet . . . it does. You spoke of destiny. There is more than yours and mine here."

"You . . . you know this terrible man?"

"I know him," Clifford said tightly. "And by your leave, sir, I will ride at once to Santiago."

He strode off to find his horse. When he was mounted, he looked down to find the old man beside him. He said again, "By your leave, *Señor* Dacis, I will be in Santiago."

Dacis said dryly, "You know how to find your way there, young man?"

There was a moment of foolish hesitation. "I must confess, sir," Clifford said, "I do not."

"You ride south until you reach the ocean. It will take you perhaps four hours. You then ride east for a day and a half, and you will find the city nestled among its cliffs, if your horse has not dropped dead under you before you reach it. Let him rest, Mr. Hawkes, for a few hours at least."

"There will be rest for neither of us, sir, until I reach the city. And once there, where will I find Adam Butrus?"

"In the Governor's palace, without a doubt. Atop the rocks above the harbor. There are mule-tracks up the cliff, find the best of them and you might reach the top, if you are not seen and promptly killed. The Governor's quarters are in the northwest corner. You think you are capable of discovering which is the northwest?"

"I am a sailor, sir," Clifford said stiffly.

"The Spaniards are not aware of it, but the walls can be climbed too . . . you should know, young man, that you ride to your certain death."

"I ride to find my wife," Clifford said furiously.

He swung the horse around and dug in his heels. Dacis shouted after him, "We will be close behind you, *Señor* Hawkes! Take comfort! We will be close behind you!"

Clifford was gone, crashing through the under-growth like a madman, and Dacis sighed. He called Linares to him and asked, "The troops, Linares, how far are they behind us?"

"Half a day at least. Perhaps longer."

"Then ride fast to them and urge them on. If you have to exhort them, as no doubt you will have to, tell them . . . tell them we attack Aguilar before his mercenaries can return. When that will be, I do not know. But speed, now, is all that matters. *Speed*, Linares."

The lank and angry man, still dressed in his rags (but carrying a rifle and two *pistoles* now, as well as a machete and, therefore, carrying more author-

519

ity than ever) rode off into the forest, riding bareback, the wiry muscles of his long legs, like tightly knotted cords, gripping his mount's steaming flank.

Butrus was indeed on his way to Santiago with Mercy.

He was riding his gray stallion at a walk, humming a tune to himself and thinking how pleased Aguilar would be with his twin successes, the one military and political, and the other—perhaps vastly more important to this ambitious man—a purely personal one.

Mercy was behind him, dazed and uncomprehending, stumbling over the trail, a rope around her waist that tethered her to the horse's saddle, her long hair falling loosely over her half-bared shoulders as she wondered, with a dulled incomprehension, why she was tied like this. It meant very little to her, though the pace was a gruelling one, and Carlotta's shoes, a little too large for her, were chafing her feet.

She was barely conscious of the passage of time, as they moved on and on and on interminably. The heat of the sun beat down on her, then the cool winds of the evening came and refreshed her. Still she stumbled on, not even feeling the pains that wracked her poor body. She knew only that she was desperately hungry.

They entered, at last, the tiniest of hamlets, one of the many that had sprung up a few miles from the provincial capital of Santiago, and she watched him dismount at a crude adobe building that had a board-outside it painted with the simple word: *Taverna*. He came to her and untied the rope at her waist, took her arm and led her inside.

It was gratefully warm there, a fire burning in the corner hearth, and one old man asleep at one of the three tables. The only other occupant of the small room was a young girl, perhaps not more than fifteen or sixteen, who sat dejectedly on a bench, doing nothing, saying nothing, thinking nothing. But she looked up, startled, when they came in, and Butrus said sharply to her, "Well, child, fetch your father. Or whoever it is owns this abominable place. I need food, I need drink, I need hot water . . ."

She wore a plain cotton shift of calico and her feet were bare. Her long hair was tied in an untidy chignon at the back of her head, her eyes large and dark and lustrous in a face that was heavily pock-marked and quite unappetizing. She could not understand what such a fine gentleman would be doing here, nor who the sad and dazed woman with him might be. She thought desperately: *Food? There is not much food, and he will beat me* . . .

She said, stuttering, "There is . . . there is little food, sir, but we have bread, freshly baked this day, and onions and chilis, and there is cheese . . ."

"Then fetch your father."

"He is not here, *Señor*. He went to Santiago to sell tapioca. He will not return before tomorrow."

"Then you will serve me. You have rum?"

"*Si, Señor*, we have rum."

"Good, bring me a bottle."

"*Si, Señor, immediatamente* . . . if you will sit down."

He stood by the fire as she hurried out, holding out his hands to the flames, his feet widely spread, the steam beginning to rise from his sweaty body. He saw that Mercy had found a seat on a bench,

521

and was resting her head on her arms across the table there, half asleep.

In a little while the young girl came back with a tray on which there was a bottle, a pair of coconut-shell cups, and a tin plate of bread and cheese. She set them down on the table and looked at Mercy apprehensively. Tentatively, she touched her on the shoulder and said, "*Señora? La comida esta preparada . . .*"

It looked so insufficient there! A half loaf of bread, a little burned at the edges, with two small onions, three long red chilis, and a piece of white cheese which would surely not be enough.

She looked at Butrus and said, her voice a whisper, "It is all we have, *Señor . . .*"

He turned his back to the fire, and stood with his hands clasped behind him. Looking at the miserable child he said, "Do you have a bath in this filthy hovel? A *baño*, *una cuba*, anything of the kind?"

"Yes, *Señor*, we have a very large tub, my father takes a bath in it very often, sometimes as much as every two or three weeks."

"Then bring kettles and put them to the fire, and fill the tub for me." He looked at Mercy and said sardonically, "This woman is covered with grime from head to foot, she smells like a pig. I want her washed and smelling a great deal better before I take her into the city. I've no wish to be seen on Santiago's streets with a scarecrow looking like that."

"*Si, Señor*, I will see to it at once. I know what to do, there was a *caballero* here only a few weeks ago who wanted a bath. *Si, Señor*, I now what must be done."

He went to the table and sat beside Mercy. She

522

was tearing at the bread in a strangely mechanical sort of manner, chewing on the hard, salted crust of it. There was a lost and distant look in her eyes, and she said, whimpering, "Where is Estrellita, Clifford? She should be with us, where is she?"

He said brutally, "Your Estrellita is dead, and so, I hope, is your Clifford. Now eat. We still have a long way to go."

"Yes. Yes, of course. You are so good to me, Clifford."

They ate in silence together and the girl was bringing kettles of water and setting them on the fire. In a little while, Butrus climbed onto the table and stretched himself out to sleep, saying to the girl, "Wake me when it is ready."

"*Si, Señor . . .*"

It was easy for him to sleep. Years of campaigning had taught him. When he woke at last to her touch on his arm, she said, "It is prepared, *Señor*, in my father's room."

He got to his feet and took Mercy's arm, and led her after the young girl into a tiny room with a floor of hard-packed earth. A single bed in one corner was made of adze-hewn planks with a mattress of cotton-covered kapok on it, a grimy blanket over it all, and a large round tub of carefully fitted wooden slats, the water in it steaming.

He said, "Soap. You have soap?"

"*Si, Señor*, we have very good soap. I make it myself."

"And towels?"

"We have one towel, *Señor*, only one. But it is very good. And clean, quite clean."

He could hear the huge tree rats scuttling among

the palm tree rafters of the roof, sounding like galloping horses.

He said disparagingly, "The lady is . . . distressed. Or, if it is easier for you to understand, she is mad. Undress her. Put her in the tub. Wash her. I want her clean."

"*Si, Señor*."

"And what do you have that we can put in the water? Lemon balm? Verbena? Or lavender, perhaps?"

"Verbena, *Señor*? Lavender?"

"Any herb," he said angrily. "Something to take away the foul stink of her."

"A herb?" She was stammering now, terrified of him. "The only herb we have, *Señor*, is garlic. But it is very good, freshly grown by my father, and taken from the ground this very day . . . we have plenty of it, it is really excellent, my father is very proud of his garlic."

He sighed. "God save me," he said caustically, "from idiots such as you."

"Yes, sir, God save you, sir."

"Show me your soap, child."

She handed it to him nervously, an eight-inch-long block of it, made with goat's fat and coconut oil and woodash, and smelling of the forest. He grimaced and said, "Well, it will have to do for the moment."

She waited for him to leave discreetly, but he did not. Instead, he said, "Well, get on with it."

"*Si, Señor*, at once."

She was very hesitant, casting anxious looks at the angry *caballero* as she stripped off Mercy's gown, bodice, and pantalettes. She helped her into the wooden tub, wondering why this strange woman was so passive and unresisting, so completely receptive to every touch, every gesture.

Butrus sat on the edge of the hard bed and watched the young girl splashing hot water over those slender and quiescent limbs, and rubbing the soap into them, the scent of coconut oil ripe on the air. He got to his feet, moved over to them, and said, pushing her aside, "Give me the soap, I will do that."

"*Si, Señor . . .*"

He began rubbing it into her shoulders, over her breasts, her stomach, her thighs, working up a lather over the little mound of downy hair there, his hand searching, questing, luxuriating. Her creamy thighs were parting to his touch and her head was thrown back, her eyes closed.

"Yes," she whispered. "Yes, there, just there, Strellita. Your hands are so soft . . ."

They were light and delicate on her body, but he was laughing quietly to himself. The young girl, stolid and unmoved, was pouring water from a coconut shell over that smooth white body, slowly and meticulously. Watching as the water found its way down through the suds in little rivulets, she wished that she herself were as beautiful as this crazed woman, with the small, tight and upstanding breasts that seemed to arouse this fine gentleman so, his lips touching them now. She stood back as he picked her bodily up and took her to the bed and laid her down there.

He turned to her and said, almost snarling: "Well, don't just stand there like an idiot, child! Either join us, or leave us."

She fled from the room, knowing that something terrible was happening here. She felt, perhaps for

525

the first time in her young life, grateful for the ugly pockmarks on her face which, she was quite sure, had saved her from the attentions of this wild and furious man, handsome though he might be.

She was very young and immature; but she had learned long ago of the self-seeking malevolence that was an inevitable, it seemed, part of the masculine animal.

Mercy lay there, compliant and expectant, and he stood above her and stared down at her, feeling a touch of regret that this perhaps—but only perhaps—would be the last time he could satiate himself on that voluptuous, comforting body.

She was waiting for him, her arms reaching out, her hips already moving in excitation, and he took off all his clothes and lay beside her. When he began to move atop her she said, urgently, "No, no, Clifford, not like that . . . the way you took me that day by the waterfall, you remember? When the purple orchid fell on us as we were loving each other. You remember?"

She raised one knee and eased her hips around, felt him searching beneath her now and whispered, "Yes, like that . . . only your lips were at my breast."

He found her breast and kissed it, moved his body down and thrust himself abruptly into her. She whimpered, "No, Clifford, you are hurting me . . ." For a very brief moment, there was a look of shock on her face, as though a sudden awareness had come; but it was gone instantly, and she was certain again that yes, this was her husband, and why should he be so harsh with her? She steeled herself against the pain, and she gasped and gasped and cried, "No, no, Clifford my love, my husband . . ."

He was aware of the momentary cognizance, and he was even disappointed that it went so quickly. She was tight around him, and very warm and all embracing as her muscles contracted in little spasms. He held himself there for a long while, and when at last he withdrew from her, he thought: *I could almost love this woman . . .*

He slept for a while. When he awoke again, he said brusquely, "We will continue on our way now. You may ride beside me, it will be easier for you."

He found the frightened young girl and gave her a silver piece of twenty *reales*. They mounted his horse together, and Mercy put her arms aound him and laid her head against his back and began dreaming again, as they rode off down the trail that would take them into the city.

CHAPTER TWENTY-FIVE

Adam Butrus was thinking: How good a thing it is to shed the *poncho* and the mud of the battlefield and relax in such hedonistic luxury!

He was lounging, scrubbed and pomaded and dressed in clean and elegant clothes in the antechamber to the Governor's private quarters, a retreat where only Aguilar's intimate friends were ever permitted entry.

It was a small apartment in the northwest corner of the great stone citadel, sumptuously decorated with hanging tapestries and drapes of the richest silk velvet in gorgeous golden color, which had been brought here from Utrecht. The three divans were covered in a heavier *moquette* of a slightly darker shade, and the chairs and stools were the more conventional scarlet-and-gilt. The floor was marble from France, beautiful amber in color, interspersed with a brilliant display of opal-like iridescence.

The cabinets and the bureaus were exclusively Spanish, very old and valuable, and even the huge gilt doors were Hispano-Moresque, taken from the palace of Oued Hassan in an earlier Spanish expedition to the North African shores.

There were fine swords on the walls everywhere, superb examples of the Toledo craftsmen's art, and ceremonial shields and lances, and battle pennants here and there, adding their bright touches of crimson and blue and green and gold.

He wore the narrow, pale-blue trousers of his dress uniform, a thin gold stripe running down their sides, with jacked-leather, loose-fitting boots and a white silk shirt open at the neck. He watched the Governor, sprawled out comfortably in the long red silk robe he liked to wear in the evenings, when his day's work was done.

They were drinking together and Aguiliar had promised himself: This night I will get drunk with my good friend.

He said, toying with his drink, a rich red wine that had just arrived from Spain, "I was worried, Adam. When I discovered you'd taken the whole of the army and left me undefended . . . and God's Blood, I'm *still* undefended! Less than fifty palace guards, it's not a position I like to find myself in."

Butrus shrugged, carelessly. "But the enemy is destroyed, Excellency. He has ceased to exist."

"And no witnesses to carry their lies to Havana, I take it?"

"None."

"Good." He sipped his wine reflectively, saying, "We had a damned official here three days ago from the capital, a junior minister sent by the Vice-Regent himself. Ha! It seems there's a filibustering expedition from the United States fooling around in the *cordillera*, led, if you please, by General Lopez, a Spaniard himself. It's all a man can do these days to discover who is on whose side. I can't think what they hope to achieve there. This damned lackey had a parchment for me to sign, reaffirming my personal loyalty! It's enough to make a man weep! But I'll tell you one thing, Adam. He was astonished to find that my army consisted of a few score palace guards, and he said to me, bowing and scraping, 'We had heard, Excellency, of an army of mercenaries . . .' "

He was lisping, mimicking and taking delight in it, and Butrus threw back his head and laughed out loud. "And you told him, I hope, 'What mercenaries?' "

"I did better than that. I told him, yes, indeed, I myself had heard those vile rumors put out by my enemies, by the enemies of the Crown. I told him to look around, and I'd give him a gold coin for every mercenary he found in my enclave. He went off with a flea in his ear, but convinced I'd never give Havana any trouble."

"And can we hope," Butrus asked, "that when the time comes for us to march there, their troops will be up in the *cordillera* chasing after General Lopez?"

Aguilar nodded. "It's a very distinct possibility. You see how kind the fates are to us? Destiny, it seems, is very definitely regarding my ambitions with a great deal of favor."

"In more ways than one, Excellency," Butrus said.

He climbed to his feet and helped himself to more wine, refilling the Governor's goblet. He said slyly, "Let me offer you a toast, a twin toast. To the soon-to-be ruler of all Cuba . . . and to the propagation of that noble lineage of yours that we discussed. And by God, sir, your new wine is quite remarkable. Allow me to compliment you on it."

Aguilar stared at him, non-plussed, and said, "The propagation of . . . what are you talking about, Adam?"

Butrus smiled and said softly, "I have found a wife for your son, sir. A fine, healthy and very beautiful English lady who is almost, though admittedly not quite, a virgin."

"*Madre de Dios*!" His eyes were wide, and his mouth was open. "A wife for my son? Surely you jest?"

"No, sir. She is already in the palace, below stairs with the servants, getting rid of the signs of wearisome travel, being dressed as befits a woman of her quality."

He could not believe his ears. "An English lady?" he spluttered. "Good God, where on earth did you find her?"

"In Cordoba's camp. And it so happens that I met her once before. I know her origins. Not noble, particularly, but from that class of distressed gentry of whom there are so many in England. She is well educated, carries herself with great dignity and, I repeat, she is very, very beautiful."

The Governor had recovered his composure and was squinting suspiciously now. "But there's a catch, Adam, is there not?"

"No, sir, not really."

"*Not really*! That means, I assume, that she knows nothing of my poor boy's affliction?"

"She has one of her own, Excellency, that renders that knowledge unnecessary."

Aguilar exploded. "By God, Adam, if you're leading me down the garden path I'll have your head on a platter, friend or no friend! What affliction, for God's sake? The pox? I won't have it!" He was striding now, agitated beyond control, and Butrus was still smiling gently, taking his time over the telling of it. He said quietly, "Not the pox, she is a very healthy young woman indeed, with that apple-blossom complexion, quite flawless, that the English are so proud of."

"Well then?"

"She is in a very mild state of . . . purely temporary derangement, a condition which I have observed is already beginning to pass. . ."

"You mean she's mad? I'm not sure I like that, it might be hereditary."

"Not mad. A state of shock, nothing more . . ."

"Well, go on, man!" the Governor said impatiently.

Butrus laughed. "Yes, if you would only allow me to. Well, she lost a friend, a very dear friend it seems, and with that loss, lost also her reason. And this, I insist, is a temporary condition. I am no medic, but I am convinced of it. Deep shock, and nothing else. It will pass."

"Well, we could talk to our own doctors about that . . ."

"It has left her . . . confused. Confused and very amenable."

"Amenable? Ah, that's good."

"She has mistaken me for someone else she . . .

533

seems to know. She trails behind me like a pet dog, she does as she is told instantly, and without objection."

"Good, good . . ."

"How long this condition will last, I can only guess. A week? A month? Who knows? I don't think it even matters."

"And you don't think she'll take one look at that monster, like all the others, and run for her life?"

"I don't think she is capable, at this moment, of making such decisions for herself."

Aguilar thought about it for a long while, pacing up and down, drinking deeply and refilling his goblet. "And she is," he said at last, "no doubt in her fifties? Her sixties perhaps?"

"Perhaps twenty. A good child-bearing age."

"And beautiful, you say?"

"Ravishingly beautiful."

"And . . . if we exaggerate a little, of noble birth."

"*Haute bourgeoisie*. Or, if you prefer the term, *petite noblesse*."

"And amenable. I like the amenable . . . unresisting, that is?"

"Completely."

"And below stairs now, you say?"

"Waiting."

The Governor said urgently, "Then bring her here, Adam! What are we waiting for?"

Butrus went to the brocaded bellpull and tugged at it. Aguilar said happily—though still a touch suspicious, not entirely believing that his fortune could be so good, "If she does indeed live up to your description, my friend, it would seem that you have done me a very great service this day."

"She surpasses *all* description. And I am not only your friend, sir," he said laconically. "I am also your most devoted servant."

The Governor nodded, understanding at once. How well he knew this man! "Yes, yes, and there's a large purse awaiting you."

A young girl knocked and came in, answering the summons, younger than Gabriella and twice as pretty. She was appraised, moreover, by Pedro Velasquez, who knew every move she made from the time she rose from her bed in the darkness of the early morning, till she sank back again into sleep, exhausted at the end of her long day's work.

She curtsied and waited. Butrus said briefly, "An English lady downstairs. Bring her here."

As she turned to do his bidding, Aguilar said brusquely, "Find my son and send him here, then send out for a priest. Get that damned fellow what's-his-name, Father Ostero. Tell him he is required to perform a wedding ceremony, here, this very evening."

"Father Ostero?" Butrus asked mildly and the Governor looked a question at him. Butrus was smiling that sardonic smile and said, shrugging, "I am not a Catholic, Excellency, but I know Father Ostero. A very stubborn and demanding man."

"And so?"

"He is what is called in your philosophy . . . a good churchman. Mistress Mercy, I fear, is Protestant. And from certain points of view, her past, perhaps, is . . . a little suspect. All that is required, really, is that a purely *legal* ceremony be pernormed, so that your grandchildren may be accepted readily." He said piously, "And there will be many of them, I am sure."

535

"God's blood, Adam, you're right, as always! Then . . . what say you? One of those damned Creole priests? As you suggest, the law would be satisfied . . . and we can't have the palace crawling with little bastards, can we?"

"We are concerned only with the production of legally acceptable offspring, Excellency. A question, if you like, of animal propagation. The so-called priests among the Creoles have been recognized by the *cortes*, it's one of the special laws they agitated so noisily for."

"Yes . . . yes, you are absolutely right! There is a fellow named Xerala, a very compliant man indeed."

He turned back to the pretty young girl. "Tell Pedro, a Creole named Xerala. Have him sent for."

"*Si, Excelencia,*" she said, curtsying, and as she turned to go, Butrus stopped her. "Your name, child?"

"Theodora, sir," she said shyly. "But they call me Tedra."

"And how old are you, Tedra?"

"I think . . . fifteen, sir."

The Governor was watching him, amused. He said dryly, "She's yours whenever you want her, Adam."

Butrus caught his eye, knowing that he was very much in favor now, beginning to count the coins already. "Then I will take advantage of your kindness, Excellency," he said. "I will admit that those little pointed breasts intrigue me."

He turned back to her. "Go about your business, Tedra. The English lady, and His Excellency's son, and tell Pedro to find us the priest. We will speak again."

"*Si, Señor.*"

They waited in silence. Aguilar was impatient now, turning at every sound, striding to the door and flinging it open at the hesitant knock there.

He grimaced when he saw his son and said, muttering: "Come in, Fernando, we need you here for a while."

He was dressed in tightly bulging purple velvet trousers, with soft white shoes and a green jacket that was split down the back. He was carrying a grotesque-looking toy, a carved and painted wooden blackamoor, with a strip of red cloth wound around it for a skirt, and he held it up and said delightedly: "They gave me a doll, Papa, a new doll. Look, you can waggle his legs."

Aguilar turned away in disgust. He said to Butrus, suddenly unsure, "In God's name, Adam . . . an idiot son and a demented woman, are they going to produce a brood of monsters for me? Is that the journey we're embarked on?"

Butrus was at pains to conceal his own anxiety. He thought of the purse and said blandly, "We are assured by the doctors, Excellency, that your son's sickness is *not* hereditary. And I know that the lady's is purely temporary."

"I hope to God you are right! Can you imagine the palace full of infant dullards like that? By God, I'll drown them at birth if they are, I swear it!"

"There is no danger, Excellency," Butrus said calmly, "if your doctors are as sure in their estimation as I am in mine."

He turned as Tedra knocked and entered, ushering Mercy before her. He heard the Governor gasp and took great pleasure in it.

He had instructed them precisely in the matter

537

of her grooming; she wore a strikingly-beautiful Empire gown of the purest white piña cloth, delicately embroidered with gold thread, a fabric so finely woven as to be nearly transparent. The very high waist was gathered closely below her breasts, and it was cut very low, so that the straight line of the neck, itself gathered and cunningly wound with gold thread, seemed to rest lightly on her nipples. Her dark hair was curled in ringlets that dropped low onto her bare shoulders, and there was a small cap of white tulle on the back of her head, tied with French knots of white silk. The long skirt of the dress was very full, so that when she moved it seemed to drift like a zephyr, and her long limbs were clearly visible. Even her shoes were white, of soft raw silk, with buckles of glittering paste.

She was holding herself very straight and Aguilar thought instinctivey of Adam's comment: "She carried herself with great dignity." He thought: *Madre de Dios*! In all my lecherous days, I never saw a woman of such startling beauty, nor one who could arouse me so quickly just by standing there half naked and innocent . . .

He threw a quick look at Butrus. "Does she speak Spanish?"

"No, sir."

"Oh."

He turned back to Mercy and felt himself quivering with excitement. He cleared his throat noisily and said in halting English, "My name, dear lady, is Manuel de Aguilar, and I welcome you to my humble abode."

The look in her huge eyes was of absolute serenity as he took her hand and bowed over it, brushing it with his lips.

538

She curtsied politely, and he could not control his avid gaze. "I am Mercy Hawkes," she said, "your obedient servant, sir."

Now was the moment of fear. He gestured and said, "This is my dear son, Fernando . . ." She turned to him and curtsied again, very correctly. He was studying her face and found there no trace of revulsion or even of surprise. He said gruffly, "Get to your feet, Fernando, and kiss a lady's hand when I present you. Where are the manners I taught you?"

The idiot put aside his doll for the moment and took her hand. He bowed over it, and licked it giggling. She said calmly, "Your servant too, sir . . ."

He took hold of the neckline of her dress, a great clumsy hand fumbling, and felt the piña cloth and said, simpering, "That is lovely material, so soft . . ."

There was no surprise on her face at all.

Aguilar took a long deep breath and said, "And Colonel Adam Butrus, of course, you already know."

She turned to look at Butrus, a smile on her face but puzzlement in her eyes. "Colonel Adam Butrus?" She held out her hand to be kissed, and said, "No, I do not think I have had that pleasure. Your servant, sir. Have we met before? I think not, I would have remembered."

"A long time ago," he said gently. "And only very briefly." He took her hand, a stranger, and touched it to his lips, looked at Aguilar and was delighted with the excitation there.

Aguilar turned to his son and said brusquely, "All right, Fernando. Go back to your room, play with your doll until I send for you."

"Yes, Papa." He paused at the door and looked

539

back at Mercy, and said, giggling, "She's very pretty, isn't she? And I simply love that dress."

He was gone and the Governor took Mercy's arm and led her to a divan and sat her down there. He sat close beside her, a hand on her thigh. He looked at Butrus and said, "Yes, you have done well, old friend. Though it seems a pity to waste such beauty on a monster like that."

He was astonished, suddenly, to find that Mercy had laid her head on his shoulder, and he put a arm around her and squeezed that nearly naked breast. Butrus said calmly, "There is, of course, the *droit du seigneur*, Excellency. The right of the first night. As you say, a pity to waste such loveliness."

"Ah yes . . . an ancient and honorable privilege. I will avail myself of it presently."

He turned back to Mercy, caressing her, and he could not control his emotions. He said hoarsely, "Will you get to your feet and stand before me?"

She answered, smiling, "Of course, Clifford. I will do whatever you want me to do."

"*Clifford*?" He was startled. "My name, Mistress Mercy, is Manuel. You are correctly supposed to address me as 'Your Excellency,' but under the intimate circumstances, Manuel will do as well. Even though . . . I have not been called by my name for a number of years now. Yes, call me Manuel, will you do that?"

"If you wish, Clifford, I will call you Manuel."

She stood up, her hand at her side, and he held her hips with both his hands. He slid them up to those glorious breasts and fondled them, saw that her eyes were half closed, her breath coming faster now. She took one of his hands in hers and slid it gently down over her body. She took his head in

540

her hands and pressed it against her, whispering, "Clifford? You have such a strange way of talking now . . ."

He could not hide his astonishment, and in a moment he stood up abruptly, his loins on fire now. He said to Butrus, lounging there with a goblet to his lips and a sardonic look on his handsome face, "Wait for us, Adam. When that damned priest comes, have him wait too."

"At your Excellency's service," Butrus said dryly.

Aguilar, panting, took Mercy's arm and led her, unresisting, into the bedchamber. She went with him in a trance, a lamb to the slaughter, knowing only that Clifford was beside her again and that her whole body was shaking uncontrollably.

She looked at the huge, carved oak bed and took delight in it. She whispered, "Oh, Clifford . . . I want you so badly now, it has been so long . . . I want you inside me. I want to feel you filling me completely again . . ." She reached and touched his face, ran her hands through his beard, and then, quite suddenly, there was a look of absolute incomprehension in her eyes. She said, frowning, puzzled, no longer sure of her understanding, "Clifford? I called you Clifford? But you are not . . . not Clifford?"

The door closed behind them.

Butrus sighed and poured himself another long drink of the good Spanish wine. He thought: God's blood, I'll miss her. Well, that pretty little serving-girl, what did she say her name was? Tedra? At fifteen years old she'll be tight as a mousetrap . . .

He lay back on the divan and thought about her.

The door to the bedchamber burst open suddenly and Aguilar was there, half undressed, clutching at his breeches, his white chest gleaming in the lamplight. There were livid marks on his cheeks, the slashing of nails...

He shouted, quite beside himself, "Damn your eyes, Adam Butrus, she's fighting me! And she's stronger than I am! God damn your eyes to perdition!"

Butrus was on his feet in a flash, all thought of the lovely young Tedra thrust behind him in the desperate urgency of his duty now. He ran to the doorway and stood there, looking at her and knowing that what he had feared might happen had indeed come about.

"*A purely temporary condition,*" he had said, full of his own arrogant assurance. "*I am no doctor, but I am convinced of it.*"

Mercy stood in a corner of the bedchamber, a bedsheet clutched in front of her naked body, her eyes wide and a look of maniacal fury on her face. There was no screaming now, but a livid, boiling anger there that was ready to explode.

The Governor was close beside him and he was shrieking now. "Amenable, you said! Unresisting, you said! And look at her! Look at her, Adam! A tigress!"

Butrus forced a tight smile, knowing that this was a very dangerous time for him. He said disparagingly, "But still a woman, Excellency. It is sometimes necessary to impress their servile position on them with a beating."

He walked across the room to her, assuming a nonchalance he did not feel. He reached out and

542

tore the sheet away from her and raised his hand to strike her savagely on the side of the head.

He could not credit the speed of her instant reaction. She slashed her nails across his face so furiously that he staggered, and he gasped as she threw herself at him and *fought* with all the strength at her command. She raked at his face with both hands, her savagery sending him reeling back, and she was on him again, raking those· deadly nails across his cheeks. He shouted a violent curse, took her by the shoulders and threw her back. As she hurled herself at him again, he struck her once, a cruel and brutal blow above her ear, hitting her as he would hit a strong man, unable now to contain his own fury.

As she fell, he reached out and caught her, then carried her unconscious body to the bed and threw it there. The blood was streaming down his face and one of his eyes was blurring alarmingly. He found that he was trembling with an uncontrollable rage.

He turned back to Aguilar, holding himself in tightly but quite unable to control his sudden loathing for her. He said contemptuously, "She can fight you no longer, Excellency. Mount her. Take her. Enjoy her. The body of a young and beautiful woman, waiting for you."

He leaned down and took her knees in both hands, and pulled her thighs forcibly apart. He said again, quieter now and beginning to recover his composure, "Mount her, Excellency. She's *waiting* for you to mount her. And then, whether she likes it or not, we'll marry her off to your son. You have my promise on it."

He bowed, trembling again at the sight of the

blood that was dripping to his shirt, remembering that other woman who had scarred his handsome face so recently. He left them alone.

When the door had closed behind him, Aguilar lowered his silk breeches and crouched over her silent body, positioning himself between those creamy thighs, looking down at himself and knowing that all his strength had gone. He began swearing volubly, furious with himself, with Colonel Adam, even with her. He lay down on top of her, hoping for resurrection, and when Mercy came back to her senses he was muttering angrily to himself as he groped at her.

She reached up and fastened both hands on his throat, tightened her grip as he tried to shake himself free of this new indignity. She rolled over on top of him, straddling him now and caring nothing about her nakedness, knowing only the furious anger that was bursting out again.

She was in a terrible rage as she thrust his head back onto the kapok pillows, her thumbs tight about his windpipe. As he struggled helplessly against her, she saw his eyes widening, his face getting redder, and he tore himself free from her and fell to the floor.

And then, the first shot sounded . . .

One of the palace guards, on his appointed rounds, had seen the shadow climbing up the wall toward the light of the upper apartments in the northwest corner of the citadel. He had fired one useless bullet and had given the alarm.

The night—was it the second?, he was barely conscious of the passage of time—had come again. The stumbling, wheezing pony, driven now only by an animal instinct for survival, lame in three legs and close to death, had forced its way up the mule-track. There, Clifford had dismounted, a deep regret upon him when he looked at its glazed and frightened eyes and knew that he had ridden it far beyond its capacity.

He cut the belly-band with the long knife he had taken from that strange man Amos Woodchuck, and fumbled off the bit, worrying about the blood at its mouth. He had turned it loose, hoping it could find some sustenance here.

The rifle was still slung across his shoulder, and for the life of him he could not remember whether or not his unaccustomed weapon was ready to fire its single lead bullet or not. He unslung it, and examined it carefully as he would have examined a harpoon gun, smelling the powder there and hoping that it was still good. He slung it over his back again, and began searching for a way to the upper story where the lights were. The machete in its leather scabbard was slapping against his thigh and it was a great comfort to him.

A patrolling sentry had almost found him, but he had crouched silently among the boulders, till he had passed.

He found a low roof to which he could easily climb, and then, with much greater difficulty, a series of protruding stones that might, he hoped, take him as high as he had to climb. He went from one to another, hand over hand, hauling himself up and not caring to look down at the waves pounding on the cliff base so frighteningly far below. He clung there like a limpet, listening to the near silence in which the predominant sound seemed to be the beating of his own heart.

The protrusions of heavy stone came to an end and he searched for a long time before he found others to explore. He went up them till he found that they led nowhere and moved down again to search once more. There was an iron balustrade above him now, just out of his reach, and he looked down at the waves pounding on the rocks down there—so impossibly far below him. He took a long, deep breath, thought of her, and leaped . . .

He seized the iron bars and hung there for a moment. It was then that the shot from below sounded.

He hauled himself up and swung himself over the railing and rolled through the flimsy *jalousie* of the window, not caring anymore about the shattering of the night's silence. He was thinking only, with a mounting fever: *She is here somewhere, and if I die in the effort I will find her* . . .

He found himself in a long, dimly lit corridor, and there was a soldier there in the brilliant plumage of the guards, reds and greens and whites everywhere, unlimbering a rifle, startled out of his wits. He saw the long muzzle pointed at him and threw himself to one side, trying at the same time, not every efficiently, to pull the strap of his own rifle over his head. He heard the loud explosion, heard the ball ricochet off the stonework a dozen feet or more to his side. He fired the gun and saw the plaster shatter a long way from his hoped-for target.

They charged at each other then, using their rifles as clubs, only the sentry had a bayonette too . . .

Clifford sidestepped the thrust, and brought the butt of his weapon around in a wide sweep, knock-

ing him unconscious to the marble ground. He
dropped his hated rifle and pulled the machete
from its scabbard, ran to the end of the corridor,
not caring where it might lead but knowing that it
must lead *somewhere*, where she might be. He did
not bother with the lock, but simply hurled himself
bodily through the door, smashing it down off its
hinges in his fury.

He found himself in a well-lit antechamber, with
golden velvet drapes over the windows and rich
tapestries hanging on the walls, and cabinets of fine
Spanish marquetry everywhere.

Adam Butrus was standing there, sword in hand,
dressed in pale-blue trousers now, gold-striped, instead of the heavy canvas trousers he had worn
aboard the *Capricorn* with a white silk shirt that
was stained heavily with blood. His face was
bloodied too, and there was a look of pure delight
in his eyes.

Clifford said hoarsely, "Adam Butrus? Adam *Butrus?*"

"*Mister Mate* to you, Seaman Hawkes," Butrus
said casually. The point of the sword, one of
several he had tried at the sound of the first shot,
unfastening them from the walls one after the
other, taking his time till he found the blade that
would best suit him, was describing little circles. Its
golden hilt gleamed in the lamplight, damascened
and studded with precious stones, with heavily en-
crusted enamel at its knuckle-bow, the steel cup
pierced with intricate decorations. It had been
made, more than three hundred years before, by
the House of Tomas de Ayala, and bore the Master's name on the *ricasso*, with the motto: "*Pago el
insulto.*"

It was a splendid weapon, a delight even to hold, its remarkable balance a masterpiece in itself.

There was a cowering, frightened man in black robes and white collar in the corner, a priest, scared out of his wits. Clifford threw him a brief glance and dismissed him, looked back to Butrus and said clearly, "My wife, *Mister Mate*, where is she?"

The scarred and bloodied face was filled with a sardonic malevolence and Butrus said, drawling: "Behind these doors, your Mercy, Seaman Hawkes, is presently being impregnated by His Excellency, the Governor of this province. Shortly she will also be impregnated by his idiot son who is, I must admit, a monster. Later, as the occasion arises, I will take her myself again. And you hope to fight me with a *machete*, Seaman Hawkes? I cannot describe the pleasure it will give me to thrust my rapier into your throat."

Clifford swung his arm up and around, hurling the clumsy machete with every iota of strength that was left in his body. It flew straight and true, like a launched harpoon searching out the body of a whale, and sliced deeply through Butrus' chest. The force of it still did not cease as it buried its point deeply into the tall gilt door that had come from a distant palace in far-off Morocco.

The beautiful rapier clattered to the ground and Adam Butrus hung there, his dead eyes glazed, his arms limply at his sides, his death so sudden that there was no time even for the last and desperate thoughts of all those things that, in the life that was gone from him now, he had loved.

Clifford strode to the door and flung it open, the body swinging grotesquely on it, the dead legs dragging over the beautiful marble floor, stained now with his copious blood.

And his beloved Mercy was there.

She was wrapping a sheet around her naked body, and there was a mumbling old man lying on the ground at her feet, naked too, save for a pair of silken breeches around his ankles, panting heavily and trying to find his senses.

For a moment, she stared and went on staring. Then, all the emotion seemed to well up inside her, and she whispered, "Clifford? *Clifford*? Is it really you?"

Neither could he believe it. He ran to her, his arms outspread, as she ran to his, reaching out for him desperately. They were clutching at each other, the tears streaming down from her eyes, her hands moving over his broad shoulders and not knowing how to assure herself that he was really here. The tears were streaming down her cheeks, quite uncontrollably, and the overwhelming flood of the relief was more than she could bear.

He was here now . . .

And even though they were together in a hostile and dangerous environment, they were—and that was the comforting word—together! He was clutching at her desperately, holding her tightly to him, thinking of the slave camp where he had lost her, and knowing that now she was in his arms again, and nothing mattered except this.

He held her at arm's length and looked at her, whispering, "In all this time, Mercy my love . . . are you hurt?"

"Yes . . . I have been sorely abused, my Clifford."

"Dear God!"

"But all is well now, now that you are with me."

"Never to leave you again, not for an instant!"

"Oh, my Clifford .. "

"And how we leave this den of iniquity and where we go now . . . I do not know, Mercy."

"As long as we are together."

"Yes, together for always."

The Governor of the province, a naked and wretched man, was stumbling to his feet, clambering toward the bed, groping for it. Clifford looked at him and said, "And this . . . this spectacle? Who is it, Mercy?"

"A powerful man," she whispered. "One of the most powerful in all of Cuba. I think . . . I think I almost killed him."

Clifford put out a foot and rolled Aguilar back to the ground again, the *potente* back where he belonged. He was in semi-coma now, still gasping for breath, his windpipe sorely damaged, no cognizance yet of what was happening.

There were the muted sounds of distant shouting coming to them from beyond the doors of the apartment, and Clifford, very calm now, picked up the whisp of piña cloth that was her dress. He said, "If you want to dress yourself now, dear Mercy?"

She looked at it with great distaste. "No, I will not wear that terrible dress again. Will you help me with this sheet?"

Together, wondering how long they might be undisturbed in this private retreat, they made a gown from it as he wound it around her slender body.

There was a thunderous knocking at the door now, and a voice calling out in Spanish. They kept deathly quiet. He crept in silence to where the

550

fallen rapier lay and picked it up, ready to see the door burst open. The knocking went on, and the voice still called out, more urgently now. Clifford held the sword ready, waiting for whatever might happen; his free arm was around her, holding her tight, and he knew that she was prepared to die with him if need be.

But now, the sounds of a new and unexpected commotion came to them from the open window, startling them, sending them both running out onto the little iron balustrade to see what was happening. Behind them, the hammering on the door stopped suddenly, and there were confused and angry shouts interspersed with riflefire.

But it was the scene below them that rivetted their attention. There were burning flares without number and groups of armed Creoles running across the palace gardens, firing their rifles as they ran and wielding their machetes. Hundreds of men and women advancing and smashing through the doors and windows as the guards went down before the sheer force of their numbers. There were others of them climbing the walls, swarming up them. And wherever Clifford looked, more and yet more of them were pouring into the citadel.

Narcisio Dacis had arrived.

He was leading a Creole army of more than five hundred men and women. Even down below in the confines of the harbor, new flares were being lit. And soon the pinpoints of light were striking in the darkness of the town itself; and the muted, distant sounds that came to them now were the cries of a city in rebellion.

CHAPTER TWENTY-SIX

Santiago was in foment.

But strangely, the violence that the Spaniards were in great fear of did not come; or at least, it came in limited, isolated form.

Small gangs of Creole youths wandered the streets for the rest of the night and the following day, looking for particular Peninsulars against whom they held personal grudges. But these, for the most part, had locked themselves in their houses and were keeping very much out of sight, leaving the streets exclusively to the Creoles.

Dacis's lieutenants were everywhere, wearing the brightly colored bandanas around their throats that signified their authority. They broke up the gangs and lectured them sternly, and insisted on Dacis's orders, firmly stated: No reprisals, and no looting.

And so, instead of guns, there were guitars and

zithers and drums everywhere. Every narrow street was filled with dancers parading around in their new found freedom and sure that all their troubles were over now that their great leader had finally come down out of the mountains to shake off for them the terrible yoke of their oppression.

He was worshipped here.

Outside the citadel that he had proclaimed the headquarters of the Liberating Army, there were long lines of women and children, carrying flowers they had grown in their gardens or cut in the mountains, waiting to lay them at his feet, merely to get a passing glimpse of the great old man.

The handful of palace guards who had survived the initial attack—twenty-seven out of the original fifty had been killed—were disarmed and stripped of the uniform that had become a symbol of exarchy, and sent into the town to find shelter among their civilian compatriots. The dead had been buried with due and very correct ceremony, and the softer sound of bare feet in the palace had taken over from the ring of jacked-leather boots on the marble floors.

The Governor and his idiot son had been imprisoned, together with Manteras, Galisteo, and the other officers and aides (including the pigeon-fancier Pedro Velasquez and a handful of servants who could not be trusted). Behind bars, they were being treated well enough under the circumstances, suffering little more than a loss of their arrogance.

For Mercy and Clifford it was the beginning of a new and exciting path for their lives, though they could not guess where that road might lead them. All that mattered, for the moment, was the moment itself; and there was tremendous gratification for them in it.

They stood in the antechamber, a little apart from each other, listening to the mumblings of that compliant and frightened Creole Father Xerala who, by dispensation of those Special Laws, was permitted to perform marriage ceremonies both within and outside the Church. So many of the Creoles had abandoned the religion of their Spanish ancestors, and had reverted to the Paganism of other forebears, Indian or Negro.

Dacis said, insisting, "Yes, my young friend, it is *legal*. Not only in the island, but recognized as such in Spain itself."

Mercy was wearing a rich and lovely gown, which she had selected from one of the innumerable wardrobes in the palace, of heavily embroidered India muslin, very tight at the narrow waist, the full skirt and the bodice and the sleeves ballooning out in fashionable fullness, its color a very pale cream (she would not wear white now), as was the long veil which fell from the little mull cap over her face and about her bare shoulders. The neckline was straight and not immodestly low, gathered at the upper arms with little ribbons of silk in a darker tone.

She looked shyly at Clifford, standing so straight and tall and handsome in the new clothes he had found for himself—long and narrow dark-blue trousers, with black boots, a blue-gray coat that hung down at the back of his knees, very flared at the waist, with a wide blue belt, a white silk shirt and a blue silk cravat. He looked so elegant, she thought! And so dignified!

The priest had stopped his mumbling and was

looking a question at them. Dacis said, smiling, "Now you must say '*si, lo acepto*,' and it will make him very happy."

"*Si, lo acepto*," Clifford said.

Soon they were embracing each other tenderly, and Dacis was pouring wine for them all. There were the happy sounds of the music outside in the grounds, the beat of a tambourine somewhere.

They drank together and made small talk for a little while, both of them fidgeting nervously now, until Dacis said at last, taking Clifford's arm and leading him aside, "You must go now with your bride and consummate your marriage. And when you return to this room . . . we will all be waiting for you, to wish you continued health."

"Yes, yes, of course . . ."

"There is a custom among my people," he said gently, "that will perhaps surprise you. I do not believe it is practiced in . . . in more advanced lands. Try not to show your surprise. Try just to accept it."

"Oh? And what is that, *Señor* Dacis?" he asked, puzzled.

The old man said, taking him to Mercy, "Go now, the two of you, and we will wait."

He felt a little foolish as he took Mercy's arm and moved with her to the adjoining room. He looked back as he closed the door; they were all standing there in an expectant circle; Dacis, and Linares, and a dozen of the others who had been privileged to witness this memorable event, all with smiles of pure delight on their dark, Creole faces.

The room had been prepared for them, a huge oaken bed with a canopy over it, the white linen sheet and the rose-colored blankets turned back

. . . and it was almost as if they have never loved before.

They undressed hesitantly, even turning away from each other modestly. But when they lay naked together, deep in the folds of a feather mattress, the ardor began to rise in both of them, and they held each other tightly, gasping out their love. She opened herself to him and knew that all that was in Heaven was being visited on them now. He was so gentle with her, and yet . . . so strong!

They lay together for a long, long time after the spasms had passed, and he said at last, still puzzled but letting nothing spoil his absolute delight, "Now it seems, dear Mercy, we have to show ourselves to them again."

"We do?"

"So I understand, my love . . . they expect it, a very strange custom."

"Oh, Clifford . . . I want to stay here forever, not moving."

"And so do I," he said ruefully. "But the wedding, it appears, is not over for them until . . . until it has been consummated. And then, perhaps they will go to their homes, and we can be alone again."

"Forever, dear Clifford"

"For longer than that, even . . ."

"I love you so much."

"My love . . ."

They dressed very carefully, Mercy leaving aside her veil now, and went to the door and opened it, a little fearfully, not quite knowing what to expect.

There was an old woman there, dressed in her Sunday best, and she was clutching a chicken to

557

her breast. She squeezed past them without a word, quite ignoring their surprise, and they looked at the circle of friends, wondering why no one spoke, nor even moved. Clifford looked at Dacis and saw a light in those strange eyes that he could only think of as signifying mischief, or something very close to it. He held onto Mercy's hand and wondered if he were supposed to make a speech, clearing his throat noisily.

And then, behind them, the door opened and the old woman was there again, brushing past them unceremoniously once more and holding up the white bedsheet for all of them to see, a bedsheet lightly stained with chicken's blood.

Immediately, the faces lit up, and everyone was clapping and moving forward to embrace them both, slapping Clifford on the back and shouting their congratulations at him, kissing Mercy on the cheeks and throwing their arms around her shoulders. There was scarcely a dry eye among them.

Mercy turned and clutched at her husband, buried her face in his shoulder, and wept.

The scented night had come again. With the perfume of the jasmine and the honeysuckle of the gardens, there came the jubilant sounds of a hundred musical instruments from the town that nestled at the base of the high cliff, pinpointed once again by a thousand flares.

There, the joyful bands were marching the streets, the dancers in all their finery prancing behind them to the muted beat of the drums, and that eerie, high-pitched ullulation of the excited Creole women sounded from time to time. There was a feeling in the air of unreality, as though all of this could never possibly have happened.

They were strolling together on the lush lawns in the palace grounds, hard by the edge of the cliff, Mercy and Clifford and their good friend Dacis.

He still had not slept, and that ancient, parchment face seemed even older than its years, though the youthful eyes were as bright as ever. They looked out over the town and the harbor and the silver sea. There was the black darkness of the mountains that stood in stark silhouette against a starlit sky, the stars so bright that each seemed to be a living, fiery force that looked down on a deeply troubled earth.

Mercy looked up and murmured, "Saturn is moving now, if my memory serves me, through the eleventh house."

Dacis's eyes were on her. "And that means," he asked, "in your philosophy?"

She sighed. "It means that friends are in need of help from each other. It is also a time of . . . of great frustration."

"Frustration?" He seemed strangely bemused, and he turned away and stared thoughtfully down at the lights of the town. He said at last, "What you see down there is exactly that. Frustration and and . . . futility."

Clifford said, echoing him, "Futility? No. They are happy now, and happiness is never futile. All of us seek it, and when we find it . . . no, it is not futile."

Dacis said fervently, "How I wish that you were right, my dear friend! But you are not, I fear."

"They have found their freedom. They are rejoicing in it."

"Yes. Because they know nothing."

There was a heavy weight on his shoulders, and he said quietly, "My spies have brought me word this day. Only a few hours' march from here . . ."

He pointed and said, "You see that mountain there? We call it *Los Pechos*, the breasts of a woman. Beyond it, on its northern flank, there is an army camped, more than a thousand men, with eighteen pieces of ordnance, and cannonballs without number. I am told that it is commanded by a fearsome Englishman who is called Commandant Olé."

"Jake Ollie, without a doubt," Clifford said tightly. "I know him well."

Dacis was searching out knowledge, peering at him. "A clever soldier, Clifford?"

"I think perhaps not."

"A strong man?"

"Physically, yes. And brutal, very brutal."

"Brutality, in a soldier, is perhaps more important than any philosophical accomplishments."

"Yes, I fear so."

"Determined?"

"Yes, I am sure of it."

"Revengeful?"

"Without a doubt." His arm was around his bride, and he was aware that she was trembling. He said shortly, "A hateful man in every respect, Narcisio. Brutal, violent and yes . . . revengeful in the extreme."

"A disciplinarian?"

"Very much so."

Dacis was silent for a while, leaning on the embrasure and staring down at the aspect of unknow-

560

ing happiness. "A thousand or more disciplined rifles," he said, "and eighteen cannon. And a thousand Peninsulars in the city who will rally to him immediately, if only for the reason that he is massacring Creoles. Perhaps I should have ordered the immediate execution of all the Spaniards here. But . . . at my age, in the last days of my life, I do not want to think in terms of death as the ultimate solution. It is a weakness, I will admit, a very Creole weakness. We think about life, not death."

He was surprised and deeply touched to find Mercy's hand in his. She said quietly, "And so, Señor Dacis, what will you do now?"

The bones of his hand were like ice on hers, a terribly restrained power in them. He said slowly, "Those of us who have guns will move out in the morning, up to the mountains. And those . . . frustrated men and women down there, yes, it is the word exactly, will move back into their hovels and hide their misery, and hope that the Spanish answer will not be intolerable. Even though they know that . . . that there will be hangings without number now, and the terrible *garrote*, and more and yet more oppression. They will remember only that for a few days they were free. They will remember that it was Narcisio Dacis who brought them this freedom. And then, they will remember that it was Narcisio Dacis who lost it for them, and they will turn against me. I know the pattern of my people, Señora Hawkes . . . and with a hundred or two of staunch followers, I will be hiding again in the mountains, going from village to village and trying once more to build an army. It will not be easy. It might even be hopeless."

561

He turned to Clifford, his questioning eyes on fire. "But there are other things we have to talk about. You, my dear friends, what will you do now?"

Clifford shook his head. His arm was around his wife, and he said slowly, "I must confess . . . I do not know. Mercy?"

"It would seem," Mercy said, "that Santiago de Cuba is not a good place for us to be."

"No, it is not. There will be a slaughter here now, and with the few guns I have . . . I can do nothing to prevent it. But I have given the problem some thought. If you wish to go to Havana, the center of the civilization which, perhaps, is yours, I can send Linares with you, though he cannot enter the city himself. There you will find a new life for yourselves, perhaps, I do not know. Certainly, if you can learn to smile and say, 'Yes, Excellency, no, Excellency . . .' you will survive, as you will not survive in Santiago. The notorious Colonel Adam Butrus is dead, and his revengeful deputy, Commandante Olé is taking his place. No, you cannot stay in Santiago."

"But Havana seems a very poor substitute?" Clifford said.

"It is indeed. But where else can you go in this accursed island, I do not know. You will find nothing but venality in Havana, and corruption, and arrogance . . . but if you learn how to bow, and scrape . . . yes, you can find safety there."

"And the alternative to Havana?" Mercy asked.

"The only alternative," Dacis said softly, "is . . . the mountains."

"With you?"

choice is not an easy one, it never has been. For some of them, it is easier to confront death in their own homes than in the forest. Whatever they choose, they will face it, inevitably. We must permit them decisions that may not be ours."

"Yes. Yes, you are right, of course. And we leave here, when?"

"At sunup."

He said hesitantly, "I consulted, this day, one of our soothsayers."

There was a small, deprecatory gesture. "We are a very superstitious people. She drew some designs in the sand, what appeared to me to be . . . a goat, and an archer, and she said to me, '*All the hope that you have . . . lies in these two symbols.*'"

Mercy whispered, catching her breath: "Capricorn . . . and Sagittarius."

The town was utterly darkened now.

The sun came up over the eastern tip of the island, gilding the mountain they called *Los Pechos*.

There were thirty-two horses laboring up the steep slopes of the *sierra* with Dacis, Mercy, and Clifford riding at the head of the column, and two hundred and sixty men and women on foot struggling on behind them.

They reached the summit, the sun still low on the golden horizon now, as its shadow crept slowly down towards the tiny whitewashed town that spread its houses over the gentle knolls and valleys.

They paused and turned their horses around, and stared down at it for a moment.

Dacis said heavily, "A vibrant, suffering people who ask only one thing of life. Happiness. I believe that they will never find it. And all that I can do is pray for them. And fight."

They wheeled their ponies around. And slowly, the long column struggled up toward the sunlight that shone on the lovely mountaintop.

Another tumultuous romantic novel
by Patricia Matthews,
author of the multi-million
copy national bestseller,
LOVE'S AVENGING HEART

Love's Wildest Promise

P40-047 $1.95

Sarah Moody was a lady's maid in a wealthy London home. But suddenly her quiet sheltered world was turned upside down when she was abducted and smuggled aboard a ship bound for the colonies. Its cargo—whores to satisfy the appetites of King George's soldiers in New York. Was Sarah destined to become one of these women? Or would she find the man she was searching for, the man who would help her to fulfill Love's Wildest Promise.

The epic novel of the Old South,
ablaze with the unbridled passions
of men and women seeking
new heights for their love

Windhaven Plantation

Marie de Jourlet

P40-022 $1.95

Here is the proud and passionate story of one man—
Lucien Bouchard. The second son of a French nobleman,
a man of vision and of courage, Lucien dares to seek a new
way of life in the New World that suits his own high
ideals. Yet his true romantic nature is at war with his
lusty, carnal desires. The four women in his life reflect
this raging conflict: Edmée, the high-born, amoral
French sophisticate who scorns his love, choosing his
elder brother, heir to the family title; Dimarte, the in-
genuous, earthy, and sensual Indian princess; Amelia,
the fiery free-spoken beauty who is trapped in a life of
servitude for crimes she didn't commit; and Priscilla,
whose proper manner hid the unbridled passion of her
true desires.

"... will satisfy avid fans of the plantation genre."
—*Bestsellers* magazine

In the tumultuous, romantic tradition of
Rosemary Rogers, Jennifer Wilde, and
Kathleen Woodiwiss

Love's Avenging Heart

Patricia Matthews

P987 $1.95

The stormy saga of Hannah McCambridge, whose fiery
red hair, voluptuous body, and beautiful face made her
irresistible to men...Silas Quint, her brutal stepfather,
sold her as an indentured servant...Amos Stritch, the
lascivious tavernkeeper, bought her and forced her to
submit to his lecherous desires...Malcolm Verner, the
wealthy master of Malvern Plantation, rescued her from
a life of poverty and shame. But for Hannah, her new
life at Malvern was just the beginning. She still had to
find the man of her dreams—the man who could un-
leash the smouldering passions burning inside her and
free her questing heart.

You've read other historical romances, now <u>live</u> one!

If you can't find this book at your local bookstore, simply send
the cover price, plus 25¢ for postage and handling to:

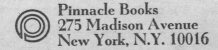

Pinnacle Books
275 Madison Avenue
New York, N.Y. 10016